ANGELS
IN THE
ARCHITECTURE

A NOVEL

ANDY JUNIPER

Library and Archives Canada Cataloguing in Publication

Title: Angels in the architecture : a novel / by Andy Juniper.

Names: Juniper, Andy, 1958- author.

Description: Includes index.

Identifiers: Canadiana (print) 20250166933 | Canadiana (ebook) 20250166941 | ISBN 9781771618489 (softcover) | ISBN 9781771618496 (PDF) | ISBN 9781771618502 (EPUB) | ISBN 9781771618519 (Kindle)

Subjects: LCGFT: Novels.
Classification: LCC PS8569.U57 A83 2025 | DDC C813/.54—dc23

Published by Mosaic Press, Oakville, Ontario, Canada, 2025.

MOSAIC PRESS, Publishers
www.Mosaic-Press.com
Copyright © Andy Juniper, 2025
Cover Design: Amy Land

All rights reserved. Without limiting the rights under copyright reserved here, no part of this publication may be reproduced, stored in or introduced into any retrieval system, or transmitted in any form or by any means—electronic, mechanical, by photocopy, recording or otherwise—without the prior written permission and consent of both the copyright owners and the Publisher of this book.

Printed and bound in Canada.

MOSAIC PRESS
1252 Speers Road, Units 1 & 2, Oakville, Ontario, L6L 2X4 (905)-825-2130
info@mosaic-press.com • www.mosaic-press.com

ANGELS
IN THE
ARCHITECTURE

Dedication

For Maureen, for providing the light and love. For our kids, Matt, Scott, and Haley, for helping — as the years pile up — to keep me current, curious, and entertained. And for Phoebe, the Wonder Dog, for supplying the requisite doses of daily hilarity.

Contents

Prologue: A Moment Unglued And Separated From Time   ix

PART ONE
Evidence Of An Angel

Crossing Paths With The Divine
And A Girl With Skinny Legs And Downy Thighs   3
Irrepressible, Irresistible Ali   10
A Continent Shy Of Hollywood   17
Pegasus, The Winged Wonder   20

PART TWO
Waiting To Derail

An Obscure Eden   29
Not Everyone Can Carry The Weight Of The World
Or, Complete Consciousness Is Overrated   33
A Person With Nothing On His Mind,
And The Power To Express It   41
There's Nothing To Get Hung About   49
The Tree From Which His Apple Fell
And Frank... Frank Never You Mind   52

Mother-In-Law Tongue	61
How Awful Of You To Even Ask	64
Serenity, Granted	69
A Thespian, A Direct Descendant of Thespis!	73
December Is Thirteen Months Long	81
Angels In The Snow	83
A Poor Penis Retracting In The Wind	88
To Follow The Fugitive Sun	92
Routines, Rituals And A Second-Hand Celica	100
Little Known Facts	104
Ali, We Need To Talk	109
The Blue Parrot Tavern	118
He's Nothing But A Fred	128
Maybe It Ain't Broke	132
The Dregs Of The Day	135

PART THREE

A Dream Come True

Ali In The Morning	145
How Should A Bird Fly? Or, Cracking The Sexual Ice	150
The Decisive Moment Or, Penis Fingers	159
If Only I Had Somebody	173
You Can Go Home	176
Two Blocks Away	181
As If The Gift Of Birth Was Not Enough	184
If Only I Had Somebody (Part II)	192

Judas Finds Pegasus Or, Solidarity	194
Hearts Broken On The Monkey Bars	199
Nights At The Round Table	203
The Cutest Kimono Imaginable	208
Not even the rain has such small hands	215

PART FOUR

Loves Lost & Found

The Beach Girl's (Almost) Endless Summer Or Roots To The Sacred	221
In The Company Of Misery	228
Not Forgiven Or Forgotten	
Biking In The Beaches	238
A Little Left Of The Dial	242
Revelations, The Beauty, The Body	247
Around In Circles	253
She Loved You, Ya, Ya, Ya	257
Until The Trail Went Cold	263
Two Broken Flowers	265
Epilogue: Angels in the Architecture	267
Acknowledgments	271
About the Author	273

Prologue

A Moment Unglued And Separated From Time

AND THAT WAS *when I first saw her. At the most mundane moment of what was destined to be but another day on life's treadmill had fate not intervened and placed me alongside a narrow, paved road that winds around the base of a hill in Toronto's High Park. Had I not been seized by an irrepressible urge to glance up. And that was when I first saw her. Atop the hill, awash in autumn sunshine, a sultry, southerly breeze caressing her in a daring and sensual way.*

She was standing beside a black duffel bag, and she was stretching like a cat that is languidly, reluctantly awakening from a delicious nap. Befitting an Indian summer afternoon in the city, she was wearing a pink T-shirt, tan shorts fashionably shortened by folds at the hem, white ankle socks and white running shoes, an outfit that was practical and casual and so seemingly unremarkable — and yet remarkable enough to become permanently branded on my memory.

In time I would document that precise, decisive moment in my life when I looked up and saw her, a moment that in my mind would become unglued and separated from time. Predictably, upon publication of that first-person account in a Toronto newspaper, I was skewered by hard-boiled critics who would not know love if it sent them long-stemmed red roses and poetry on a whim, and by a particularly skeptical soul named Harland (Hap) Hazard. Amongst assorted other things, the Hazard questioned how I could have possibly discerned (let alone been mesmerized by) her beauty considering what he deemed the "prohibitive distance" that separated us; the Hazard would dissect this scenario — her on the hill, me down below, what I saw, what

ANGELS IN THE ARCHITECTURE

I could not possibly have seen — with the tireless tenacity of a conspiracy theorist questioning the whole dubious JFK/grassy knoll/lone-gunman scenario, to the degree where late one night he drunkenly demanded a reenactment. A request initially sloughed off with laughter and then, once determined that he was actually serious, indignantly rejected.

Furthermore, I was derided by critics for my flowery *choice of words and phrases*: namely, the "almost otherworldly bronze aura" I suggested surrounded her, and the "slivers of sunlight" I asserted were reflecting off the strands of her silky brown hair. They accused me of flaunting, indeed flogging, poetic license. They insinuated that I could not possibly have felt — that instantaneously, that powerfully — the connection between us, Cupid's arrow piercing my heart. Detractors in mind, I'll stick to the bare facts regarding what happened next...

She knelt beside the black bag. After a moment's hesitation, she then fully reclined, supine on the grass, and placed her arms across her chest like a mortician customarily arranges the arms and hands of a corpse. Then, with an elbow, she gave herself a push-off and began rolling down the hill.

Rolling. Her body rotating like the rollers on a steamroller, quickly gathering momentum on the steep descent. Rolling, rolling, rolling... right on into my life.

And in that dizzying, impetuous moment, I was reborn. Would I believe in love at first sight? Yes, like the beat-keeper for the Beatles sings, I'm certain that it happens all the time...

Part One

Evidence Of An Angel

Crossing Paths With The Divine
And A Girl With Skinny Legs And Downy Thighs

Hunkered down under a small, sturdy wooden table in the hallway of a Florida coastal cottage that is creaking, trembling, leaking and under siege. Clothes damp and gritty, skin clammy from humidity, perspiration and fear. Muscles tremulous and cramping and nerves frayed. Thoughts creep into dark and uncharted corners of the mind as the assault begins to exact its inevitable toll and extract its proverbial pound of flesh.

Hours earlier, Hurricane Iris, sweeping in off the Atlantic Ocean and only beginning to flex her grotesque muscles, downed power lines and transformers, knocking out the area's telephone service and, in many areas, electricity. Now, in the thick of the hurricane, in the dead of night, Daniel (Storm) Baker is enveloped by claustrophobic darkness, eerie, dense, and absolute.

Table legs shimmy, rattle. If not for his steadying hand gripping one of the legs, the table would jitterbug down the hallway. His ears ring, ache and repeatedly pop. Pain, raw and piercing, emanates from the site of an old root canal at the back of his mouth. Dehydrated, he strains to swallow and counteract the radical drop in barometric pressure that has produced a peculiar sensation: that at any moment his head may explode.

A surreal cacophony. Sounds startle, torment, sounds akin to those documented by correspondents in war zones. The humming and fitful sparking of electrical lines, bursts of broken glass, awnings and tin trash cans clanging down deserted streets of the ghost town and the relentless, strident wailing of alarms as automobiles across the disabled landscape are effortlessly flipped and broken, their security systems breached. The sounds are intermittently punctuated by explosions, each detonation setting his heart frantically pounding.

ANGELS IN THE ARCHITECTURE

Be over. Be over.

Now but a quiet plea, a needy mantra whispered across parched, cracked lips, uncertain even in his own mind whether he is referring to the hurricane or what has become his life.

Outside, Iris is heightening, gathering force and fury. Having effortlessly conquered the beachfront, she is resolved to pick up the ocean and drive it right down the quaint main street of the vulnerable town of Turtle Key. Surge waters carpet the hardwood floors and are starting to edge up the walls. Torrential, horizontal rain hammers the house, propelled by savage, screaming winds.

In time, on a night when time loses all definition — when seconds grind into minutes and minutes pass themselves off as hours — the very sounds scrabbling at his senses and threatening to push him over the edge become precisely what he yearns to hear as every sound becomes buried by a constant, disorienting and punishing roar. The scream of the world's suffering souls; the howl of the dead.

Packing winds of more than one-hundred-and-fifty miles an hour and energy akin to a one-megaton hydrogen bomb, the storm is capable of (and, he is convinced, intent upon) reducing the overmatched cottage to kindling. Numb with fatigue and overwhelmed by both the astonishing intensity and stamina of this natural phenomenon, Storm surrenders. In the days and months to come, when afforded an opportunity to reflect, he will contend that he surrendered not to the hurricane, or to sleep, or even to a prevalent variety of storm-induced cabin fever, but, rather, to a vision. To the most real, alive, electric, and lucid vision ever experienced. In that moment, he is visited by his wife, Ali Reynolds Baker.

The *late* Ali Reynolds Baker. Ten months deceased and what sometimes so sadly seems like a lifetime removed.

For an ephemeral, energizing instant, time stops. Mercifully for Storm, the moment has the feel of an eternity during which the hurricane's assault is arrested and, for the first time in ages, the world is right-side-up, orderly, just and safe. For the first time in ages the world is as it was, as it should be, as it should have been forevermore, Storm and Ali.

He stares at her in childlike, wide-eyed wonderment, awed by this incandescent apparition. Although unable to rationally grasp what he is witnessing, he is oddly unafraid. Because the apparition is unquestionably Ali, encased in a calming, merciful, bleached aura and because, inexplicably, it feels so natural, like it is commonplace to be crossing paths with the Divine. The vision is as beautiful as it is humbling, as humbling as it is poignant.

She smiles. God, how he has missed that smile, at once innocent, bewitching, mischievous, sensual. A smile that over the course of a brief conversation could effectively disarm strangers and buoy friends. A smile virtually tethered to his heart. What he would do, what Faustian pacts would he sign in his own anemic blood just to have her back.

She does not speak, but the radiance surrounding her shines nourishing, healing light into the pervasive darkness. Her presence alone after such an unbearable absence replenishes, begins filling the void of his loneliness, makes him feel for the first time since her death as though he is not all alone in a desolate world. Further, her presence plants within him a small seed that, if nurtured, has the potential to germinate into nothing less than a desire for life. It's a desire that, following Ali's death, was turned to ashes and delivered by a late-autumn breeze across a verdant hillside back in High Park, in the west end of Toronto, the neighborhood they had so contentedly called home.

Iris, as though suddenly mindful of Ali's presence and incensed by the angelic disruption to her earthly devastation, tears a plywood sheet off the outside of the kitchen window, shatters the glass and hurtles jagged shards across the house, through Ali, piercing the being of light. Storm winces at the surreal violence of the image. And in that instant, she is gone.

Nevertheless, vestiges of her remain, a reassuring warmth that slowly spreads throughout his body – like a shot of bourbon taken straight-up on a cold winter night — and a trace of her indomitable spirit. And Storm Baker, who had come within a whisker of truly convincing himself that he no longer cared whether he lived or died, a broken man who had disregarded a series of hurricane warnings, pleas from family and friends, even subsequent emergency evacuation orders — purposely placing himself in the path of the storm and, in essence, daring it to get him — finds himself negotiating with God.

He has never been a religious man. Contemplative, certainly. Spiritual, perhaps. But not religious. Following the godless events that stole his mother and that later tore Ali from his life, he found himself questioning the very existence (or, at the very least, the motives and logic) of God. What kind of higher being would allow such a grievous fate to befall two of His own angels?

ANGELS IN THE ARCHITECTURE

There have been days when the imposing weight and darkness in his world have been incapacitating, when Storm could do nothing more than dolefully conclude: If God exists, He is a heartless being. Or, in the more mortal and blasphemous terms employed when despair, anxiety and insomnia had him tossing and turning in an icy sweat late into the night: If God exists, He is a real prick... And yet he finds himself asking that heartless being, that prick, a supreme being, any supreme being, to deliver him from this force, this virtual hell on earth. His mumbled bartering is truncated when he registers a new sound that has abruptly replaced the din of past hours.

A hush. The sound is silence.

Cautiously, his ears still ringing and unable to immediately accept the sudden cessation of noise, Storm eases out from under the table. He cannot believe his fortune. That his prayers have been answered. That he has been spared. He stands tall and momentarily lingers, stretching to the fullest and unknotting cramped, fatigued muscles before groping through the darkness, sloshing down the hallway through ankle-deep water toward the front of the cottage. The pressure that for hours has made it virtually impossible to even open a door, has abated. He opens the door and peers out. All clear.

He steps outside into a dreamlike, nighttime calm. Everywhere, pools of water, debris that furious winds have scattered, and the ocean has disgorged, regurgitated from its churned-up depths onto the sandy soil. Everywhere, mayhem, destruction. Trees, boat parts, portions of out-buildings, cars that have been toyed with and tossed aside, and overmatched houses that have been left in tatters. Birds chirp madly, like they are giddy with relief, or childishly heckling the forces that dared unleash such wrath upon them. A slight breeze caresses his face. It feels so heavenly it might be the sweet breath of an elusive God.

Storm gazes heavenward into the pie-shaped face of a brilliant moon. Myriad stars and constellations wink conspiratorially at him, one in particular — Pegasus to the north, he thinks with wonder — is exceptionally prominent in the night sky. For a time, he simply stands unmoving, taking in deep, stabilizing, cleansing breaths of air laden with an indescribable scent never previously experienced. Old-timers, hurricane veterans who dwell anywhere along the Sunshine State's thousand-odd-mile coastline, would suggest that he is inhaling ozone. He believes he is inhaling life itself — primordial, pristine life.

ANDY JUNIPER

In his sanctuary, in his corner of the ring, a boxer's handlers remind their charge: keep your guard up. Never drop your guard. Because the instant you drop that protective fist is the instant you find yourself victim of savage fists — flat on your back, down for the count on the canvas, bloodied and drifting in and out of consciousness. Storm is the boxer who has endured too many rounds in a glaring mismatch, and his guard is down. If it were daytime, he would be able to observe that, despite the deceptive calm, the ocean continues to angrily churn. He is ensconced in what amounts to a tunnel that has formed between the heavens and Earth. He is not at all braced for the backside of the storm.

As abruptly as the calm arrived, it departs. The hurricane's vortex charges northward, continuing its devastating stampede up the coast. Change is instantaneous. Ominous, swirling, bruise-colored clouds block out the moon and stars and harmless breezes are overtaken by winds gusting in the opposite direction to which they were moving prior to the hurricane's break. Storm is jolted back to reality by an astonishing sound and light show — fulminating thunderclaps, swiftly succeeded by lightning so charged, the flashes momentarily blind. In that instant he again thinks of Ali, phobic and scared witless by thunder and lightning even when they were safely off in the distance. Turning back toward the house, his path is crossed by a thick, three-foot-long corn snake, driven out into the open by flooding and slithering for its life to the safety of higher ground.

Storm manages to return inside and force the front door closed behind him. As he treads through the water toward the hallway, toward relative safety under the table, the wind strips away another sheet of plywood, this time from the living room's vulnerable bay window. The windowpane surrenders without a fight and the incoming rush of air bullies a television set off its stand and onto the floor, glass and brittle guts shattering. When Storm is only a few feet from the table, time ceases marching forward in straight lines. It is as though his mind, under attack and taking flak, bails out. And then free-falls. A thought parachutes in through the backdoor of his consciousness, seemingly unrelated to his predicament, or life and death, but of his Grade One teacher.

Although he often reminisces about a particular soft, sweet-smelling element of her class, he has rarely thought about Ms. Balls over the course of the past twenty-odd years, so erasable was the impact she made on him. And yet, there she stands at the head of the class in Room One at

ANGELS IN THE ARCHITECTURE

Tompkin Public School, the grossly corpulent and wholly inept instructor with the lamentable name that, to the endless amusement of the giggling schoolchildren in the schoolyard at recesses, was so naturally converted into the various synonyms for testicles. She is wearing her favorite flower-patterned dress, which catty moms were often heard whispering amongst themselves, may well have been her only dress. Her hair sits like a hard, gray helmet atop her head. Redolent of talcum powder at odds with perfume that has been too liberally applied and perspiration, she sweats prodigiously as she reads to the class: twenty school children fidgeting around three long tables. It's a familiar and befitting fable, the story of Chicken Little.

Storm has few fond memories of those younger school grades. It was not a particularly easy childhood, not when your home life is fractured, when you are small and frail and awkward, count-your-ribs skinny and bespectacled. Not when you are considered to be unusual, weird, an odd, introverted and seemingly overly sensitive boy.

Storm was the butt of daily jokes and a punching bag for the school's alpha bully, a cruel and detached brute whose surname of Haven seemed purposely dipped in irony. Storm was one of those tormented children who would have merely been facilitating the inevitable had he just stuck a "Kick Me" sign on his own back each morning as he unenthusiastically dressed for school, anxieties cavorting in his mind, butterflies in his belly. If anything saved him from the daily harassment in those younger grades at the hands of Mark Haven and his clique of oversized underachievers, it was a brawny, athletic, older brother who occasionally found fit to come to his aid, an older sister who unfailingly stood up for him whenever she was in the vicinity and, for a brief period, a girl. She was a newcomer to Storm's hometown and, with one warm, passing smile on the first day of school, she hooked and reeled in his young heart.

She was his first love. Other than Ali, he swears, his only love. She was a compassionate, benevolent girl. Granted, compassion and benevolence are not what appropriate a six-year-old boy's heart. She was a pretty girl (get a boy all fluttery-in-the-stomach, all light-in-the-head pretty) with shoulder-length sandy-blonde hair and playful blue eyes and a wide smile that left all but the boldest boys stammering, if not outright speechless.

Christian Matthews, a girl forever clad (or, rather, forever frozen in Storm's mind) in colorful, quirky dresses, white socks, and black patent-leather saddle shoes, at which he spent many hours staring, precociously noting the care, the shine of the buckles, the polish on the shoes. Christian Matthews, a sweet girl with skinny legs and downy thighs and the upbringing and propriety to sit with her legs properly pinched together at the knees.

In the heartbeat before he is cracked on the back of the head by a small, hard object propelled by hurricane winds, he envisions himself in that classroom setting. In one of those peculiar, synchronous moments that mysteriously thread together the errant strands of life, he sees that in that first-grade classroom he is situated precisely, protectively where he would like to be now. Under a table.

Apparently with the approval of Ms. Balls, who was clumsily surfing the crest of a wave of apathy right on into retirement, under the table was where he spent most of his time. As the projectile crowns him, as his body crumbles and his mind begins sinking deep into unconsciousness, Storm's memory flashes in recall. How day after day he hid under that table from those cavorting and crippling anxieties, from enemies, and from life itself. And he remembers that, for comfort, he used to clutch young Christian's leg. Because he loved her. Because she always smelled of the freshness and promise of spring. Because the skin on her leg was unspeakably soft and smooth and more comforting than any security blanket he had ever caressed. And because, with magnanimity and empathy, she let him.

Irrepressible, Irresistible, Ali

IF ALLOWED TO play God, and empowered to make meaningful choices in life, most people would prefer to die suddenly. Not violently, mind you. Granted, if violence is fated to be part of the equation — a doomed soldier in wartime, for instance — wouldn't most still favor the clean, instant kill of a sniper's bullet over a protracted, life-slowly-seeping-out-of-you death in a bloody trench? Discard the notion that each moment of life is precious, that each breath is a gift. If the moments are shrouded in the befuddling fog of Alzheimer's, if the breaths are corrupted by cancer, if a morphine pump has become the only relief, if the life that remains possesses no dignity, no joy, no hope, no light... most people would prefer to die suddenly....

Furthermore, most people would prefer to die at home rather than in a sterile, soulless institution where the majority of deaths occur, and preferably in old age after a lengthy and fulfilling life. It's a paradox with which Storm is too familiar — that the preferred abrupt death (particularly the *premature* abrupt death) is the most traumatic and difficult for the survivors, those afforded no time to brace themselves for the loss of their loved one, and who are left behind to pick up the pieces and to wonder for the rest of their natural lives: why?

Ali Reynolds Baker died a sudden death. She claimed from early on that this was her destiny; she said she knew "practically forever" that her lifeline was regrettably short.

Ali possessed what she called, tongue-in-cheek, insider information: a sixth sense that translated into presentiment. She said that even as a child — a precocious being, by all accounts, but a child nonetheless — she was able to peer around, or gaze beyond the accepted notion of time perpetually moving forward in linear fashion. Playfully, she would enlist the likes of people as disparate as poet T.S. Eliot and the writers of *Star Trek* to help her explain. In Eliot's words:

"Time present and time past
Are both perhaps present in time future,
And time future contained in time past."

"Or," she would say, "just think of it like this: everything has already happened, or everything is happening now, concurrently – the proverbial 'space-time continuum', if you're a Trekie. Consequently, all information about everything is 'out there', it's just a matter of unshackling your mind from the constraints of preconceived perceptions and, if you'll pardon the television analogy, discovering what channel the information is on…"

Did she truly believe in clairvoyance and her gift in this mystic realm? How else to explain why a woman who shunned the traditional and conventional – who had to be cajoled into even opening a bank account, and to whom money seemed inconsequential ("I guess we have enough," she'd say, if asked: "The bills are being paid." – furtively invested in a substantial life-insurance policy. Her agent was in touch with Storm shortly after her death, explaining how the policy assured "a lifetime of financial piece-of-mind." Yes, she truly believed. And even if you are not a gambler, if you find yourself at the racetrack with knowledge of which horse is going to win, you'd be a fool not to wager on the race…

When presented the facts, even non-believers would be forced to admit that minimally she was more intuitively in touch, more acutely attuned with the world (and the other-world) around her. More likely, she was genuinely psychic: accurately (and sometimes chillingly) predicting occurrences through indescribable, albeit unshakable feelings and signs. Feelings? Signs? Until her death, Storm Baker would include himself among the legion of skeptics. So much mystical mumbo jumbo; too much Shirley MacLaine. It all seemed wishy-washy, vague, difficult to explain and impossible to prove.

One night in the cozy confines of The Blue Parrot Tavern in Toronto's west end, during a protracted debate on the plausibility of human clairvoyance, the unceasingly and unrepentantly cynical (and, in this instance, uncharacteristically somber *and* sober) Harland Hazard curiously sided with Ali. He said he believed that prophetic people walked this Earth and then added, with a deft and almost theatrical touch of flare and mystery, that he had personal experience to support his view. Equally as curious to Storm was Ali's less than warm and welcoming reaction to the Hazard unexpectedly elbowing his way across to her side of the debate: Ali, shifting in her chair, apprehensively biting her lower lip and unconsciously tracing her fingernails up and down her arm, healthy nails leaving red tracks along her skin.

"Not surprisingly," the Hazard recounted, "I was a ridiculing, mocking non-believer. That is, until the day I was converted, the day my skin was saved by... Feelings. Signs. It was years ago. A lifetime ago. I was in Florida, scheduled to fly to Nashville to meet two record-label snakes. The morning of my flight, the young woman I was with at the time woke me. She was feverish and panicked, saying that she'd experienced a premonitory dream in which the plane went down."

Talk of gooseflesh. Imagine the rise across the Hazard's fair skin as he watched the network newscasts repeatedly, ghoulishly airing amateur video footage of the Nashville-bound plane on which he was scheduled to be a passenger – a bystander's slightly out-of-focus, grainy, bouncy film capturing the sheer terror of the moment as the crippled bird, thick black smoke billowing from an engine, tumbled awkwardly out of the sky.

"Seventy-seven dead in the charred, twisted wreckage and me still alive and left to wonder what the last moments must have been like for those poor passengers, all because this woman had had the dream and had then taken full advantage of my white-knuckling nature to convince me not to fly. And," he needlessly added, "consequently, not to crash."

Admittedly intrigued, Storm remained unconvinced.

"I'm sure that people dream about planes crashing all the time and planes crash all the time. It doesn't mean the two are connected by some grand cosmic cable network that these preordained psychic dreamers are able to access."

Which explains why all her matter-of-factly issued prophetic soundings and psychic alerts proved ineffectual even though she repeatedly forewarned him of her own death. While her predictions assuredly spooked him to his core — in the way a seemingly implausible, outlandish nightmare nevertheless terrifies the dreamer and leaves him unsettled even in the hours after awakening — they failed to convince him (did not fully believe, would not fully believe) that she would die young. Consequently, they did nothing to cushion the blow. Her death was tantamount to being impaled on a rusty, double-edged sword. One day she was there, the very next day he awoke from a brief, fitful sleep to find himself not only decimated by grief, but also virtually alone. The one person who truly knew him to his core, who loved him — unconditionally, wholly — and who was strong and stable enough to pilot him through his pain, being the very person who had been torn from his life.

Understated, it's been a daily struggle that he has lost more often than won, futilely attempting to keep muzzled and at bay what Winston Churchill aptly described as "the black dog of depression." Adrift on what Carl Jung termed "the night sea journey," the passage that follows the abrupt cessation of life's meaning. Living life atop a base of emotional quicksand. Wondering whether grief can be a cause of death. Whether a man can literally die of a broken heart. Whether life with a broken heart is a life worth living.

It has been his experience that beyond attempting to patch or mend the gaping hole in his heart and simply finding a reason to breathe, the most difficult, demoralizing aspect of life-after-Ali has been coping with the possibility that he may one day forget her or forget certain things about her. Petty things, precious things. Fretful that in time memories will be misplaced, recall will recede, she will inevitably fade, and he will eventually lose the very essence of Ali.

He has traveled this road before. He has experienced that inevitable fade, awakening one morning to the disturbing realization that the contours of his mother's face, the waves of her beautiful black hair, the distinction of her voice that he'd always found so soothing and reassuring were being lost to time. Within days of Ali's funeral, he became reacquainted with the harsh reality that death distorts, sends cracks shivering up the mirror of memory, altering images that, for the sake of his very sanity and survival, he believes he must keep clear in his mind forever.

What did she look like — precisely? Because to him, detail and precision in such matters are essential. What did she look like when she was asleep in her T-shirt and underpants, in those rumpled, softly lit and serene day-breaking moments as he rested beside her, watching the peaceful rise and fall of her breath, content to simply watch his wife? He knows he will never forget that in those moments, as she hugged her pillow and unconsciously treasured the last moments of sleep before beginning another day, he felt blessed beyond belief, a man fortunate enough to have found meaning and purpose in life, a place in the world and someone with whom he could share his life. Blessings and good fortune aside, what did she look like? Precisely...

How did she look when outdoors in the sodium light and biting grip of a cold winter day, when damp, predatory winds whirled off Lake Ontario and painted her face a robust red? In summer, when the city, overheated and on edge, became a suffocating blanket and she could be found on their apartment balcony overlooking High Park, listening on her Walkman to a cassette exactingly compiled for her by the Hazard (songs he'd blended with Ali in mind, according to mood, style, artist association, or assorted themes). Or, Ali on that balcony reading – time traveling back to the days of the Bronte sisters, or marveling at the inherent modern-day sensuality of Leonard Cohen's poems in *Death of a Lady's Man*, or the beauty and craftsmanship of F. Scott Fitzgerald's *The Great Gatsby*, or simply leisurely thumbing through an issue of *Modern Photography* magazine?

Ali, young, irrepressible, irresistible. Ali, bursting with health. Ali, embracing the prickly heat so many others in the metropolis were anxiously plotting to escape. Ali, in a brief cotton sundress, skin tanned, brown hair bleached by the sun and carelessly lifted off her shoulders and clipped at the back with a barrette. Invincible Ali guiding a cold, perspiring bottle of water up and down the length of her neck. Ali glancing up, seeing her husband, and smiling broadly. Ali, free. Ali playfully flipping up the front of that sundress.

"New undies, hon, you like?" Unaware of the reach of the myriad tendrils of her sensuality, the power of her sexuality, and the tantalizing allure of those lacy white briefs. He *liked*. God, how he liked.

Ali. How did she look when naked, lissome, lovely, bending and running a razor the length of those athletic legs, or tilting her head back in the shower to wash her hair, breasts rising to meet the runoff of soapy water? How did she look when making love? Specifics. Slender feet slipped inside black, heeled shoes, lean legs in lacy-topped white stockings. The enticing, hugging fit of high-cut underwear and lacy bra worn to further inflame, as if that fire ever needed further fueling. Her face, her comely visage — accentuated by thin lips, hazel eyes and the most adorable nose — up close, as they stood facing each other, exploring lips, mouths. Lost in each other's scent, lost in lust, in love, and ecstatic at being lost.

Remembering... The smell of her hair. The soft curves of her ears. The plucked arch of her eyebrows. The perfumed spot she loved him to nuzzle on her neck, the contour of the collarbone along which he would glide his fingers. How her fingers would frolic, her lips, mouth adroitly wrapping his excitement. How his heart would threaten to break out of his chest when she stepped out of her clothing. How he would have gladly died in the moment as she slowly turned away — his hands following her form, from shoulders to the small sensual hollow of her lower back. Bending, hips rising, summoning. Entering her world, *other-worlds* altogether. Penetrating love, body shivering, arching, in spasm beneath him, in union with him.... And her song, a barely audible, back-of-the-throat, feline purr. How he could make himself insane within the padded walls of this Catch-22: driven mad with desire if he can clearly remember; driven mad with grief if he cannot...

Her scent. Habits. Mannerisms. Essence. The very sound of her voice. He is like a child at a beach, resolved to keep the incoming tide away from the sand-castle city over which he so arduously toiled, over which he sacrificed exposed flesh under a fiery summer sun. He despairs at the inevitable, at every castle that is destroyed, memories being washed out to sea. How it weighs on him, memories being all he has left. He knows what she would say — that she left behind something more tangible than memories. He has photographs, albums and shoeboxes full of photographs: some snapshots casually shot, others artistic portraits painstakingly and passionately taken.

Ali was a photographer. She called this medium of communication 'the language of mankind', and she believed in the camera's power, in its potential to act as a witness to the world. Case in point, she would cite two harrowing photographs credited with swaying public opinion and stanching the bloody tide of the Vietnam War: Eddie Adams' still-frame of a Vietcong officer's assassination by a brigadier general (shockingly brutal, close-up, bullet to the skull); and, of course, Nick Ut's picture of Phan Thi Kim Phuc, nine-years old, naked, flesh melted off her bones, running toward Ut's camera and away from a U.S. napalm strike on her village.

Personally, Ali believed that of all photographic images — and in this world, she would note with contagious wonderment that never dulled even with accumulated age and experience, there exists more photographs than bricks — the simple snapshot came closest to truth. Each shot a specific, spiritual moment. Immortalization via images. The few times he has forced himself to view the personal portion of her work — captured memories; frozen, snared slices of time — he has bled until the only conclusion he could draw was that the photographs had not immortalized the woman he loved so much as they had immortalized all that he had lost.

It is imperative to his survival to continue remembering her in life and at no time was she more alive than when they made love. Fiery, consuming passion. Sexual, spiritual — worshipping, as he was, at her alter as frequently and for as long as the day-to-day rigors of life allowed. He remembers her lack of inhibition, her curiosity and inventiveness, her lust, her joy, her ability to fully immerse herself in a moment, her fingernails teasing his skin, her feather-light kisses caressing every inch of his flesh.

Kiss and tell. She was good. She made love with the fervor of a woman possessed, a woman conquering (or, perhaps, expelling) demons. Experienced beyond her age. Experienced beyond her experience. She philosophized that the way to become a better lover was not through making love. Rather, through living life.

A Continent Shy Of Hollywood

AND NOW WHEN *we make love, only in my mind's eye, I can see — and I swear I can almost touch — the beautiful gold necklace and pendant that so sensually fell on her chest, riding the gentle, lapping waves of her breaths.*

Remembering our first official date, time stolen on a weekday...
What would you like to do? What would you *like to do?*

Eventually finding ourselves at an outdoor cafe in Bloor West Village, lingering over a coffee, an herbal tea, sharing a heavenly, honey-laden slice of baklava and opening ourselves up in conversation. Finding common ground and sifting through endless options. Pleased to discover that, together, we could do nothing and be more than content.

It was a perfect late-autumn day, crisp but comfortable. We strolled the length of the Village, pausing now and then to window shop, to browse amongst the dusty wares in a used bookstore (Ali alight at the discovery of an early, absurdly under-priced hard-cover edition of Salinger's Franny & Zooey*), to test our sense of smell at a candle store, to sample small squares of decadence at a chocolate shop, and all the while sailing on a steady sea of unforced conversation.*

"What is it with women and chocolate?"

"Have you heard about the twelve-step program women chocoholics must live by?" she asked, a sly, sweet grin playing on the corners of her mouth. "Never be more than twelve steps away from chocolate..."

Late afternoon. Spotted in a jeweler's window, the necklace and pendant: a gold coin bearing an imprint of the image of Pegasus, the winged horse of Greek mythology. Listening as she related the myth with which she had become familiar in a youth spent as an only child, entertaining and educating herself — an insatiable bookworm burrowing deep into various libraries across the country; emulating, she would say, one of her fictional heroines, Francie Nolan, the precocious young protagonist in Betty Smith's American classic, A Tree Grows in Brooklyn. *Ambitious Francie was apparently determined to read all the books in the world, beginning with every book in her small, shabby neighborhood library, and meticulously doing so in alphabetical order and, Ali chuckled, "not skipping the dry ones."*

I'd like to submit that I was listening, attentively, politely, but was I?

Honestly, no. I was entranced by this young woman, by the intoxicating, heart-skipping-beats reality that we had found each other and that I was out with her (how those fickle gods were suddenly smiling on me now). Consequently, beside her, all words — and even the centuries-old myth of Pegasus — paled. I wanted to touch her, to kiss her, right there in broad daylight in front of anyone who happened by. I didn't care. I was an adult, feeling every inch as smitten and anxious and inexperienced and embarrassingly flushed as a fourteen-year-old with a high-school crush; I was overwhelmed by the urge to feel her lips against mine, her heart beating against my chest. Still, snippets of the ancient tale were nonetheless absorbed, through osmosis, I suppose, because I really wasn't listening...

The winged horse was born the son of Poseidon, God of the Sea, and the gorgon Medusa. Shortly after his birth, from the neck of Medusa, Pegasus struck the ground atop Mount Helicon with his hoof and on that spot a spring began to flow. This spring became sacred to the Muses and was believed to be a source for poetic inspiration. And the fate of Pegasus? Everyone longed to catch and tame the magic steed — and many tried, in vain, but no one more than Bellerophon, prince of Corinth, for whom Pegasus became an obsession....

Nodding, I touched my obsession's cheek, her hair — for me, advances uncharacteristically bold. I struggled to read her body language which offered no sign as to whether she wanted me to come closer, to kiss her, absorbed as she was in the recounting of the tale.

On the advice of a seer, Bellerophon spent a night in the temple of the goddess Athena. As he slept, the goddess appeared before him with a golden bridle that she indicated would help him capture the winged wonder. With that bridle, Bellerophon easily caught and tamed the horse. In time, Pegasus steadfastly assisted Bellerophon in perilous adventures against the Amazons and the Chimaera...

Surely feeling in my guts like Bellerophon mustering the courage to take that initial step toward Pegasus, I held my breath, mentally zeroed in on her lips, then closed my eyes and moved forward. My lips toward her lips. Short, sweet, hopelessly awkward, a continent shy of Hollywood. Still, that clumsy kiss, that collision, nevertheless left me short of breath and unsteady on my feet. I awaited her reaction, which followed not in words but in small gestures. A demure tilt of the head, a sly sidelong glance and crooked half-smile, then her hand coming into mine. Fingers becoming electrically entwined.

Here is what she neglected to tell me: Bellerophon was to be undone by delusions of grandeur, by his own ego, his own pride. Winged horse under his control, he felt immortal. Attempting to fly to the top of Olympus to join the gods, the sagacious steed bucked him, leaving him disconsolate and doomed to wander eternity… As for Pegasus, he found refuge in the Olympian stalls and was enlisted by Zeus to bring him his thunder bolts and lightning rods.

Here's what she did tell me: "In time," she said — thankfully, I can still remember the words, even the timbre of her voice — "Pegasus became a constellation in the northern sky, a symbol of strength, swiftness and the special bond between a man and a woman." The bond between like souls, kindred spirits.

The next day I returned to the jewelry store and purchased the gold chain and pendant. That night, on our second date, I brought her Pegasus. A symbol of strength, swiftness and the special bond between a man and a woman. A gift she joyfully accepted, openly adored, and wore religiously. A gift, I would learn, that was not without a trace of irony: Pegasus, eventual courier of thunder bolts and lightning rods, around the sensual neck of a woman so wholly petrified of… thunder and lightning.

Pegasus, The Winged Wonder

"Suffering shit. Man, oh man. You most obviously had something special looking over your shoulder. Or you've got a giant horseshoe lodged up your backside..."

Slowly surfacing through a tunnel of aqueous and infinite darkness, most everything is fuzzy. Sounds, vision, memory. All that is clear (at least, steady and constant and in rhythm with his heartbeat) is the throbbing inside his head.

"I mean, hum-doggie, think about it." The weathered, whiskered face is so close, the man's raspy voice threatens to crawl inside Storm's head and take up residence. Storm shrinks from the breath, soured to repulsion by whiskey and pipe tobacco. His empty stomach grumbles with discontent. He resists the urge to close his eyes and once again surrender to beckoning sleep. With effort he becomes increasingly conscious of where he is, clear on what has happened and what is occurring around him.

He is on his bed, which has a damp and gritty feel beneath him. Everything around him is sodden. The man hovering over him is his neighbor from a few doors up the unpaved road. Tellingly, he is unsure of the man's name — Brady, Brandy, Bundy? — even though the neighbor had gone out of his way to introduce himself on various occasions. However, to Storm, in past months, he's just been the inordinately amiable old-timer who would pluck the ubiquitous pipe out of his mouth and offer up a goofy wave in greeting umpteen times a day. Every time they laid eyes on each other, as though they were fraternity brothers and had not seen each other since college.

"You've got a nasty goose egg on the back of your head," the old man says. "Now think about it logically," he continues, his words accompanied by animated actions. He acts out his working hypothesis with hirsute hands and muscled arms like he is a hybrid of Popeye and actor Peter Falk's television detective, Columbo, on the brink of solving a particularly puzzling mystery. "You get knocked on the back of the head, clunk, you fall flat on your face, unconscious, right? Then you drown. The water gets you, fills your lungs, steals your breath. End of story." He shrugs. "No, sir. I found you right-side up. Right-side up. I carried you to your bed. You're light. Could use a few pounds, my friend."

There follows a moment of silence during which the neighbor contemplates dumb luck or divine intervention and to aid his contemplation he fires up another match to relight his pipe. Storm considers immediate needs. Water for a parched mouth, painkillers for his aching head, a shower, his toothbrush and toothpaste; how he would delight in the luxury of scrubbing away the hurricane grit that has invaded his mouth, eyes, nose. Saturated beach sand clogging every pore.

Glancing around, the neighbor reports: "House fared fairly well. Busted windows, water damage, a minor roof leak in the back bedroom, that's about it. Insurance should take care of it, provided you've got some coverage."

From Storm's dry mouth, one word: "Good." Good.

Regardless of the desolate crannies into which his mind had been edging, he was never beyond considering others — consideration, like civility, bred deep into his bones by his mother, a trait he is destined to take to the grave. And this quaint, beach-side Turtle Key cottage belongs to Harland Hazard who has been Storm's closest friend for almost as far back as he can remember; blood brothers from grade school onward. Blood flinchingly drawn from pricked fingertips onto the blade of a pocketknife and then mingled in a solemn ceremony amid overflowing ashtrays and drained whiskey bottles in the Hazard's garage.

A few weeks after Ali's funeral, Harland couriered him the keys. The Hazard, intuitively sensing and responding to the needs of his friend, extending an olive branch, or, perhaps, attempting to escape the weighty yoke of guilt. A note and a detailed map to the property were enclosed in the envelope along with the key. Written in the Hazard's nearly illegible chicken-scratch, the note read: "It's yours. Follow the fugitive sun. Fly south, recover, recoup, and then come back. Storm Baker, I need you in my life."

ANGELS IN THE ARCHITECTURE

He needed Storm because Storm was his best friend. Perhaps his only close friend. Because his brittle world, like his fragile heart, was broken. And because he loved her, too.

Storm palmed the key. Although a telephone call and a few words could have gone a considerable distance toward clearing the air between them, to lightening the burden the Hazard was carrying upon his narrow shoulders (justly or unjustly), Storm did not pick up the phone. Instantly and overwhelmingly enamored at the thought of packing up and heading south, he began making necessary arrangements. Unaware that it would not have mattered anyway, that Harland Hazard was long gone.

Although Storm no longer cared about himself — in his mind, he had already been blown away — he nevertheless felt duty-bound to protect the Hazard's house from the hurricane. As the storm collected its thoughts and summoned strength off the coast, residents headed inland in cars hastily packed to their hoods. As long lineups of antsy, frustrated, and short-fused motorists formed at the two local gas stations, Storm engaged in what other residents had been frantically doing for the previous two days: nailing plywood sheets over windows, moving lawn furniture indoors, shutting off gas, electricity and water, unplugging electrical appliances. Generally preparing the cottage for the battle of its young life.

While the vast majority of the town's residents heeded the evacuation order, a small fraction balked: merchants who refused to abandon their livelihoods and leave their futures in the hands of the hurricane and, afterwards, looters; hurricane neophytes who gazed out at the horizon on the days before the storm and were duped by the beguiling azure skies and calm conditions; and hurricane veterans like Storm's neighbor who had weathered such storms in the past, were reluctant to go to the time and expense of evacuating, and had no patience for the government bureaucracy that invariably followed evacuations. Getting back into one's home was oftentimes more challenging than packing up in haste and getting out.

However, those remaining behind — to be categorized and castigated in an editorial by the local newspaper, *The Turtle Cay Packet*, as "the stubborn, the apathetic, and the idiotic" — took basic precautions to protect not only their properties, but also themselves. They stockpiled food and batteries (for flashlights and radios to pick up emergency broadcasts). Filled containers with drinking water and bathtubs with water for washing. Prepped first-aid kits and readied coolers for maintaining fresh food. Conversely, once he had the Hazard's house storm-ready, Storm discontinued all preparations. On the day the hurricane was expected to reach land, he took a lawn chair, a thermos of strong, steaming coffee and went outside to maintain a storm vigil. Waiting, simply waiting, for the hurricane's imminent, early evening arrival.

From his vantage point on the gravel walkway in front of the house, he witnessed in the distance the transformation of the waves as they multiplied in size and became increasingly violent, breaking against the beach and washing tauntingly, menacingly farther inland. He saw the thick, threatening clouds gathering over the Atlantic, felt the winds slowly rising. He watched the storm's initial approach with utter fascination and tugging fear. Watched, mesmerized, until the fringe of destruction was nearly upon him, until the palm trees lining the road began doing the limbo, bending unnaturally in the wind. Until stinging bits of gravel lashed his face. Until a primal survival pang — emanating not from his head, but from the pit of his guts — compelled him to get off that walkway while he was still able. He stood in retreat and the lawn chair he'd been sitting on was at once propelled down the road.

God's wrath, he thought. As if God hadn't done enough already.

"Personally, I lost a good whack of everything," the old man says. "My old, war-built, shit-shack couldn't take the punishment. But I can rebuild, I've done it before and at least Iris didn't get me. I hung out in the can. It's one of those great survival tips that no one ever seems to mention cause it ain't all that dignified: you can most always survive a hurricane if you camp out in the shitter...." He pauses, scratches the grey-flecked stubble on his chin, then philosophizes: "You know what they say: what doesn't kills us only makes us stronger, or smarter, or whatever the hell that saying is..." Sighing, he adds: "Next time those dolled-up, eyebrows-plucked, snazzy-suit TV weather types start talking about us taking a direct hit, I'm evacuating. Going to find me a nice, dry, safe Marriott somewhere inland with a well-stocked mini bar. Honest to god, I'm too old for this crap."

Storm is transported inland to County General Hospital. A brief stay for concussion treatment. Poked, prodded, observed and assessed by various besieged nurses and doctors to determine the overall status of his health. The headaches continue, as does a vague feeling of disorientation, a disconcerting fugue state. Past hours remain unreal, a hallucination, an incompatible combination of dream and nightmare.

ANGELS IN THE ARCHITECTURE

After forty-eight-hours he is deemed fit for discharge; compared to other hurricane victims who have been wheeled into inundated County, he is a picture of robust health. When a Dr. Morton Brown (himself a tanned, transplanted Canadian, or so he jovially announces) shakes his hand and delivers the discharge — replete with a stern warning for Storm to take it easy for two weeks to a month — Storm finds himself contemplating for the first time in ages precisely what succeeds the past.

What comes after Ali Reynolds Baker? What follows the limbo in which he's been living? Where to go, what to do? Physically, he has been living the life of a beach bum. In all other ways, he has been living like an escape artist, on the lam from life. Does he turn himself in, or keep running?

Admittedly, he is in no shape to make consequential, life decisions. He has been through hell, a hurricane, and a hospital: the sterile sights, sounds and smells of the modern medical facility having further distorted his reality by launching him back to an excruciating hospital vigil that he had endured at the bedside of his mother in what now seems like a previous century.

Storm is in his hospital room, pleased to be changing out of the institution's standard issue of an absurd, baby-blue, backless Johnny and into his street clothes — cleaned, pressed and smelling fresh out of the hospital laundry — when a young, ebullient nurse he knows from a previous introduction as Carlotta Swift raps on his door and enters with his personal belongings.

"Met your friend yesterday," the personable Carlotta says as she gently tosses his possessions onto the bed. Storm thinks of the grizzled old-timer who brought him in and, he assumes, came to visit. "You were sleeping. He sure asked a lot of questions. He said he would come back, but I didn't see him return," she adds. She is summoning the nerve to question whether the friend who visited is single — because lately her shifts have been long, her social life wanting, her needs unfulfilled — when she notices that Storm is not listening. The nurse misinterprets his expression and disbelieving eyes as confusion. She doesn't know what to make of the sharp intake of breath.

"Procedure, just for safe storage," she hastily explains. "We take incoming patients' valuables and lock them up as soon as they are…"

Heart launched into his throat. Goosebumps spider-walking across his skin. Suddenly he's hyperventilating. Can't breathe, can't think lucidly.

The room spins. Blood to his head in a dizzying rush. Knees buckle. He clutches the arm of a padded chair to steady himself, then collapses into the chair's cushiony grip. Carlotta Swift to his side, thinks what she is witnessing is pain.

"Storm, Mr. Baker, are you okay?" She is holding his arm. But in that instant, he seems unaware of her presence, impervious to her concern and to everything around him save for the few valuables on the bed. Wristwatch. Wedding ring. Gold pendant and chain. Imprinted on the pendant, the image of Pegasus, the winged wonder. The very pendant and chain that had inexplicably vanished on the day she died.

Head supported by his own clammy hand, voice but a cracked whisper, he stops Carlotta from buzzing for a doctor. Reassures her and asks her to hand him the pendant.

The pendant. Reverently holds it up to the light flooding in the window like it's a rare artifact. Carlotta Swift feels uncomfortable, as though intruding upon a moment of gravity that is not only awkwardly personal but bordering on spiritual. Places it unsteadily into palm of his other hand, closes his eyes, runs his fingers gently over its contours. Carlotta Swift, now a voyeur to an act of intense, sensual intimacy, feels she should be averting her eyes but cannot. They're transfixed. Further, she feels flustered, flushed, and oddly aroused. His eyelids begin fluttering. He cannot hold back the tears even if he had the presence of mind to try.

"Everything is going to be alright. Everything... alright."

It takes a few minutes of her soothing words and unbridled, unfounded optimism ("Isn't all optimism unfounded?" the Hazard had often questioned) before he can collect himself.

He says that he needs to make a telephone call. Unthinkingly, by rote, out of the habits bred (and reflexes refined) in nearly life-long friendship, he is driven to contact the Hazard for the first time since Ali died. Tell him that his Turtle Cay cottage survived. Tell him that his old friend survived. Tell him that, honest-to-God, he saw Ali, that she was with him, and he now has proof in a pendant.

Mind racing, he is also thinking that he should enlist the Hazard to help track down Ali's mother. Because Storm Baker has been seized by an imperative need to visit Janeen Reynolds, to feel close not only to the spirit of Ali, but to what he believes to be the sole remaining connection to her flesh and blood.

ANGELS IN THE ARCHITECTURE

Carlotta hands him the telephone off the bedside table. He dials, Florida to Toronto, gives an operator his calling card number and waits for the connection to be completed.

In Florida, Carlotta Swift fans herself with an old and faded *Life* magazine that was resting on the windowsill. Storm Baker sits on the edge of the chair, still shaky, mind reeling with possibilities and what are, to him, indisputable realizations. In Toronto, a shrill telephone ring is absorbed into the dusty silence of an empty, abandoned home in the upscale Baby Point area, west of High Park.

As he listens to the second ring, an image flashes in Storm's head. The image that won't die, that not even time will kill, that remains too clear, too distinct, too definitive despite its age and the eerie autumn mist that surrounds it. And with the image — eyes sting, and the familiar lump (of sadness, anger, disbelief, betrayal) begins its slow journey up his throat. Why, Harland, why? He cradles the receiver, severing the connection before the emptiness can answer. He whispers to himself: "You bastard, I'm coming home."

Part Two

Waiting To Derail

An Obscure Eden

AND WE CAME *to find ourselves in an obscure Eden — a ten-acre park, carved out of northern Muskoka wilderness — our senses arrested by nature. Around us, ponds fed by natural springs, botanical gardens, and majestic red pines. Directly in front of us, seventy steep flagstone steps leading up an incline to a magnificent stone monument.*

"The beauty," Ali said, shaking her head in wonder, "it's beyond words." She plucked a Pentax 35mm camera from her photography bag, holding it for a moment like a preacher cradling a bible as her eyes scanned for ideal light and interesting angles. Then she began capturing the monument which, having penetrated the cloudless blue mantel, appeared to be poking the sky.

Unlike the handful of other visitors in the park on that late-spring day, we had not come in search of the monument, or even the park for that matter. We had simply stumbled upon the scene. As usual, we were lost. If there were signs posted, we missed them. Granted, we often missed signs, typically because we were not paying proper attention to where we were going — or, deep in conversation, any attention whatsoever. I will always regard our recurring state of being lost as "an Ali thing," not solely because she was a hopeless navigator, but more because she had this philosophy by which she lived: that one of the ways that people could best find themselves, was to lose themselves.

When asked what she wanted to do on days when we found ourselves with free time, she would often answer: "Let's get lost." Which meant she craved escape, to hop into my beat-up old Dodge Dart and abandon the city, responsibilities, deadlines, inhibitions. And on those impromptu road trips she would insist that we travel off the beaten path and that we carry no map, no itinerary, oftentimes no baggage (save for the ubiquitous camera bag which she rarely left home without, brimming with all the technology necessary to "capture all beauty that comes before me.") In Ali's words, our road trips were *"unencumbered by the baggage of expectations."*

Although against my nature, she helped me realize that I could travel without creature comforts or expectations — that I could let myself go and experience the assorted surprises, disappointments, and delights of such spontaneous journeys as they occurred. That said, I admit to having had some innate, ongoing difficulties traveling minus the map and itinerary.

"Honest to god. Would it kill us to know approximately where we're going?"

In the time we were together, we got lost in two countries, a handful of American states, assorted Canadian provinces and in charming cities like Halifax, Quebec City, Montreal, Vancouver, even in our home base of Toronto, and in San Francisco, New York and Savannah, Georgia, where we actually spent an enchanted night wandering in the garden of good and evil. Some destinations were assigned to us via work; others, such as Lexington, Kentucky, (thoroughbred horse capital of the world), and Hilton Head, South Carolina, were chosen purely for pleasure and often on a whim. Our future — never realized— would surely have included further travels, other continents and other cities that she often spoke of with dreamy, faraway eyes...

"Picture us in Paris," she would say. Or, "Picture us in Rome." Or, "Picture us on a beach in Fiji." I pictured us, right up until she died. Then I had trouble even picturing myself, alone, anywhere. Without her, nothing was capable of captivating, and nothing seemed to fit... particularly me.

Closer to home: for two glorious weeks one sunbaked summer we vacationed in one of the Hazard's 'investment properties', a striking baby-blue cottage just outside of Goderich, Ontario, that sat, postcard-perfect, atop a hill and overlooked a pristine stretch of beach on the seemingly endless sandy shores of Lake Huron.

Ali on the beach — barefoot, in shorts, a bikini, or jeans rolled up her calves, walking for miles, chasing waves in and out, finding flat stones and skipping them out into the lake, collecting driftwood, marveling at the shapes that perpetually moving time and water had created, collecting wood for a fire; Ali late at night, staring into the fire, or roasting a marshmallow to golden brown perfection as campfire smoke curled around her.

At Ali's urging we often got back to nature and spent nights camped out under the stars. Faced with inclement weather on a road trip we would sleep in the car, cramped and uncomfortable, or in sleeping bags atop the flea-bitten beds of cheap, roadside motels (not daring to even consider, let alone investigate, what may have been lurking beneath the bedcovers). Despite my *intrinsic leaning toward comfort and higher-end accommodation, I never (okay, rarely) complained because I sensed that we were fashioning enduring memories, and I knew that I was having the time of my life...*

So, how did we come to find ourselves facing those seventy, steep flagstone steps leading to the monument, Ali enthusiastically snapping pictures? One minute we were on a highway outside of Huntsville, about one-hundred-and-forty miles north of Toronto, the next we were on one of the Muskoka region's characteristic rollercoaster roads, grinding up hills the old Dart barely had the guts to climb, speeding down the other side, and careening around hairpin turns. We came to an old stone schoolhouse and turned off the main road onto a back road that Ali said was beckoning. From there we followed a sandy track that mimicked the tortuous curves of what we would learn was the Big East River. And then we found it. Or, as Ali suggested, it found us...

Dyer Memorial. A forty-two-foot-high granite obelisk built by Clifton Dyer, a prosperous Detroit lawyer, as a memorial to his wife Betsy. In 1916, the Dyers honeymooned in the area and fell in love with what the locals have always proudly pronounced to be "God's Country." They canoed on the Big East River and portaged around Young's Rapids, which brought them to the site upon which the monument would eventually be erected. In 1936, they celebrated their twentieth wedding anniversary with a canoe trip that culminated in the purchase of a substantial parcel of the land they so adored. Four years later they built a log cabin that still stands on the bank of the Big East River.

In 1956, Betsy Dyer died. Consumed by grief, her husband decided to build a monument to his wife and to their love. A Detroit architect designed the memorial and local stonemasons built it in the center of the park, an area graced by the gardens and ponds. Clifton Dyer died shortly after it was finished, and his ashes were placed alongside his wife's ashes atop the monument.

"Take my hand," Ali said, easing the camera back into the bag. Hand in hand, we began our ascent up the steps. At the top, the monument, and at its base the inscription: "Erected in fond memory of Betsy Browne Dyer by her husband Clifton G. Dyer as a permanent tribute to her for the never-failing aid, encouragement and inspiration which she contributed to their married career, and as a final resting place for her ashes..." And upon reading those words, Ali faced me, and she hugged me — tighter and with more urgency and for longer than I'd ever been hugged before — like a mother squeezing a final goodbye out of the flesh of her child as she sends him off to kindergarten for the very first time.

ANGELS IN THE ARCHITECTURE

When her grip finally relaxed, she spoke, her mouth so close to my ear I could feel the warmth and moisture of her breath: "Swear, Storm Baker, that you'll never forget me, no matter what happens." Then, turning to run a pensive finger across the monument, she added: "And that you will always love me this much..."

Two blue jays noisily fought over a shelled peanut, a bubbly girl giggled as her father hoisted her onto his shoulders and her family began climbing the flagstone steps, a seaplane sputtered in the distance, and a trickle of sweat ran down my back. I told her what she wanted to hear. The honest-to-God truth...

"I already love you more," I said, kissing an errant tear off her cheek.

Not Everyone Can Carry The Weight Of The World
Or, Complete Consciousness Is Overrated

THE LAST TIME he saw her was at the funeral where they paid their final, formal respects to his wife and her sole offspring, Ali Reynolds Baker. Predictably, she was tardy, delaying the service and flustering a delicate and excitable bible-hugging minister whose facial ticks became more animated and whose ears and once alabaster skin burned a deeper shade of red with each minute Storm requested the opening prayers be delayed.

Janeen Reynolds had never really possessed any real sense of time. To her way of thinking, she had to wonder why in the world would a woman with her irrefutable sense of presence and impeccable sense of timing have any need for a sense of time?

She had been difficult to locate. Faithful to her wandering, bohemian nature, she uprooted herself after her daughter died and naturally never bothered with a detail as mundane as leaving a forwarding address. After Storm returned to Toronto from Florida, it took a week of persistent sleuthing and full utilization of his honed investigative skills, before he discovered that for the past five months his mother-in-law had been residing at the CrossRoads, a high-rise apartment complex in west Toronto. Coincidentally, less than two miles from where Storm and Ali had lived.

Driving to the CrossRoads, he is dogged by uncertainty. Memories — wonderful and warming and yet at once unsettling and destabilizing — are triggered by geography, by proximity to their former neighborhood, an area so overpoweringly steeped in Ali that he has consciously avoided it since returning. Further memories are triggered by the calendar and prevailing weather.

ANGELS IN THE ARCHITECTURE

The car heater hisses on low. Outside it is autumn ugly and autumn cold, with winter lying in ambush just around the corner. As he parks his Dodge on a side street across from the high-rise complex, he considers that capricious autumn will forever be a trigger. Because to Storm, autumn was Ali. It was when they met, when they married and honeymooned, and when she died. On this autumn morning the memories triggered are those of her funeral. Regressing in time, nearly one year.

Thankfully he has slim and selective recall of that November day, protectively wrapped as he was in a cocoon of numbness, and as proficient as the mind is at entombing unpleasant memories just as it shamelessly embellishes and enshrines the good. Thankfully no photographs exist to immortalize the occasion. Not a single picture was taken by anyone despite Ali's repeatedly voiced conviction that cameras should be on hand at funerals just as they are at picnics, parties, vacations, weddings and births (post-delivery/after clean-up, naturally, the actual birth being too bloody a reality). It was her contention that family photo albums, which generally present such a false, rosy sense of life — devoid of horror, hatred, sadness, sex and death — should, rather, reflect the truth of existence, or what she described as "mankind in the bathroom with pants bunched around the ankles..."

"Remind me not to show up for Family Photo Night at your house," Harland Hazard would retort. "At least, not sober."

Prior to the funeral service, Storm had been overcome by an irrepressible, almost frantic need to steal a moment alone. He located a side door and slipped outside. The sky was a depressing mantle, steel-wool gray, the air misty and distinctively autumn as he, a southern Ontarian, had always known the season. Smoke emanated from a pile of damp leaves being burned behind a residence down the road. On the road in front of the home, boisterous teenagers were playing touch football, young men and women taking advantage of every opportunity to bump and touch without consequence; and on this day, even the usually pleasing, nostalgic thump of the ball being booted sounded mournful. The early afternoon chill burrowed into his bones, making him feel as though he would never again be warm. He stood shivering, uncomfortable in his clothing, miserable in his own skin, longing for escape, for sunshine, for warmth.

Naturally he wondered whether Harland Hazard would show up, and what they would possibly say to each other if he did. What words could be used to bridge the awkwardness, the anger, the Judas chasm that had opened between them? What words could justify those actions and ever assuage their effect? In Storm's mind, nothing under the sun — not desire, desperation, not even fragile mental health, or a regrettable, reckless mixing of assorted antidepressants, anodynes and alcohol — could rationalize such behavior. What could he possibly have been thinking? What?

That said, there was a part of him that could not imagine the Hazard missing the funeral. There, for appearances, as Storm's best friend. There as the man who, late one night at a regular gathering of friends at Ali and Storm's apartment, during an ill-advised round of the juvenile Truth or Dare, let the medications and white rum excavate a best-buried, slurred confession.

Truth.

Dramatically pushing his chair back, rising with effort, confessing. He had this fantasy, the two of them, star-crossed. Her playing Daisy Buchanan to his Jay Gatsby, Zelda to his F. Scott…

A faux pas that stunned, rendered speechless: for certain it was a discomfiting game-ender, and it definitely had potential to also be the stake driven through the heart of the party. However, even in his state, he was cognizant that he had broken the code and crossed the line. Even in his state, a not altogether unaccustomed condition, he had the mental agility, the practiced wherewithal to know that he could save himself, as he most always saved himself, by tossing out into stormy seas the lifesaver of levity.

"Oh fuck, how about you?" And here he pivoted: pointing to the doe-eyed Sally Hayes, a close friend of Ali's who was seated beside Storm. "Beautiful you, Sally-girl, for one glorious night as Mia Farrow to my Robert Redford…" Followed by that infectious grin, he resuscitated the party he'd nearly killed. And once again he was golden.

Storm contemplated the funeral. He hoped that he had made the right decisions, unclear in his own mind of precisely what Ali would have wanted and uncertain of what he could endure. She had advised him in advance regarding the basics such as no church service, a non-sectarian minister…

And what a surreal dinnertime conversation that had been: a youthful, healthy, lively woman who so embraced life, prosaically reiterating her morbid presentiment that she would die young, instructing her husband on funeral arrangements and, could he please pass the homemade Thai

ANGELS IN THE ARCHITECTURE

salad dressing. She said that she was entrusting him to ensure that her funeral would not turn into a media circus and that it would contain no talk of religious trappings such as the pearly gates and The Great Hereafter, which she believed sounded a phony note and made heaven sound like a celestial Club Med resort. Like her girlhood fictional hero, Holden Caulfield, she had an intense distaste for things that were phony and all.

"And, honey," he had said, when he could no longer endure the conversation, "what type of casket would you like? Perhaps we could go to Shady Happy Willow Acres tomorrow and pick one out together. I'm partial to mahogany, with ornate brass handles and kind of an Elvis-esque red velvet interior. And then there's always the headstone..."

"I get your sarcasm, Storm Baker, and it's funny as hell, it really is. All I'm trying to do is prepare you. And, by the way, remember I want to be cremated." And as she uttered the word "cremated," she glanced up from her salad and saw her husband's ashen face, tremulous hands clamped over his ears. She dropped her fork, took gentle hold of his wrists and guided his hands back down to the table.

"Hon, I'm sorry."

"I'm sorry, too. But I can't... This isn't normal. Every time you start this, I hear Michael Stipe, in my head singing, mumbling, *Talk About The Passion*. You know that line, 'not everyone can carry the weight of the world.' I can't carry... I'm just not that strong..."

Not strong enough to face one of the most painful fears known to man: loneliness. Clouded vision, a heart so heavy it felt like the weight of the world. Not everyone.

"Come on, babe, you start the bath and light the candles and I'll get the bubbles. I bought a new sandalwood mixture..." Ali's tried and true remedy; to simply steam and soak away whatever weight was dragging them down.

"There are few things a hot bath won't cure," she once recited, "but I don't know many of them. For the less-literary types in the room, that's a quote attributed to Sylvia Plath."

"Didn't she commit suicide?"

"Not after a hot bath, she didn't."

Despite her attempts to prepare him, he remained steadfastly unprepared. Funeral arrangements had quickly become overwhelming, the details boundless and extending far beyond her basic wishes.

ANDY JUNIPER

Storm's father appeared at the doorway, summoning him back inside the funeral home with a short, stiff wave. Like a youth forced for the first time to exchange his familiar, patched play clothes for a confining suit and tie, the enduringly happy-go-lucky Pete Baker appeared incongruous and hopelessly ill-at-ease in this setting; appeared as though at any moment he might bolt for the parking lot and squeal off in his Mustang to a local golf course for a quick round, or to a pub for a perspiring brown bottle of relief.

At that moment a chevron of Canadian geese flew overhead, serenading Storm with their plaintive flight song. He was envious of their apparent good fortune and conveniently blind to their actuality. On this day Storm was unable to even consider the myriad possible misfortunes awaiting the geese on the course of their long journey south. He would not allow himself to think of the eager, camouflaged hunters, whiskey flasks, guns and jowly, salivating hounds at the ready. On this day, the geese were simply the lucky ones, leaving behind the chill and the oppressive autumn gray, flying toward boundless azure skies, curative warmth and sunshine.

What Storm also remembers clearly and with a measure of fondness and disbelief is what his mother-in-law was wearing that afternoon when she finally made her grand entrance through the back door of the funeral home and marched by the gathered media, friends and relatives toward where he was seated at the front. Her entrance and attire created a stir that fractured the ponderous silence, produced whispers and, for an instant, cracked open Storm's cocoon of numbness and allowed into his world a bracing whiff of air laced with sweet and communal sorrow.

There she stands in his mind's eye, Janeen Reynolds looking like an adventurous and deviously potent tropical drink in a clingy and loud lime-green dress that spanked conventional conservative funeral attire just as surely as it clashed with both the occasion and the gold Jackie Kennedy-pillbox hat crookedly perched atop an imposing mountain of orange hair. If not for her undeniable natural beauty, she would have effectively rendered herself hideous.

She had always possessed a flair for the dramatic and she had always been partial to bold, flashy makeup — wild slashes of war paint — which, the Hazard once quipped, appeared as though it had been applied with a trowel. She loved clothes that coordinated with little beyond her demeanor: outrageous clothes, big hats (ten-gallon cowboy hats were a fashion favorite) and really big hair (mercilessly teased and *poofed*) the color of which she dramatically altered on a regular basis. Any time they were anticipating a visit from Janeen, Ali and Storm would place friendly wagers on how high the hair, and what color? Granted, anticipating a visit from Janeen was a fool's gamble. A frequent no-show, her style was a more impromptu, drop-in, typically, at the most inopportune moment.

"Oh, Ali, you look ravishing in that black teddy you're trying to hide under your kimono." Then, playing the innocent to perfection: "Now, what are you kids up to tonight?"

Once at the front of the funeral home, she eased past Storm's immediate family — his father and his siblings, Mackey and Paris — and sidled up beside her son-in-law. She took his arm in her hands and, with her long, thin fingers, applied pressure indicating that she was feeling nowhere near as strong and composed as she appeared. She was acting. Because she would forever think of herself as an actress and this mournful setting, this grim, grievous reality had become her stage. In a cloud about her, the scent of perfume scuffling for prominence with the odor of chain-smoked Lucky Strike cigarettes. When she glanced up at him, he also got a whiff of the gin that had been imbibed, no doubt to fortify her performance. He watched her eyelids and long, black lashes fluttering rapidly, butterfly wings in flight, beating back tears.

"You know, I've never looked good in black," she said, quietly acknowledging the wave of whispers that had yet to crest. "And this particular occasion is not at all endurable sober. I truly believe," she added, "that complete consciousness is overrated."

How could he possibly argue? Grief naturally numbs, but not nearly enough. Personally, he had further anesthetized himself with a pill produced by his physician and friend, Dr. Redic Mackenzie, who had made a compassionate, unsolicited house call at Storm's apartment on the morning of the funeral.

"Librium," the general practitioner had informed. "A minor tranquilizer. At this strength, prescription calls for two every six hours. It should help you to eliminate some of the anxiety, some of the edge, without knocking you out."

"Take a hammer to my skull, Redic… I'd prefer to be knocked out."

However, when it came time to swallowing the manufactured 'chill' with the glass of water Redic fetched, Storm was reluctant, and of the attitude that the occasion was actually crying out for an edge. In the end he took only one of the pills.

ANDY JUNIPER

When silence at last descended upon the funeral home, Storm nodded for the minister to begin. The beleaguered pastor extracted a precisely folded white handkerchief from his suit jacket, dabbed the heavy beads of sweat from his forehead and, with lips quivering, began twitching through his opening remarks, welcoming the gathered and then asking everyone to pray. As all heads solemnly bowed, Storm Baker squeezed his eyes shut and prayed for the obvious and the impossible. Make these recent days disappear, God. Make it so they never happened.

At various times during the service, the pressure of Janeen's grip on Storm's arm increased. He could physically feel her sorrow, just as surely as he felt her painted fingernails intermittently digging into his flesh. Sadly, he was unable to comfort her in any way. He was petrified of surrendering to his emotions, petrified of precisely where that surrender might lead.

New grief invariably inspires reminders of old grief. Years ago, Storm Baker had lost his mother. Now, like then, he was certain that he had lost everything.

In front of all the people in the world who mattered to him — some who had known him all his life, many who knew him intimately and who loved him and whose arms were open and whose hearts were bleeding with him and for him — he stood tall, erect, fiercely in control. It was a performance that an actress like Janeen would have been able to appreciate and applaud had she not been preoccupied with falling apart.

Granted, there were two fleeting instances when Storm nearly relinquished that control: the moment he allowed thoughts of the conspicuously absent Harland Hazard to encroach upon the blank white screen he had raised across his mind's eye, and upon which he was determined to remain focused; and the instant when he glanced down at his mother-in-law and witnessed mascara and tears mingling and trickling down her cheeks — that is, the moment he felt the full, piercing force of her pain. Until then, he had selfishly assumed that his anguish was unrivaled.

"How could she be dead?" Janeen would ask no one in particular at the intimate, impromptu wake that sprang to life at the Harbour Castle Hotel where Storm's family was staying. Unable to stand the confining funeral attire, the cloak of mourning, for another moment, Pete Baker had aligned himself with the Irish as a proponent of the boozy wake as a glorious celebration of life. He changed into more casual clothes and effectively commandeered the mini bar in the room he was sharing with his eldest son, Mackey, who many people considered to be "a chip off the old block," albeit with a little less of Pete's jocular, infectious personality.

Mackey meanwhile commandeered the television, obliged by his very nature to watch "the big game", although from his constant channel changing and the undulating voices of various announcers, Storm never got a clear sense of which sport's big game his brother felt compelled to watch.

"No disrespect," Mackey would mutter in commercial breaks, "but I think Ali would have wanted it this way, life going on and whatnot…"

Storm had requested there be no reception following the service. Intuitively he knew he would be unable to stomach the tart punch, the crustless sandwiches; unable to endure the clumsy condolences, the pressing of flesh, making the rounds and simply being in the same room with grief, dressed up. Although he did not embrace the thought of returning to the apartment he had shared with Ali, he nevertheless wanted to go home just so that he could be alone and bury himself in sorrow. Paris Baker, his sister who flew in from London arriving only hours before the funeral, would have none of that. In retrospect, he would be grateful for his sister's insistence, her good sense, and her love.

"A child is not supposed to die before her mother." Janeen continued, nursing a gin and dabbing at her bloodshot eyes with a crumpled Kleenex (drag, sip, dab). "It's not the way of things, Storm. It's not natural. It's not the way the circle of life goes round…"

Outside the Harbour Castle, across the harbor and the island airport and out into Lake Ontario, night was descending. Grief works the night shift. Hurt souls are infinitely more vulnerable when surrounded by darkness. Storm Baker was a hurt soul, an open wound.

As the supplies in the mini bar ran low and his father called the hotel's room-service personnel for refills, as Mackey nodded off in front of the television, as Paris dexterously manipulated the knotted muscles in Storm's shoulders, Storm held his mother-in-law's hand and stared out the hotel room window into the dying light. Through his sorrow and disbelief and his childlike fear of a future that seemed even more unappealing than it was uncertain, he agreed with Janeen. How could she be dead? How could someone so full of life, lose life? More silent prayers for the obvious, the impossible. More demands on Our Maker. Fix it, God.

A Person With Nothing On His Mind, And The Power To Express It

OUTSIDE IN THE imposing shadow of the CrossRoads stands a community bulletin board. Procrastinating, Storm stops to peruse the clash of postings by local peddlers and prophets, including one that dominates by its bull's-eye positioning, its size, and the boldness of its print. It reads:

**Please Join
The League of Decency**

And under the plea, right across the League's telephone number, a local armed with a thick, black marker and considerable attitude has scrawled:

Fuck You

Entering the CrossRoads, Storm is met by feuding smells of coffee, assorted fried foods and cigarette smoke and by a fire alarm sounding a strident alert. The entry-level of the drab and architecturally uninspired twenty-two story concrete complex houses a compact shopping concourse replete with a handful of prerequisite fast-food restaurants, a ubiquitous Coffee Break coffee shop, a convenience store, a liquor store, and a Brief Encounters lingerie-chain outlet. Not a single uplifting beam of natural light has been permitted to permeate the concourse, the architect alternatively opting for fluorescent lighting that casts everyone in a sick, ghostly pallor.

A heavy-set, heavy-eyed uniformed security guard on duty by the elevator doors reluctantly breaks from mining his ear with the antennae of his static-screeching walkie-talkie to inform Storm that the elevators will remain out of service until the all-clear is issued by the fire department which, he adds, has yet to even respond. He also perfunctorily states that it is his duty to inform people that they should be evacuating, although it's apparent that few are choosing this prudent course of action, and the guard isn't exactly corralling anyone out the doors.

"So," Storm innocently asks, "do you think it's safe on this level?"

"Do you smell smoke?" He chuckles sardonically at the rube. "Where's your turnip truck, man? Not from around here, are you? Man, if I had a dime for every alarm in this building..." He shakes his head. "I'd have a lot of fucking dimes..."

Storm wanders through the concourse, past the convenience store with its wall-long racks of skin magazines and shelves overstocked with Asian-imported dollar bargains, past the unwashed, tottering vagrants tremulously awaiting the opening of the liquor store, past the predominantly tasteless and crotchless merchandise in the window of the lingerie store. Like the security guard, everyone seems unmoved and altogether unconcerned by the fire alarm.

Still, not prepared to scale potentially smoky stairs en route to Janeen's nineteenth-floor apartment, Storm ducks into the Coffee Break. He is not displeased by the delay. He craves the caffeinated encouragement of a coffee and a part of him desires to postpone meeting Janeen indefinitely. Understandably, he is uncertain of the reception he will receive from his mother-in-law considering that he bailed out on her just as surely as he had bailed out on life itself, and Janeen has traditionally been prickly and unpredictable even at the best of times. Storm did not telephone in advance to arrange a convenient time. There is a certain freedom and comfort in not committing, in being able to just wake one morning and drive north to the CrossRoads unannounced, and gamble on her being home.

Stepping in line to order at the front counter, he is blind-sided by a baby stroller — one wheel smacks his ankle while the body of the stroller clips his knee along a fine scar-line, a permanent (albeit faded) reminder of a surgical rebuild he underwent years ago. The pain is minimal but personal medical history has made Storm overly sensitive and defensive when it comes to that vulnerable joint. The chubby and visibly frazzled force behind the stroller — a squat woman clad in white sweat socks and running shoes, black spandex workout tights and a white, oversized CN Tower T-shirt — begins profusely apologizing, spitting out words, waving her hands and flapping her flabby arms, semaphoring flags of flesh gesturing for absolution. In mid-apology she suddenly recognizes the man she has crashed into.

"*You*," she says, almost accusingly, and loud enough to ensure that her voice is the center of attention in the coffee shop, "you *touched* me." She is oblivious to how this peculiar declaration must sound to the other patrons who shift uneasily in their seats as they weigh whether to watch what may develop into a scene, or remain true to their Torontonian natures and simply stare into their coffee cups. Or, better yet, bury their faces in their newspapers and pretend that nothing at all is happening.

"You touched me here," she continues, clasping meaty, sausage fingers over her left breast. As though cued, the pudgy infant in the stroller whimpers, alerting imaginative minds to the possibility that this incident may climax in a juicy revelation. Perhaps his touching her in that particular soft and ample spot in some way precipitated or inspired the conception of this sorrowful bundle of joy. Storm attempts to speak but is cut off by the woman's bubble-headed ebullience, her quick, practiced tongue, and another eruption of words.

"I'm Oral, by the way, like composition, not sex," she titters. "Oral Bannon, and I'd heard that you'd left Toronto and that you were a mess, a real basket case, and my best friend, Trisha-Rose Bowman-Hinchberger, but, well, you don't know her, bet me that you'd commit suicide within a year. Suicide! Within a year!

"She said that she could accurately predict your future, as short as it was, by reading between the lines of your last column. She's always been pretty good since way back in high school, Runnymede Collegiate right here in Toronto, when she was still a Bowman and not a Hinchberger — well, Bowman hyphen Hinchberger because she's kind of a feminist and all — with tea bags and tarot cards and palms and that. But I knew better, and I told her that I didn't give a flying fig what her old Ouija board confirmed or did not confirm. I know you, Storm Baker and, my word, you touched me."

She pauses only for an instant to catch her breath, a prudent move considering her face has turned an unflattering purple from effort and oxygen deprivation. Then, as an aside, she exhales: "It's been a year now, hasn't it?"

In what now seems like a lifetime ago, Storm Baker was a journalist. Specifically, a newspaper columnist, or what *New York Times*' celebrated editorialist Russell Baker (Storm's idol, his namesake) once wryly described as "a person with nothing on his mind, and the power to express it."

Storm's column appeared prominently on Page Two of the Monday, Wednesday, Friday, and Saturday editions of *The Toronto Times*. And over the course of six-plus years his essays garnered three National Newspaper Award nominations (one win); the Stephen Leacock Medal for humor for a compilation of some of his more off-beat essays (*Storm's Rising!*); and a modest book offer from a Winnipeg-based publisher seeking to expand its reach into the east.

Although difficult to pigeonhole, the *Times* was (and remains) a thick and oftentimes imposing morning newspaper with liberal leanings, an impressive daily circulation of half-a-million readers (650,000 on weekends), and a notable identity crisis; this being a publication with a tortured history of being unable to decide what direction it wished to proceed. Whether to dedicate itself to being saucy or high-minded, entertaining or enlightening. Which direction would earn awards and respect? Which would lure more advertisers and sell more copies?

During his tenure, Storm never became accustomed to, or comfortable with, being confronted by readers, critics and admirers alike. People who recognized him from the headshot that accompanied his "About Metro" column. Ali critiqued the photograph as being "inexcusably grainy and barely recognizable as you, but nevertheless cute as all get out." Storm refused to have it retaken. It was his hope that an inexcusably grainy and barely recognizable photograph would result in less recognition in public. Besides, he reasoned, there were worse things in this world than being considered cute as all get out.

The *Times*' zealous marketing department, which in the minds of the overworked editorial staff, had an enviable surfeit of time and budget on its hands, conducted endless readership surveys that reaffirmed that Storm Baker's column was one of the newspaper's more popular features. Up there with the likes of Ann Landers and Jim Unger's twisted Herman cartoon. Furthermore, apparently many of these Baker Loyalists liked him enough — or, to Harland Hazard's oft-voiced way of thinking, were pathetic and lonely enough — to actually consider him to be a friend, someone they felt they knew personally. After all, he did periodically mine his personal life in his column, especially after he met Ali, and hadn't these readers so generously invited him into their breakfast nooks every morning for years?

ANDY JUNIPER

With the passage of time, the Hazard's sonorous voice has taken up permanent residence in Storm's mind, his words becoming an integral part of the soundtrack that now accompanies his memories from childhood onward...

"Breakfast nooks?" he can clearly hear the Hazard questioning in that rich, narrator's tone, a perfect radio voice if not for the occasional cigarette-induced scratchiness: "Don't flatter yourself. For half of the Big Smoke, you're the comfort people reach for when they're ensconced in the washroom and *People* magazine isn't available. People in The Big Smoke rely on bran muffins, strong coffee, and you to help keep them regular."

In a summary that was *howlingly* ridiculed by the newspaper's department heads, the marketers concluded that readers perceived Storm to be a "regular guy," an agreeable alternative to the abundant arsty-fartsy, or radical-feminist, or political-animal, or family-life-chronicler columnists at the *Times* and Toronto's other dueling dailies. Letters to the editor and letters personally addressed to Storm further revealed that readers believed he was a suitable confidant, a guy with whom they could share intimate everythings or, at the very least, someone they could slap on the back in a hearty greeting and maybe even buy a hot coffee or a cold beer: talk about the Leafs, the Jays, the Argos, or how about those bumbling morons down at City Hall, and what the hell's up with that goddamn property tax increase?

When it came to reader mail, Storm felt a kinship with Nick Caraway, the narrator of Ali and Harland's favorite novel, *The Great Gatsby*. In particular, he could relate to F. Scott Fitzgerald's description of how people were always opening up to Caraway and making him "the victim of not a few veteran bores" with their unsought confidences and intimate revelations... Revelations that were always "quivering on the horizon."

Dear Mr. Baker, you don't know me, but I feel as though I know you... Followed by the treacly. The private. The outrageous. The delusional and worrisomely possessive. The unstable and the volatile. And when inappropriate outpourings went unrequited, the threatening.

One complete stranger, a woman with the unlikely name of Elizabeth Still, was convinced their one-way communication – he'd politely answered her initial letter but none of the dozens that followed over the next two years – was, in fact, a real relationship; her salutations transgressed from Dear Friend to My Lover (followed by parenthetic advice: be careful your wife does not see this... we mustn't be caught!") in under ten letters. And while his colleagues and the Hazard were united in mining the humor out of her creepy obsessiveness, he (and, at times, Ali) felt more threatened and stalked than amused. When he answered his ringing telephone and silence greeted his hello, he was convinced it was her. Likewise, when their apartment buzzer sounded at 3 a.m. He came to dread the arrival of the mail and her handwriting on an envelope had the power to nauseate. And at times when he was alone, he wasn't sure he was alone. He was forever feeling eyes on his back.

Suffice to say, this is an area he has not missed since resigning his post. He can't imagine ever missing being cornered in grocery stores, applauded or taken to task by witless, insensitive interlopers for something he wrote. Or miss having to change his telephone number, unlisted but nonetheless uncovered once or twice a year by crank callers and early morning, prank-playing disc jockeys engaged in another lame "Call Of The Day." He certainly will not miss being slipped unsolicited column fodder as he relieves himself at a urinal in the washroom of a downtown restaurant. And, just as he could have easily done without Elizabeth Still, he could also have done without this repellent encounter with Oral in the Coffee Break coffee shop at the CrossRoads.

"Let me tell you a little something, Storm Baker," Oral Bannon says, stooping over the stroller to quiet her baby with a honey-dipped soother she's fished from a Tupperware container in her purse. "I know you didn't rip-off that New York writer's words because you had so many neat words all of your own." Storm considers forgoing the coffee and beating a retreat: the prospect of risking his life on nineteen smoky flights of stairs is becoming increasingly appealing. "I know exactly what you were going through. I lost my husband around the same time you lost your wife. Only my guy left me for the office skank and...."

"And my wife died," Storm says, pouncing on a pause and finally managing to cram a sentence into her interminable monologue. "Died tragically. Oh, and it has not quite been a year, so don't even think about collecting that bet because..." He hesitates and, for effect, grins maniacally like he's Jack Nicholson plastered on the poster for *The Shining*, before adding: "You never know..."

It's a technique he learned from Sting, during an hour-long interview that inexplicably veered wildly off course. At one point the musician/

songwriter and then-frontman for The Police related how he'd been confronted late one night in a secluded area by an incensed drunk.

"Do you know what to do in such a situation, how to vanquish meddlers or disarm drunks?" he'd asked. "Act crazy! Recite Shakespeare, if only because it is sure to give the impression that you are crazier than they are..."

The tactic works, effectively silencing the woman who stares at him, silently reassessing. She is unaware that Storm is acting on the advice of a popular icon, or that journalists tend to share a sense of humor with ambulance attendants, hospital ER workers, undertakers, and people like Harland Hazard. Humor noir.

Thoughts turn tortured circles inside her head, like mad dogs chasing their own tails. Maybe her best friend Trisha-Rose Bowman-Hinchberger was bang on. Maybe the man she thought she knew so intimately is but another of those unbalanced, suicidal, writer types. Like that brutish bullfighting bore, Ernest Hemingway, that fruitcake Plath woman, who stuck her head in the oven, and — her mind blanks — well, some of those other unbalanced, suicidal, writer types...

A further welcoming silence envelops the coffee shop. Not only has Oral Bannon been hushed, but the fire alarm has also been disabled. About the only sound that can be heard comes from deep within the stroller: the frantic sucking of the baby working double time on the soother.

"Bout goddamn time," someone mutters.

"There'll only be, what, two or three more alarms today?"

"Welcome to life at the CrossRoads."

Storm's erstwhile admirer nods curtly and purposefully steers her baby stroller toward the exit, pausing only briefly to hike up her long T-shirt and tug at her workout pants that have inched uncomfortably up the crack of her buttocks.

Storm cannot stop himself; he feels obligated to state to her departing back, just for the record: "That guy was Russell Baker, columnist for *The New York Times*. To me, he was, *is* a God. I grew up loving his work, idolizing him. He's why I became what I became. And I did rip off his words. I committed the ultimate sin for a journalist: I plagiarized. Consciously, subconsciously, whatever. I'd lost my wife, I was under stress, the paper suggested I take a leave, and I refused. But all of that is no excuse." He sighs, then states the truth: "I've held myself accountable."

ANGELS IN THE ARCHITECTURE

He resigned. Because he was fully aware that when he lifted Baker's words from the muddle and murk of his mind — when he appropriated two-plus paragraphs and claimed them as his own; when those paragraphs were put into print and out into the public for consumption — he had effectively torpedoed his career. Forget that they ran for only one little-read edition before a perceptive editor, relaxing over a whiskey on dinner-break, came upon words, the alarm-tripping familiarity of which stopped him cold. And forget the innumerable mitigating circumstances. In the industry's unwritten code, plagiarism is ultimately unforgivable.

Storm's actions unwittingly sired an exchange in the newsroom between two hardboiled editors, softened by the knowledge that the death knell had sounded for a man they liked personally and admired professionally.

"He always wanted to be Russell Baker," the one editor said, running fingers through what little remained of his hair.

"Well," the other replied, following a deep, pensive drag on a cigarette, "for one fucking day, he was…"

Oral is out of the coffee shop. Storm calls out a final thought: "And Oral, you should know. Oral is the same, whether it's composition or sex…"

Although she does not look back, Storm knows that he is being harrumphed. Harrumphed because Oral's favorite writer, whose words and thoughts had frequently been posted on her refrigerator alongside *Redbook's* postpartum dieting tips and clippings containing the wisdom of Ann Landers, has fallen to Earth, if not lower.

There's Nothing To Get Hung About

WE TALKED FANCIFULLY *about one day owning a home. Cape Cod-styled with shiny hardwood floors, a roomy kitchen designed for the comfortable entertaining of friends, a finished basement replete with a billiard table, and a cozy family room with a wood-burning fireplace and wall-to-wall bookshelves so that on cold winter nights we could cuddle by a crackling fire, surrounded and comforted by familiar literature. Outside our dream home there would be a doghouse (for aesthetics only — as if Ali would ever let a pet sleep outdoors), gardens in which Ali could plant her green thumbs and, in the back, an in-ground pool bordered by stately cedars. Ali would swim lengths, and I would be happy to sit on a comfortable chaise and watch. Out front of the house, a smooth asphalt driveway and a basketball hoop — aside from the pool table, my only real contribution to the dream. All that said, honestly, we were in no rush.*

We loved the High Park area and were mindful of how far removed we were from being able to afford even a matchbox in that section of the city. Besides, we loved our apartment that I'd secured through dumb luck, with a little help from my new colleagues.

Following a stint as a feature writer and second-string columnist at a newspaper in Thunder Bay, Ontario, I was hired by the Times. Management put me up at the downtown Holiday Inn as part of a relocation package, although they stipulated that there would be a two-week limit to their munificence. Under pressure to find accommodations, while at once working extended hours and attempting to become acclimatized to both life in the metropolis and work at a metropolitan newspaper, I got wind that an old family friend was leaving Toronto to take a job in the U.S. My shrewd colleagues were quick off the mark with advice in fundamental matters of money tossing (how much, in what direction, at whom), which substantially increased my chances.

ANGELS IN THE ARCHITECTURE

Frankly, I knew little of the area, or the apartment for which I was vying (a trendy residence, I would learn, in a fashionable area), and I knew less of the cutthroat gamesmanship involved in apartment acquisitions in Toronto. In retrospect, it should have been obvious considering that the city had an atrocious annual vacancy rate of about zero-point-something percent that constantly had civic activists up in arms. After I'd signed the lease and moved in, I determined from the envious responses I received when asked where I lived that I had unwittingly managed something of a coup.

Down the road I met Ali. Farther along that road, she moved in and began working magic within the apartment walls, infusing the sterile cold with warmth and beauty and a much welcome feminine touch. And when she was finished giving the entire residence a creative and thorough makeover, there remained only two things that were truly hideous within the walls of what we comfortably called home: the refrigerator and the stove (sorely, standard issue for every apartment in the entire complex; an eye-assaulting green).

"Like an eclipse," she said, upon laying eyes on the appliances for the first time. "Stare directly at them and you'll go blind."

"I just don sunglasses whenever I reach for a glass of milk..."

"I wonder what they call this hideous shade of green?"

"Exorcist barf, I believe..."

"It's not easy being green..."

"You quote Kermit the Frog?"

"At length, whenever appropriate... Sometimes even when it's horribly inappropriate. As Kermit once said, 'Time's fun when you're having flies.'"

Ali endeavored to conceal or at least offset the Linda Blair barf with enlarged photographs and refrigerator postings. The photographs were prints of whatever she happened to be working on that week, or snapshots of people we knew. The postings were a mishmash of casual philosophy, motivational words, catchy phrases, borrowed lines of lyrics or dime-store poetry and quotes she gleaned from the work of artists, poets, musicians and others who had in some way inspired her. She wrote the postings in black marker on a sheet of plain white paper and then secured the page on the refrigerator with magnets; Muppet magnets, if you must know. Some of the postings were obvious, some ambiguous, cryptic.

"Most of what matters in our lives takes place in our absence..."
"If a man travels too far into the desert, he becomes sand..."

> "Everyone wants to go to heaven, but no one wants to die…"
> "Beauty comes from the soul…"
> "Don't pay the ransom, honey, I've escaped…"

I was familiar with some of the quotes and could attribute them to artists Ali was reading, or listening to, or to people she simply admired.

> **Leonard Cohen:** "A scar is what happens when the word is made flesh…"
> **Kurt Vonnegut:** "So it goes…"
> **Carl Jung:** "The fate of neutrals is to be abused by both sides…"
> **Harland Hazard:** "You've got to be happy with the skin you're in…"
> **Alice Walker:** "Being happy is not the only happiness…"
> **John Lennon:** "There's nothing to get hung about…

Others were unfamiliar.

> "Too much cleverness could kill a man…"
> "The more I think, the less I know…"
> "I believe it, because it is absurd…"

I don't know where she got them, or if they were Ali originals. But I knew that the words spoke of the woman I loved, one week's posting the very antithesis of the next. One week it was quirky, almost school-girlish Ali up on the fridge, the next it was an insightful, profound, old-soul Ali confronting me each time I entered the kitchen.

I can't clearly recall the first posting, but I vividly recall the last….

The final act before saying one last goodbye to the apartment: taking down and boxing the photographs, then removing the last posting — pocketing the Miss Piggy magnet, folding up the paper and placing it in the back pocket of my blue jeans, all the while feeling a bitter stinging in the eyes and a sadness threatening to further shatter an already broken heart.

F. Scott Fitzgerald's epitaph. Painful, fitting. The last lines of The Great Gatsby:

> "So we beat on, boats against the current,
> borne back ceaselessly into the past…"

The Tree From Which His Apple Fell And Frank... Frank Never You Mind

COFFEE BREAK PATRONS reluctantly return to their morning pick-me-ups, immersing themselves in private thoughts, sluggish conversation, or their newspapers, disappointed that the scene fizzled and with barely any of the potential fireworks. Distancing himself from the episode, Storm steps up and orders a large coffee. Once served, he pays and cautiously penguin-shuffles toward a free table, the agreeable and addictive aroma teasingly steaming up from the cup.

It's then that a woman's voice, thick and gravelly wafts through the coffee shop, barely clearing the cover of cigarette smoke. It's a late-night voice. Or, rather, what remains of a voice after an extended evening of gin, chain-smoked Lucky Strikes and animated conversation conducted over live jazz.

"My daughter died, too, hon. So, don't go thinking you're flying solo in this whole overblown mourning, martyr production of yours."

Heads naturally crane toward the source of the froggy utterance to hear the revelations the voice is delivering, or perhaps just to be enveloped in the raspy, seductive sound. And there she is, tucked into a back corner of the coffee shop, slouched on a chair under a pot-light that is humming and intermittently blinking off and on like a lighthouse beacon. She is wearing a ratty, mauve housecoat and pink, furry, flip-flop slippers that are balding and badly in need of a wash. So disheveled, she prompts a mental comparison to the bag ladies residing in cardboard shelters constructed in the stairwells and alleyways around the CrossRoads, or the subway vents along the Yonge-Bloor line. No particular thought paid to appearance, none of the customary makeup. Her big hair is uncharacteristically tame, ordinary brown, roots asymmetrically graying, all unusually unattended, fallen, flat across her scalp. Following a formidable and fearless drag off a cigarette, a cup of coffee embarks on a shaky journey toward her lips.

Storm takes a steadying breath, then moves to greet her. Coffee laps up over the cup and onto his hand, stinging skin. And as he winces and curses under his breath, he fleetingly considers how blissful it would have been to have just remained asleep that morning. In the fetal position. Buried deep beneath the covers in his warm and oversized bed at the Harbour Castle, the site of his wife's wake and his current, temporary home until more permanent digs can be found.

Storm kisses her cheek, then sits across from her, dabbing at the coffee spill with napkins. He senses that she is examining him with unsettling intensity. It's akin to being under the scrutiny of a suspicious border guard, turning red-faced and self-consciously stumbling over the nothing-to-declare declaration even though, honestly, he has nothing to declare. In particular, he senses that she is studying his eyes, gauging his expression and his reaction. The ensuing, clumsy silence is eventually truncated by Janeen who takes another careless drag off her cigarette and exhales a thought that he construes to be laden with reproach.

"The merry-go-round didn't stop just because you got off the ride..." She pauses, accurately sensing that he is not getting her drift. "*Me*," she says, emphatically stabbing the air between them with her cigarette. "While you were taking your temporary leave from reality, I awoke one morning and found myself on the slippery slope. I've never been the most observant woman in the world, but damn it, I know me. I admit in my past to being a bit of a mirror junkie. These days I am not at all enchanted with my reflection. I can see corrosion. I can see decline." She says it as though it is two distinct words, like it's an official name, like it's country singer Patsy's non-existent sister, De. Cline. And Storm can see decline. Obvious, disturbing decline that, regretfully, he has failed to keep from registering on his face. She is not that old. Since first spotting her, he has been mentally fumbling with the math and coming up with fifty-five, sixty-years-old maximum.

It is not surprising that he does not know her precise age; Storm and Janeen have never been very close. From their initial encounter onward, Storm instinctively felt that a close relationship with his mother-in-law would be virtually impossible considering her aloof temperament, elusive nature, and the fact that she was rarely around for more than a brief visit — breathless, unannounced, a quick drink or two to wash down some engaging, provocative conversation, and then *poof*, gone.

That said, there exists between them obvious, undeniable bonds. They've both been through a living nightmare. They've both suffered unimaginable loss. She *is* his mother-in-law. And, in the words of Harland Hazard, obviously incapable of subtlety, words uttered to Storm before he married Ali: "Crazy Janeen is the tree from which your apple fell." To Storm, Janeen was not crazy, although she quite handily qualified as enigma and an outlandish, grander-than-life character.

Janeen, ribald raconteur, suspected fabulist. Unsubstantiated Janeen, according to none other than Janeen...

In the 1960s, her shapely, unclad backside was the subject of a stunning erotic painting by a then-youthful James Minstrel that proudly hung for six months in the modest but influential Queen Street Art Gallery as part of an exhibit of "hip" and "up-and-coming" young artists; this was before an uncensored smorgasbord of hallucinogenic drugs, as prescribed by Timothy Leary, the prophet of LSD, and glorified by Ken Kesey and The Merry Pranksters, destroyed the mercurial Minstrel's ability to put color to canvas, or, for that matter, coherent thoughts into words. This was before he was committed to a psych ward, coincidentally located on the very same street as the art gallery, albeit in a seedier and less trendy district.

"This was when James Minstrel's bony hands were channeling higher sources," Janeen would say. "And there it was, my every curve, crack and dimple on display. Larger than life and in living color for six audience-wooing, critic-delighting and, it goes without saying, pervert-pleasing months..."

In the mid-1970s, her "full", "ample", "milky" breasts became the subject of a rather ridiculous, idolatrous, erotically explicit — or perverted, depending on your tolerance for such things — poem by the outspoken and ostentatious Irving Layton.

"Never met the man," Janeen would recount. "Apparently, or so the story goes, the poem was written with Mr. Layton viewing a photograph of me – fully clothed, I should mention — given to him by a friend of a friend." And was she pleased with the outcome? "It's a poem," she would laugh with gusto. "My breasts have been *personnetfied*."

ANDY JUNIPER

Janeen Reynolds, a woman who loved to play. With words, with things, with people. A woman whose very soul had been purportedly explored by philosophers, poets and politicians alike.

Unsubstantiated, Janeen, according to Janeen...

At one time or another, she alleged to have enjoyed (really, really enjoyed, she would intone, with sass that proved as irritating to some as it was intriguing to others) a romantic liaison with Pierre Elliot Trudeau, prior to his marriage to Margaret Sinclair and his memorable tenures as Prime Minister of Canada. She motivated (in untold, albeit slyly implied ways) the solitary genius, pianist Glen Gould. She was the inspiration for a rather charmingly naughty and unrepentantly ribald and risqué mother in a Mordecai Richler novel (a bar mitzvah, a gift that included a woman in the nude, Richler fans are doubtlessly familiar with the scene in which she was featured). She briefly shared a stage with legendary crooner Tony Bennett, not to mention an "enchanted evening" (and a suite) with Frank... "Frank Never You Mind!"

And never you mind that she may well have fabricated each of those exotic experiences. She could get away with weaving such bold yarns simply because Janeen was Janeen. And whenever Janeen narrated a story, she drew from her wealth of life experience and she never failed to make her audience at least consider the possibility of there minimally being a pinch of truth in the tale. And for the chronic disbelievers...

There was a day when Ali, whiling away an hour in the *Times'* library while waiting for Storm to be sprung from yet another rambling editorial meeting, ran a little fact check for the sake of curiosity on one of her mother's oldest and boldest claims. She burrowed into the newspaper's archives and came away shaking her head. Sinatra had indeed been in town at the time Janeen had insinuated that she and Old Blue Eyes had "connected on a higher level." Further, there was the more tangible matter of the photograph on the society page: a photo that featured Frank in the foreground, standing on the St. Thomas Street sidewalk in front of the Windsor Arms, chivalrously offering a hand to a woman exiting the luxurious lair that is the backseat of a Bentley. According to the cutline that anchored the photograph, Frank was assisting "an unidentified woman", who bore a striking resemblance to...

"He was such a cupcake," Janeen would say, her voice wistful, her bewitching green eyes dreamy. "We dined at the Courtyard Cafe. Coincidentally, we had a table beside another delicious cupcake, Leonard

ANGELS IN THE ARCHITECTURE

Cohen, who was dining alone but hard-pressed to enjoy his meal as young sirens kept coming up brazenly offering him their telephone numbers — scribbled on their panties, for goodness' sake! Leonard, what a tiny doll, forever insisting he was all of five-feet-five-inches tall. Sure thing, and I'm a natural blonde. Anyway, imagine, Frank and Leonard working one room. I'm telling you, from the female perspective, there wasn't a dry thigh in the house! The turtles were all out of the giggle patch!

"Frank laughed at all the giddy women, saying that would have been him receiving those panties had I not been on his arm. But I was on his arm, and if I had been wearing panties to begin with, well, he'd have long ago melted them with his charm. We talked, we smoked about two packs of his dreadful Camels fired up by his famous Zippo lighter, we drank, and after more Jack Daniels than I care to recall, he opened up like an exquisite gardenia. That's right. Macho, steely, mob-connected Frank, a flower. As we were about to leave the restaurant, he picked up a napkin, a beautiful blue napkin, and he said in the most sorrowful, waif-like voice, 'this is the color my eyes used to be when I was a kid...' This is the color my eyes used to be. And I swear, as he stared down at that napkin, he had tears blurring those baby blues..."

She intimated that unfailingly every year on the anniversary of that night they spent together, he would send her a gift, a little something special that somehow found its way to her from destinations around the world, regardless of where he was and regardless of how many moves she had made in between. She liked to joke that regardless of whether Frank did indeed have mob connections, he definitely had connections high up in the post office on both sides of the border. When doubters tactlessly hinted around for her to produce the gifts as evidence to support her claim, she would shrug, wave a hand dismissively, and say that nostalgia was a graveyard she was not keen to enter. Besides, they were packed away somewhere amongst her possessions.

Janeen, grander than life. Conversely, before him now is a character diminished, nearly dwarfed by an everyday coffee shop scene over which she would once have held court. Over which she would once have dominated.

She has lost weight. Always slender in the way of a busy woman who smoked heavily and whose eating habits were spotty at best (meals frequently forgotten, skipped, sometimes in favor of a stiff cocktail), she now appears gaunt, face pinched, skin lined, cheeks puckered. Always a force, she now appears frail, a mere whisper of the woman he left behind when he followed the flight song of the geese to Florida. Oddly, one eye bloodshot. Hands tremulous. A word slurred here and there. He wonders whether she has already been drinking at this early hour. He doesn't know what to say. But is aware that she is waiting for him to say something. Lie? Support an awful truth? Be blunt and ask her exactly what is on his mind: whether she has sought medical attention? Or just stay up on the balls of the feet and dodge?

"You've misplaced your big hair this morning," he says, dodging, albeit not artfully. "And your outfit — Lagerfeld?"

She cackles, until an over-ambitious drag of cigarette smoke gets snagged in the cackle and chokes her. A full minute passes, gasping, sputtering, hacking, Storm on the verge of calling out for help, before she is again able to talk. "And you," she says, "I heard through the grapevine that you'd misplaced your mind..." This sets her off again. Standard Janeen, he thinks. Humor noir. No added cream. Definitely no sugar.

When the laughter is spent, she fidgets in her chair.

"As for the outfit: remember, clothes wear us. I think it was Virginia Woolf who said that." She places a hand atop of Storm's, and her expression grows pensive.

Entering this, their initial encounter, his plan was to actively avoid the pensive, the serious, the solemn. There would be a time and place for that down the road when he feels stronger, healthier, and better able to cope. He adopts a forced smile, rummages through his thoughts for something to say. He would settle for a light-hearted gesture that could be coughed up as comic relief, but he finds the weight of this meeting, the circumstances, the setting, and her hand resting on his all to be prohibitive. He is a widower blindly attempting to navigate out of the woods. She is a disheartening sight. And the CrossRoads is a soulless mix of hapless, loitering youth, moribund dreams and life going nowhere in a hurry. Small-talk seems inappropriate; the light-hearted gesture feels incongruous, even clownish.

"I would curse you if I had the energy," she says, languidly glancing around the coffee shop with a vacant expression on her face. Her gaze returns to him. "Oh, hell, I'd probably pop you one if I had the energy." She makes a bony fist and shakes it at him. "Ten months without a call, a letter..."

"If you're going to pop me, Janeen, tuck your thumb under your fingers. Honestly, you're making a fist like a girl, and you're going to end up with your thumb broken." This elicits a grudging smile. "And you," he adds, "you moved without so much as a word, no forwarding address, nothing."

She shrugs. Fair enough.

"What brought you back?" she wonders. "What finally brought you back to Toronto and now here to me?"

"I honestly don't know. Something directed me. Some kind of need, an inexplicable pull." It's an effort to find the words, the means to articulate what he has experienced. "Really, some kind of vision." He blurts. "I saw Ali."

Ali, celestial Ali, the divine vision that appeared at a crucial moment in his life, that inspired, that connected heaven and earth and offered Storm Baker a lifeline, a reason to live. Ali, the humbling, radiant vision that also caused him to fear for his own sanity.

One of his first things he did once back in Toronto was visit a psychologist. The callow, prosaic practitioner fully believed he was putting a widower's distraught mind at ease when he dismissed that angelic vision with a cursory wave and the earth-bound explanation that it is common for the bereaved to experience what he called "hypnagogic, half-waking or pre-sleeping hallucinations"; further, the downhearted souls who experience such illusions typically suffer significantly more loneliness than those who don't. All researched, duly documented, undoubtedly recorded in dry, erudite language in an overweight textbook. All about as underwhelmingly ordinary as your common cold.

Storm, defensive, standing up for his vision, for its uniqueness, its power and presence, and its significance in his life, snapped at the doctor, requesting that he try to rationalize the physical reappearance of the pendant of Pegasus. "Another hypna-whatever hallucination?" Time was up, the session over. Money spent. The psychologist smiled, a patronizing smile. They would, he assured, delve into that in the next time they met. They never did any such delving. Storm dismissed the doctor as a condescending quack and never returned...

Janeen casually nods, as though she has not heard what he has said concerning the vision of her daughter, or else angels draw people to her on a regular basis and the whole process is becoming tiresome.

"I still call her, you know. Every week."

"Call her?"

"Ali,' she snaps. "*Ali.*"

Storm flinches against the raw, abrupt anger in her voice. She releases his hand and lights another Lucky Strike with her battered Bic lighter, oblivious to the cigarette still smoldering in the ashtray. Inhaling, her eyes glaze and her face slackens, a mudslide of muscles.

"Every week," she says, "every Sunday, just like always. Simply checking in. Then that horrible woman comes on the line..."

Storm closes his eyes, nods. Because Storm Baker is personally acquainted with the horrible woman.

After Ali died, it was Storm — with support from his sister Paris — who boxed up an abbreviated lifetime of worldly possessions. Caught between wanting to trash and treasure it all, each item a potential floodgate of reminiscences. Books and records that sparked memories and spoke of her essence. Personal papers, letters, diaries dating back years. Jewelry, knickknacks, and ordinary, everyday everythings that were suddenly fraught with previously unimaginable significance, forcing Paris to question, for instance: Do you really want to keep her toothbrush? Her makeup bag? Her hairdryer? Her favorite perfume, the scent of which was like a debilitating punch in the gut. All very Ali, but... Clothing. Clutching the silkiness of a blouse to his cheek, lingering over her scent on a sweater, fingering her lingerie with a sorrow and longing that physically hurt. Eventually keeping a little of this and that, depositing a handful of boxes in storage and surrendering the rest to charity.

It was Storm who broke the lease on their apartment, knowing in his heart that despite his love for the High Park area he could never return. With regret he handed over the assorted apartment keys to the superintendent, a virtual stranger in a grimy grey mechanic's uniform, who nevertheless offered a parting handshake gripped with grease, accompanied by a pitying, you-poor-bastard look. It was one of the reasons he had to flee. Everyone knew his tragic story. His life had been laid bare on the front pages and no matter how well-intentioned, the cloying compassion of strangers was more than he could take.

Finally, it was Storm who had the telephone disconnected. Then he said goodbye to family and friends, who unanimously thought the idea of his isolating himself in such a way was a huge mistake. He pointed the Dart toward the U.S. border at Fort Erie and headed south. Which is where the sightings began.

In Florida, Ali. He was certain. At times during the day when lightness and darkness dance, cavort and conspire, at dawn, at dusk, in the shadows, in the half-light, Ali. From behind, from the side, from a distance, Ali. And he would approach, heart pounding in his throat, only to have that heart hammered back into his chest. Then there was the night when, like Janeen, he called that number, called on a whim what used to be home just to see if she would answer, to see whether what he had been living through was simply a hell from which her voice would rescue him.

Janeen's voice fades. In a hoarse, smoky whisper, she mimics: "The number you have reached is not in service... Fuckers," she says, in a disquieting voice, employing an expletive he had rarely heard her utter, "they've disconnected her. Fuckers have disconnected my daughter."

Mother-In-Law Tongue

SHE COULD BRING things back to life. It was her nature, it was her essence, it was Ali — to nurture and to love, to not only cheer for, but to assist the underdog and offer a helping hand to the down-and-out. Ali volunteering at the Daily Bread Food Bank. Ali dishing out her savory homemade minestrone soup and thick, buttered slices of fresh, crusty French bread at the Christian Mission of Hope shelter for the homeless on Jarvis Street.

Ali Reynolds was the type of person who would adopt neighborhood strays. That's how we ended up with Fred, the cantankerous, flatulent, one-eyed tomcat, and Sandy's Summer Dream, an orphaned Palomino. If the tenant code in our building had allowed for dogs, I'm sure our home would have become a canine sanctuary, a cushy and infinitely safer alternative to the pound.

Before I met Ali — in a spasm of domesticity, out of a desire to create a homier and less stereotypical "helpless-bachelor" ambiance to my apartment — I purchased a half-dozen house plants at a popular flower shop on Bloor Street. The first time Ali set foot in my apartment she was aghast at the condition of those plants. In various rueful states of decline thanks to a knockout combination of neglect and ignorance (specifically, neglect born in ignorance; honestly, I wasn't killing them on purpose!), the plants were by then unwittingly heightening the whole helpless-bachelor vibe.

"Gardenia," she said, fingering the dry, brown-tipped, curling-up-in-a-Billy-Idol-snarl leaves of one plant. "Rarely successful as a house plant. Not enough humidity, too many drafts and way too temperamental. You've bitten off more than you can chew with this pampered princess...."

"An African Violet," she said, examining another plant. "Needs light to bloom. This dark corner amounts to a death sentence..."

ANGELS IN THE ARCHITECTURE

"Look," I said, with forged enthusiasm, *"this one ain't doing half bad."*

"Ficus," she replied, dismissively. *"Your basic rubber plant. It's almost impossible to kill one of these, unless you tie it up to your bumper and drag it for miles..."*

"I'll give that a shot."

"I'll bet they told you this at the store. A Ficus is basically idiot proof..."

"Hang on," I said, mentally plotting my defense while simultaneously attempting to ascertain whether I'd just been labeled a simpleton. Then I made the mistake of noting, *"They're plants..."*

"They're alive and they are under your care and you," she said, pointing an accusing finger, *"are killing them..."* Her tone elevated me alongside the likes of Charles Manson. *"And if you don't care about them personally, Storm Baker, you should at least know that these plants can help you live a healthier life. They convert carbon dioxide to oxygen, and they trap and absorb pollutants. NASA uses plants aboard space missions..."*

On a white wicker stand in the bathroom, she found the one plant that had thrived under my so-called care, a robust, three-foot-tall beauty that the clerk at the flower shop had advised was *"ideal for 'black thumbs'."*

"Perfect," Ali laughed, *"Sansevieria Trifasciata, a plant that actually thrives on neglect. They even do well in bathrooms, like this, where there's no natural light. Do you know the funny thing about these plants?"* she asked. Honestly, I didn't know anything particularly funny about any plant.

"Well, they're potentially deadly if ingested...."

"And that's riotously funny how?" I wondered.

"Wait, I haven't got to the funny part. Because of their long, thin leaves, they're known as 'snake plants', and because of the sharp and potentially dangerous tips of those leaves, they're also called, get this, mother-in-law's tongue..."

It became a fact that I never tired of mentioning to Janeen whenever she dropped in to see us. Carting the plant out of the bathroom, I'd innocently ask: *"Janeen, do you know the nickname for this prickly plant?"* And for that, I was mercilessly 'oh poof-ed'; once I caught her in a particularly foul mood and she, in turn, caught me across the back of the head with her umbrella.

With Ali's savvy touch, the apartment soon became a greenhouse (or, in the words of Harland Hazard: *"A regular Amazon Rain Forest, right here in Toronto."*) Plants brought over from her apartment when we moved in together, a few additions purchased here and there, and many more simply grown either from seeds, or from slips she'd taken from other plants.

ANDY JUNIPER

Her pride was a Dieffenbachia, (a.k.a. Dumb Cane, because of its poisonous sap), a stunningly green, wide-leafed plant which, under her care, outgrew three pots, eventually touching the ceiling and earning the nickname "Big Ben."

How I loved watching Ali at the kitchen table, the antique-styled, round wooden table protected by old spread-out newspapers ("Finally, a noble purpose for your column...") Ali, preparing a mixture of sand and peat moss in seed pans. Planting seeds, moistening the seed-bed, then anxiously awaiting like an expectant mother — three weeks, sometimes longer — for the seeds to germinate. Ali, watching over the seedlings, replanting, fertilizing, and taking tremendous joy in having had a hand in the process of life.

After she died, before I headed south, as I boxed up our memories and our lives, Paris and I gathered Ali's beloved plants, packed them into the back of a rented cube van and we delivered them: to local library branches that Ali had frequented (Annette, Runnymede, High Park), to area nursing homes, hospices, hospitals. Big Ben – now a whopping, sturdy, seven-feet tall, or so I'm told — ended up in the lobby of Bartlett House on Jamieson Avenue where to this day it stands watch over all the troubled souls who enter the women's shelter.

There are times when I get anxious, wondering whether the plants endured being moved, survived life post-Ali, survived without her practiced, gentle touch, her green thumb, her love and passion. Conversely, there are moments when I take comfort picturing them in their new homes, converting carbon dioxide to oxygen, trapping and absorbing pollutants, brightening up the world around them, and carrying on her generous, giving spirit.

Don't forget to water. To fertilize. To always pamper, and prune as need be....

How Awful Of You To Even Ask

IN-LAWS SIDE BY side in an elevator that reeks of urine that overpowers even the smell of harsh cleaning disinfectants. The doors close and with a raw gnashing of gears that inspires assorted safety concerns, the elevator surges to life and begins to rise.

"Like Jesus, ascending into heaven," she mutters, as she pulls the Lucky Strike pack and lighter from her housecoat pocket.

"Unless city bylaws have changed since I left town, you can't smoke in here."

"Actually, I can smoke wherever I please. What?" she says, nudging him with a bony elbow. "Are you going to make a citizen's arrest? Call the ciggy piggies?" There is a welcome defiance and teasing vigor in her voice that was absent for the most part in the coffee shop. She lights up and greedily inhales, her lungs, overall health and (in her word, "Draconian") municipal bylaws be damned.

"Oddly, these days whenever I think of a biblical character, any biblical character, in my mind that person looks like that big boob Charlton Heston. Is there a bigger, more self-righteous fool on Earth? Needless to say, it's rather disconcerting and it definitely spoils the thought for me." After a contemplative pause, she adds: "I wonder what a psychiatrist would say about that? Or a casting director for that matter."

By the time the elevator grinds to a halt on the nineteenth floor, Storm is perspiring, queasy and on the verge of an anxiety attack. Presumably he could have tolerated the trapped cigarette smoke and the elevator's gagging stench, but the confined quarters and the unsettling, jarring pauses — "More bumps and grinds than a burlesque show," according to Janeen — proved to be more than a borderline claustrophobic could endure.

Cigarette dangling from her lips, Janeen leads the way off the death trap and down a dimly lit hallway, slippers scuffling along faded, once-maroon, discount carpet. Again, the building's pervasive fish-market smell. Storm wonders whether anyone at the CrossRoads actually bothers to use a toilet, or does the tenant code require everyone urinate on the building's musty carpets?

"Janitorial crew on holidays?"

"Seemingly so. Ever since I arrived," she shrugs, stopping in front of an apartment door. "Lucky 1913." She touches the doorknob and is zapped by static shock.

"Merde! Every damn time." Then, in a grand and exaggerated motion, she swings open the heavy door, which promptly smacks into the wall behind with a paint-and-plaster-chipping thud.

"Your superintendent must be fond of you."

"Home sweet home." She motions for Storm to enter.

"Janeen, this isn't Mayberry. Don't you think you should lock up when you go out?"

"Oh, poof." She dismisses the notion with a wave of her hand.

The apartment is tiny even by contemporary, cramped, bachelor-model standards, and actual living space is further reduced by clutter. Contributing to the disorder are random piles of newspapers, Hollywood trade publications and gossip magazines, and trashy tabloids that promise in thick, bold headlines to make public the private lives of celebrities. There is everything from well-thumbed issues of *People*, to the venerable *Variety*, to *The Hollywood Reporter*, *OBN* (Off Broadway News), *The National Enquirer* and other assorted fonts of sensational journalism.

Wrinkled clothes are strewn about, intermingling with junk-food wrappers and soda pop cans and overflowing ashtrays. Furniture is sparse: two threadbare, albeit comfortable-looking armchairs plunked down in front of an old television, a round mahogany coffee table between the chairs. Atop the dusty table are more magazines, including a handful of *TV Guides*, a pair of eyeglasses that Storm has never seen before (he was unaware that Janeen even needed eyewear), an ashtray, and more empty cans and wrappers. Janeen has evidently taken a shine to Canada Dry Ginger Ale and Hickory Sticks.

The apartment conspicuously lacks any personal, homey touches. No flowers or a plant to be found. The walls are bare, save for newsprint smudges and paint chips. No artwork, no photographs. There are no bookshelves. In fact, nowhere to be seen is Janeen's formidable book collection. Throughout her life she has been a voracious reader with eclectic interests extending far beyond the trashy fare now strewn about her apartment; as a reader, she once proudly called herself a snob, scorning the wildly popular writers of her era, the Sidney Sheldons and Harold Robbins and Irwin Shaws, with the notable exception of Shaw's war chronicle, *The Young Lions*, which she reluctantly read, loved, and deemed "a masterpiece".

Likewise, nowhere to be seen are her prized LP records, or any sound system on which to play them. On more than one occasion he'd had the pleasure of thumbing through her sizable, enviable, eclectic and invaluable record collection, with records ranging from classical to popular to jazz to big band standards to Frank, a reverent abundance of Frank, both commercial-issue and bootleg.

The apartment, indeed the building itself, belies the reality that Janeen has money. Throughout her life she has worked. She also received a monthly check, the mysterious, anonymous source of which she was never inclined to reveal to anyone, not even her daughter. Consequently, she has always had enough money to live comfortably, at least during those times when she was able to reign in her spend-thrift behavior. Storm also knows for a fact that she received a life-insurance inheritance when Ali died. He knows that she could easily afford bigger, better.

To his right is the bedroom. To the left, a barely functional kitchenette with a stove, a refrigerator/freezer combination, the thigh-high size typically found in hotel suites, a sink piled with unwashed dishes and enough space for a slim, nimble person to maneuver and cook a meal, provided the preparation did not require more than breadboard-sized counter space.

Straight ahead is a vertiginous wall of windows. Storm crosses the dusty linoleum floor and gazes out at a depressing, decaying, Dickensian cityscape: a dilapidated abandoned factory (windows broken, graffiti sprayed across its red brick), train tracks, and a stretch of moribund mom-and-pop retail outlets. He leans against the window, pressing his face against the cool pane, and looks down to the street.

Extreme vertigo, to the point where he has the sensation that the window has failed to support him, the pane has shattered, he is falling and is but a heartbeat from splattering on the pavement below. Her voice yanks him back up to safety.

"I've been meaning to clean up a bit," she says, not at all self-consciously, more just a statement of fact. "Pile the magazines, corral the dust bunnies, that sort of thing. Mind you, I wasn't expecting guests. I'd hire a maid, but I'm afraid the temptation of snooping through my stuff, lingerie drawers alone, would be too much to resist." At this point Storm is thrilled to hear that she is not completely oblivious to the mess. Confessing that she likes to nibble when she watches television, she brushes a few wrappers and a lacy red brassiere off one of the chairs and offers him a seat.

Storm would never have pegged Janeen to be either the nibbling or television type. He remembers her assorted diatribes aimed at mesmerized television worshipers, people she said would do well to get off their couches, step out into the world and see an actual theater performance, or a live set of jazz up at the Top o' the Senator, or the latest exhibit at the Royal Ontario Museum, or simply explore one of the city's funky art galleries, hang out at the Harbourfront, or even just get out and people watch in Yorkville.

Janeen leaves him alone. As he sinks into the chair's worn cushions, his senses begin tunneling out of the clutter that has assaulted his eyes. It's then that he notices the smell. Not overwhelming like that encountered on the elevator, but persistent enough to subdue the odor of stale cigarettes; an odor that wafts into the nostrils, wraps its tendrils around unsuspecting olfactory nerves and then loiters. He wonders whether the windows in the apartment have ever been opened, or whether food may be going bad. Worse, he wonders whether some small creature recently met its maker and is beginning to decompose in this very room.

"You haven't got any pets?" he calls to her. Under his breath, he adds: "Or *had* any pets?" She is in the bedroom, he assumes – or, at least, he hopes — changing out of her sleepwear.

"Animals? How awful of you to even ask." Storm hears her mumbling something about "woodland creatures" and "as if..."

Five minutes pass. Still no Janeen. Every minute or so, Storm hears a beep. Not piercing, or urgent, but loud enough to distract and frequent enough to annoy. Each time a solitary sounding. Beep.

"What is that?" he finally asks.

"What is what?"

"That noise. The beeping."

"I have no idea. But, you know, it's been going on for about a week now and I've been meaning to get to the bottom of it because it's becoming irksome to say the very least."

ANGELS IN THE ARCHITECTURE

Storm locates the source: emanating from the ceiling outside the bathroom, a smoke detector with a low battery that is intermittently beeping to alert occupants that it's time for a replacement. This particular alert sets off an alarm in Storm's head: how a person could live with that kind of grating noise day in day out for and not do anything about it?

"Janeen," he says, with growing impatience, "are you okay in there?"

Receiving no response, he approaches the bedroom and reluctantly peeks in. Along the far wall is what appears to be her book collection, contained in dozens and dozens of stacked liquor boxes, a box here and there ripped open, a book or two on the floor. Along the wall to his right is her record collection, hundreds of records stored in old milk crates. Then there's Janeen. In bed, under the covers, fast asleep. Storm whistles softly.

Serenity, Granted

PERSONAL EARLY WARNING signs. Akin to strobe-light flashes or the appearance of an aura for migraine sufferers. Shortness of breath. Energy being siphoned from his body. Muscle bands along his chest quivering uncontrollably. Icy, hostile, predatory grip on skin, gradually, spitefully penetrating into brittle bones. Dark veil descending.

Leaving Janeen to her mid-morning nap, he finds himself back in the living area, amid the disconcerting disorder, and is abruptly overcome by helplessness. An encompassing sadness. Mind in turmoil. He knows from experience accrued over past months that he is but one inescapable black thought away from a full-blown attack, what has the feel of a mental meltdown. Sensation of losing control, equilibrium. Bleak, undermining, unnerving sense of doom. Inability to produce even one remotely comforting, positive thought.

He slumps onto the floor, leans back against a wall. It's Janeen. Janeen and this awful, godforsaken apartment, every inch of which forewarns of hazardous, impassable road ahead. He believes that whatever spirit guided him here, was misguided. Feebly he argues against himself because he hungers to believe that he is not an emotional cripple, that he is his old self, vital and able. He chides himself to get a grip and unnecessarily reminds that you help someone who is on this road, you don't just turn and run. However, instinct, in tandem with the nauseating waves of panic that are upon him, says screw it. Run. Because he believes that only the healthy and the whole can truly help the sick. And in his heart, he feels miles removed from the desired states of good health, or wholeness.

Storm closes his eyes to block out the apartment. Labors to terminate his mind's frantic racing. Into black thoughts he forcefully imposes a vision of Ali, as he saw her nearly every morning they were together. Hair still saucy and uncombed. Unchanged out of her bedtime T-shirt and undies. Ali, assuming the lotus position on the carpeted floor in the living area of their apartment and beginning what she called her "morning measure of serenity", the meditation she passionately practiced once and sometimes even twice a day, and which she encouraged him to practice.

"Ali, I'm in your hands." A whispered plea.

He crosses his legs; the lotus position remains beyond the restraints of his flexibility. Ali inhales and Storm follows, taking in a breath so needy it feels as though the oxygen bypasses his lungs and is sucked directly into his gut. They exhale simultaneously. Easy, she counsels, slowly. It feels so familiar, Storm thinks, unconvinced of whether he is yet able to be comfortable cloaked in the skin of the familiar. Focus on the breathing, she directs, deep, cleansing breaths. In-hale. Ex-hale. Liberate your worries. Anchor your attention in the present. The here and now. Pick up your mantra, your focus phrase, and let it be the broom that sweeps the mind clear of all other thoughts. A meaningless sound, a meaningful phrase, whatever. It's personal, it's yours.

Formerly, when they meditated together, it was Serenity, Granted. Today, on the in-breath, in his mind, Storm whispers Let, and on the out-breath, Go. The phrase surfaces like an air bubble from the murky depths of his subconscious. About to take her leave and allow her husband the space he needs, Ali suggests that not unlike the body, the mind intuitively knows what it needs. Inhale. Let. Exhale. Go.

Storm has been unwilling to even attempt meditating since losing Ali, the very act being so intimately associated with her, the focus, the concentration and discipline required having been lost with her.

In time, although Ali would remind that time has absolutely no place in the process, Storm reconnects with the sacred. He loses himself to another world in which the gritty film of panic and anxiety and despair is washed away by a rejuvenating rain. After an indeterminately prolonged session, Harland Hazard opens the door and allows himself into the cleansed space of Storm's mind.

"Maharishi," the Hazard says, gently touching Storm's shoulder. "Earth to the Maharishi, wakey, wakey." Storm opens his eyes to a disheartening reality, the disorderliness of Janeen's apartment and the fact that he is alone in this room.

"Harland, I meditated," he wanted to say. "First time since Ali... It felt..."

And right there, the Hazard would have cut him off.

"You start talking about finding yourself, and inner peace, or any of that mystical mumbo jumbo and you'll be looking at my back. Don't forget she had me doing that for a while, too." Storm remembers. Considering that he walked in on them meditating together in their underpants, his odds of forgetting are remote. He would also vividly recall Ali's frustration when the Hazard, who could be as indolent as a dog day in August, said he preferred medicating over meditating because it requires less concentration, less effort.

Storm stretches his legs out in front of him, muscles prickly with sleep. With effort, he gets himself back up on his feet. Although his head is clear, and he is enjoying a certain welcome and long-overdue calm, he can't escape the tugging weight of loneliness.

He begins cleaning the apartment. Because in a world where life is fundamentally unpredictable, where control is an illusion and vulnerability an inescapable actuality, Storm Baker has come to include fastidiousness, neatness and order — once simple, intrinsic character quirks — among life's prerequisites. Necessary, just to stay sane.

"In the designs of Providence," Pope John Paul II once wrote, "there are no coincidences." The designs of Providence – or, perhaps it's Jung's theory of synchronicity, of meaningful coincidence – is hard at work, toiling alongside Storm in Janeen's bedroom as he quietly and carefully empties box after box of her books. He is painstakingly lining hard-cover and paperback volumes alphabetically by author on the floor along the wall (thus far spanning, William S. Burroughs to William Butler Yeats), and then loading the empty boxes with the old magazines collected from the living room.

As he contemplates where best to purchase easy-to-assemble bookshelves for Janeen, he lifts a heavy hardcover out of a box. The poems of Robert Burns. He randomly opens the weighty tome and reads the title of a verse inked some two-hundred-years previous by the beloved Scottish poet. It's called "*Man Was Made To Mourn*," and eerily opens: "When chill November's surly blast, made fields and forests bare...."

As he reads, as chills tingle nerve endings, Janeen awakens to discover him in her room. Sensing her eyes upon him, he glances up from the book and their eyes meet. She recoils and lifts the bedcovers protectively higher.

ANGELS IN THE ARCHITECTURE

"Janeen, it's just me. Sorry to startle you."

Her stare is vacant. She does not seem fully conscious. Reminiscent of the grandmother in *Little Red Riding Hood* initially encountering the big, bad wolf, she lifts a hand out from under the covers, aims a crooked finger at him and demands: "And who are you?"

Spooked, he stumbles to explain his presence in her room. Although she seems satisfied and more trusting of this dream-crasher, she still appears to be a wake-up stretch, or a cold shower or, Storm can't help but think, a stiff gin, shy of complete consciousness. She peels away the covers and swings her legs over onto the floor. She wiggles her bare toes. The movement appears to amuse her to a childish degree.

"So then," she says, tugging the hem of her nightie to cover her knees, "you are you, but who am I? Who the hell am I."

She giggles and reaches for the Lucky Strikes on her nightstand.

A Thespian, A Direct Descendant of Thespis!

OVER THE COURSE of her lifetime, it was a question that was repeatedly posed by a variety of people with various motives. However, typically, few truly bothered to excavate deep enough to unearth the answer, and even those willing to do the necessary digging tended to find themselves (or lose themselves) in a maze of detours or diverted by red herrings. Ali maintained that her mother strategically planted the diversions because she was intrinsically averse to anyone ever discovering the true Janeen Reynolds.

"I don't know whether I even know the true Janeen Reynolds," she said. Then, after a moment of further consideration: "Honestly, I don't know whether *she* knows the true Janeen Reynolds. Uncovering the true Janeen is equivalent to a chameleon trying to determine what color she really is.

"My mother desires or needs to be both outrageous and mysterious," she continued. "She can be a regular aloof, enigmatic Greta Garbo, although obviously without any of Garbo's reclusiveness and disdain for the spotlight. Janeen never met a spotlight she didn't like. Personally, I think she equates being outrageous with gaining the attention she so covets and being mysterious with being different. My mother has always had a penchant for being different, apart from the pack. Honestly, who else do you know whose mother *insisted* from childhood onward that her daughter call her by her first name? While all the other girls were going to the park to teeter-totter with mom, I was off to bohemia to do heaven-knows-what with Janeen.

"At a relatively young age she sat me down and explained that, in her mind, the label 'mom' had been taken and substantially abused and devalued by the stuck-up, self-righteous, finger-pointing, back-stabbing, submissive stay-at-home types — high-heeled foot soldiers in what she called 'the apron army' — who were forever judging and condemning my mother in malicious whispers behind her back. That is, when they weren't busy overprotecting their poor children and spouting their inane mom-isms, like: 'If you fall out of that tree and break your leg, don't come running to me!' Not that Janeen held anything against a woman who stayed home in the noble pursuits of keeping house and rearing children. So long as that woman was *happy* at home; in other words, at home by choice, not by dictate, societal or otherwise, and so long as that woman wasn't lording her conventionality like a hot iron over Janeen.

"Suffice to say, she has always been determined not to be like everyone else. She can be confoundedly full of contradictions. We're talking about a woman who one minute speaks eloquently, quoting the likes of Socrates or Shakespeare and the next is cursing like a carpenter who's just nailed his thumb with a hammer. She needs to be the center of attention, but at the same time she keeps everyone at arm's length. She can be exasperating. Infuriating. I'm not a shrink. I don't know why she is the way she is, but that's my take."

Not surprisingly, Janeen's take differed.

"People are basically slothful," she said. "They don't really want to see anything save for the superficial: what's in plain sight, what's simply found, what is right there on the surface, particularly when it comes to assessing women. If a woman has a heart of gold and a wart on her nose, she is forever known as the woman with the wart on her nose. If a woman has a heart of gold, a wart on her nose and big breasts, she's forever known as wart face with the big tits. Coarse, but true… Karl Marx once suggested that a society's cultural progress could be measured by the social position of plain-looking women. We are nowhere. Nowhere."

What people saw on the surface with Janeen was a force as unpredictable as nature, combined with what was to many an infuriating unwillingness or incapacity to conform and a desire to be contrary. These traits naturally made people defensive in her presence and resolute in their insistence on classifying her, and often made them malicious in their assessments. Judgments ranged from those suggesting Janeen was erratic or unstable (a "quirky bird", a "daffy duck"), to her being one giant leap over the acceptable edge and, as such, an unfit mother.

"As if these people even know me," Janeen would retort. "Like anyone knows anyone. I've always contended that autobiographies are distorted by ego, and biographies by ignorance." She observed that it was usually women, or men whose romantic advances she had rejected, who were the most severe in their judgments.

"Forget the notion of a united sisterhood. Forget the whole notion of the 'fairer' sex. Women are socialized to be in perpetual competition against other women, particularly in matters of men. Consequently, women are absolute bitches to each other. As for scorned men, well, hell hath no fury... Please, don't get me started on scorned men. I could write a book. Or, better still, perhaps a play..." And here she would shake her head and lament, "I honestly don't know whether it would be a tragedy or a comedy."

The bottom line remained constant: although an easy target for potshots, Janeen Reynolds was virtually impossible to pigeonhole. Just when people thought they had her pegged, just when all were certain she would zig, she would gleefully zag. While never fully supporting the laws of logic, her way has always been to think outside the box, or to not even bother acknowledging the box.

It's been Storm's first-hand experience that she can be at once intelligent, charming, witty and endearingly entertaining, or prickly and brusque, moody and immature. He has never known anyone who could take such childish pleasure in infuriating people and in rankling those she thinks deserve to be rankled. He's witnessed first-hand her arguing that black is white and white is black just to get a rise. She has never suffered fools gladly if she bothers with them at all. And yet, she has been known to play the fool when the part served her purposes. To Storm Baker, Janeen Reynolds has always been an enigma, an intricate puzzle that may well be missing a piece, or two.

Before meeting her for the first time, Ali — futilely forewarning and endeavoring to prepare him — said that while growing up she routinely heard people branding her mother an incurable eccentric. Storm was never convinced. Unquestionably Janeen fit the basic definition of eccentric, being peculiar and unconventional. However, she did not wholly match the classic personality profile. Certainly, she was a loner, at times egotistical and always robustly humorous to those who shared (and were not altogether offended by) her oftentimes dark and bawdy sense of humor. However, she could hardly be characterized as being particularly carefree or overly cheerful, nor (he would ruefully discover) would she live the extended life afforded most eccentrics, longevity which experts attribute to eccentrics' very eccentricities. Janeen was no blithe spirit. She definitely had her demons.

Rather than actually being an eccentric, Janeen always seemed to Storm to be more like an intelligent, fiercely independent, highly opinionated woman *acting* eccentric. Or, as Janeen once readily acknowledged: "Given the era into which I was born, given that I was a single mother raising a daughter, given my circumstances and my refusal to be subservient to men, I was simply a self-reliant woman acting like a man…" Needless to say, Janeen Reynolds has spent the majority of her life not quite fitting in, being ostracized, being an outsider. And, she has spent the majority of her life acting.

Storm recalls that initial meeting with Janeen with amusement, although at the time he found the encounter to be anything but amusing. It was before he and Ali began cohabitating. One night he was at Ali's cramped basement apartment in Swansea when Janeen unexpectedly dropped in. Rather, she entered the scene, Stage Right as it were, found her mark in what served as the living room, stood directly beside Storm, who had risen to introduce himself, and grasped his right hand between her hands. The hair. Good god, it was all Storm could do to rally his thoughts to rise above the hair. Flaming orange, untamed and piled high, as if it had been randomly styled by near lethal jolts of electricity.

"It's the latest 'windblown look', straight out of New York fashion magazines," she informed, answering the obvious but unasked question.

"A little too much wind, a little too blown," Ali opined.

Ignoring her daughter's barb, Janeen queried Storm in an affected, amplified voice. As she questioned him, her gaze intensified until she appeared to be staring right through him. Ali would later sheepishly explain her mother's tendency to play scenes in everyday life as though performing on stage. Naturally she did not simply speak to the actor opposite her, she addressed the entire audience. Projecting, always projecting.

"I'm assuming that you are the new beau," she said. "I've been versed, but I cannot for the life of me recall what it is that you do."

"I'm a columnist for the…" Before he could finish his sentence, Janeen interjected, grandly: "I'm a Thespian, a direct descendant of Thespis!"

Storm glanced at Ali, his expression questioning: Who the hell is this woman? Seriously, who speaks like this? He was unable to discern whether Ali was smirking or cringing into her hand, which was cupped over her mouth. Thoughts tumbled into his head: had this woman been drinking?

Was she high? What was he getting himself into? Considering his intense feelings for Ali, he knew that he had no choice but to cling to the hope that in the intricate design of genetic wiring, dottiness skips a generation. He turned back to his future mother-in-law.

"A Thespian," she repeated. "A daughter of Thespis."

In retrospect, Storm would think that perhaps this was one of the keys to unlocking Janeen. Unmarried — unapologetically unmarried — she held numerous odd jobs over the years. At various times she was a seamstress, a saleswoman (peddling aphrodisiacs, thinly disguised as "restoratives", door-to-door to lonely and, it goes without saying, concupiscent housewives), and even a bank teller, a vocation that lasted precisely three days, the number of shifts it took her male companion at the time to repeatedly visit her, case the joint, and then rob it (he was subsequently caught and she, an "unwitting accomplice," was eventually exonerated).

Nevertheless, she never thought of herself as a common seamstress or a lowly product peddler, or a teller, but, rather, as an actress, a potential leading lady of the screen and stage (she never discriminated between the two) whose star had been inexplicably, unjustly overlooked. An actress simply mastering roles: seamstress, sales, teller, unwitting accomplice.

"A woman of theater. A true tragedienne," she said to Storm. From prior conversations with Ali, Storm knew it to be true, knew that Janeen had indeed performed for — or starred in, to hear her version of events — more Little Theater troupes in more small towns than either she or Ali could possibly recall.

In the early 1960s, she briefly resided in Toronto where she found the local theater scene to be a hard nut to crack. At the time there were only a handful of professional theaters in the entire sprawling metropolis. In subsequent return moves to Toronto — the precise timing and duration of which have been lost in time (Ali and Janeen would spend considerable time debating to no firm conclusion precisely when they had been where, and for how long) — she found the city blossoming into the third-largest theater center in the English-speaking world, behind only London and New York, with some two-hundred professional theater and dance companies performing nightly in nearly one-hundred venues.

By then there was ample work to be had in the theater.

"If you had a pulse, a voice, and the ability to memorize, you could find work," Janeen would note. Granted, the pay was niggardly, if not outright insulting, particularly for the sort of gigs she tended to land. Chiefly secondary roles, performed primarily in the Annex Neighborhood and Bathurst Strip, a theater district that offered what were deemed to be "fringe and alternative productions." Or "pretentious, obscure drivel," depending on whose opinion was sought and valued.

"It's true that I was, for the most part, denied by politics, pretensions, and petty jealousies the opportunities of the Downtown Theater District, or the East End Theater. They said, unjustly, that I was 'difficult'. Well, poo on them. I think my body of work speaks for itself.... Loudly. Proudly. Like a peacock's brilliant plumage. Like... oh rot, I'm fresh out of analogies. Regardless, in repertory, one summer up north in cottage country, Huntsville or Gravenhurst or some Port something-or-other backwater, I accomplished a Tennessee Williams' double bill. In one night, I played Maggie Pollitt in *Cat on a Hot Tin Roof*, all palpable sensuality and butterfly neuroses, and Blanche DuBois in *A Streetcar Named Desire*, all delicate and mothlike precisely as Williams envisioned, only better... Over the course of my career on the boards, I played Juliet innumerable times... Heavens, I even had the theatrical cojones to play Romeo on one occasion, in a pinch..."

"You'll have to excuse my mother," Ali said. "She has an obvious flair for the dramatic and, apparently, a weakness for gin. By the way, the reason she and her theatrical cojones had to play Romeo in a pinch, even though she had originally been cast in some forgettable bit part, was because in dress rehearsals she stumbled and accidentally blind-sided the real Romeo, knocking him clear off the stage and out of fair Verona. Janeen was the only thespian around who knew all his lines by heart so, for one night while the poor man recuperated from his concussion, she was it. Romeo Montague."

"Oh poof! He was far too delicate a man to have been cast as Romeo in the first place. A Nancy-boy who couldn't stand up on his own two feet and, my, my, what a bleeder... And, yes, dutiful daughter of mine, I will have a gin, since you're up and pouring." As Ali went to mix drinks, Janeen continued.

"I played Jo March in *Little Women* and gave a performance that was sinfully delicious. Critics said that my body language was poetic and my face, and I quote, was 'a refulgent beacon of theatrical expression.' They understated. I made Louisa May Alcott bolt upright in her grave and express regret at not having written a sequel... I was that good!"

"Let me revise my last statement to read that my mother has an apparent weakness for both gin and hyperbole," Ali called out. Back in the room, the daughter then refreshed her mother's selective recall, reminding her that the ill-fated production in question closed in under two weeks, and if the ghost of Louisa May Alcott was doing any bolting it was doubtlessly to distance herself from the whole fiasco.

"All good plays alienate some part of the audience in some way," Janeen retorted, before dismissing Ali with a wave of her hand and an unspoken, but obviously implied: "Oh, poof."

Over the years, mother and daughter repeatedly relocated. Ali would insist that regardless of how often they moved, or where they resided, while she was growing up there was always an abundance of love and guidance and even a sense of security and home. Nevertheless, there was no denying that it was an odd, unstructured, nomadic existence, leaving infinite indelible impressions, but planting no roots.

Frequently they found themselves but one slippery step ahead of creditors. In matters of personal finance, Janeen was bankrupt. She had a knack, which she would slyly spin as being a "a gift," for squandering every cent of her mystery money and her own earnings, oftentimes in advance of her actually being in receipt of that income. Impulsive, compulsive, she loved to shop, which she considered a genus of hunting, and she loved to purchase, which she likened to the kill. For Janeen Reynolds there was no such thing as window shopping, or, heaven forbid, placing an item on layaway. When she saw something, she liked she simply had to have it now, regardless of the status of her bank account, which more often than not was on life support.

"Fortunately for the Reynolds," she was fond of saying, "I have close friends high up in the banking industry."

"You dated a branch manager in some rustic outback," Ali would remind, "for one or two dates, about one-hundred years ago. Not exactly close friends, or 'high ups.'" Facts for which she was mercilessly, 'oh poofed'.

Other times mother and daughter were but one slippery step ahead of the law. Janeen was never discerning when it came to the character of the characters with whom she associated. For every upstanding man the likes of Pierre Elliot Trudeau there were two or three Wayne (Knuckles) Knight. She was hopelessly addicted to the adrenaline rush and she was not particular if that rush came from an ephemeral association with Frank

ANGELS IN THE ARCHITECTURE

You Know Who, or a slightly more protracted relationship with the likes of the infamous Knight, currently serving the second half of his quarter-century stint in Kingston Penitentiary for armed robbery, resisting arrest, and for ignominiously removing the pinky finger of his arresting police officer with his notoriously sharp, beaver-like teeth.

And the direct descendant of Thespis' greatest role, which she played time and time again, until her precocious daughter outgrew her part and made the whole overblown production superfluous, was the role of the brave, optimistic and comforting mother.

"Everything's going to be all right," she would say, with wrenching conviction that she was not particularly feeling. "Let's just get our things packed. We need to be out of here."

"When?"

"Yesterday, if not sooner."

"Why? I don't understand. I've made friends here, you know. I finally have teachers who actually know my name. Mr. Meadows, the school librarian, lets me have first crack at the new books that come in. Mr. Gillespie says I'm a natural and wants me on his cross-country team..."

"It's like the milk the other day, sweetie. Life here has passed its prime. It's gone sour. Now be a dear and pack up..."

By nature, and necessity, thespians are chameleons. The day they allow themselves to be pigeonholed is the day they are typecast. Condemned to the hell that is playing the same role over and over and over.

December Is Thirteen Months Long

ON JANEEN'S INSISTENCE Storm retreats from the CrossRoads. And in retreat there is a tugging sense of déjà vu, a feeling akin to that experienced so many years previous when he would burst out of the doors of the palliative-care ward at the hospital after having spent time visiting his mother. Although ecstatic to be busting out of what he had heard tactless nurses call the House of Pain, or, worse, Death Row, he was nonetheless acutely aware of the ephemeral nature of that happiness, a happiness undermined and mocked by both the guilt the healthy feel when they leave the dying behind and by obvious fears and concerns over the inevitable path the future was following.

Once Janeen had gotten up and about, she seemingly transformed. She shook off the cobwebs, became lucid, sharp and even somewhat caustic, convincingly cloaking herself in the role of the cantankerous in-law. Rather than thanking her son-in-law for straightening up and cleaning her apartment, she griped that she would never be able to find anything amidst all the "confounded order."

"Everything had its place," she protested.

When Storm patiently suggested that she now look in the cupboard instead of the sink if it was a cup she was after, she indignantly harrumphed him and then said it was time that he moseyed along. She insisted that she had things to do, people to see — for starters, she said she was going to the hairdresser for "the works" — and he could not argue that she seemed fine. Like the old Janeen. Energized and full of piss and vinegar.

"That's the second time I've been harrumphed today. Somebody call Guinness. So, you're making me mosey?"

ANGELS IN THE ARCHITECTURE

"You deserve to be royally harrumphed, picking on me and that poor, beleaguered mother in the coffeeshop and, yes, I am making you mosey..." Then, in a tweaked voice: "I can not, will not have you hanging around all day baby-sitting me." She touched his arm in an uncharacteristic, almost motherly gesture, then sharply added: "If I need a diaper change, I'll call."

He crosses the road toward the side street where he parked his car. A belligerent wind has picked up, corralling brittle leaves and propelling them about in swirling gusts, reminding Storm of Robert Burns: "When chill November's surly blast, made fields and forests bare..." It won't be long until snowflakes will be kissing cheeks and playing tag in the air; until those flakes will acquire support and staying power and begin gathering on the ground; until time marches out of autumn and into what amounts to an annual endurance test for the soul.

Considering hurricane season has passed for another year, he wonders what he could possibly have been thinking when he exchanged Florida for this: for dead leaves underfoot, sounding like sandpaper scratching against rough wood, for another imminent, interminable Canadian winter with not enough warmth and not near enough sunlight to properly sustain healthy life. Although he grew up in the infamous Southern Ontario snowbelt, Storm Baker has no affection or even patience for winter. Possibly it's just an accumulation of age and loss because he was not always this way. He warmly remembers a time when he and Mackey and Paris would dance around their parents' bed like elves on a sugar high on the morning of the season's first snowfall, making elaborate plans for snow forts and toboggan runs and an ice rink, even though what had fallen amounted to a meager dusting of the precious powder.

And, of course, he spent a handful of winters with Ali, who bear-hugged each season. Although, in enduring a Canadian winter, even she had occasion to stare out a frost-etched window into a gray, threatening sky and quote countryman, poet Alden Nowlan: "December is thirteen months long. July's one afternoon."

He nostalgically remembers those long months of December, and grows misty at the thoughts...

Angels In The Snow

ON MORNINGS AFTER *a fresh snowfall she would rush to dress in layers of outdoor apparel. It seemed she was always the first one outside celebrating the snow's arrival, quicker off the mark than the neighborhood dogs who loved to bound out and tunnel and discolor the white blanket, and even quicker than the children who were so eager to frolic in the inviting powder.*

There was a courtyard at the south side of our apartment, nestled between three other identical buildings. In summertime, tenants from all four high-rises used the grassy, protected area to dress down to next-to-nothing, stretch out on blankets and worship the sun. In winter, the area was generally deserted, save for the odd straggler shuffling along the narrow path that led to a convenience store. Consequently, that's where she would head first, to the courtyard, to that pristine canvas of snow.

Typically, I'd be deliberately slow getting ready, busy with a column I was writing, or procrastinating with an odd job I would convince myself needed to be immediately addressed; in other words, not always sharing her unbridled enthusiasm over the snowfall. My mindset was more tethered to the pragmatic: how the hell was I going to get to work/a meeting/an interview later that day/ the next day? Restrictive, unproductive thoughts that she worked diligently to reshape, if only by example. On those occasions when I managed to remain behind, if only for a while before being overtaken by the enticement of wanting to be with her and share her joy, I'd look out our balcony window and see my Ali, flat on her back in the snow, christening the courtyard, making angels. Even from that distance, that height, I swear I could still see the smile stretched across her face.

One winter, for a protracted period of time, it didn't snow. Not even a spirit-lifting dusting to offset winter's terminal, godless grey. Soon the lack of

ANGELS IN THE ARCHITECTURE

white began to weigh on her. She got cabin fever. She could be found wistfully staring out our apartment window at depressing, corpulent clouds that refused to burst, that in effect were hoarding the snow, her snow, and under her breath she could be heard cursing: the gods and the greenhouse gases.

"It's global warming, that's what it is... We've screwed ourselves over. We've raised the temperature by degrees and now we're destined to live through these dismal, soulless winters without snow. There's a column for you, Storm, tell them how we've screwed ourselves over. Tell them that this is not an anomaly, it's an omen..." Flustered: "I'm going to make a pot of chamomile tea, lace it with serotonin, and meditate under a bright lamp... Call me when real winter arrives."

It reached the point where she became so antsy that even I began to pray for a huge blast of good, old-fashioned winter. That blast came in mid-January, in the form of back-to-back bruising storms that effectively shut down the city. I'd rarely seen Ali so giddy.

Throughout every winter, she insisted we keep a snow shovel in our apartment.

"It's an apartment," I'd remind, needlessly, but working hard to nail down a point. "We don't need a shovel sitting in our hallway for half the year. Maintenance crews shovel for us. Besides, every time I go near the door I crack my toes on it and knock it over."

Logic aside, that shovel found a home in our hallway. And on snow days, long after the sun had set and the neighborhood children had retreated inside for cups of hot chocolate and a few minutes of homework or television or a chapter of a book before bed, she could be found under the pale glow of the streetlights, walking up and down neighboring streets, camera slung around her neck, shovel in hand, photographing winter's wonder between good-Samaritan stints of helping people dig out stuck cars, or drifted-in driveways. She said she was just being neighborly — and I'll grant you, she was on a first-name basis with neighbors for miles around. But more to the point, she was just being Ali.

Other winter memories include our lopsided but lovable snowman that stood nearly six-feet high and that miraculously survived nearly a month in our capricious climate as the centerpiece in the courtyard... A snowball fight in High Park that pitted us against a half-dozen tenacious neighborhood grade-schoolers who handily won the battle by scoring more direct hits — although more than once I detected snowballs suspiciously flung at me from the flank manned by Ali.... Ice skating in the park on Grenadier Pond until sunlight waned and/or our faces numbed, and feet froze...

"Do you feel that?" she once cryptically asked as we skated circles around the bumpy ice surface.

"Feel what?"

"Their eyes," she said in a creepy voice." Their eyes upon us."

"Whose eyes?"

"Their *eyes*," she whispered, mysteriously, taking hold of my hand as we weaved between assorted tykes on skates.

"Legend has it that during The War of 1812, British soldiers practiced maneuvers right here in the park. It was considered an essential plot of land, partly because this pond, this very small inland lake feeds directly into Lake Ontario. One day during a raging snowstorm, British Grenadiers were defending the area from an American invasion when some of the soldiers became separated from their regiment. And, the story goes, these men crashed through the ice on the very pond we're skating on, sinking and drowning in the murky depths, never to be recovered... Hence, Grenadier Pond. Do you feel it, Storm Baker?"

"Thanks a lot," I said.

Because, by then, I did feel it. The power of suggestion, and their eyes upon us...

Then there was the Sunday afternoon she lured me into a road hockey game that was in progress on a side street by our apartment with an enticing offer of a night of hot chocolate and marshmallows and massage and candlelit conversation and "wherever else hot chocolate, marshmallows and massage and candlelit conversation might possibly lead..."

I hadn't held a hockey stick in my hands in an eternity, let alone played in a game with competitive players years my junior. When the game dissolved around dinnertime, Ali and I (exhausted, bruised, sweaty, my bum knee swollen and sore) went home with an open invitation to come and play anytime, offers tendered by young men who seemed appreciative of Ali's road hockey talents and altogether infatuated with Ali who, admittedly, was undeniably adorable in her Toronto Maple Leaf jersey (an oversized, old-time Dave Keon, number 14 model). That night, as the marshmallows began their slow melt in the hot chocolate, Ali asked if I'd had fun that afternoon. I replied, truthfully, that I could not remember the last time I'd had that much fun.

On particularly cold nights, nights when most people with any sense at all simply refused to go outdoors — naturally preferring to stay inside and gripe

ANGELS IN THE ARCHITECTURE

about the weather — Ali would suggest a walk. I remember Bloor West Village, late at night, deserted, brittle and frozen under a guardian moon; the sound of our voices in conversation, underscored by snow crunching under our boots as we traced our usual route, along Bloor to the Humber Theater on Jane Street, and then back. I remember exposed skin — face, ears — tingling. I remember her breath, my breath, mingling and kissing in the cold. Her mittened hand in my gloved hand. Her hand bringing my hand to her belly.

"You know that some day I want to have one." We were approaching a maternity shop. We stopped in front of the store, gazing in at the impossibly tiny apparel and baffling paraphernalia. She pressed my hand more firmly into her belly. "Your baby, my baby, our *baby, growing right here."*

I pulled the glove off my hand and placed a warm finger over her lips, not wanting her to go further, because we had traveled this road so many times before and it was trying. She would say that she wanted one, maybe two, maybe three, because she loved children — and doubtlessly would have been a fabulous mother.. Then she would remind that time was not on her side, and wonder aloud: would it be fair to bring a child into the world if you knew you'd never see that child through all the monumental milestones (birthdays, graduations, new jobs, marriage, the birth of their own children, et al), or that you might not be there to simply bandage a cut suffered in a fall, or help with math homework, or cheer them on in their first hockey game, or dance recital? Ali, considering the fate of our children, already fretted over, albeit not yet conceived. Rare occasions when she could be heard not living firmly in the here and now.

Despite her reservations, her fears of not being there for her offspring, she'd long since taken herself off birth control. Yes, we were trying… Often, diligently… But despite our persistent efforts, my boys and her girls had yet to dance. There was talk on my part of both of us getting tested, but Ali was sure fertility wasn't the issue, so much as fate.

"If I'm not pregnant yet with the amount we've been mauling each other, somebody's trying to tell us something."

Fat flakes of light snow began to fall on our faces. She caught a flake on her tongue I kissed one off the tip of her rosy nose before it had a chance to melt.

"Let's go home."
"And make love…"
"And make love…"
"All night."

ANDY JUNIPER

"Till the cows come home..."
"There are no cows in the big city, babe..."
"Perfect..."
Despite the memories, I believe that it was Ali Reynolds, not winter in the city, which granted those moments their pressing clarity and beauty and stamina.

A Poor Penis Retracting In The Wind

APPROACHING HIS CAR, Storm espies a man urinating on the back passenger-side tire. Heavy woolen trench coat flapped open, pants and gray underpants around his thighs. He's about to rebuke the offender, but intuition reigns him in. There's something about the slouching figure, a forewarning and menacing air of instability that extends beyond indecent exposure. Clothes threadbare, a sleeve of that cumbersome coat affixed at the shoulder with duct tape curling up at the corners in a nasty snarl. Eyes, glassy, staring blankly into space. Face unshaven, contorted. Lips twisted in a permanent sneer. And a hirsute hand on the trunk, for support.

Ever since moving to Toronto, Storm has magnetically attracted the intimidating and the unstable. On various occasions they have approached him out of the blue — risen out of the gutters, crawled out of alleys. Not wanting to seem paranoid, but he can't help but think that they have targeted him ("It's like they hold meetings," he once wrote in a tongue-in-cheek column, "strategy sessions: a united, militant fellowship of the addlebrained.") How else to explain the frequency of these unsettling encounters, or why these people crisscross busy streets and pick their way across crowded sidewalks just to get at him?

He's been sworn at, spat on, and compelled to dodge errant punches. Once he had his ears boxed by a hulking half-wit on a street corner — it was all he could do not to wet himself. Another time he was boxed-in on a streetcar seat and showered with sweat, spit and abuse by an apparent psych-ward escapee, a sickly reed of a man, railing on about "his personal savior, Jesus Christ" and the "imminent Apocalypse", a rant that held Storm hostage, lasting a good ten minutes and carrying him several stops beyond his intended destination.

Most haunting, however, was the late-night subway incident that would play over and over in his mind for months to come, disturbing Storm to his core and causing him to question his own instincts and makeup…

Storm and Ali rattling underground along on the Bloor line, a car to themselves, animatedly discussing the inspiring grand opening of a photography exhibit they'd attended at a mid-town studio featuring the work of one of Ali's friends. The subway screeches to a stop at a station along the line and into the car lurches a lone man, a young, hulking figure in a black headband, army fatigues and clunky, black army boots. With every seat in the car available, he naturally collapses into the seat directly across from them, the chair protesting under his considerable weight. Unwashed, scruffy beard, sweating profusely, greasy hair plastered to the headband, he glances across at Storm with eyes that sear, then leers at Ali. Perversely, predatorily. His eyes tread slowly down her body: frilly white blouse, flirty black skirt, black-stockinged legs, black heels, before settling in her lap.

The man reeks: body odor, cigarettes, pores oozing alcohol. But all Storm Baker can smell is his own pungent sweat. His heart is pounding, guts are turning over. He's sweating pure fear. The man opens his foul mouth.

"I smell cunt." He stares at Storm, his expression an aggressive dare. Do something to stop me, asshole. "Do you smell cunt?" he asks Storm, although his eyes are again riveted on Ali. "You probably don't cause you're a pussy." He laughs mirthlessly at his own juvenile wordplay. From the depths of a pocket of his fatigues, he pulls a switchblade, fingers it open and points it at Storm. Wordlessly, menacingly. At once he takes his free hand and rubs his crotch, thick, grotesque, animalistic arousal evident.

Storm is frozen. His existence suddenly a slow-motion nightmare, every helpless, nauseating second lasting a lifetime. While a part of him commands action, another voice reasons: the guy is six-foot-some-odd-inches of intoxicated and armed insanity.

With effort, the man stands, slowly bringing himself to his full height, legs apart as he battles for balance against the subway's rocking motion. His hand buffs his crotch. If he'd previously undressed Ali with his eyes, those eyes now have her naked form spread out on the aisle of the subway car.

"You make me hard," he whispers, feverishly. His hand now a blur on his crotch, the other hand stroking the air with the knife. "That's what you are, that's all you are, cunt, cunt, cunt." His eyes close. Across his face an expression of pain, like he's being stabbed, or in the full throes of a seizure. There follows relief, closure, in a brief spasm. Metal on metal squeal as the subway jars to a halt at the next station. He opens his eyes, snaps the knife shut and pockets it. And as suddenly as he lurched into their lives, he lurches out: practically throwing himself out of the subway car and onto the platform, turning briefly to look back not at Ali, but at Storm, blowing a kiss to the cuckold.

Later, Ali, at home. PTSD retriggered, shivering. Storm wanting to talk about it. Ali wanting no part of the discussion. She knew from experience what she needed.

"I need a bath just to get warm and to wash his eyes off me. He made me want to crawl out of my own skin." Then, en route to the sanctuary of the bathroom – the candlelight, smoldering incense, her music, the tub full of inviting warm, bubbly water — she answers the unasked question: "You did the right thing, ignoring him."

However, he senses something in the tone of her voice, in the fact that she did not even look at him when she spoke. It will haunt him. He hears water running in the bathroom and is left to wonder whether she was sincere in saying he'd done the right thing, or whether she actually blamed him, considered him spineless for not standing up to him, for letting him use her and abuse them both.

He asks the Hazard what he would have done.

"Gone fucking postal on him." Without hesitation.

"But he'd kill you."

And he shrugged, as if to say, you do what must be done. Damn the torpedoes. Screw the consequences.

Not coincidentally, or surprisingly, it was following that rocky underground ride that Storm decided to investigate purchasing a car, truncating a long-standing, near slavish reliance on the Toronto Transit Commission.

****

Storm sidles up to his car and attempts to inconspicuously slip the key into the lock, hoping to slide in unnoticed. No such luck. Not yet fully zipped, the man nevertheless feels uninhibited enough to pound the trunk with his hand and then charge. Storm throws himself into the front seat and barely closes the door before the guy is madly thumping the driver's side window. In the time it takes Storm to turn the key four or five times to coax the temperamental diva into starting, he discovers the source of the man's vitriol. Apparently he has been personally and aesthetically insulted by Storm's car. The nine-year-old, third-hand, Dodge Dart. Specifically, the fact that it's not in showroom shape and, as such, is — What? Storm wonders, *is what*? Bringing down property values in this otherwise classy neighborhood?

"Fucking car. Bring that fucking shitbox, piece of shit, shit fucking car around here you asshole!" Words strung together, slurred, like necessary medications have been neglected, or replaced by or combined with alcohol or street drugs, and each word is accented by an apelike, hairy-fingered fist smacking the window.

Storm fears the fist is about to crash through the window, that shattered glass is going to rain down around him and that the hairy hand will then be pounding on him, or those simian fingers will be navigating the narrow contours of his throat. Although he knows nothing about automobiles, he is fairly confident that he has flooded the car that is admittedly a shitbox by any standard.

Suddenly something clicks. The car belches exhaust then revs to life in a thunderous roar. Storm yanks the gearshift into drive and tears forward, his concern of running over the man's feet dwarfed only by his dread of the man. Departing in a sputtering, smoky burst, he takes a huge breath of air redolent of burned rubber and burned oil and panic laced with perspiration, and he glances in his rearview mirror to determine whether the madman is following on foot. Thankfully, he's not. He's just standing there, still shaking a fist at Storm and Storm's altogether offensive automobile, and still swearing; his pants are off his hips, half-mast, his poor penis retracting in the brisk, biting wind.

Pulse still pounding, body still jacked in fight-or-flight mode, Storm Baker manages to utter three words: Hap goddamn Hazard.

To Follow The Fugitive Sun

Memories of a teenaged Harland Hazard and a distant afternoon over which hung the threat of a premature snowfall. You could see that threat in the pregnant, bruise-colored clouds. You could feel it in the damp, brisk winds. And the farmers who worked the neat parcels of land surrounding the Highlands Golf Club in the village of Innerkip just outside of Storm's hometown — wise, weathered men whose livelihood and sanity demanded they stay in tune with the capricious swings of Mother Nature — would tell you they could smell it.

Unsurprisingly, Storm Baker and Harland Hazard were the only golfers on the course which, technically speaking, was closed for the season. Although, to the Hazard's way of thinking: "If they really wanted to close up for the season, they would have erected high electrical fences and hired security — pit bulls, sharpshooters and such…"

It was the Hazard's idea to play a round under such inhospitable and contrary conditions. It wasn't that he was cheap and wanted to avoid paying green fees, or that he was one of the zealots the game routinely attracts. In fact, he was a casual duffer who played only a few times each year, his playing time relegated to inclement outings because he refused to golf in traffic. In explaining why he shunned the general golf population, he would quote Linus Van Pelt from the Snoopy cartoon: "I love mankind, it's people I can't stand." Consequently, to get his turn on the course, the Hazard had to outwait even the fanatics who played well into autumn. Until playing was not only unpleasant, but bordering on unbearable.

To the motorists speeding along the rural sideroad that curved around sections of the course, Storm and Harland were just two manure-for-brains high-schoolers lacking the good sense on such an uninviting day to stay indoors, or go hunting – it was duck season, after all. Many passing motorists sacrificed time out of their busy schedules to roll down their windows and share their considered opinions.

"Morons!"

"Stupid fucks!"

"Get off the course, assholes! It's fuckin' freezing out!"

"Like we don't know that," the Hazard said, struggling to stay hunched under the protective collar of his windbreaker as he bent over a four-foot putt. "Like the village people are telling me anything I don't know. Like... shit." He flubbed the putt, leaving the ball perched teasingly on the lip of the hole.

To Storm, it did not seem like a particularly momentous moment. A lapse in concentration, a failure to properly read the frosty green, a simple matter of hands being too cold to manage an honest grip on the putter. Or just your basic crappy putt. To the Hazard it apparently was something else altogether.

The pond off the hole was not yet frozen. A paddling of unsuspecting ducks was leisurely splashing about in the water hazard — one duck nearly decapitated by the Hazard's putter as the club sailed over its head before slicing into the water. Still ensconced in their bulky golf bag, the rest of the clubs followed. Producing an unspectacular splash before slowly disappearing into the murk.

As Storm and Harland stood side by side silently staring into the pond, as though expecting the clubs to miraculously rise from their watery grave, a flatbed farm truck drove idly alongside the course. The beshitted vehicle had "Zepher Hog Farms" painted on its side, a ubiquitous logo in the area. The driver, presumably a bona fide Zepher, or at least a trusted Zepher farmhand, was hanging a hefty arm and his disproportionately large head out the window, that pie-shaped countenance crowned by a black-and-gold Zepher Hog Farms baseball cap. Turned backwards, naturally.

"Stupid golf fuckers," he shouted, flipping off Harland and Storm. The words ominously hung for a moment in the biting air before encountering an even frostier response.

"Pig *fucker*," the Hazard shouted back.

"Oh, Christ," Storm muttered. "Are you out of your mind?"

And in a confirming glance, the Hazard replied that, yes, somewhere on the frozen links he had indeed lost at least a few of his marbles.

ANGELS IN THE ARCHITECTURE

The truck skidded to a stop in an arching, furious patch of burned rubber. The Hazard did not wait for the driver to emerge from the truck's cab. Without a word, with alacrity, he plucked his ball off its perch on the lip of the cup and threw a blazing fastball at the truck. What an arm! Upon impact, at the sound of the windshield shattering, the Hazard grabbed the end of Storm's golf bag — the other end still strapped to his friend's shoulder — and they were off. Fleeing the scene. Wisely not waiting to see if the pig fucker was picking shards of glass out of his fat face. Or, worse, was jumping out of the truck in pursuit.

"It's like when you broke the school window with the baseball," Storm shouted over the clatter of the clubs.

"Like when you busted old man Barker's front window with the marble," the Hazard replied, gasping, already gassed. The Hazard was naturally fast, but to him any run beyond a twenty-yard dash was an Iron Man test of endurance. It did not help that he was already a heavy smoker, a champion of marijuana, and a very social drinker. "Remember how that crazy old coot came after us with an oar? A frickin' oar!" It was an odd, incongruous moment for nostalgia. But as they ran for their lives, inexplicably nostalgic was what they were feeling.

They reached the gravel parking lot by the clubhouse and tossed Storm's clubs into the trunk of his father's red Mustang, circa 1965. Still panicked — they knew that no Zepher hog farmer would ever surrender a windshield without seeking swift and severe retribution — they piled into the car and were off in a rush of adrenaline and a wheel-spinning hail of loose gravel. Whooping, hooting. Matched souls. Blood brothers for as long as Storm could remember, virtually since the day the Hazard had moved from his birthplace, St. Paul, Minnesota, and into Storm's neighborhood, prior to both beginning Grade Five. And from that point onward, they were bonded, best friends, always together, always in cahoots, forever sharing innermost thoughts, secrets, camaraderie, and an us-against-the-world attitude.

There were times back in those grade-school days when Storm — and Storm's protective mother, too —considered the Hazard to be a savior of sorts. By high school, they were inseparable. And they remained inseparable until the moment when they were sure that they were alone, certain that the pig fucker had abandoned pursuit or was lost somewhere in the distance they had put between them. It was then that the Hazard announced, in a voice that was wistful, weighted and weary beyond its years, that he could not endure any more local Zephers, another semester of school, another Canadian winter. That he was leaving.

It was a deflating announcement, one that sucked the ecstasy, indeed, the life right out of the car. It was followed by a prolonged silence, eventually broken by Storm wondering aloud if things at home were really that bad. Firing up a cigarette, the Hazard said that home and his old man had nothing to do with anything. Had he even mentioned home? Had he even mentioned that prick?

Within a week, without fanfare or formal good-byes save for a tearful farewell with Storm's parents, he dropped out of school, packed his life into one small suitcase, strapped his six-string Guild Dreadnought into its case and onto his back and quixotically quit Canada for the United States. Going, he told Storm in his lyrical way, to follow the fugitive sun.

The Hazard crisscrossed the American Sunbelt. A month or two spent here, a month or two there. Sleeping in motels when he had the funds, overnighting in hostels or couch-surfing in the homes of acquaintances when he didn't. For cash, he busked on street corners, bus stations, train depots, or took on odd jobs befitting a struggling artist.

"I did a bit of everything," he would relate years later after he and Storm were reunited. "I waited tables, bused tables. I got dishpan hands and a grotesque skin rash from double shifts up to my elbows in greasy dishwater. But I drew the line at prostitution, drug dealing, or taking any job that required me to wear a hairnet. In this life you must have a backbone and stand up for what is morally right."

Flippancy aside, it was a lonely, dispiriting existence. There were always people buzzing about the Hazard, like bees to the hive, but none that really mattered to him, or cared enough to remain around for the long term. Consequently, he was virtually alone, and he was hungry, in every sense of the word. Harland lost himself in various altered states, attained through his music – songwriting, performing – through casual and frequently regrettable sex, through a smorgasbord of drugs and alcohol.

In all his years away, he proved to be both unrepentantly unprolific as a letter writer and, with his nomadic lifestyle, an elusive target for U.S. postal workers. Storm's rambling, late-night, introspective missives to his friend, pecked out on an antiquated Smith Corona typewriter in whatever city his schooling or career led him, were frequently returned unopened.

ANGELS IN THE ARCHITECTURE

And even when they did not boomerang back-to-sender, he could only hope that they had reached their target and not ended up in the dead-letter-office. As time passed, Storm became discouraged by the whole process; he wrote Hap less and less.

He was nevertheless able to keep track of his friend and the bare bones of his assorted comings and goings via news briefs and entertainment stories in newspapers, magazines and occasionally in the latter years on television clips. Through that six-string Guild Dreadnought, to which he remained sentimentally attached — through two underdog albums sated with lyrics that *Rolling Stone* compared to the likes of Cohen, Waits and Simon, and music that *On Track* magazine gushed was "at once a festival and a funeral of beautiful noise" — his childhood friend's star had risen. In indie music circles, his 'simple yet stunning songs' were revered; he became something of a cult figure. To some an enigmatic icon, to others a reluctant indie god.

The Hazard did little to champion his status, his behavior forever wavering between temperamental, erratic, and reclusive. Any success he ever had was despite himself. He routinely shunned the media and rejected interviews or simply antagonized the interviewer. It wasn't that he was a prima donna so much as that he simply did not suffer fools gladly. He had no patience for trite, stupid questions, or trite, stupid questioners for that matter. He abhorred playing games. He was a musician who just wanted to be left to his music. He wanted to shut up and simply let his music to speak for him. That said, despite the apparent death-wish he wielded like a knife to the neck of his career, he was briefly bestowed west-coast status of "minor celebrity," primarily on account of his name being dropped in the media by a group of young actors then redefining west-coast *Tiger Beat* petulance and bad boy/bad girl cool.

"For thirty days I was their flavor of the month."

Aside from being a favorite of the Brat Pack — in particular, Molly Ringwald who gushed to *People* magazine that Harland was "a sensitive soul, a beautiful loser, one of those guys you just want to take home and mother half-to-death... and then boink." — he was also a darling of critics who were enamored with his glaring talent and the fact that he had not sold himself down the lazy, polluted river that is mainstream music.

"I was a little 'left of the dial'. Uncool enough to be considered cool. On the acceptable edge of the unacceptable. But, believe me, critics be damned, if I could have found the mainstream, or, rather, if the mainstream had found me, I'd have been in my dinghy paddling down it. Despite what so-called music rebels say, songwriters *want* to have their songs heard. That's the point, right? Not pouring your soul into something that no one will ever hear. Like, fuck that…"

With one powerful and unfathomably enriching exception, he was generally ignored by the Dick Clarks and Casey Kasems and Top 40 America. That exception was a song he wrote called *So We Beat On (All Apologies To F. Scott)* that was covered, and sugar coated to distraction, by one of the era's prominent Pop Tart princesses. The Hazard loathed everything about the over-produced, over-polished, saccharine rendition. Apart from the mind-boggling, life-altering royalties it produced and produced and produced…

"They even changed the name of the song on me. I always pictured the meeting of the minds. Dim record execs and their obsequious marketers right out of *Spinal Tap*: 'So We Beat On' doesn't work! We need something catchier, less obscure, less cryptic, easier to understand. I mean, 'So We Beat On' just raises questions. So We Beat On *what*? What the fuck-hell are we beating on?'"

The Hazard's history with record execs — 'label stiffs', or 'record weasels', or 'industry snakes' as he routinely called them — was long, turbulent, and disappointing, to say the least. When feeling nostalgic, he would relate his first meeting with the breed: two guys listening to his demo, one paying no attention whatsoever, and the other shaking his ratty ponytail and remarking: "The audience simply isn't going to *get* your songs. If you have anything that's not quite so clever, we'd love to hear it…"

"You *want* me to dumb it down?"

"Oh, yes. Considerably."

Harland Hazard in the news. A highly publicized barroom punch-up in The Sunset, the famous Sunset Strip nightclub. John Lennon played the venue in its heyday. The Doors and Zeppelin, too. However, by the time the Hazard arrived in Los Angeles, the landmark had been reincarnated and reduced from rock palace to dance club and had subsequently become a celebrity hangout. The in-place for the fickle in-crowd. Actors, actresses, models, musicians. In short, all the beautiful people.

"I stepped into the Sunset once in all my time out there, just wanting to pay homage, to be in the same room where Lennon played and, wouldn't you know it, all hell breaks loose. Some yahoo accuses me of hitting on his girlfriend, I accuse him of being a total dipshit…"

When unprovoked and sober the Hazard was no fighter. The punch-up resulted in the Hazard's nose being broken by a daytime TV star. "Daytime TV star — now there's a rich oxymoron," or so he was quoted in *The Enquirer*. A subsequent court appearance on assorted mischief charges saw him being placed on probation for one year.

Then there was a rumored tryst with blossoming actress, Winona Laura Horowitz, a.k.a. Winona Ryder, who years later would come to be known more for her kleptomania and ravenous appetite for shaggy bastards of rock and roll, than for her considerable acting chops. The rumors were followed by a fairly blunt denial issued by the Hazard ("Winona's what, sixteen?"), a denial that to Lotus Land's pretzel logic was either viewed as no denial at all, or else a smokescreen. The bare bones of these stories would not be fleshed out until Storm and Harland reunited. After Storm met Ali.

Until that fortuitous reunion, he had no idea that his childhood friend was even back in Canada let alone residing in Toronto, coincidentally only a few miles west of Storm's apartment. Likewise, the Hazard had no idea that his blood brother had ended up in Toronto.

"You're Storm Baker, Small-Town Man. Rustic beyond redemption. I never thought you'd end up anywhere that boasted a population of more than 30,000."

"Don't you read the newspaper?" Storm would question. "I'm in there you know."

"Hey, your rag ain't the only game in town." Then, sheepishly, "No, I don't read newspapers. They're full of propaganda. And they make my fingers black."

Undoubtedly the two had narrowly missed running into each other innumerable times at various places: grocery stores, coffee shops, liquor stores, restaurants and the like. The setting and circumstances surrounding their actual reunion would become a conversation piece, the type of coincidental encounter that would have people recalling classic Thomas Hardy plotlines so heavily hitched to fate, or that would simply leave people shaking their heads and wondering, what are the odds?

Ali, an eyewitness to the reunion, would side with Hardy, saying that it was predestined – just another of life's meaningful coincidences. The Hazard would only say, "It was just plain, bloody embarrassing, Storm here busting in on us doing yoga in our skivvies, and let's leave it at that..." In lighter, and/or more-inebriated moments, he would add that on the positive side, at least he'd been wearing clean underwear. And, as a whispered aside to Storm: "At least I didn't have a boner..."

Over the long course of their intertwined history, there would be moments when Storm Baker believed that he knew everything there was to know about Harland Hazard. Alternatively, there would come a time when he believed that he knew next to nothing about his friend. In moments of more honest and frank reflection, he would concede the possibility, the probability, that his friend was the type of person that no one could ever completely know... "Like anyone ever completely knows another person," he could imagine his friend weighing in... Nevertheless, there was never a time when Storm did not believe that he knew more about the Hazard than anyone else in the world.

Routines, Rituals And A Second-Hand Celica

ALTHOUGH HE WOULD never make money the measure of a man — for all the embarrassingly obvious reasons, print journalists rarely do — Storm knew with certainty, for what it was worth, that his friend could afford to drive a sports car or a luxury automobile. Such vehicles were well within his means. Disinclined to discuss personal finances, the Hazard did once confess that while he was not quite what the casually philosophical Kurt Vonnegut would characterize as "fabulously well-to-do", he was nonetheless "a more run-of-the-mill, garden-variety well-to-do." Not an unenviable position for a man who made no secret of the fact that he was "creatively constipated", and who, consequently, has not worked in years. Unless endorsing royalty checks can be categorized as work.

Regardless, sports cars and luxury automobiles were never the Hazard's style. His taste, as dictated by personal philosophy and personal paranoia, tended toward older, previously owned vehicles. In fact, it was the Hazard who sold the Dodge Dart to Storm after the Hazard found himself in love with a seven-year-old, second-hand, shiny-grey Celica he espied on a used-car lot.

"I hate to say goodbye to this sweetheart," the Hazard said upon handing the Dart's keys and ownership papers over to Storm. "I bought it second-hand three years ago and it's truly a piece of work. You'd have to drive a stake through its heart to kill this beast."

"It's a shitbox, Harland. Out of sheer desperation, I'm taking a shitbox off your hands."

"Yeah," he admitted, "it's a shitbox. But a classic shitbox."

A temperamental shitbox that only started if and when it was in the mood.

As for the Hazard's preference for older automobiles, like the Celica and the Dart before it: he theorized that the chinks in an old car's armor were but minor irritations when compared to being beaten, robbed, and possibly even held hostage at gunpoint by trigger-drunk punks weaned on guns and cartoon violence. Which, he contended, was what invariably happens to people who tool about in cool sports cars or luxury automobiles…

Storm and Harland. Harland and Storm. Lives intertwined. Common interests. Rundown cars. Ali. Of course, Ali.

There was a period when they also shared the same physician, Storm's good friend, Dr. Redic Mackenzie. Granted, Storm only visited Dr. Mack on a professional basis a handful of times over the years while the Hazard, who suffered from over-concern — if not full-blown hypochondria — saw him on a more persistent and nagging basis. To the personnel at the doctor's bustling Bloor Street West clinic – and, similarly, the staff at The Blue Parrot Tavern — the Hazard was simply known as "the regular."

They also shared some of the Hazard's various "therapies." Basketball, or what the Hazard called "hoop therapy", for one. A juvenile, albeit calming pursuit, born in high school and picked up as adults after their reunion in Toronto. Hoop therapy. Shooting baskets on the Hazard's driveway. Being sedated into a drug-like stupor by hours of mindless repetition: grab basketball, square-up to the basket, set, launch shot, rebound, repeat. Barely speaking. About the only sounds heard being the occasional scuff of a sneaker on the asphalt, the *thunk* of the ball careening off the backboard the Hazard had mounted on his garage, the clunk of an arc-less shot hitting the rim, the occasional thunderous crash and subsequent reverberation as an errant shot bounced off the already dimpled garage doors… Oh, and Harland doing his best impression of famed announcer Marv Albert ("Yes!") whenever he swished a shot. Hoop therapy, even in the off-season, on days when it was too damp and too cold to get a decent feel for the ball. Which in Toronto, was half of each year.

"Never too cold for hoop therapy," the Hazard theorized. "And you don't need to get a feel for the ball, the ball will get a feel for you."

"How very Zen."

For as long as Storm has known him, the Hazard has engaged in various forms of therapy; he has always had his rituals. In retrospect, it's obvious that some of those rituals were beneficial to his health and well-being, while others did not serve him well at all. As a young teenager, for instance, he seldom went to bed until he'd watched Johnny Carson's monologue on the *Tonight Show*. It was a nightly ritual that only served to escalate the hostilities between Harland's bickering parents (his father enraged that his mother, upon whose shoulders fell the responsibilities of child-rearing, was letting him stay up that late), many missed first-period morning classes, and Hazard dozing off like a narcoleptic in various other classes throughout the day.

More recently, there has been "therapy, therapy," as the Hazard termed the period when he was seeing two psychologists on a regular basis. Regardless of what one said, he thought it essential to secure a second opinion.

"For all I know, these head doctors may be a quacks. Keep in mind, it's my subconscious we're peeling here, not an onion."

Typically, the Hazard played one shrink against the other, accepting from each only what he wanted to accept, hearing only what he wanted to hear. Consequently, he was just spinning his wheels with both. For his part, the Hazard steadfastly maintained: "They are getting to the bottom of me. It's only a matter of time. Look how long it took Dr. Landy to help Brian Wilson."

Then there was the ritual he shared, or, rather, had in common with Ali. The ritual he called "hydrotherapy." In other words, baths. Long, steaming baths to dissolve tension, to soothe whatever ached and help turn tight muscles to putty. The Hazard could lay claim to being one of the cleaner people on the planet. Honestly, who could argue? He routinely filled the tub with water as hot as his skin could tolerate, then immersed himself up to the armpits. He would stay like that for prolonged periods of time, intermittently reheating the water, until his poor, pink skin had shriveled, and he was nearing dehydration.

Aside from torturing his skin, he regularly did one of two things in the tub: he returned to *The Great Gatsby*, which he said never failed to rip at his guts with its monumental beauty and heartbreaking themes of unrequited love and the death of dreams, or he listened to old Beach Boy records. In time, with the help of a female friend — or so his story always went — he had come to comprehend, appreciate, and believe in the genius of Beach Boy Brian Wilson. After years of openly and vociferously scorning the man and what he perceived to be nothing more than a vaporous west coast pop music sound, the Hazard claimed to have discovered, in an assisted epiphany, the brilliance of the artist, and the haunting, ethereal nature of the man's music.

"This young woman helped me to realize that there's a spiritual soul inherent in the songs," he asserted, "and a deep and underlying melancholy that lurks everywhere in the music, even behind those godless 'Fun, Fun, Funs.'"

It was the Hazard's contention that he needed rituals to keep calm and grounded and to merely keep functioning. In his mind, they were what kept him from going over the edge. In time, they became the diversions, the distractions, the obstacles that he erected between himself and his craft. After Storm found Ali, and after he was reunited with the Hazard, he was often left wondering just when was the last time his friend had practiced his craft, or even thought about picking up his guitar?

Little-Known Facts

IT'S A LITTLE-KNOWN *fact: equine history is some fifty-five-million-years old. Furthermore, the relationship between humans and horses is about six-thousand-years old, and scientists believe that horseback riding predates the wheel by some five-hundred years...*

About the only television show that Ali watched with any regularity was the Boston bar-based sitcom Cheers. She loved the cast and the chemistry, particularly that shared by Sam (Mayday) Malone and Diane Chamber, as played by Ted Danson and Shelley Long. Further, she could do an uncanny imitation of Cheers' regular Cliff Clavin, actor John Ratzenberger's delusional know-it-all, a hapless postal worker who often prefaced his trivial, and woefully misinformed outpourings, with the words: "It's a little-known fact..."

"It's a little-known fact that cows were domesticated in Mesopotamia and were also used in China as guard animals... There's no rule against postal workers not dating beautiful women, it just works out that way... If memory serves, the umbilical cord is ninety percent potassium..."

Ali delivered the aforementioned equine history facts, in her finest Bostonian Clavinese, from her saddled mount atop Sandy's Summer Dream, a beautiful and behaved five-year-old Palomino. We had been together about six months when she slyly suggested one sun-splashed Sunday morning in springtime that we sign up for a trail ride at Five Star Ranch, a horse stable located northwest of the city that had recently been featured in The Times' leisure section.

I watched in awe as she declined the foot-up offered by Matt Wendall, a grizzled Five Star stable hand, then effortlessly mounted the Palomino, like she was cowgirl Dale Evans in her prime boarding Buttermilk, or, as Matt whispered, "like she was born on the back of a horse." My awe emanated from my own failed, almost farcical attempts to mount the horse that I'd been assigned, a gelding ironically named Tiny — Tiny being the largest, goofiest and most awkward organization of horse flesh assembled at the ranch. Even with Matt's helpful foot-up, I inexplicable ended up not atop Tiny as intended, but, rather, dangerously underfoot, the quick-handed Matt dragging me out of the path of Tiny's hooves, clumsily sifting through the dirt.

"How did you do that?" I asked a smirking Ali. "You've done this before!" I accused. I glanced at Matt, who just scratched the graying stubble on his chin and grinned affably. "She said she's never done this before... That's how she got me here, on the condition of mutual ineptitude, that we would make complete fools of ourselves together."

"Never before, I swear," she laughed. "I guess there's just an inherent bond between women and horses. It comes naturally." And with that she clicked her heels into the horse's flanks and was off, out of the paddock and into the sunshine, following one of the trail guides down a dirt road toward a handful of other riders who were waiting to begin the trail ride, and leaving Matt and me squinting at the sun's rays glinting off Summer Dream's shiny, golden-blonde coat. As we watched Ali's backside gracefully rising and falling in sync with the motion of the horse, Matt looked at me skeptically and said, slowly, as though his voice was reined to the pace of an aging school horse: "I do believe she's pulling your leg. She's ridden before.... Nobody's that natural."

Turns out, she was pulling my leg. She would fess up that night as we shared a bubble bath that, in an overzealous attempt to appease aching muscles and saddle-sore backsides, was too bubbly and too hot. She had ridden before. Apparently, like so many young girls, she grew up with a love of horses.

"There were no Tiger Beat pinups in my life as a kid. I grew up in bedrooms adorned with horse pictures that I'd clipped out of magazines and saved over time. As much as we moved, I never really felt at home until those pictures that I'd so carefully packed inside the covers of books, so they wouldn't get crinkles were located, unpacked and thumb-tacked back up on my walls.

"I watched horse shows on TV, went to horse movies at the theater. I dreamed about owning a horse, taking care of a horse, even having an opportunity to name a horse. Most times in my mind, I'd settle on Smoky, like the lovable nag Lee Marvin's Kid Sheleen rode in the movie Cat Ballou, one of my all-time favorite movies. First time I saw it, I wanted to be Jane Fonda.

"I read horse magazines Janeen occasionally brought home and I read horse books I picked up at libraries. Books by writers like Maxine Kumin,

ANGELS IN THE ARCHITECTURE

Elizabeth Atwood Lawrence and Vicki Hearne. I read Misty of Chincoteague *by Marguerite Henry,* Smoky the Cow Horse *by Will James, and* My Friend Flicka *by Mary O'Hara, which was actually a series of excellent books. I fell in love with Walter Farley's* Black Stallion *and John Steinbeck's* Red Pony. *I read* Black Beauty *about a dozen times. It's a little-known fact,"* she chuckled, cupping a handful of bubbles and blowing them my way, *"that by the time I was born,* Black Beauty *was the sixth best-seller in the English language. Not bad for a novel chronicling the life of a horse and told from the horse's perspective."*

She took a sip of wine. I rolled a perspiring bottle of beer across the sweat beads gathering on my forehead, and she continued...

"About the only thing I liked about our constant moves was poor Janeen's inevitable guilt." She closed her eyes, smiling at memories conjured. "Every new town, every new city, Janeen, feeling just terrible about having pulled me out of another school and away from friends I'd just made, would say that she was taking me out for a treat. We'd drive out to the nearest stable and she'd pay to let me have the works: groom a horse of my picking, take a lesson, go for a long arena ride or out on a trail..."

"Janeen rode horses with you?" I asked, incredulous.

"God no. She'd watch for a while, teetering in the dirt on a pair of heels, then she'd quickly tire of the sights, sounds and smells of the barn — particularly the uncivilized smells — and she'd leave me in the hands of the stable staff. She'd go out to the car to read a book, or listen to the radio, a jazz station she could pick up out of Chicago and empty a flask of whatever medicinal she'd brought with her." She paused, brushing an errant strand of damp hair off her face. "So, Storm Baker, did you like riding?"

"More than I liked falling," I admitted. "I don't think I'll ever again walk normally or sit without pain. Hey," I teased, "you don't have to feel guilty about nearly being the cause of my ultimate demise. *You* should, but *you* don't have to..."

Eventually Matt had managed to get me atop Tiny. And eventually, with the coaching (and coaxing) of a patient guide, I caught up to the pack. Although I was by all accounts, "stiff as wood up there," an unbalanced, ungraceful sorry sight. Holding on for dear life, joints locked, pinching my legs together like a human vise in an attempt to remain aboard the tired, old horse.

The trail guide led us along a scenic, wooded path that meandered around the expansive Five Star property. Past a pond and up a ridge, the peak of which offered a panoramic view of the surrounding area, then back toward the main road, past golfers on the back nine of an adjacent golf course and past an old Anglican cemetery, granite tombstones and memorials sparkling in the sun in memory and honor of the departed. Even with Ali offering advice, which I was simply too helpless to take, I had difficulty keeping up with the others; that said, I was taking a certain amount of pride in not falling too far behind.

Pride was bucked when Tiny — the big, stupid baby — came to a moribund creek that was all of an arm's length wide and only half as deep and refused to cross. I tried everything I could think of. Everything I'd ever seen in westerns from coaxing to cursing to digging in with my heels, but the big oaf wouldn't budge. Ali finally came to the rescue, circling back, dismounting, and literally pulling Tiny, me, and my public humiliation across the small spit of water.

Horses, by and large, apparently don't hold a whole lot of affection for water, or so Matt Wendall would later tell me (taking, I thought, a little too much pleasure in hearing the tale of my misadventures). And to boot, Matt would add, Tiny happens to be one of those hapless creatures that walks God's earth petrified of his own shadow.

"We've got barn kittens with bigger balls than this big guy..."

Ali would become a regular at Five Star, getting up to the ranch as often as her schedule would allow, which was never often enough for her liking. She found this return to her girlhood pastime therapeutic.

"Riding," she would enthuse, "takes me outside myself. You know how when kids play, they get so absorbed in what they're doing, they get lost in time? When I ride it's like that, like there's nothing else in the world, just me and the horse."

One night, Matt called with the unsettling news that Sandy's Summer Dream was up for sale. The owners of the stables felt that, as a school horse, her potential was not being realized. Ali spent a long weekend in a quandary: it wasn't the money so much as the commitment. She didn't want to buy the horse unless she could dedicate enough time to its well-being.

At the time, Five Star had a loosely knit club for its young female riders called Five Star Pony Pals. At a meeting hastily convened by Ali in the ranch's cramped and over-stocked tack shop, she offered a deal to the eight adoring faces staring up at her: she would lay down the two-thousand-dollars for the horse if they would help her care for Sandy's Summer Dream. Muck her stall. Feed her. Groom her. Clean her tack. And give her the exercise she needed by riding her as often as possible— which, naturally, would be as often as their parents would volunteer to bring them to the barn. Giddy shrieks of approval

ANGELS IN THE ARCHITECTURE

from eight young girls who felt like they'd just died and gone to heaven signified that the deal was sealed.

Finally, up out of the bubbles we flopped on top of the bed, naked, side-by-side, supine, pink-skinned, over-heated, light-headed. In the comfortable silence between us, I considered ways of making love with Ali that I knew my inflamed aching muscles would probably never allow. Ali, apparently, was considering other things altogether. Like, little-known facts. Which is why, when I turned my head toward her, she was wearing that familiar Clavin grin...

"It's a little-known fact," she said, "that around the world today there are more than sixty-million horses..." A perfect pearl of Cliff.

"Ahhh," I replied, adopting a barely passable Clavin voice, "it's a little-known fact that the tan became popular in what is known as The Bronze Age..."

We spent the night watching classic episodes of Cheers *that Ali had taped and, later, making only the slow, cautious, tender love that our muscles would allow.*

Ali, We Need To Talk

A DAY OF remembrance. As if remembrance required tethering to man-made calendar time. As if any need existed for a date to be set aside and observed. As if each day of the past year was not spent remembering, to the point of distraction and despair. Remembering, until he barely remained afloat, the undertow of memories and loss simply toying with him; remembering, and in time enshrining her memory, whisking her up beyond the clouds into the heavens to a resting place amongst wished-on, worshipped, winking stars. A perfect angel, Ali.

Subsequently, when he slowly surfaces from sleep on the first anniversary of his wife's death — opening heavy eyes to a spider crossing the ornate plaster swirl of the bedroom ceiling in his rented digs at the Harbour Castle — he is resolute in thinking that he will not bow to a calendar date or allow the day to wield any subversive power over him. No special significance, no superficial ceremony. It will be but one more day on the road to recovery. One step forward on the journey back to life, back to an existence that he can stare in the face and deem worthwhile and, one day, perhaps even normal, should something resembling 'normal' still exist. Even in rare moments of optimism and hope, on days when the clouds unexpectedly part and rays of sunshine briefly pierce the darkness, he cannot help but think that for every forward step taken on the journey, life throws a sucker punch and knocks him back a few steps...

He's shaving, on his face an unsightly mixture of shaving cream and blood from multiple razor nicks on sensitive, razor-shy skin that he inherited from his father who used to shave each night before a workday just to give his face time to recover. The telephone rings. He leaves the call to the hotel's answering service as he persists with the removal of the patchy shadow on his face. After the shave, a hot shower, and a light breakfast delivered by room service, he checks his messages.

Janeen. In a peculiar voice, void of emotion, flatlined...

"Happy Anniversary." A pause, a snort (the stifled, choked-up beginning of a laugh or cry), muffled sounds. Silence. Then, "Listen, if you're there, when you get this, I'm thinking we need to do something. Be close to her. Let's go to that establishment she adored, The Blue Bird Tavern, or whatever. Call me, Storm Baker. You call me..."

Blue *Parrot* Tavern, Janeen, Blue Parrot.

Janeen. Time spent with her every day at the CrossRoads and out and about in the city whenever he was able to coax her out of the dreadful high-rise and away from her creature comforts: Hickory Sticks and Ginger Ale and, on television, the lecherous Bob Barker and his leggy assistants on *The Price is Right*. Storm has noticed that she has transformed into something of a homebody, increasingly content to cocoon, reluctant to socialize. That said, they did share a memorable night at The Rex Hotel, a prominent jazz house on Queen Street West, where she was greeted upon her arrival with patron fanfare akin to that commonly received by barfly Norm whenever he entered the sitcom tavern of *Cheers*.

Norm!

Janeen!

Between sets by a local ensemble known as The Jazz Age, Janeen regaled those gathered around her — including a particularly attentive man named Cotton ("Just Cotton"), a lanky saxophone player and, evidently, an old friend. She spoke of other memorable nights in jazz clubs across the country and even down into the States; apparently there had been more than one impromptu and epic road trip down to Bourbon Street in New Orleans, fueled in equal parts by alcohol, adventure, and a love of jazz. Storm watched her with fascination: Janeen, reveling in the music, the atmosphere, and the attention. Janeen infused and positively giddy with life. However, near midnight, giddiness dissipated. The night sputtered.

"Janeenie, where have you been?" Cotton asked, attempting to pilot the conversation out of its tailspin. "You haven't been around the Rex in ages. You just drop off the face of the Earth now and then without a word and it leaves everyone wondering and worrying. Nobody knows where the heck you're at."

"I've been around... busy..."

Storm sensed an annoying, "Oh, poof!" quivering on Janeen's lips.

"Well, honestly girl," Cotton added, taking hold of her hands, "I've seen you looking better."

"And honestly, Cotton, I've felt me feeling better." Her skin had turned a waxy gray under the unflattering bar lights. She forced a laugh. After Cotton kissed her cheek and stepped up on stage for the ensemble's last set of the night, Janeen turned to Storm and said in a drained voice: "Stick a fork in me, handsome. I'm done..." In the taxi on the way, she admitted that she could barely keep her eyes open, and that her head was pounding.

A week later there was an interesting spur-of-the-moment shopping expedition. Late in the afternoon they were unenthusiastically discussing dinner options when Janeen blurted out of the blue: "Forget relieving our hunger, we need to shop. My fall and winter wardrobe is past its expiry date..."

Which is how Storm came to find himself in GladRags, a self-promoted "funky" Queen Street West boutique that proudly caters to the willowy-thin, perky-breasted and unrepentantly trendy — to women three or four full decades Janeen's junior. Janeen deftly parked Storm by the changerooms on an uncomfortable, pad-less iron chair, the chair's grooves immediately creating a waffle design on his backside, while she deliberately mixed and matched her way into one of her signature outfits. Storm wondered how many other men over time had been cast by Janeen in this very role of supportive shopping partner, or sad-sack dupe just waiting for the agony to end so they could get on with their day.

"Janeen," Storm called to her back as she returned to the changeroom for the umpteenth time armed with more eccentric fashion possibilities, "I think your ultimate goal should be to find clothes and colors that actually match." Sound advice nevertheless greeted by a scornful, what-the-hell-do-you know retort.

"Oh, poof!"

Finally, to a sales assistant named Sarah, an orange-haired and infectiously giggly twenty-something: "I'll take this, this and this. Oh, I'll be needing new panties. Scanties, of course..." Then, in an exaggerated whisper feigned as a covert aside to the salesclerk: "Oh look, Sarah, we're making my date blush! The panty-word got my Stormy-boy going. Honestly, who knew he had that color in him?"

Taking Sarah by the arm, Janeen added confidentially, girl to girl: "There are a couple of p-words that always get men going, and the c-word can always be called upon if you want to turn him purple. And, you know, the mystery of men: if dirty talk is their thing, the word 'nipple' for some reason always gets a rise. Nipple, for heaven's sake! Honestly, go figure…"

Storm could not discern whether Sarah was embarrassed, amused, or shocked. Personally speaking, the dirty talk exchange flustered him only half as much as when Janeen began to theorize on the link between female shopping and female sexual arousal.

"It's true. Shopping is often a precursor to sex. Remember all those trashy 70's novels, the Harold Robbins, Jacqueline Susans, Sidney Sheldons? Of course, you wouldn't, they were way before your time, lucky you. Anyway, they all catered to, and ultimately cashed in on, the entangled female urges for attire and intimacy. At the time there was a genre that publishers called 'shopping-and-shagging novels.' It was Freud, that costive old windbag, who formulated this theory. And I can tell you that in this field I've done exhaustive research…"

Then there was the topic she turned to as she made use of the time it took for Sarah to ring in the purchases at the cash register. Glancing at Storm, she announced that it was high time he got back out there, back up on that horse. She said he would do well to gather the gumption and ask the Sarah out on a date; this exchange within obvious earshot of the mortified salesclerk. Embarrassing, crawl-under-the-chair moments aside, for the most part they found themselves enjoying each other's company. In the short time he's been back, Storm senses they are already becoming closer, that she is slowly letting him in, although he remains cognizant of the barriers that she unconsciously erects around herself and that he has yet to scale.

Still, he frets. At times she seems vibrant and full of her old independent self, other times she appears reliant. Worn, shaky, frail. Mentally she has seemed stable. Albeit temperamental, forgetful, flighty, intoxicated. Even when he is certain that she has not been drinking.

"Janeen, are you on any medications I should know about?"

And despite the time that has past, even on her good days he is unable to shake the impression that was so vividly shaped in his mind on that first day at the CrossRoads. When he closes his eyes at night, he envisions the dust and clutter in her apartment. Out of the blue he hears the infernal beeping of her smoke detector. Likewise, the shock of seeing her across the room in the coffee shop remains fresh. It was with that image entrenched in mind that he initially broached the subject of her visiting a doctor, only to be rejected with a wave of her hand. Janeen professes little faith and less regard for the medical profession, or what she deems the "high-priced hocus-pocus" practiced by the profession. Nevertheless, when he witnessed her having trouble lacing up a pair of fashionable boots — staring down at those laces, befuddled, like she had never before encountered anything so intricate — he knew that Janeen refusing medical attention was no longer an option.

It's as he is dialing her number to respond to her invitation to the Blue Parrot that he initially feels it, a pull over which he holds no control. The lure of the day, the draw of the calendar, like a siren's call to the adrift sailor, the liquor bottle's seductive invitation to the parched alcoholic. Irresistible. Conscious thought and determination be damned, he is sucked in. Once finished confirming plans with Janeen, he grabs his windbreaker, departs the hotel, and soon finds himself confronting what he has so willfully avoided....

Retracing their steps, visiting old haunts and places where together they experienced both the mundane — day to day life (a library, bank, record shop, coffeeshop, grocery store, bookstore, the dry cleaners, the neighborhood convenience store) – and the more monumental... Standing on the congested Bloor/Keele street corner where he first summoned the courage to express what was by then obvious to everyone, that he was in love with her, and where she so animatedly reciprocated, arms thrown around his neck.

"Storm Baker, I have *always* loved you..." And then a kiss, the passion staggering. Storm remembers the cars speeding by en route to or from Lakeshore Boulevard, the Gardiner Expressway or the Queen Elizabeth Way, gawking motorists honking and making crude gestures and hollering lewd remarks out opened windows.

Storm Baker, turning up the collar of his jacket against the chilly wind along their stretch of Bloor Street, scarcely acknowledging and occasionally even avoiding the familiar faces of shopkeepers, erstwhile neighbors and acquaintants, apprehensive and reluctant to actually stop and converse.

ANGELS IN THE ARCHITECTURE

He shudders to even imagine the regressive steps the conversations would take. Teary eyes, shrugs of sympathy, remembrances and fleshy hugs wrapped in emotion. Frankly, he's not up to it.

Storm Baker, today taking the full emotional wallop, to the head, to the heart, to the gut, of the geography and personal history of this area of Toronto.

Storm Baker, walking through High Park. Where they met, played like kids, exercised, strolled hand-in-hand, where her ashes were eventually surrendered to a city breeze. Walking, virtually everywhere that was Ali. Storm Baker, standing in the shadow of the apartment they shared, staring up the sheer face of the high-rise and succumbing to the need to sit on a bench before dizziness dragged him face down onto the walkway. Storm Baker, on that bench, in the throes of an anxiety attack that has him rumpled, sweating and shaky, gasping for a decent breath of air. Storm Baker, reassuring a diminutive and elderly Asian lady — communicating in frantic gestures and fractured English — that he is okay. No, no need to call 911, but thanks…

"Hey, babe. Brought you a dozen red roses from your favorite flower shop. One for every month.…"

At the gravesite. On bended knee, addressing *her*, and her modest granite memorial.

He recalls the funeral director, William Thomas Day, a tall, pencil-thin man, well-versed in grief etiquette and death decorum, impeccable in his dress and manner and intuition of when to interject a comforting word, when to smoothly slip out of the casual and into the formal, when to place a reassuring hand on a mourner's arm, and when to respectfully retreat and allow space for a breath of air, for a lagging thought to play catch-up. He can feel William Thomas Day's fingers gently coming to rest on his forearm, can see his perfectly manicured fingernails, flawless half moons, as he explained that the ashes are placed in an urn and that the urn is typically buried in a burial plot and marked with a proper tombstone or memorial. All taken care of, should he desire, by the funeral home.

Storm informed him of Ali's wishes. Did he detect an eyebrow furrowing as the director surely considered why a healthy woman of Ali's age would have had "wishes"? He told him of his intentions to scatter the ashes — not saying where, doubting that such activity was legal in the park. To which the funeral director replied, in a tone as somber as death itself: "I believe, Mr. Baker, that it won't matter that the urn is empty, that you have chosen to scatter her ashes. That, naturally, is your decision. However, it's been my experience that there will come a day when you welcome the formal grave as a memorial to your wife, a physical place where you can go, sort through your thoughts, and commune with her in spirit."

The day has not yet come. He is not welcoming the gravesite, and yet he is here. The roses he purchased fanned out across her plot, his fingers tracing the grooves, the lettered indentations on the tiny, simple memorial, in grave contrast to Mr. Dyer's grand obelisk to his wife. Storm's thoughts and emotions racing. What exactly is he doing here? Seeking closure? Acknowledging the anniversary of her death? Celebrating her life? Or is he here against all logic, all common sense and everything in which he believes, or everything he believes he believes? He's here, his tears watering the manicured grass, waiting on an appearance. The appearance of an angel...

"Ali can you hear me?" he blubbers to the cold stone. "I need you to hear me. And I need to see you. Ali, we need to talk..."

And then and there, in the small Anglican cemetery named after St. Paul, in a countryside setting that Ali adored just north of the city across a quiet, gravel road from Five Star Ranch, Storm Baker swears he feels her presence. Welcome, divine. Swears that the movement, the rustling, the gentle midday breeze blowing between grave markers, playfully batting about dead leaves and debris like a kitten having its way with a ball of yarn, is the spirit of his wife. He believes that even the squirrels, abruptly ceasing their assiduous preparations for winter, feel her presence. He shivers. A chill sets down his spine. He hears her voice, a faint whisper piggybacking on the breeze and being whisked through the graveyard. He basks in her presence. Smiles when he first feels eyes upon him and senses he is being watched and nearly jumps out of his skin when a hand softly touches down on his shoulder.

He screams and bounds up from where he was kneeling. She shrieks and leaps away from him. He stares, she stares, both slack-jawed, wide-eyed. Like they have seen a ghost. They take a moment to collect themselves, mutually embarrassed by their outbursts, still shaken at having had the daylights scared out of them.

"Who are you?"

ANGELS IN THE ARCHITECTURE

"You're Storm Baker."

"I know who I am. It's you I'm wondering about. You nearly gave me a heart attack."

"Natalie. Natalie Wilkins. We met at the funeral."

She formally offers a hand and a smile that is at once trusting and warm, wide and winsome. As he buries the small hand in his, Storm strains to recall ever having met this young girl. His memories of the funeral are limited, most faint and admittedly there are gaps. Still, the face is naggingly familiar. Certainly, she would have been dressed differently then than now. Nobody, not even Janeen — well, perhaps Janeen — would wear a cowgirl outfit to a funeral: night-black Stetson, a white collared shirt with fancy embroidering around the collar and cuffs, a purple vest, black jeans, and polished cowboy boots. And more than likely, given the way children grow in leaps and bounds, she was even smaller than she is now, a mere slip of a girl. Storm still cannot place her amongst the mourners at the funeral.

"Wait a minute... Natalie Wilkins." It's the name rather than the face that suddenly registers. "You were a Pony Pal."

"Still am," she says, running a hand proudly across her riding clothes. "We've got a show today. Last one of the season. Would you like to come over and watch, even for just a while?"

"Are you riding..."?

"Sandy's Summer Dream," she nods.

"I'd love to come and watch."

She takes his hand and guides him out of the cemetery. He cannot feel his body but is aware of a hollowness where his guts should be. His mind is a million miles away. However, he trusts young Natalie Wilkins implicitly, and his trust is blind.

"She was a great lady. I still have framed pictures she took of me and Summer Dream on my dresser in my room. I dust them myself because they're special to me. My parents took me to her funeral. It was my first. They said I should pay my last respects. There sure were a lot of people paying last respects. My mom said that showed she was popular and well-loved.

"A few days after the funeral we heard from Matt Wendall at the barn that she had willed Summer Dream to the Ranch and had even set up a fund to pay for her board and feed and vet bills and everything... We were all crazy happy and still sad at the same time. I didn't know until then that you could be crazy both ways all at once. I'll bet that was why I saw you crying. Because she was a great lady, and you must miss her with all your heart." Natalie Wilkins, insightful, precocious, diminutive philosopher.

"My dog Mandy died last winter. She was a Sealyham Terrier, and she was the specialist dog ever, even though my dad said her breath smelled like rotting garbage, and she had all these problems with her bum. Itchy glands or something, the vet said. She got run over by a neighbor's car because of her itchy bum when she stopped to scooch right in the middle of the street. I still feel sad about her every day. My dad told me that I'll see Mandy again when I die, that we'll get to play together in heaven. I'm not sure it works that way and that he wasn't just trying to make me feel better. But sometimes, even though I know it's wrong, I kind of think that it would be nice to be, you know… dead. To be with her and to play with her. Do you ever feel like that?"

Storm Baker closes his eyes. Unable to speak. Barely able to swallow.

She *was* a great lady. And, yes, all too often he feels precisely like that.

The Blue Parrot Tavern

"The rumors are unfounded," she quips as Storm props open the cumbersome wooden door for her. "The Age of Chivalry is *not* dead..."

She flits past him like a butterfly, creating a mild breeze redolent of liberally applied perfume and lingering Lucky Strikes. Out of the cold and into the warm congenial embrace of The Blue Parrot Tavern. Janeen Reynolds, decked-out for a night out: tan Stetson, dark-brown bomber jacket (a gift received years ago from a smitten, former Royal Canadian Air Force pilot), flouncy purple skirt and knee-high boots.

When Janeen suggested the tavern in her early morning voice message, she was oblivious to the abundant history of the place and had no idea to what degree Ali, and Harland Hazard for that matter, still palpably, hauntingly existed between the tavern walls. If she knew, and was residing in her right mind, she would never have suggested it. Storm had agreed to rendezvous at this haunt that he and Ali had so adored, but not without reservations and an ulterior motive. Unbeknownst to Janeen, he'd asked Dr. Redic Mackenzie, good friend, general practitioner, and sympathetic and understanding soul, to stage a chance encounter with them later in the evening.

Upon entering the tavern, Storm realizes how delusional he was in thinking that he could withstand the emotional rigors of a night in the Blue Parrot. The tavern's ambiance has been altered by events and the passage of time into something cloying and unwelcome like an impertinent embrace from a stranger, or a wet kiss forced upon unsuspecting lips at the conclusion of a date on which no connection was made.

The Blue Parrot Tavern is but one in a long line of venial mistakes made in his recovery. Already there have been too many hours crammed into this day, each hour arduous and emotional. Circuits long ago overloaded, incited by his tour down the memory lane of Bloor West Village and by the sight of a collected Natalie Wilkins aboard Sandy's Summer Dream, en route to three blue ribbons. Young Natalie, throughout each stellar performance, discomfortingly appearing to Storm like a youthful version of Ali. Like Ali Reynolds long before he even knew her. Like Ali with her whole promising future stretching out before her.

Storm hears phantom voices. They are like pesky mosquitoes buzzing around his head under the dark cover of night. Cannot quite locate them or elude them. Certainly, has no power to make them stop.

"Hey, Hap, what'll it be. The usual?"

"Provided you haven't lost the recipe."

And he sees his estranged friend plain as day, larger than life, settling into his favorite cushiony chair in the corner and wrapping himself in the confines of the establishment.

"Ice cubes, white rum, bathed in Coke?"

"*Gently* bathed," the Hazard specifies. The waiter winningly grins at his favorite customer. "The cubes and rum must be gently bathed."

"Gently," the waiter repeats. "And what about your friends?"

Janeen orders a gin and ginger ale, Storm a no-frills domestic beer. Ali would have had her usual dry white wine, her taste partial to time-tested French wines although upstarts from California and Niagara were winning her approval. Only on sultry summer days did she occasionally deviate from her usual order, opting instead for an ice-cold beer or, when the mood was just right, a gin and tonic.

"Gin and tonic," the Hazard would smirk, winking like a pervert. "Ahhh, the Panty Peeler..."

Storm makes a concerted effort to focus on Janeen, to not torpedo the night by envisioning his wife. Ali, appearing right at home in hip-hugging blue jeans and her beloved Toledo Mud Hen T-shirt (a birthday gift from a sportswriter friend of Storm's), relaxing under a bold moon on the Blue Parrot's back patio, sipping a gin and tonic. He cannot even consider the path such summer nights frequently took, what with the tinderbox coupling of their desires and that gin. The natural tendency has been to place such idyllic nights, which surely must have come with their own intrinsic blemishes and flaws — unpleasant humidity, a damp breeze, mosquitoes, summer city smog — up on the pedestal of infinite promise and perfection.

ANGELS IN THE ARCHITECTURE

Janeen. Focusing on Janeen.

Unlike her daughter, whose approach to total body-and-mind health was holistic, passionate, and proactive, Janeen has never been remotely health-conscious. On the contrary, she has lived life pleasantly health-oblivious. Any steps ever taken toward wholesome, fit living — taking a walk, for instance — were unintentional and dictated by circumstances: the taxi never arrived, the next pub on the crawl was just down the road; the city's provincial closing time was creeping up on the evening and last call was beckoning. And even those unintentional steps were invariably sabotaged by alcohol, cigarettes and undesirable lifestyle-dietary habits...

"I eat what I want, when I want. And if that means Chinese takeout at two a.m., then bring on the sweet-and-sour chicken balls. And don't be stingy now..."

Storm is realistic regarding his planned encounter between Janeen and Redic, fully aware that no doctor could ever be expected to diagnose a patient without a proper and detailed examination, blood-work and likely a battery of unpleasant tests — the very invasive poking-prodding investigations, bereft of human dignity, that served to make Janeen leery of the whole profession in the first place. However, he hopes his friend can at least converse with her, gain her confidence and trust, and perhaps even formulate a rudimentary hypothesis as to what could possibly be ailing her. And, aside from destructive doses of the obvious — grief and loss siphoned from a brewing cauldron of frustration, helplessness, and anger — what has aged her so radically over such a short period of time.

"My what a stylish establishment," Janeen says in an affected snobbish accent. She carelessly lights a cigarette; her lighter is set high and the flame bears resemblance to a blowtorch that comes perilously close to alighting her rusty-red hair and the hat that crowns it. Before she can deposit the lighter back in her purse, Storm grabs it and adjusts the flame. She merrily mocks his "Smokey the Bear-ishness..."

Drinks arrive. Storm pays.

"Cheers," she says, raising her gin. "You know, I've been here before." She warms at the pleasant recollection. "Once or twice with Ali and young Harland. Harland called this his home away from home, and I felt obliged to tell him that I loved what he'd done with the place... I miss Harland, precious handful of times that I saw the waif, I was quite taken. Charmed. I know Ali was, too."

Storm stiffens with Janeen's verbal pairing of Ali and Harland, with the mere mention of their life before him, with the automatically triggered vision of them here together without him. It's a bitter jealousy — childish, he knows, but nonetheless suffocating — that sustains these discomfiting, unfounded images he carries of his Ali swooning at Harland's feet, like a bobbysoxer at the mere sight of Sinatra, and her being swallowed whole by his infinite, honey-like charm.

"He did, I must say, have this certain sadness about him. A world-weariness, *weltschmerz*. I've met plenty of women who carry this sadness, but few men. It was in his eyes, I suppose. Have you heard from him?"

Storm shakes his head. Not a single word. Storm considers that "certain sadness" his friend had about him. He wonders to what degree he may have exploited it as a means of attaining what he desired. He wonders how many women cradled him in their sheltering arms and pressed his head to their breasts, intent on mothering that sadness right on out of those baby blues.

Janeen continues talking and Storm endeavors to concentrate on all that is occurring around him. Janeen's words, the brisk serve-and-volley banter at other tables, quiet laughter, a couple nuzzling in a corner whispering and making plans and promises to last a lifetime, ice tinkling in a glass, waiters coming, waiters going. It's like attempting to keep his eyes on the ball during a fast, furiously competitive table-tennis match. Sadly, his mind is incapable of keeping pace. Since Ali's death, his attention span has been frustratingly reduced to that of a child. He frequently catches himself feigning attention, nodding and gesturing at what he can only hope are appropriate times and in a pertinent manner, to camouflage the fact that his mind is adrift in orbit. Ground Control to Major Tom. Since entering the tavern, he has been on edge. The ambiance is overpowering, all cherry-stained wood paneling, flickering candles, soft and fuzzy shadows, and memories.

The Blue Parrot Tavern was the Hazard's discovery and his hangout, an ideal off-the-beaten-track getaway on Davis Drive, a mile or two north of his Baby Point home. Close enough that he could do the late-night walk (or weave) home if the bartender on duty deemed that he'd had too much to drink. Occasionally he brought Ali here in what he dubbed her "IBSE" (Illustrious Before-Storm Era), an era Storm preferred to pretend never existed. After Ali met Storm and Storm and Harland were reunited, all three would congregate at the Blue Parrot, catching up on the day's happenings, immersing themselves in conversation about anything and everything: contemplating current culture, occurrences in the world of sports, mulling over the news of the world and changing that moribund world over a few drinks. In time, Storm and Ali started frequenting the tavern on their own and it became one of their places, akin to High Park or the length of Bloor West Village.

At the time when he was ensconced in that universe, that beautiful life, he took those places for granted; they were simply a part of life's day-to-day landscape. However, as he whiled away days walking barefoot, restlessly and aimlessly along a seemingly boundless stretch of white Florida beach — walks that afforded him plenty of time to labor at capturing elusive perspective — he came to comprehend how special and integral to their lives those places had become and how they provided the setting, the very pages upon which their story was written. When living in Florida, he found it exhausting to even think about such settings as saturated as they had become in personal history. Until today when he was drawn out of the Harbour Castle and deposited back into their former world by an inexplicable force, he had been reluctant to revisit them, their powerful pull repelled only by the even greater remembrances that they triggered.

"Ali used to love it here," he said, uncertain and not caring whether his words were at all apropos of the current conversation. "So unpretentious, so nothing-to-it, no loud music, invasive noise, no wall-wide televisions, no arcade games, no trendy gimmicks, no topless waitresses or bottomless bartenders, no hot-wings Wednesday, no godless disco balls or mechanical bulls, just the dim lights, candles, tables, comfortable chairs, friends, food, a glass of white wine and conversation. She feared the death of conversation but said that in places like this the fear seemed unfounded. Conversation was alive and, at times, electric." He pauses, Ali, Ali, Ali. He could easily reach out and touch his mother-in-law, his friend Redic will soon be meeting them, and yet moments like this continue to dog his existence. Moments in which he feels stricken and alone. Grief, he once wrote, is the loneliest experience imaginable.

"This is my first time here since coming back and everything's the same. And yet, everything's completely different..." It's all he can do, see her face.

Not wanting Janeen, a few familiar faces, or even the anonymous tavern staff and patrons to see him like this, he removes his owlish wire-rimmed glasses and slowly rubs his eyes. Like the problem is that his eyes are fatigued, irritated by smoke. Like he is not simply concealing the fact that they are blurred by tears welling up. God, he does not want to blubber.

To Storm, a man once able to conceal emotions with a stoic face, public blubbering is akin to uninvited and unwelcome intimacies delivered in incongruous social settings; the sort of revelations that are lobbed at you from out in left field and that leave you with nothing to say and nowhere to look. He has personal experiences that have left him wincing. The evidently costive acquaintance who detailed over a morning bagel and coffee the assorted problems he was experiencing with his bowels: "Donkey bowels, man... I can't get them to move." The inebriated lifestyle reporter who unashamedly divulged at a *Times'* Christmas party that her "G-spot Orgasms" — evidently often attempted and seldom achieved — had somehow become affixed to a classic Stevie Wonder song played at thunderous volume, and to an acrobatic position depicted in *The Joy of Sex*... Then there's the man who continues to blubber twelve full months after the death of his wife. Nothing to say and nowhere to look.

Time is a healer. Time heals. Or so he has heard, more times than he cares to consider. True, time has managed to downgrade the pain from something wholly unbearable to a more tolerable, although nevertheless persistent and gnawing ache.

Since returning from self-imposed exile, he has been bombarded from all angles with advice. Advice that reverberates off the inner walls of his skull deep into the night, further contributing to already established insomnia. Unsolicited advice heaped on suffocatingly high and often wrapped and presented like gifts in clichés and maxims of the "time heals" genus. Friendly, well-meaning advice. But to Storm, at this juncture in his life, undermining and extremely grating.

Friends urge, in staccato outbursts. Get busy. Jump back into things. Get on with life. Create a new life. Don't dwell in the past. Live for today. And, don't you know, tomorrow's another day. Like uncoordinated, B-squad cheerleaders. Carbonated, bubbling over, and shaking their pompoms in his face.

Former colleagues look him up at the Harbour Castle, intent on persuading him to return to the *Times*. They say his 'slip-up' is understandable and ultimately forgivable; they miss him, miss him about the office, miss his popular ramblings on Page Two. Apparently, readership is down, and they generously attribute this dip to his absence rather than the escalating intensity of the city's fierce newspaper wars — the basic

ANGELS IN THE ARCHITECTURE

consequence of too many daily newspapers in the city (more than in either New York or Los Angeles) — and not enough readers. They say that, although it's wonderful that he is back in Toronto, it's a waste the way he is letting his talent wither on the vine. He should return to the business. More pep talks, more cheerleading, more pompoms in his face.

Add to the advice, add to the reverberation off those inner walls, the voice of the lost Harland Hazard. Cannot seem to forgive, but nor can he forget. In the past, whenever Storm was down about anything, the Hazard would don his patented half-smile and do his Dr. Feelgood — raise a depleted rum to his health, offer him a suspicious pill of some vague strength and description, and casually, philosophically advise: "Do what you have to do."

In the past, regressing as far back as the shared period of their childhoods, the Hazard has been an unlikely buoy. In the present, Storm finds himself thinking about the Hazard — his depleted drinks, his pills — and wondering and worrying what exactly it is that the Hazard thinks that he must do. After all, he also lost Ali. Storm wonders whether his friend has become addicted to the post-surgery analgesics, wonders for how long a man — always playing the child's game of hide 'n seek with all he is feeling within his diminutive, vulnerable body — can hide behind a jauntily dipped baseball cap, a joke, a quick comeback, or that lovable, infectious grin.

Where on God's Earth are you, Harland?

Then there's Janeen. Relaxing in her apartment one night, she nurses a drink, nibbles on Hickory Sticks and deals advice like cards across a table in a serious game of poker.

"Do you think she would want you doing nothing?" she chides. "Listen: you are a writer..."

"I *was* a columnist. Big difference..."

"You are a writer," she persists, "who has in his possession, in his heart and in his soul, the very thing that writers hunger to have. More than notations in a notebook, more than words, phrases, more than bare-bones ideas... a story." Storm closes his eyes and strains to peer inward. He sees no story in his heart or in his soul, only emptiness...

Before Harland Hazard came riding into town on the proverbial white steed and rescued him from himself, young Storm Baker was a loner. A child who preferred to exist indoors within the walls of the elaborate worlds he was continually creating inside his head. Few things possessed the power to draw him outside, the exceptions being the bicycle he received as a gift from his parents on his eighth birthday — a sleek, gold, sports model with high handlebars and trendy banana seat — and, oddly enough, construction sites.

No amount of stern lectures and dire warnings from his mother regarding the innate dangers of such sites could deter him, not even the ever-fresh memory of a terrifying altercation on such a site discouraged him. Simply put, Storm loved visiting new-housing developments, absorbing the distinctive smells, the steady, purposeful and oftentimes rhythmic sounds and the businesslike atmosphere. He would sit, perched on the seat of his bicycle for hours on end, simply observing the daily progress and the process of home-building with a precocious appreciation that bordered on awe... A lot cleared, a foundation dug and later poured, a frame constructed and on and on, step by step as the structure methodically rose from the ground.... Watching, watching, watching, such was his fascination.

If construction occurred in the damp of spring or autumn or in the chill of winter, once the walls were up, the builders would often nail or staple-gun lengths of plastic sheeting to cover the various window and door openings. Invariably, in time, a corner or a whole length of that plastic would be torn away, inadvertently by workers, or by stormy weather, or at night by delinquent youths. Busy with other chores, or simply oblivious, the workers would leave the plastic like that for days, unattended to flap in the wind.

In recent times, whenever Storm Baker peers into his own heart, whenever he turns the mirror on his own soul, what he sees is this image extracted from boyhood: the frame remains standing, but there is this vulnerable covering (once secure and whole) flapping eerily in the night with the whims of the wind.

"It would be a love story, Storm. The love between my daughter and you. Think about it. It could become a bestseller, be adapted for stage, or even made into a screenplay." He examines her face, seeking clues as to whether she's delivering a sincere inspirational address and goosing him into action, or just having her way with him. She sighs, exhaling cigarette smoke and luxuriating for an instant in dreamy contemplation of who would be cast to portray her, and whom she would be cast to portray. Surely not herself.

ANGELS IN THE ARCHITECTURE

Undoubtedly someone younger. Playing young, after all, has been this chameleon's forte.

"Granted," she continues, "by contemporary, western-world ways of thinking, it would be a story about a love that is star-crossed, like Romeo and Juliet, ill-fated and destined to end tragically. Personally," she pauses, fingers a fallen strand of hair and stares out her apartment window, looking down on the city illuminated by streetlights, "personally, I believe that all loves are star-crossed."

Storm wonders whether this belief is drawn from the well of personal experience. She elaborates.

"Consider: unless two lovers grow blissfully old together and then expire at the same precise moment, painlessly and in their sleep — and, honestly, what are the odds? — then their love will obviously end tragically with one partner heart-broken and pining the loss of the other. And if that isn't star-crossed...."

Janeen and Storm sit quietly, both fully aware of what Ali would say. She would assert that the love of Ali Reynolds and Storm Baker was not star-crossed. On the contrary, it was blessed, a rare and priceless gift. Although she would surely have to concede that a phase of their love was tragically (even horrifically) truncated, it would be her contention that their love transcends tragedy. Because she believed that their love was absolute, immeasurable in human terms, not bound by flesh and blood, not tethered to time and place, a love shared by kindred spirits and existing eternally through the ages.

Curiously, Ali Reynolds rarely spoke the words: "I love you." Aside from not wanting to devalue those words, she said that love existing between soul mates need not be spoken; it was implied in thoughts and expressions and gestures, making words seem not only small and insignificant, but also redundant.

"You say you love me so many times each day," she once said. "The other morning when I was in hurry and on my way out the door, you handed me a lunch you'd made for me. Well, that whispers love. When you did the laundry on my laundry day. Instead of a heaping hamper, I found clean clothes in my drawers. You hand-washed my blouse. My word, Storm Baker, you even neatly folded my unmentionables and put them away. What could shout love louder than freshly laundered and neatly folded undies? And yesterday, when I came home and was out of sorts after the photo shoot at the Harbourfront had gone all wrong all day long, you poured me a glass of wine and a steamy bubble bath. In the tub, you told me to close my eyes and then while I soaked, you read to me from *The Beautiful Game*. Wine, bubbles and Leonard Cohen. Love, love and love..."

... And when the water eventually cooled, after her skin had turned a wrinkled pink, he put down the paperback and offered her a helping hand out of the tub. He attentively caressed her dry with a bath towel, then dropped the towel onto the tiled floor and led her by the hand into the bedroom. He ensured that she was comfortable on the bed, the lioness contented and cozy in her pillowed lair.

He massaged her feet with an aromatic honey-butter cream, massaged until his fingers cramped from the effort. He kissed her feet, kissed her ankles, kissed her calves, and continued kissing and caressing his way up her smooth legs. When he at last reached the spot where she truly loved to be kissed, he took a mint upon his tongue, then he kissed and he lingered. Inflamed, intoxicated by her scent, procuring pleasure from pleasure, her whispered song, her open desire, he continued to kiss, kiss, kiss...

And yes, she was moved to confess, those intimate kisses and curled toes screamed love a million times louder than any brown-bagged lunch or folded panties. In the afterglow, she held him, arms locked around his chest, legs locked around his legs, and she told him that she had loved him even before she met him, that he had always been her lover, and that he would be her lover for now and forevermore. Ali would doubtlessly say that she continues to love him from her current place in the cosmos and that one day they will be together again, reunited, possibly reincarnated, unquestionably in love.

A beautiful conviction.

Granted, it was a conviction that provided scant relief in the days, weeks, and months succeeding Ali's death. A few grudging drops of rain in a severe drought. Although he could clearly hear her voice inside his head assuring that they would be together for all eternity, his only truth, the reality in which he was floundering, was that they were not together in the physical present, in the here and now.

That she was gone and that she had left him all alone.

He's Nothing But A Fred

ALI AND FRED *awash in the eerie orange safelight of the darkroom. Ali, immersed in her work and Fred, asleep on his favorite blanket spread out across an Ikea bench. Rubber gloves protecting her hands, lines of concentration crinkling her forehead, Ali dips a pair of tongs into a tray of chemicals and coaxes a photographic image to life. Muscles intermittently twitching, Fred dreams of his previous life, of tomcatting in the park, of mice hunts and risky nights spent under the stars.*

Although she jokingly referred to the darkroom as "The Dungeon," she said that it was where she felt most at home, and I struggled not to be petty and childish and take offense. She said that each time she stood in the darkroom — surrounded by the seductive darkness, the orangey glow and the distinctive pungent odor, which she had not only come to tolerate, but had actually come to crave — every time she bathed a print and watched the images emerge and become defined in a chemical bloom, she believed that she could relate to the way pioneers in the field of photography felt nearly two centuries previous upon seeing a photograph for the very first time.

In its infancy, people were unabashedly amazed by photography, which they viewed as a triumph of human ingenuity and imagination, and a way of placing art in the hands of anyone who could master its techniques. Personally, when I watched her at work and witnessed the images magically rising off their chemical bed, I was envious of both the depths of the passion she possessed for her craft, and the control she wielded over the whole process. She had within her grasp the ability to manipulate an image, an outcome, to achieve the result she desired.

When she lived on her own, she used the bathroom in her basement apartment as a makeshift darkroom, an imperfect and inconvenient setup at best. Once she moved in with me, she sought a more permanent refuge to set up shop where she would not have to concern herself with shifting photographic supplies and equipment each time anyone wanted to shave or shower or, in Janeen's case, simply powder her nose. She found what she was looking for in the basement of our building, an unused maintenance room down the hall from the laundry facilities and just off the entrance to the underground parking. She said it was perfect. About ten-by-ten feet of space replete with the requisite sink and water supply. She sweet-talked the rental office staff into letting her have it for a nominal monthly fee which, by our calculations, barely covered utilities.

And while I was pleased to reclaim our bathroom, I wasn't thrilled with the idea of her spending time alone in the bowels of the building; there had recently been a much-publicized rape in the stairwell of the high-rise situated kitty-corner to our apartment, and less than a mile north of us there had been a late-night shooting that had left a teenager paralyzed. Following the rape, police had gone door-to-door in the area warning women to be on alert, to take the appropriate safety precautions and to buddy up wherever possible. Obviously, I would not be home every time Ali needed to venture down to the darkroom. And, knowing Ali, she would never have allowed me to accompany her each time even if I were home. She assured that everything would be fine.

"I can take care of myself. Besides, I'll have Fred with me."

Fred. Not doubting the ornery old tabby's heart, or the ferocity of his spirit, or his willingness to step up for Ali, but his days as a champion fighter were over by the time Ali found him on a dirt pathway in High Park, slipping in and out of consciousness and bleeding from various ugly gashes about his body. She wrapped him in her worn sweatshirt and carried him out of the park and back to our apartment. Together we drove him to The West End Veterinary Clinic. It was the best guess of the vet on call that Fred had been overmatched in an encounter with one or more of the park's burgeoning number of bold urban coyotes or foxes. It was the vet's best advice to put him down.

"He's old, he's hurt. He's lost an ear, an eye..."

Ali would not hear of it. She had the vet stitch him up and then we took him home and Ali began the consuming process of nursing him back to life. Everything from eyedroppers of warm milk and medications to sleeping on the floor beside him so that he wouldn't awaken disoriented, frightened, and alone. At some point in the recovery process, she christened him Fred because...

"Just look at him, he's nothing but a Fred!"

ANGELS IN THE ARCHITECTURE

Which is how we came to inherit a boarder, a one-eared, one-eyed retired tomcat with considerable attitude and a permanent bald spot on his backside that gave him the appearance of a casualty of nuclear testing gone horribly awry.

From day one, Fred loved his surrogate mother. Purred whenever Ali entered a room. Possessively sat on her lap, wholly un-tomcat-like, when she sat down to read a book. As for me... Perhaps he instinctively picked up on the vibe that I had never been a big cat lover. And while he didn't outwardly disdain me in typical cat-fashion — no hissing, no flagrant displays of aggression — he had ways and means of making me feel that he certainly had it out for me.

"He hates me..."

"Nonsense. Fred loves you. You're his daddy..."

"He bodychecks me. Throws me a hip every time he walks by..."

"It's a sign of affection..."

"It's a sign that he's trying to knock me over..."

"You're paranoid..."

"You want paranoid. There are times when I catch him staring at me with what I swear is a one-eyed, f-you look on his fuzzy face..." Other times, if he encountered me embracing Ali, he'd swat at me with a paw, as if to say, move on, buddy, move on. And then there was the matter of how he greeted me whenever Ali was out, and I entered the apartment...

"Total nonsense," Ali proclaimed. "Cats don't fart. The nature of their diet, the slow way they eat, never taking in much air, their particular digestive system, it all adds up to very little gas..."

"Trust me," I countered. "Fred farts. Boomers. At will... First, he looks up from wherever he's sleeping to see whether it's you coming in the door. Then, when he determines it's me, he lets one rip. And if you want the whole butt-ugly truth, he actually points his ass at me before doing the deed.... That's right, he aims!"

Ali and Fred awash in the eerie orange safelight of the darkroom. Ali, immersed in her work and Fred asleep — sleeping the eternal sleep — on his favorite blanket spread out across an Ikea bench. Fred, forever dreaming of his previous life, of tomcatting in the park, of mice hunts and risky nights spent under the stars, of being given a second chance by a gentle and compassionate human being.

ANDY JUNIPER

A knock on the apartment door. I open the door and there she is with Fred, wrapped in his favorite blanket, cradled in her arms. A sob escapes, sorrow through clenched teeth.

"He's gone... died... dead... in his sleep... Right there while I worked..."

I hug her, a dead tomcat stiffening between us, because it's all I can do. In time she will follow Fred, and I will be the only one left in the apartment. Left alone, without comfort, hugging myself.

Maybe It Ain't Broke

THE PRESENT PERPLEXINGLY mingles with the past. The here and now of the Blue Parrot Tavern blends into Storm's reveries and the evening starts to grow fangs. It's nearing closing time and save for waiters hustling about on clean-up, and a few hard-core regulars slumped in chairs nursing nightcaps, they have the tavern to themselves.

Storm is alone at their table. Janeen is standing, elbow propped up on the bar, engaged in animated conversation with bartender, Zach (Easy) Flannigan and Dr. Redic Mackenzie, with whom she has famously connected despite immediately seeing through the flimsy fabric of their alleged chance meeting.

"Oh, Storm," she drolly announced when introduced to Storm's friend, "how nice of you to set me up with a fine young man, and a doctor no less..." She then waved a finger at Redic, warning him to not even contemplate any meddling, and to forget about initiating any medical line of questioning because no answers would be forthcoming. Then she stated emphatically with more determined gesticulating: "You don't fix what ain't broken..." And no amount of logic was likely ever to convince her otherwise. Can't tell her that it may well be broken or, less harshly, that a measure of proactive maintenance may well prevent complete breakdown. Because she has her head buried in the sand, right up to the shoulders.

Predictably, Storm has spent the night hopelessly immersed in the past. Nonetheless, he feels the present weighing on him. He's tired. His bed at the Harbour Castle is beckoning, its covers neatly turned back by hotel housekeeping staff, and he would like nothing more than to call it a night. He can practically feel himself slipping between those cool sheets.

For the moment, thankfully, the future retains its elusiveness. For now, he cannot see himself and Redic in tomorrow's grey daylight hours, ensconced in a corner booth at Fran's Restaurant, a popular diner on St. Clair Avenue. Thus, he cannot see the doctor picking at two over-easy eggs or hear him sharing his observances and offering interpretations.

"What a grand lady," he says. "I had genuine fun last night. I could listen to her for hours. Come to think of it, I did, and consequently sleepwalked through rounds this morning." Then, after a moment to collect his thoughts and plan his words, he wades in: "Storm, I know you want me to be frank. From talking with her, I saw obvious signs of disconnects. There's assuredly something happening with her, neurologically speaking." Storm listens, his stomach soured by bitter coffee and concern, his temples pounding the drums of anxiety and fatigue. "If you want my guess, I'd say we're looking at a dementia-onset scenario, probably vascular dementia, and I say that not as a MD making a rash, stab-in-the-dark diagnoses after one social meeting, but as a son whose father lived with, and was eventually killed by, that precise thing. Storm, you know that story, and we both know that it's not pretty…"

A death sentence. Impossible to swallow that early in the morning.

Storm watches Janeen having a ball, engaging the men in what amounts to the literary equivalent of a pissing contest. Easy or Redic recite from memory a classic poem, or an excerpt from a novel, or even an evocative song lyric, and she responds by attempting to one-up them with a recital from a play from the catalogue of work by the prolific William Shakespeare. From her over-painted lips soar sonorous, near-perfect soliloquies.

Storm's head is in a fog. Listening to those words, written by Shakespeare and delivered by this daughter of Thespis some four centuries later, virtually anything becomes possible, believable. Maybe she is a good actress. Maybe it ain't broke. Never a big drinker, he considers that maybe he should not have ordered that last beer or agreed to a Manhattan nightcap.

"Your turn, doc. Anything but *Gray's Anatomy*, dear. Anything at all."

He hears Redic, in a resonant voice, saying how Gatsby believed in the green light, the orgiastic future that year by year recedes before us. Redic, quoting from Fitzgerald's masterwork, *The Great Gatsby*. Who knew Redic had *that* in him. The doctor continues, "It eluded us then, but that's no matter — tomorrow we will run faster, stretch out our arms further… And one fine morning — So we beat on, boats against the current, borne back ceaselessly into the past."

Storm could cry. Fitzgerald's haunting, poetic words. Words he had so often heard the Hazard and Ali reciting back and forth to each other, like it was their personal, private language, a cryptic code and the words were wrapped secrets that only they could open; sometimes she would kiddingly call him, "my Scott", and he would endearingly answer with, "my Zelda", and Storm would feel very much the odd man out. The lulling image of boats against a current, being borne back ceaseless into the past is impaired by a jealousy at times so petty it incites personal contempt.

Storm Baker yearns to be borne back into his past. At once, he also yearns to shed the cloak of the past and be borne into the future. What he wants, honest to God, is to feel okay, about himself, about his life. To have one unburdened breath, one moment without pain.

Janeen's voice rises. What she's saying seems to make no sense. Storm figures he's just too distanced from the voice and their conversation, and too tired to comprehend. Then he notices the frown on Easy Flannigan's face and he hears Redic's respectfully suggesting that maybe she's had enough gin for one night. Which naturally gets Easy working on the math. Best that he can remember, she's had only two drinks all night, and the second is still sitting there...

Storm Baker reenters the cluttered labyrinth of his own mind and is lost to Blue Parrot Tavern, lost to the world. An incongruous, goofy smile parts his lips. Because suddenly rising through the fears and the fog is a recollection, of what his wife came to call "the decisive moment" in their lives. As usual, that recollection gets him contemplating how a man, who had been deemed "non-marriage material" by a so-called relationship expert, suddenly became a beautiful woman's dream come true.

The Dregs Of The Day

INSIDE AN AILING head, glass shatters.

She stands naked before the vanity in her bathroom, cupping in her hands her once proud and upstanding breasts and frowning at the mirror and the unfamiliar creased face frowning back at her. She lets her breasts drop, discouraged by the inevitable sagging fortunes of aging flesh. With tremulous hands, she adjusts her wig (according to the label, "Burning Bush Red"), then positions a white Stetson precariously atop the still-lopsided hair. Frown lines deepen. Frantically she rummages through what she calls her "magic kit" – her makeup bag, propped up in the sink. Near the bottom of the bag, she finds what she needs. A slick mascara brush. Carelessly she applies the mascara to embolden eyelashes, but in the process, pokes herself in the eye. There's obvious pain, a paroxysm of expletives. When the sting eventually abates and she is able pull her hand away from the teary, bloodshot eye, she clutches a lipstick tube awkwardly in her palm and applies two quick slashes of bold red. She seems satisfied with the results and oblivious to the mascara streaking her cheeks.

"There... Much better."

She presses two fingers across her reddened lips, kisses them, then plants the two-fingered kiss on the mirror.

"Nobody," she tells the smudged mirror image, "not even the rain, has such small hands..." She smiles. "I think that's e.e. cummings, but what the hell do I know anymore? Could be Burton Cummings." Never a follower of sixties or seventies' pop/rock, or classic Canadiana for that matter, she cackles at the eclecticism encompassed by her own wit.

ANGELS IN THE ARCHITECTURE

Opening the entryway closet, she yanks a trench coat off a hanger. The hanger clangs onto the floor. She cloaks her nakedness in the trench coat, fumbles for an eternity with the buttons until they are all done up, although not all buttons are in the correct corresponding holes. She steps into her furry slippers and calls out an inordinately cheery "adieu" to the empty apartment. She closes the door behind her, naturally not giving a thought to locking up. Walking down the musty corridor, she sings. *Fly Me To The Moon*. Enunciating each syllable. Just like the pride of Hoboken, New Jersey. The Chairman of The Board, Old Blue Eyes, Frank You Know Who.

It's 11:55 p.m. And she's decided to go out for a walk. On a snowy winter night. Alone, in Toronto.

Just to see what's up...

****

He sits on the edge of his bed staring down at a photograph of his wife who is naked and in what the god-fearing would surely consider a blasphemous pose. Christ on the cross, minus the wood. Arms outstretched, head lowered (chin to collarbone), eyes closed. Forsaken. The deed, fait accompli. Christ has died.

Questions course like the runoff of snow down a mountainside in spring filling his mind to overflow. Not the least compelling question emanates from what she inscribed in dark, sanguine ink under the self-portrait; the enigmatic caption: "Christ Will Come Again."

Jesus. Christ.

The whole night has been slowly, methodically devoured by a less severe strain of the anxiety that since her death has frequently threatened to consume him with all the speed, strength and virulence of a flesh-eating virus. Despite being muddle-headed and bone-achingly tired, he did not go to bed. He knows how elusive sleep can be, particularly on nights like these, and he figured what was the point in even trying? He paced about the hotel room. Caged animal, tight quarters.

The room is immaculate. Everything in its place. Because earlier the maids had worked their daily magic, efficiently and professionally cleaning and straightening. And because, by rote, whenever he is anxious, he obsessively, almost unconsciously tidies, procuring a slim measure of calm and comfort in fastidiously creating and vigilantly maintaining order.

Which is how he came to find the photograph. In his obsessive vigilance. While straightening a pair of running shoes in the bedroom closet, he noticed that a side-flap zipper on one of his suitcases perfectly parked on the closet floor was not fully zipped. Despite himself, he could not let it go, could not leave that flap only partially closed. Bending into the shadow of the closet, he saw the corner of a glossy black-and-white print poking out of the flap.

He was staggered by the find, and her stark nakedness, and her chosen pose for this stunning self-portrait, and the thought that the suitcase and the picture had accompanied him throughout the past year...

The photograph reminds him of how, during their time together, there were moments of insecurity, self-doubt — self-defeating moments when he would question why and how someone as wonderful and winsome and beautiful as her could ever have ended up with him. There were times when he felt certain that, despite their obvious and irrefutable closeness, he could never fully know her, never completely understand her. There were times when he wondered what could possibly be going on inside her head, and times when he could only conclude — a conclusion that left him rattled — that he had no idea...

"There are times," she would counter, "when I think you want to have more than my heart, my commitment, my love. Times when you want to possess me. And that scares me. That's not healthy. Two hearts may beat as one, but there remain two hearts beating..."

But... "Christ Will Come Again"? What was she thinking? Motivated by what? Did she feel forsaken? Was this supposed to be ironic? Funny? A joke? Because if it was a joke, he desperately needed to be in on it. He needed to get it. Was this art? Because if this was art, shouldn't he — husband, lover, kindred spirit — possess the intelligence and aesthetic sense to understand and appreciate its meaning?

An undercurrent of guilt runs beneath the stream of questions. Guilty, of what? Voyeurism? Masochism, he thinks, his eyes refusing to leave the photograph. Perversion, perhaps? Because he's unzipped his blue jeans and is experiencing an uncomfortable strain against his fitted boxer shorts. And isn't it a measure of depravity, for a man in a fierce, prolonged period of mourning to become aroused over his deceased wife, posed naked as a crucified Messiah?

He reaches over to the dresser. Bottom drawer forever reserved for lingerie that survived the apartment clean-out and that has traveled with him, Toronto to Florida, and back. He fingers a pair of her black panties, remembering the promise they once held. Silky smooth. He shivers. This is not what he wants. Fuck it. He lowers his boxers. He wraps the soft nylon panty around his hand, his hand around his excitement.

Within minutes he's crying her name into the void, into the loneliness of the hotel room, a plaintive wail.

****

"A teenage symphony to God."

The enigmatic words mumble down from his perch atop a rattan barstool and crash land below. He's at his regular place, in his regular pose. Slouched over a half-empty glass at the bar in the beach-front Sunset Grill, situated beside the Paradise Hotel just outside of Long Beach, California. In daylight hours, the bar overlooks a magnificent stretch of the Pacific Ocean; at night, the view is lost in an infinite sea of India ink.

"Sorry, Rocky, you talking to me? Couldn't hear, I'm cleaning up. Almost closing time, my man..."

Rocky. It's what B.J., the young, affable and gregarious bartender (part-time student, skateboarder, philosopher, upright-bass player for the band Reach 4 The Ska) has taken to calling him, in the absence of him ever anteing up his real name. He needed to be christened *something* as he evolved from being a stranger into a Sunset Grill regular.

B.J will never forget when Rocky first darkened the bar's doorway. A stray that one night came in out of the darkness looking like something that the tide had unceremoniously deposited on the shore. Unkempt in a faded Hawaiian shirt and wrinkled Bermuda shorts and sandals, ashen-faced, haunted, eyes sunken and anchored by thick dark lines that gave rise to the nickname, Rocky, after Rocky Raccoon. With a hint of drama that was not unbecoming, Rocky called himself an exile. Said he was living in a rented beach house just beyond the nearby Santa Clara pier. Beyond that, even after he became a regular, he remained reticent, rarely saying much of anything to anybody. Apparently absorbed in his own thoughts, existing in his own world.

In time, when questioned, B.J. will remember that Rocky always ordered the same drink: ice and white rum, "gently bathed in Coke."

That's what he always said, "gently bathed in Coke." Always sat in the same place. Always requested that the seat beside him remain empty. Apparently one of many quirks.

Now he glances up from his drink, appearing surprised to discover someone else in the room. He points above B.J.'s head to the speakers over the bar. Because it's late and close to closing time, the annoying thump-thump dance music that each night brings patrons together in a lusty froth, has been mercifully forsaken in favor of a classic pop station out of Los Angeles.

"Beach Boy Brian Wilson," he says. The bartender marvels at how his words remain crisp and precise, despite all he has consumed. But that's Rocky's style. From an extended, prodigious period of stone-cold sober to... *blotto*, every night, and seemingly in the wink of an eye.

"Genius. Between 1962 and 1968, he wrote and produced fourteen albums, more than one-hundred-and-twenty songs. And this, this perfect pearl, is *God Only Knows*. Paul McCartney, a guy who knows a thing or two about music, called it the greatest pop song ever written. Was on the seminal *Pet Sounds* album. 1966." He sighs, shakes his head. "I was just a kid. Before the band recorded *Pet Sounds*, Wilson said that it was his desire to create a teenage symphony to God. Isn't that beautiful?"

"Beautiful, Rocky, but a little before my time..."

"Shit, man," he retorts. "It's a little *ahead* of everybody's time. Besides, beauty like this isn't tied to time. There was a period in my jaded, narrow-minded youth when I couldn't stomach Brian Wilson, when I thought the Beach Boys were mindless west-coast crap. One day I had an epiphany. I was up to my armpits in the bathtub, with a woman, for the sake of the story, and she helped me tune into, and clue into the brilliance of Brian. The haunting, ethereal nature of the man's music.

"Flash forward a few years and I actually met the man. In a recording studio. I was coming, he was going. Got up the nerve to speak to him. Told him I loved him like a brother. Told him that he helped me through some dark times and that I could feel the spiritual soul inherent in his songs, and the deep and underlying melancholy that lurks everywhere in his music, even behind those godless 'Fun, Fun, Funs.' Know what he told me?" Rocky doesn't wait for an answer. "Think he dished out sage advice? Fuck no. He took my shoulders in his hands and told me to... watch what I eat. Said, food can be a real killer. Then he left the studio and disappeared into the night..."

ANGELS IN THE ARCHITECTURE

B.J.'s taken aback by the outburst, by the both the passion with which it is delivered and by the sheer number of words strung together. Rocky takes a long tug, emptying the glass. Forlornly rattles the ice around in his glass. Runs his fingers through his hair. Dirty-blonde, over-grown and flirting with his shoulders.

"Nightcap?"

"Double, times two... And remember, B.J., gently bathed...."

"Watch what I eat. Fuck..."

Once the drinks are delivered and tabbed, B.J. returns to his cleanup. Rocky back to his rum. And to the incessant sounds in his head.

Inside Rocky's head there has always been music. Since he was a child. At night, during sleep, in his dreams, in all his waking hours. Music that not even his father, a pugnacious bureaucrat with an alcoholic gene and a short fuse, could beat out of his stubborn skull. Rhythms, faint strains of melody swimming within the walls of his skull, waiting to be hooked and extracted from the muddy waters of his mind. He still hears the music, but for some time now he's been inexplicably unable to reel it in.

Brian Wilson likewise heard music in his head. He called it his gift. Then, one day he suddenly found that he could no longer write. Said there was too much pain and sadness inside him. So, he withdrew from life. Turned his den into a sandbox. Rarely left the house and then only if it was sunny — what he called "a blue sky that offered hope." Quit changing his clothes. Gave up on personal hygiene. Ate until his weight ballooned to three-hundred-and-fifty pounds. Smoked five or six packs of Marlboros a day and drugged himself into dense fog of paranoia.

Rocky now wonders what Brian Wilson lost. Pain and sadness. Don't even get Rocky started on pain and sadness.

"He was a genius... A fucked-up, ballooned-up, drugged-up, fucking genius."

"You still on that Beach Boy?" B.J. asks. "Listen, Brian Wilson's got nothing on you, man."

"You've never heard my music."

"Who's talking about music?" He laughs. "Hey, Rock, I'm kidding. It's a joke. Shit, you okay?"

Because Rocky has turned to face the ocean. He's staring with glassy eyes out into that endless India ink. His face is flushed, and he is sweating heavily. Sweating rum. Sweating sadness and loss. He cranes his neck, straining to hear the mournful voice of the Pacific. He craves the soothing rhythm of the waves lapping up onto the shore. Waves he'd like to run out and embrace.

He whispers — and now the words are slurred, the voice unsteady and full of longing, need: "She would have loved it here."

"She who?"

He shrugs, waves him off. Answers, with impatience, annoyance.

"*She*...."

Part Three

A Dream Come True

Ali In The Morning

SHE COULD BE *quixotic and impetuous. There were times when it seemed she was living life on a whim, bound for wherever the wind blew her. She said she tried to live life as it was meant to be lived: mindfully, day to day, moment to moment, savoring each precious second and cognizant of, but unbowed by, the inherent fleetingness and fragility of our existence.*

"*What do you feel like doing today?*"

"*Rollerblading.*"

"*You must have a vague recollection of the freak spring snow that blew in yesterday.*"

"*You asked me what I wanted to do, and I told you. Rollerblading...*"

"*Ice on the streets. Wind chill. Freeze your backside, break your tailbone.*"

"*Not here, silly boy, in South Carolina. Hilton Head. I saw an ad in the paper, last-minute availability for an ocean-front condo. I investigated, and it sounds incredible. Unfortunately, there are no direct flights. So, we fly into Savannah, rent a car, forty-five-minute drive and we're on the island, rollerblading by midday. Come on, babe, let's do it. Like my man sings (she sings, operatically): 'I want to feel... sunlight on my face'.*"

To the consternation of a costive Retirement Management Consultant — who mothered his financial institution's money as though it were his own — we cashed-in a RRSP ("You'll pay through the teeth in taxes if you cash this now," he direly warned, shaking a crooked finger at the irresponsible infidels). The following day, after a stretch of white-knuckling turbulence over the Alleghenies, and a long, circuitous car ride from Savannah (actually, a short ride extended by a vague *map and our inept navigational skills), we were seizing the day in Hilton Head. Seventy-seven glorious degrees, the entire island abloom and redolent of spring rebirth and rejuvenating sea breezes.*

ANGELS IN THE ARCHITECTURE

Two pale tourists slathering on tanning lotion and buckling rollerblades onto their feet, to the endless amusement of the locals...
    "Crazy goddamn Canadians..."

Quixotic. Impetuous. Conversely, in the mornings she was all staid routine, this being the foundation upon which her busy days were built. Her morning schedule rarely fluctuated, and then only depending on the demands and vagaries of whatever freelance work was slated for that day. If she was needed at an early photo shoot, a meeting, presentation, or such....
    Rise early. Yoga for thirty minutes and then meditate. All the while appearing charmingly rumpled and irresistibly sexy in her bedtime T-shirt and undies. I was encouraged to join her morning routine and frequently did. However, as I came to view it, my main responsibility upon which I endeavored to remain focused was to restrain myself from interrupting her with untimely invitations to fool around. In other words, my job was to refrain from thinking or acting in anyway like I was feeling. Admittedly, there were moments during mediation when I would cheat, open an eye a slit and watch my wife. Ali in the lotus position, swallowed by serenity....
    Following meditation, she would shower. Some days, under the pretense of pressing conversation, I would sit on the bathroom floor, bare back pressed against the cool tiles, and I would watch her through the rising steam and glazed glass. There were mornings when she would invite me to join her. We would make wet, soapy, steamy, awkward love. We considered it an embraceable reality: shower sex was squeaky and slippery – slick love fraught with bad angles, poor footing, and danger. On the upside, the day would be off to a start that no traffic jams, car troubles, editorial meetings, pending deadlines, antsy editors, or column concerns could tarnish.
    Breakfast was always simple. Ali was a fan of the fruit smoothie. While I tended to the hot beverages — black coffee for me, assorted herbal teas for her — she would get out the blender and prepare the smoothies using various combinations of fruit. Her favorite combination involved peeled and seeded mangos and papaya, fresh raspberries, a splash of orange juice and a handful of ice cubes, blended to a kind, cool, sensual, mouth-pleasing consistency – a nutritious start to any day, save for the one morning when the Hazard, infernal meddlesome wise-ass, sabotaged wholesomeness by secretly spiking the smoothies with vodka.
    "Ah," he cackled when we caught on to his treachery: "Breakfast of Champions!"

ANDY JUNIPER

For variety, we'd sometimes forego the smoothies in favor of fresh fruit diced and mixed into plain yogurt, followed by toast and Ali's favorite, raspberry jam. On weekends it was eggs (soft boiled, over-easy, poached) and fresh bagels that I'd run out and retrieve from The Monastery Bakery. And each morning as we ate, we would discuss and interpret our dreams from the previous night.

Ali considered dream analysis, like meditation, to be an essential bridge between the conscious and unconscious worlds. A bridge that offered an opportunity to experience dimensions of our minds that are infinitely wiser than our normal consciousness. She had become a self-styled student of dreams when she was a Technicolor-dreaming teenager. As a high school student she was also a voracious reader who was spongelike in her absorption of ideas and information. In the various cities that she and Janeen called home for varying periods of time, she would visit local libraries and peruse books on dreams, weighing opinions as diverse as those of Nostradamus, Freud, Jung and The Sleeping Prophet, Edgar Cayce. At some point, she began devotedly maintaining a dream diary, documenting and interpreting her dreams on a daily basis. She came to place tremendous credence in the prophetic nature of dreams. Eventually she took her cue from the Senoi, the Malayan tribe whose people articulated and examined the previous night's dreams as part of their breakfast ritual. She introduced me to this routine shortly after we started sharing a bed.

While I typically voiced the prosaic and earth-bound opinion that — just as a cigar is sometimes just a cigar — dreams are usually just dreams, Ali suggested that my attitude was based on (or mired in) a journalist's fundamental cynicism, and in my personal shame over the nature and roots of my own sleeping cinema. She said that my reluctance to explore the obvious metaphorical images that played over and over in my dreams each night was understandable. Cannons. Cupboards. Umbrellas. Roses.

"Pervert," she would tease. "Perv person, perv dreams. What next, perv boy, wild horses?"

Perv person, perv dreams?

Is it any wonder why I never disclosed the details of the recurring dream I experienced almost monthly throughout our marriage? Me, on a train. Rather, me as a train. A sleek silver bullet speeding up, down and around sheer, treacherous mountainous terrain. Rocketing, like a rollercoaster car, careening perilously around hairpin turns, precariously, miraculously, defying laws of gravity and physics, managing to stay upright and maintaining the slimmest contact with the rails. Then, a turn so sudden, my stomach would flip, and I'd

ANGELS IN THE ARCHITECTURE

begin a steep descent toward a dark tunnel in the distance. Only as I neared could I discern that the tunnel was...

Ali.

Nude.

Straddling the tracks, the tunnel a gynecologist's view of her vagina.

The dream always ended just as I was entering the tunnel. Just as I was being swallowed whole. My word, she would have had a field day...

It was an uncharacteristically somber Ali who one morning told me that she had dreamed about a house being boarded up, one window at a time. The following morning, she said the disturbing dream had made a return engagement, only this time after being boarded up, the house was demolished. Leveled, imploded in a heartbeat by strategically positioned explosives. This was not some condemned, dilapidated shack, she said. It was a new home, a good home.

"Dreams are just dreams," I said, thinking: at least you didn't get swallowed whole by your wife's vagina. "No need to over-analyze...."

A couple of weeks later, during another breakfast session of dream analysis, Ali confessed to having experienced a recurring dream that she had been understandably reluctant to discuss. She took my shoulders in her hands, fixed her eyes on mine, and offered a sliver of history: In the months preceding World War II, Carl Jung had horrifying anticipatory dreams of blood-drenched battle grounds. Similarly, Ali ventured, she had been experiencing her own blood-soaked dreams. Not distant battle grounds, mind you. The grounds saturated in her dreams were much closer to home.

I did not believe. Was not convinced. To believe, to be convinced, was to concede the unthinkable. That I was to lose what I had spent a lifetime seeking, what was now so precious, what had become such an integral part of me. That I was to lose love, lose Ali.

"Come on," I said, "dreams can spring from anywhere, can mean anything. Whatever's been on your mind during the day. The last thing you think about before sleep. Fantasy. Wish fulfillment. Spicy food, or even cheese before bed. Anything." Hadn't Ali herself once said that in dream interpretation there was a recognized rule of opposites, that dreaming of death could actually symbolize a rebirth of some sort? Our marriage. Our starting a family. Whatever.

Blood-drenched battle grounds.

"God, maybe the metropolis of Toronto is preparing to go to war with Buffalo. Who knows?" Wishy-washy. And all-so vague.

Ali dissented, vehemently, and a hurtful, palpable tension descended around the topic. She would not simply let it drop. In my own best interests, she wanted me to begin facing what she perceived to be a reality.

"I've told you," she said, "the importance of a dream is in direct proportion to the impression the dream makes on the dreamer. I'm not throwing this at you to shake you up. You know I'm no high school drama queen. My dreams come true. If they're recurring and persistent and impactful, they come true."

"When? When have your dreams ever come true?"

For a moment her jawline tightened in anxiousness as though muscles were being drawn taut by a memory with which she wasn't wholly comfortable; in the next moment, muscles slackening, the stress lines of Ali's expression just as suddenly eased. With her spoon hovering over a slice of succulent grapefruit afloat in a creamy sea of plain yogurt, a pleasant memory inspired, my wife smiled, her hazel eyes sparkling playfully. She nodded at me.

"You," she said. "You. I dreamed of High Park, very vivid, very clear to the point where I could feel the heat, the sunshine, the barely-there breeze. I could feel the day and smell autumn in the air, just around the corner. And I dreamed about the hill. And I dreamed about you at the bottom of that hill. Do you get it, Storm Baker?" She beamed. "You are literally a dream come true…"

How Should A Bird Fly?
Or, Cracking The Sexual Ice

THEIR LOVE. UNCORK the champagne of maudlin love metaphors. Play the soundtrack of silly love songs. Generously apply the rich, thick, gooey language of love. The boastful exaggerations. The glorious oxymorons. All the inevitable (oftentimes antithetical) analogies. Intoxicated words. Sober words. The timeless, meticulously crafted language of the poets, words that sound bombastic, saccharine, trite… until you find yourself in love, at which time they pierce your palpitating heart and ring precise and true — perhaps even seeming understated.

In the words of Harland Hazard, a begrudging witness to his two friends falling fast and hard for each other: "Oh, fuck, forget the champagne of love metaphors. Uncork all the clichés. Break out the oysters, the honeydew-flavored condoms and the Barry goddamn White."

Their love. Two like-souls, destined to find each other.

"How should a bird fly, except with its own kind?" Ali would say, respectfully appropriating the words of Rumi, the 13th Century Persian mystic poet.

Their love. Two like-souls euphoric at having found each other (again, the Hazard was inclined to replace "euphoric" with "insufferably giddy, like tittering schoolgirls…"). Two like-souls salvaging lost time, bestowing meaning to what was once a void, giving heat to the cold, light to the darkness. Two like-souls by a crackling fire, kissing deeply into the night.

Their love. Love at first sight.

"Doesn't it sometimes appear," Ali once wondered aloud, "that fate went to great lengths just to orchestrate our coming together?"

Their love. A force of nature. An unpredictable reaction of human chemistry. Instant, undeniable attraction. And accompanying it, the sense of being born again, or of truly being alive for the first time. The sense that life has finally been brought into focus and the future can now be viewed with clarity. The feeling that a perilously overpopulated planet has abruptly been reduced to just two human beings.

What once seemed so important becomes irrelevant. What once was trivial becomes magnified in its significance. What once was two hearts, two histories, two lives, become fused as one. Life's erstwhile order is flipped upside down and shaken until it becomes unrecognizable. And two people, one with a powerful predisposition toward attempting to maintain control in his life, are only energized and exhilarated by the chaos that abounds.

Their love. And in that love, they are rendered conveniently blind to any forces that could possibly conspire against them. In many aspects they are not birds of a like-kind; conversely, they are opposites, as incalculable successfully paired people are complementary opposites.

"Opposites?" the Hazard would question. "If you're the Stones, then she's the Beatles for god's sake." And could the Stones and the Beatles not have aligned, created something moving and momentous and made beautiful revolutionary noise together? "Definitely not. Keith could never stomach Paul and John and Mick would have killed each other…"

Their love. Overwhelming, consuming. Unable to think about anything else, unable to keep their eyes off each other, unable, simply unable.

"Just go to the Poconos for a sleazy weekend and get it all out of your system. I mean, honest to God, I don't even want to see you guys again until you figure out a way to pull your faces apart. It's sickening, it really is."

Their love, its tendrils effortlessly extending into all areas of each other's lives. Their love, subsequently chronicled, interwoven into Storm Baker's first-person, casual accounts of life in the city — wolfed down by readers of *The Toronto Times* on weekday mornings and consumed more leisurely on lazy weekends.

Six months before Storm met Ali, Lydia Beaver, the female half of the *Times*' dueling Between the Sexes columnists thoughtfully went out of her way to inform Storm that he was "about one ephemeral year shy of reaching official 'confirmed bachelor' status."

ANGELS IN THE ARCHITECTURE

Storm wondered whether the notorious Ms. Beaver, clicking across the newsroom in stiletto heels — sounding like a Doberman with unclipped nails crossing hardwood — then interrupting Storm in the grip of a looming deadline and imparting this arbitrary information, apropos of nothing, was in her own peculiar way hitting on him, again. It would certainly be an odd way of expressing interest. But then, Lydia, an officious and insufferable know-it-all, was one curiously *odd* organization of female flesh. Within minutes of being introduced to this bizarre creature at a Times' Christmas party at The Royal York Hotel, the occasionally insightful Hazard rechristened her 'Labia Beaver'; this after Lydia ruffled the socially unflappable Hazard with a tendered invitation to slip away from the maddening crowd to a stall in the ladies' room for a private unveiling of her new bikini wax.

"It's like my cookie got a Mohawk," she gushed, before detailing just how excruciating the grooming procedure had been. Follicle by follicle.

Storm did not for one minute believe that his over-sexed colleague had any notion of what the word "ephemeral" meant, nor had he ever previously concerned himself with any of the various vacuous opinions she held on any particular issue.

"The feminist movement," she once spouted, "was formed so I could wear skirts this short! Without shame, or fear, or guilt, or panties for that matter!"

Storm liked to think of himself as a tolerant man whose upbringing had taught him that "it takes all kinds." Where Lydia was concerned, he probably would have been better off focusing on another of his mother's favorite momilies, that being, "consider the source." Storm found his tolerance level for the likes of Lydia to be nearly as shallow as Lydia herself.

He could not help himself. He was naturally impervious to the interminable yammerings of a woman who was forever articulating an insatiable desire to be taken seriously as a journalist while nevertheless arriving at work each day wearing diaphanous blouses over plunging, padded bras, micro-miniskirts, garter belts and flashy patterned stockings, impossibly high heels and pancake makeup that made her appear like she was en route to a Mary Kay Cosmetics convention, or a porn shoot; this was a writer who each week in her inexplicably popular essays stretched the envelope of editorial acceptability for a family newspaper, graphically detailing her weekly dalliances. In particular, she like to spell out for her readers specifically where she ate, what she ate, and oftentimes, *who* she ate on each of these titillating sexcapades.

Lydia Beaver was a vocal proponent of sex toys – imposing, pliant, pulsating playthings — oftentimes to the exclusion of men, if no man happened to be around. Or, if the man who was around, upon seeing her treasure-trove of toys, took his flaccid feelings of inadequacy and fled. In various columns, Lydia advocated frequent female masturbation ("Like a turkey in the oven at Thanksgiving, women need to baste in their own juices!"); an (attempted) orgasm a day ("They're like multi-vitamins!"); an underwear-free society ("Let your cookie breathe!"); and open relationships ("Like the great philosopher said, 'the more the merrier.'") She also recommended that couples give each other "a brisk spanking on the first date just to crack the sexual ice."

"I'll tell you why her column is popular," the Hazard ventured. "It's the penned equivalent of a massive train wreck. And as ugly as the outcome will inevitably be, you can't help but look. Or, in this case, read."

Despite Storm's low opinion of his colleague and her revolutionary sexual ice theories, he could not help but detect and take to heart that to the term "confirmed bachelor" she applied the same belittling connotation that has historically been attached to the word "spinster." Long after Lydia had teetered back to her own desk, long after the smell of his colleague's overwhelming perfume had finally dissipated, even after the day's deadlines had all been met and the newspaper had been put to bed, her words and their damning connotation still hung in the air like a threat, wearing on Storm and eventually sinking him into dispirited consideration of a life spent alone. A life lived without a romantic partner.

Storm Baker was not altogether unhappy. Most days he could quite effortlessly convince himself that he was basically a satisfied and content human being, particularly when he compared his charmed life to that of others he frequently encountered while covering the streets of Toronto. Specifically, the city's burgeoning army of homeless, hapless, depressed, destitute. Suffice to say, he never took being content for granted, nor was he ever inclined to undervalue such a commodity in life.

Storm was successful, his profession challenging, his daily work engaging and not without just rewards. He wasn't rich and knew he'd never know affluence as a columnist, but neither was he deprived. He could afford the essentials without anxiety and extras such as books, music, movie and theatre and restaurant outings without fretting about checks bouncing or credit cards being ceremoniously sliced in half by some condescending, ponytailed artiste moonlighting as a waiter in the theatre district. His sense was that his life was not completely full. However, in comparison to innumerable malcontents around him, it was nowhere near empty.

Professionally and socially, he was active. In any given week he would have days that were lacking not in activity, but in hours. That said, there were times, in moments of brutally candid reflection, when he was achingly aware that something was missing in his life. He craved more; he fully expected more. For Storm Baker, being basically satisfied and content was simply not good enough.

Typically, those moments occurred on listless nights when Storm lacked the energy and desire to work out or venture out. Nights before meeting Ali, before being reunited with the Hazard. Nights when all available options were unappealing and Storm found himself disappointed by a novel that, given his state of mind, never really possessed any chance of capturing his interest. Nights when he would mindlessly click up and down the channels of the television, seeking something, anything worth watching, and loathing himself for this blatant waste of the precious commodity of time. Nights spent flipping through his record collection in search of an album with edges dark enough to mirror his mood. Empty nights. Sketching future columns, jotting notes, essentially filling the void until he could, without shame, call it a day. On such nights, he could reach out and touch his own loneliness.

Loneliness was pervasive in the city. Urban critics theorized that it was fostered by the city's sprouting population and its soulless concrete sprawl. To Storm, loneliness was the unwanted companion on the couch beside him, arm draped possessively around his shoulders. And in those moments, thoughts of life without love were everything — the black clouds over his head, the pang in his chest and the wistful, sinking feeling in his gut.

As a print journalist, Storm Baker toiled in a profession that had been aggrandized and glamorized in the wake of the whole Nixon/Watergate fiasco. In reality, it was an odd, incestuous and afflicted industry generally void of any elements even remotely resembling glamour. It was, in the Hazard's words, a "mutant industry", chock full of "mutant people" doing "mutant labor" (*this* from musician). An industry in which encumbrances such as eccentric personalities, prolonged working hours and elevated levels of workplace stress combined and invariably proved detrimental to socializing and disastrous to relationships.

"Put it this way," the Hazard remarked after meeting many of Storm's colleagues at the Christmas party: "I looked around the Royal York and, stoned as I was, I did not see a whole lot of Woodward and Bernstein material. Honestly, I didn't even see anyone the likes of Redford and Hoffman capable of *portraying* Woodward and Bernstein."

In the introduction to his column compilation, *There's A Country In My Cellar*, Russell Baker confessed that most of his editorials in *The New York Times* were "written under the influence of desperation, which is the newspaperman's normal state of mind. Deadlines do that to him. He lives in a world where time is forever running out..."

Struggling to simply keep their heads above water in that frenetic world, many of Storm's coworkers had never found time to truly fall in love, let alone get married. Among the wedded, bliss was uncommon; marital meltdowns — trial separations, separations, divorces — were prevalent. Office romances, while not unusual, were ill-advised and ill-fated: convenient pairings of people mired in similar predicaments with little more in common than the day's top stories, the rat's nest of petty office politics and a need to commiserate over the assorted negative aspects of their lives. Storm could only imagine the grinding gears of their logic:

"We're overworked, overwhelmed, unable to dedicate time to ourselves, let alone each other. You're cute, your ass is passable, you have relatively straight teeth and a commendable commitment to personal hygiene. Maybe we should move in together..." After a few days, weeks, months of overkill, of seeing each other day-in and day-out, they invariably loathed the sight of each other, which made life at work unpleasant and, at home, unbearable. It all added up to a surfeit of surly single people spending inordinate amounts of time under one roof, in a perpetually shrinking environment with thin, transparent walls and Big Brother's all-seeing eyes.

Compelling and contrary statistics and scientific evidence be damned, Storm believed (cerebrally, if not viscerally) that single people had an honest shot at happiness, that unmarried life could be agreeable, productive, healthy. Although around the newsroom were abundant walking-wounded reminders of the pitfalls inherent in living alone. Certainly, Storm did not have to look far to see unmarried men and women who had so patently become lost in themselves. Become narcissistic and self-absorbed. Become isolated, disenchanted, embittered. And many, many who had simply become so very, very... odd.

Which is not to say that the newspaper world was devoid of warm and personable people, engaging and colorful personalities, and men and women who were on Storm's wavelength and with whom he struck-up loyal, lasting friendships. Every workplace has its peculiar people, and *The Times* was certainly no exception, although the Hazard would contend that the newspaper business in general, and *The Times* in particular, actually acted as a magnet in attracting "crazies" (again, *this* from a musician).

"Seriously," the Hazard opined, "I'm telling you, most of these people you work with give everyday dysfunctional a bad name. Honestly, they might as well go out now and buy the cats. That's obviously as good as it's going to get..."

Truth be told, Storm Baker feared becoming lost in himself. Dreaded faltering, becoming too rigid, inflexible, and set in his ways. He was petrified of becoming a 'confirmed bachelor,' with all its dated, spinster-like connotations. Although he would never outwardly acknowledge the fact, in matters of the heart — in regard to finding someone with whom he could spend the rest of his life — he felt like he was beginning to stare down the barrel of a deadline. How else to explain the occasions when he would come tumbling out of character and do what would previously have been unthinkable? And he did the unthinkable almost unconsciously: words over which he seemingly had no control, simply blurting out of his mouth. The next thing he knew he was on a date with Lydia Beaver, wearing brand-spanking-new briefs and fully anticipating an unstoppable assault on his backside as Lydia went about cracking the sexual ice.

"What were you thinking?" the Hazard questioned when he eventually met Lydia and discovered, in the form of a sheepish revelation by Storm, the passing personal history she shared with his friend. "You dated her? What, had you been commissioned to write *The Desperation Handbook* for single males?"

Naturally the Hazard wanted to know how the date played out. He demanded all the sordid details in part because he could be a real snoopy s.o.b. But also because there were times when he was powerless to prevent himself from endeavoring to create little rifts between Ali and Storm, aware that a fissure here, a fissure there, could well add up to a seismic, catastrophic quake in the relationship.

"I was home by eleven," Storm recounted. "She picked me up at nine, dressed like, well, let's employ the kind euphemism, 'an escort.' She insisted that the night's agenda was in her manicured hands. She also said that she believed in being upfront with a man. To that end, she told me that if I played my cards right, I would find myself in her apartment where she promised, or threatened, to handcuff me to her headboard, treat me to a reading from her sizable collection of Anais Nin erotica, and then have me dip into her overstocked 'toybox.' Then she chauffeured me to a downtown strip club on Yonge Street. Gentleman Jim's, or Horny Hal's, or some such.

"As luck would have it, it was amateur night, so we had the gross misfortune of being titillated by a procession of awkward, gorky exhibitionists peeling. As further bad luck would have it, after about four Grasshoppers, Lydia decided it would be the bee's knees to take a turn up on stage…"

"And?" the Hazard prodded. "And?"

"As luck would have it, the establishment had an emergency exit in the back near the washrooms. I slipped out just as she was about to go all Edison and become carnally familiar with a 60-watt light bulb. My escape set off security alarms, and seriously detracted from Lydia's gyrations, something for which she swears she will never forgive me. Hey, I wrote it off as just another night of playing the role of the meat in the dating grinder…"

Storm had been through the dating grinder, but then most singles his age had some experience at being ground into social mincemeat. By the time he reached thirty, he felt equipped to write a book on dating disasters. He'd even had a light-hearted, wine-fueled discussion with a publisher at a colleague's book launch about that very topic, although both agreed it was a row that had been thoroughly hoed (publisher's pun, intended).

Too bad. He could have dedicated the book — tentatively titled, *Ain't No Dignity In Dating* — to Miriam, the blind date who greeted him at the door of her apartment on her knees, in a ratty blue housecoat, reeking of vomit and still too drunk to stand up, let alone coherently speak; her slurs adding up to something about a really bad day at the office, and a torrid affair with a boss that had somehow soured.

To Clair, who became increasingly obtrusive as their date wore on, eventually working up to a confession. She was actually a "minion of

God", and she made it painfully clear that she viewed poor lowly Storm as nothing more than a reclamation project for her and her personal savior, Jesus Christ.

To vivacious and equally vacuous Sandy, the walking uterus. Before the end of their virgin sail down dating waters, Sandy asked about the health and hardiness of his "little men," convinced as she was that she wanted to (and *would*) bear his babies: "Six!" she exclaimed. And then she proceeded to give the gaffers names.

Or, to Sonja, the raven-haired ice-princess who genuinely liked everything about premium Canadian whisky save for the price (he paid, all night) and who, with each ounce imbibed, became incrementally more bellicose. By night's end she was virtually snarling sentences, stating that she abhorred sex because it was "too messy" and warning him that if he attempted any "funny business," she would take his scrotum and staple it to his forehead. Now there was a mental image for Storm to savor. In Sonja's defense, she did phone the next day to apologize for her prodigious alcohol intake and her anger, admitting that she was "hormonally bananas, PMS-ing big time." She also mentioned that she had a handful of minor issues with men that she was sorting through with the help of a therapist; oh and that she was unapologetically "custodial" when it came to her "tunnel of love."

The book would have contained whole sections on the women who, over candlelight and costly dinners, proved to be agonizingly garrulous or excruciatingly quiet. Women whose opinions and preferences and basic personalities clashed with his to the point of mutual embarrassment, or repulsion. Over the years there were no real 'steadies,' no relationships inching toward cohabitation, and certainly none venturing anywhere near marriage.

The Decisive Moment Or, Penis Fingers

IT WOULD BE Ali's contention that Storm's mounting sense of desperation, and likewise his fears, were born in susceptibility and in the knowledge that he was already far along the road toward becoming the creature he did not want to be.

What could Storm say? No reasonable argument sprang to mind. Before Ali entered his world — thankfully flipping his life upside down, breaking him out of the shell in which he was becoming imprisoned — he was an obsessive personality, and his obsessiveness was manifesting itself in a perfectionism that definitely possessed a dark side. In retrospect, it would become obvious to him that his need to be in control was spiraling out of control: rapidly approaching the point where his need to manage life (specifically, life's risks) was crippling him and rendering him unable to fully appreciate his relationships with others, his life, and his place in the world.

Storm was confronted by the unpredictable nature of life at a relatively young age: an age when most healthy young adults are still pleasantly oblivious to reality; when most innocently believe that they are invincible and that life, consequently, is a forever proposition, and that the sole purpose of human existence is a good time; an age when a young man is governed by the whims and dictates of rampant hormones.

Storm Baker lost his mother when he was eighteen. In that single moment, he was force-fed two of what he believes to be unassailable truths: that most of what is important in your life takes place in your absence, and that as hard as you try, it is impossible to control your own existence. It's trite, but true. Shit happens. Human beings are vulnerable. Absurdly vulnerable.

ANGELS IN THE ARCHITECTURE

Although he paid regular lip service to these truisms there nevertheless existed a contradictory force within his subconscious that propelled him to spend years subversively denying this reality. To maintain a sense of peace and hope — for the sake of his own sanity — Storm needed to embrace the myth that he was an exception to the rule, that he could control his life. It was this blind embrace of such brittle logic that allowed him to wake each day and get out of bed with the necessary assurance that in an instant of inattention, in a moment of lapsed vigilance, his existence would not be in some way obliterated. That someone he loved dearly and unconditionally would not be ripped from his life. The myth became rooted in his psyche. And it grew. Imagine the impact (the chip, chip, chipping away) on that myth when Ali began prophesizing her death. Imagine the fiery hell in which it perished on the day she died.

Control. A sense of control. Beginning with self-control, which he equated with discipline and structure. In the sedentary profession of print journalism, in the noxious environment that was *The Times*' newsroom — an environment where stress was king, caffeine queen, and every day the air of their royal dominion was annexed by cigarette and cigar smoke (for this preceded smoking bans in such places) and the repulsive smell of food fried right on site in The Bulldog, the newspaper's own greasy spoon, Storm was an anomaly. Storm minded his health.

As a columnist it was not essential that he work each day in the office. So, once or twice a week he would work from home – initially phoning in his completed commentary and dictating it to the rewrite desk; later, as technology evolved, faxing in his work — thus avoiding the whole harmful work environment.

Secondly, he ate right. Unlike the vast majority of his colleagues, he did not dare exist on a diet of toasted western omelets, under-cooked burgers and greasy fries, spicy sausage sandwiches and heaping schnitzel platters, all chased with another Coke, or more lukewarm coffee (known as "Bulldog piss"), or a barely chilled beer from the Hungarian Schnitzel Hut across the street. To the unending amusement of his colleagues, Storm was a brown-bag guy. The fact that he brought his own food to work made him an aberration. The fact that the food he bagged was nutritious made him something of a freak.

Furthermore, he existed in a world of chain-smokers, in the realm of the truly addicted. Many of his colleagues could not sit through a meal without lighting up for a few craved puffs between mouthfuls. Like nicotine was a digestive tool.

Russell Baker once noted that in the newspaper business, "high blood pressure goes with the territory, and alcohol is an occupational hazard." Storm never had any blood-pressure issues. He wasn't a heavy drinker, and he never took a drug more potent than regular-strength Tylenol. Not that he was a member of the earthy, crunchy-granola/my-body-is-a-temple congregation so much as he was concerned — to the point of paranoia — about how any given substance might react with his body and mind and possibly send him careening out of control, like a car on black ice.

For as far back as memory served, he had kept himself fit, fitness being an implement in his childhood survival kit. As an adult he took up weightlifting: light weights, for definition, not bulk, desiring to be strong, but not awkward or muscle-bound. He walked, he jogged. And when, in a one-month span, a second news editor was transported out of the newsroom on a gurney with a suspected heart attack — after the news staff gave a collective shrug, lit up another smoke, slugged back another coffee, and began wryly calling the newsroom The Cardiac Ward, and themselves The Cardiac Kids — Storm rededicated himself to good health. Walking farther, running longer.

Storm lived in a sparsely furnished, immaculately kept — everything has a place, everything in its place — one-bedroom apartment on the fifteenth floor of a high-rise building directly across from High Park. From his balcony he could see the expanse of the park and bare witness to its seasonal transformation: alluring, lush and green in summer; arrestingly colored in autumn; a barren and forlorn skeleton in winter until snow arrived and beautifully blanketed its acreage; and spectacularly reborn bud by bud in springtime. Beyond the park he could see the grey and ceaselessly choppy waters of Lake Ontario, typically appearing frigid and uninviting and, in season, flecked with sailboats.

Storm's life routine included daily exercise that revolved around High Park. One day he would briskly walk in the park, the next day he would jog on the streets surrounding it. Usually he jogged before work, early in the morning as the city awakened. His various routes, meticulously measured out in a friend's borrowed car (this being before his reunion with the Hazard and his union with the Dodge Dart) and selected on any given morning depending on his ambition and energy levels, on how much time he felt he could spare, and on the level of tenderness in his knees, took him along the city streets and through several of the small, ethnically diverse neighborhoods that comprise the west end of the city. Heeding the call of his erudite and ebullient editor, Patricia (Penny) Lane ("To properly cover this city, we've got to be out there!"), Storm would suit up and get out there, into the intricate mosaic of cultures.

On good days when he hit the perfect running rhythm, when his stride was relaxed and fluid and the motion almost effortless, he had the strength and endurance — in runner's terms, he had the legs — to cover considerable territory. A single outing might find him running alongside the building traffic on Keele or Bloor streets; darting between early bird shoppers in Bloor West Village; mingling with the shopkeepers and residents of Little Poland, a strip of shops and delicatessens on the east side of the park along Roncesvalles Avenue; and, at various times, hearing snippets of animated conversations in English, German, Ukrainian.

The next morning, regardless of the weather and throughout all seasons, he would escape the city and enter the park for a long walk. Giving his knees needed rest from jogging's pounding; startling the ducks and geese on Grenadier Pond; striding past Colborne Lodge, the grand 19th century Regency-style cottage turned museum.

Situated less than four miles from Toronto's downtown core, High Park — like Hyde Park in London or Central Park in Manhattan — offered what surely seemed to city dwellers to be a rustic retreat from urban life. Having grown up in somnolent, small-city southwestern Ontario – the type of place that had only recently been graced with its first McDonald's and had yet to be lit-up by a Cineplex or dazzled by a shopping mall — Storm understood that the park, albeit a welcome and inviting sanctuary, was a far cry from rural and was not quite representative of the boondocks.

In the boondocks you would not typically find Shakespeare being professionally performed under the stars on muggy summer nights, actors competing for audience attention with pervasive, pesky mosquitoes; a botanical gardens redolent of roses and replete with sculpted hedges; or a mini zoo — stocked with barbary sheep, peacocks, rabbits, raccoons and buffalo, among other creatures — which children found riveting, but which Ali and Storm, when they began the process of comparing notes, both found hopelessly depressing.

And in the boondocks, you would not find people who, despite the relaxed setting, still appeared unable or unwilling to totally unwind or truly slow down. Even in the park, Torontonians typically continued to move at the speed of the city: people striding with purpose down the park's vast network of fitness trails (not walking so much as *walking...*), or racing over to the swimming pool, or off to the tennis courts for an early morning match. Most mornings Storm figured that about the only serene people in the park, about the only people who seemed to be taking time to figuratively smell the flowers in the bountiful gardens, were the handful of elderly Asian gentlemen he frequently greeted on his way through the Bloor Street gates who, weather permitting, were engaged in the postures and balletic exercises of tai chi.

The park naturally attracted people simply seeking pleasure and doubtlessly grateful to be outdoors; men and women out for exercise, families on an outing, dog walkers and the like. But it was also a congregating place for mischievous youths and more menacing riffraff. On any given wooded trail, regardless of the time of day, Storm could encounter people getting high or even shamelessly amorous — typically, youths caught up in a moment, bare-assed, thrusting and trusting thin foliage to camouflage their awkward couplings. Once he interrupted a pair of middle-aged adventurers flailing about, a judgment-blinding mid-life crisis in full bloom.

Although Storm never really felt afraid in the park, he did have moments of apprehension. Which is why he was always on alert against potential danger. Shortly after moving to Toronto, he instinctively developed a previously unimagined awareness, a sixth sense, a vigilance that he lacked or simply deemed unnecessary when living elsewhere. At night, nothing could lure him into the park. At dusk the whole complexion of the parklands changed, and every activity took on an edge. Drunks went into the park to get drunk and stayed to sleep it off. Heavy drugs were dealt and used, needles and assorted paraphernalia scattered along the paths. Illicit sex was sought and procured. Gangs of youths went into the park to have it on. And on occasion, urban legend had some poor soul entering High Park under the cloak of darkness and never coming out.

The autumn Storm met Ali was characteristic of the season in Toronto. The weather was as fickle as that encountered any time of year in storied San Francisco, with all seasons potentially making guest appearances on any given day. Temperatures and conditions fluctuated wildly, sometimes hourly. Prepared parents ushered their children off to school dressed in

ANGELS IN THE ARCHITECTURE

layers with instructions to shed or add layers as became necessary, and about midday the unprepared would receive a castigating telephone call from the school's harried secretary requesting they deliver appropriate clothing to the school, their child's attire that day being ill-suited to the prevailing elements.

In mid-October, a brief, flirtatious warm spell goosed temperatures and spirits. Indian Summer. Brandishing caulking guns and listing under the weight of tool belts and honey-do lists, area homeowners took advantage of the unseasonable warmth to prepare their houses for the inevitable onslaught of winter, the farsighted actually hanging Christmas lights so they wouldn't be caught up a ladder in the dead of December. Meanwhile the carefree flocked outdoors — soccer balls, footballs, Frisbees, or baseball paraphernalia in hand — knowing that at any moment the weather could again turn against them and force them back indoors, cooped-up and claustrophobic, sniffling and sneezing until spring.

On the morning of October 18th, it was downright summerlike. Lethargic heat and hazy smog originating in the American industrial heartland migrated north and hung over the city. In High Park, the white-collared crowd could be espied exiting The Grenadier Restaurant following breakfast meetings that were becoming increasingly trendy. A group of business types, appearing equal parts incongruous and uncomfortable in their dark suits and dress shoes, kicked a soccer ball around the parking lot, trash-talking and acting half their ages.

Ubiquitous end-of-season wasps – moribund, seemingly angry, and stunned — swarmed garbage cans, buzzed about the heads of park visitors and stung anything that got in their way or that dared defensively swat at them. Summer whites could be seen rushing the nets at the tennis courts. Sun worshipers sat on the park benches, heads cocked heavenward. It wasn't hard to imagine the migratory birds and ducks and geese flapping about on Grenadier Pond contemplating postponing indefinitely any plans for their annual southern sojourn. The tai chi gang was in shorts and tank tops. Storm Baker was in thin, worn track pants and a faded grey Huskies Track Club t-shirt.

He had already been in the park for more than two hours and had covered considerable territory. The digits on his sports watch were an illuminated reminder that first-edition Bulldog deadlines were not that distant and that he had better begin making his way back home to shave, shower and face-off against the blank, taunting screen of his computer. As he walked, his mind focused not on the beauty of the park, or the splendor of the day, or on the magnificent paint-splash of autumn colors, but on work. He was mulling over possible wording, phrasing and punchlines that could be employed in a week-long series of columns he was writing celebrating the city's flourishing comedy scene — from the renowned Second City improvisational theatre to the handful of smoky, stand-up comedy venues, to local comics currently making considerable hay south of the border. He reached the park's zoo. Preoccupied, his mind still grinding and hard at work, he lingered by the animal pens.

A few preschoolers were feeding the docile, defeated animals with parents or grandparents or nannies supervising and advising on the best way to present the food without sacrificing fingers to a greedy bite. An elderly couple perused one of the posted signs that outline the origins and offer a brief history of the species in that particular penned-off area. An indolent, flatulent buffalo, patchy coat caked from rolling in muck, craned its imposing head toward Storm and stared at him with coal-black eyes. Always in awe of these creatures, and appreciative of the opportunity to encounter one up so close, about all Storm could think about when locking eyes was how the once mighty and plentiful creatures had now been reduced to this sad, waning existence by a lethal combination of stupidity and avarice.

A male peacock strutted into his vision, its rainbow-colored tail upright and fanned out. Nearby, a mother explained to her young, inquisitive son that the bird was preening, simply showing off. The boy suggested they hit it with a rock to see if it could fly.

In subsequent days Storm will think of the mother, about how she rolled her eyes and bit her lip as she struggled to suppress laughter, and how she glanced over at Storm as if to ask: Can you believe the preciousness that spills out of this child's mouth? How she knelt with all the love and affection in the world to patiently explain why you do not strike birds with rocks just to see if they can fly.

Storm was envious. Leaving the area, he waved a social goodbye to the boy and his mother, the sort of wave that was common, polite and expected back in his hometown, but exceedingly rare in the metropolis. He still had a considerable walk back to his apartment and a steep hill to ascend before getting back to the main entrance of the park. His thoughts were a jumble of Toronto comedy, preening peacocks, death-row buffalo, impending deadlines, all vying for his full attention when his full attention was abruptly arrested by no thought at all. But, rather, by a vision.

And that was when he first saw her, at the most mundane moment of what seemed destined to be but another ordinary day. Had she not been atop the hill, awash in sunshine, standing beside a black carrying bag that she had placed on the grass and that contained, he would learn, valuable photography equipment.

She was stretching like a cat upon awakening from a long, lazy nap. She was wearing a dark pink t-shirt, beige shorts, white ankle socks and white running shoes, an outfit that was unremarkable and yet remarkable... Because how could you explain how something 'unremarkable' ever managed to become so permanently seared into a man's memory?

Skeptics like the Hazard would later question whether he could possibly have discerned (let alone been mesmerized by) her beauty from that distance, as Storm would claim. And what about the "bronze aura" that he alleged surrounded her, or the "slivers of sunlight" he would assert were reflecting off the strands of her brown hair? Could a sultry southerly breeze honestly caress a woman in such a daring, sensual way, or was he by then flaunting, flogging poetic license? Could he possibly have felt, that instantaneously, that powerfully, the arrow piercing his heart?

She held a hand across her eyebrows to reduce the sun's glare and gazed down in his direction.

He waved. Then immediately wondered: what am I doing? He crammed the offending hand deep into the pocket of his track pants to ensure that it did not repeat the transgression. I don't even know this woman, he thought, and this is Toronto. She waved back.

She waved back!

Following that wave, she knelt beside the black bag — putting something in, pulling something out, he could not tell.

"Ha!" the Hazard would exclaim, in his thorough and combative cross-examination. "You could not discern from this distance whether she was putting something in or pulling something out of the bag and yet, from that very distance, you claim you could discern her beauty! I'm calling bullshit!"

She hesitated for a second, leaving him spellbound and curious. What is she doing? Then she reclined on the grass and rolled over onto her back, her eyes looking up at the heavens. She placed her arms across her chest, positioned like an undertaker sometimes positions the arms and hands of a corpse. There was a pause — and in that still moment, Storm would swear on his mother's grave, a voice whispered inside his head: "Life is about to change." And then, with an elbow, she gave herself a gentle push-off and began rolling down the hill.

And how she rolled, her body rotating like the rollers on a steamroller, quickly gathering speed on the steep descent, her unabashed peels of laughter filling his ears, the park, his world; the very spinning movement of her body actually making *him* dizzy, vicariously. He could not help but feel that as bizarre as this behavior appeared — and to the somewhat staid Storm Baker, it *was* bizarre — it was somehow fitting and fateful: this woman simply rolling right on down into his life. That descent into his life seemed to last an eternity.

Upon hearing the story of how Ali and Storm first met, Janeen Reynolds, veteran thespian and seasoned stagehand, would suggest that at the moment Storm was watching Ali roll, he was experiencing what actors call a *liminal* moment. A moment that passes through the threshold of what is perceived to be real, that somehow becomes unglued and separated from time. Because he was so engaged in what was occurring around him, time, in effect, ceased to exist.

And it would be Janeen's daughter who would suggest that at that very moment both she and Storm were experiencing what photographer Henri Cartier-Bresson termed "the decisive moment"; specifically, "the fractional period when all elements in a photograph work in harmony." At some point in time the term entered the lexicon, cloaked itself in more casual connotations, was adopted by sportscasters and the like and became, simply, a pivotal moment in time. A moment after which nothing remains the same.

She slowed and came to a stop at the bottom of the hill, only a few feet from the road. She remained still for a moment then unsteadily rose, her head surely still spinning, and began brushing off twigs, bits of grass, dirt. The boy who would hit birds with rocks raised his voice in approval.

"I want to try, I want to try. That lady's crazy fun, I want to try…"

By then Storm was beside her, openly wearing his adoration and, he was sure, the smile of a simpleton pasted across his face. Staring, and admonishing himself not to stare, and staring. She was beautiful in a breezy and unconventional way. Hair adorably mussed, skin soft and lightly tanned, playful hazel eyes, thin lips. His heart pounded, a bass drum thumping madly in his chest. His thoughts scurried like harried mice

ANGELS IN THE ARCHITECTURE

in a maze, frantically searching every narrow corridor, every far-off nook and cranny of his mind for those, those *things* he so adroitly employed every day to earn a living. Words. That's right, words. The few words he managed to retrieve from the recesses of his mind seemed inadequate and inane and would have been of no use anyway for his tongue was tied.

He watched as she fluffed her hair with her fingers to extract the tangled remnants of her roll. Every movement, he thought, sensual, alive, athletic without any aggressive edges, poetic, all fluidity and grace. When she tucked an errant wing of hair back behind her ear, about the only thoughts he could muster were of how he would like to run *his* fingers through that hair; how he would like to kiss the lobe of that uncovered ear, kiss a path right down her neck to her collarbone. And when she looked directly at him for the first time and smiled, Storm's face flushed. Fretful that she was reading his mind. His heart accelerated, and his knees weakened. "White flags," he would say, "were raised in unconditional surrender." His defenseless heart belonged to her.

In his head he heard the off-key voice of Ringo, beatkeeper for the Beatles, answering the question: Would you believe in a love at first sight? Yes, I'm certain that it happens all the time. Storm swears it was that immediate, that uncomplicated, or that incredibly complex, depending on your thoughts on a notion as divisive as love at first sight.

There is a popular concept that is supported, if not by science, then by tabloid media, talk-show television, and assorted diluted television Movies of the Week, that in the instant before you die, your entire life flashes before your eyes. There is another notion, what French philosopher Jean-Paul Sartre termed giving birth to yourself, that suggests a human being can be 'born' more than once in a lifetime. The moment Storm Baker saw Ali Reynolds at the crest of that hill in High Park, he was reborn. And in the moments that followed that rebirth, he insists that he saw his *future* flashing before his eyes. Thankfully, the future that played in his mind was more idyllic than portentous, more Rockwellian white-picket-fence than prescient — who could possibly cope with the vision of love abruptly found being abruptly lost? In those ephemeral moments he saw himself conversing with her, their fingertips accidentally, electrifyingly touching. He foresaw their first embrace, envisioned their first kiss…

"What I saw," he would say, "was certainty. That I was going to spend the rest of my life with this woman. That regardless, I would die loving her. I saw it all. From the first date to the wedding, to us walking through the park together as a family and me kneeling to explain to one of our kids that you don't throw rocks at the peacocks just to see if they can fly. And right on through to us growing old together. I saw the rocking chairs side by side on the front porch of the rest home, Happy Shady Acres, or whatever..." Wild, fanciful visions from such an earthbound soul. However, he would insist, these were not dreamy, fantasy visions: these were crystal clear...

A liminal moment. A decisive moment.

However, because human beings are involved, even such rare and momentous moments are not without incidents, accidents, folly, not without the imperfections that define and afford distinction — pimples, pockmarks, scars — to the creamy complexion of life. When Storm finally recovered his voice, it was cracked and tweaked an octave higher than desirable, but he believed that employing that squeaky pre-pubescent voice was nevertheless better than remaining inappropriately and idiotically mute.

"Hi, I'm Storm. Ah, nice roll." Nice roll? Hi, I'm Storm and I just tumbled off the turnip truck and you have no way of knowing that I actually make a living with words. Nice roll? He had mortified himself. "Down the hill. Nice roll down the hill..." Oh, God, he thought: I stood a better chance as a mute.

Again, that smile, crushing him with openness.

"Thanks. I don't know what came over me. But other than the odd rocky bump, it was fun." She held out a hand. He stared at the long, delicate fingers belying the hand's strength. They shook, Storm's mind remaining focused on her fingers.

"You have pianist's fingers." Pianist's fingers? With all the marbles in his mouth, his words, as they mockingly reverberated around the insides of his head, sounded more like... You have penis fingers. Storm felt the lump rising in his throat, the cold sweat trickling down his back, sensed the perspiration ringing his underarms. Penis fingers? And if there's a hole nearby, I think I'll just crawl into it.

But she kept smiling. She shook her head.

"I did play guitar when I was growing up. *Four Strong Winds, Day Tripper, Leaving On A Jet Plane*, that sort of thing. Simple songs, basic chord changes..."

"Well maybe that's it." Oh, you blithering idiot. You silver-tongued twerp. Maybe that's what?

ANGELS IN THE ARCHITECTURE

"Maybe," she laughed, endearingly, like she was encountering a star of the stand-up comic scene Storm had been researching. Like she was face-to-face with the funniest man on earth.

"My hand, Norm," she grinned. And it was at that deflating moment he realized that not only was this woman under the impression that his name was Norm, but he was also still shaking her hand. Had been for an eternity. Because he loved the feel, the warmth, the power, the potential, the connection. Because he loved being that close to her, fast becoming intoxicated and disoriented in her scent — a healthy, outdoors, woodsy scent, he would describe.

"Oh, for god's sake!" the Hazard would cry at the description: "Healthy? Woodsy? You were outside, you moron! With fucking woods all around you!"

Self-consciously, he dropped her hand. That's it, pull the plug on the life support. Call it a mercy killing. He was about to correct her on his name when she set into an introduction.

"My name is..." she began, but at that instant her attention was diverted. Eyes abruptly averted, muscles suddenly coiled — a sprinter, in the starting blocks, on the starter's 'set' command. She was staring behind them at something back up on the hill... "Shit."

Admittedly, it took the love-struck and love-stunned Storm a witless moment to determine the obvious. That she was *not* telling him that her name was Shit. First, or last, or perhaps a nickname? That she was in fact cursing something. In that moment, as he turned to determine the object of her ire, she was gone. Without a departing word. In a flash, up the hill. All long legs, explosive speed and resolve, after the punk making off with her camera bag.

Storm lost precious moments contemplating what had transpired. Lost further time standing idle, his head in the billowy, perfumed clouds of infatuation, mindlessly admiring her form as she powered up the hill, before he belatedly took up the chase. Although he was in splendid physical shape, there were elements working against him such as her head start, her fit legs, and the fact that an operation performed years ago to rebuild his knee had slowed him down considerably. Storm Baker could be counted on to run forever, but if speed were a prerequisite, count him out. His strength was conditioning and endurance and his natural tenacity, or what the Hazard called his "dogged, bordering-on-pig-headed, stick-to-it-iveness."

ANDY JUNIPER

As he scaled the hill, she went over the top and disappeared from view. When he reached the peak, he got her back in his sights: there in the distance, those legs still determinedly churning, steadily closing the gap between herself and the thief, who appeared winded, waning, and impeded by the cumbersome camera bag. They ran about half a mile along the grassy paths; Storm's despair growing in direct proportion to the widening gap between them. Aside from his desire to help her, he did not want to lose this woman. He did not know her name and she did not know his. In a city of some four-million people, he could only assume that she would be impossible to locate.

Increasingly anxious to ditch his relentless pursuers – stealing a camera bag with god-only-knows what inside was never supposed to be this challenging — the thief made a calculated beeline into the thick woods. Ali crashed in after him. To Storm, now trailing by some four-hundred yards, eyes still riveted on her back, it was as though the trees and brush simply consumed her. By the time he reached the spot where he thought they'd entered the woods, there were no signs of anyone. Storm stopped for a second to listen for telltale sounds but heard only his own labored breathing. Felt only the burning in his lungs. He entered the woods, altogether uncertain of which direction they may have run. For all he knew he was putting further distance between himself and her.

Storm Baker had a history of what renowned psychoneuroimmunologist Joan Borysenko coined 'awfulizing.' That is, the tendency to mentally escalate a situation to its worst possible conclusion. By the time the exposed tree-root on the overgrown path caught his foot — twisting his ankle, stretching elastic ligaments, and sending him sprawling — he was certain that finding her had become an imperative matter of life and death. In his mind the punk had finally quit running, turned to face his pursuer and...

Storm pulled himself off the floor of the woods and limped back to the clearing. He was a sight, bruised and swollen cheekbone, scratched face, mud, bits of brush and leaves festooned to his clothes like harpoons on a hunted whale. He hobbled across the restaurant parking lot in search of a telephone.

The police took twenty-five minutes to arrive. A vet and a greenhorn, a male and a female respectively, both unmistakably underwhelmed by the situation Storm was so animatedly describing. Frustrated, Storm offered more detail, as though it was the dearth of specifics that was making them underestimate the gravity of the crime. When he rambled on about her hair, her hazel eyes and thin lips, the cops glanced at each other. Storm detected smirks and definite eye rolling when he mentioned that adorable nose. When he described what she was wearing, the female half of the dynamic duo glanced up from her notebook and repeated...

"Brown hair, shoulder length, maybe a little longer, dark pink t-shirt, beige shorts, white running shoes... We passed a match to that description as we entered the park, Bloor Street gates, leaving, heading east and, you know," she added with a smile, "I'm quite certain she was carrying a black bag."

Ali Reynolds, the then unknown, unnamed woman, heading east. Gone. Love found, love lost.

If Only I Had Somebody

THE WALLS ARE mauve, faded, chipped, smudged, pleading for putty and a fresh coat of paint. Hung askew at odd heights are paintings donated by well-intentioned patrons: two fighter planes skirmishing; a close-up of a cow's ungainly head, impervious coal-black eyes; an ancient mariner in full rain gear, perched atop a wave-lapped rock, scanning the horizon while pensively inhaling the pipe smoke that will surely turn cancerous the susceptible cells in his throat and lungs.

Handrails screwed into every wall. Handrails in an adjoining bathroom, its heavy door flung open. Grey lockers along one wall. And beds lined-up, barrack fashion. Crisp white sheets, alternately green or pink covers. Bedside tables. Water pitchers. Styrofoam cups. Straws. Pill packets. Flowers: fresh, brilliant posies. Flowers: aging, neglected bouquets.

Pervasive, opposing smells skirmishing in mid-air, not unlike the fighter planes in the picture. Fresh-cut flowers. Vomit. Powerful disinfectant. Human waste. Bland food and instant coffee. Indignity and decay. Skin creams and perfumes, liberally applied and fragrant but still unable to fully mask the smell of fear, the distinctive stench of death.

Dehydrating electric heat. Stifling hot, causing shocks and prompting the opening of windows, allowing into the ward wild rushes of icy air and just enough whiffs of the outside world to pitilessly tease the infirm and incarcerated and to prompt the demand for extra blankets, continuing the absurd cycle. Hot. Cold. Hot. Cold.

A woman lies in bed and weeps, dampening her pillow with tears, snot, and despair. Condemned, she says aloud, to no one, to everyone: condemned to die. Everyone wants to go to heaven, you see, but no one wants to die.

ANGELS IN THE ARCHITECTURE

A cleaning crew goes about its morning routine with no visible sense of concern or urgency. Dirty floors are not going to kill these people. Ginger Ale spills on bedside tables are the least of their worries. And the puke beside Bed #4A? Relax, some sawdust, scoop it up, disinfect, no hurries, no worries.

Beepers summon. Mundane announcements, spliced with an occasional coded alert, over a scratchy, dated P.A. system. Outside the hum of traffic, beeping horns, the occasional squeal of brakes, acting as a reminder that the outside, while so very close, is a world away: far enough removed that you and you and you – deep down, at some brutally honest level of consciousness, you all must surely know who you are – may never again be a part of it. That outside world becomes nothing more than a mirage.

More godless sounds. The beeping, belching, whirring, farting, gargling, grinding, excruciating sounds of machines laboring to prolong, what? Agony? Meaningful life? Anguish?

"It's a big world out of there," the woman condemned to death moans, continuing the morphine-driven, self-pity-laced soliloquy, "but there's no one in it for me… Jesus," she cries, shaking a fist at the heavens, "I thought you had my back. Lord, I don't care about dying, if only I had somebody. God, it's a big world out there, but there's nobody in it for me…"

"Mae," a passing nurse comforts by rote, patting the patient's feet under the covers, "you're not dying and you're not alone. Your sister was here an hour ago and your husband called for an update and is on his way."

"I don't *care* about dying," Mae continues her disconnected lament unabated, "if only I had somebody."

A man enters the ward, a vacant expression on his blotchy, unshaven face. He is clad in the standard-issue Johnny, no housecoat, but seems pleasantly oblivious to the fact that his saggy, wrinkled ass is exposed, and he has a wet stain up-front, crotch-level. He shuffles over to Storm because, as Storm had once documented, 'they' always beeline straight for him. The man gets face-to-face with Storm — not aggressively, more child-like curious — and exclaims: "My god, you look sick. You need a doctor. Somebody calls the doctor. This man is sick." The man's moribund breath, the smear of egg on his cheek, urine on his Johnny. Storm feels closed-in. Trapped. Indeed, sick. His morning coffee somersaulting in his guts. He's sweaty, lightheaded. He really needs to sit.

"Mr. Blair," a nurse says, pleasantly, hitching an arm through Mr. Blair's bare arm, "you're wandering again, you sneak. You're not supposed to be in here, remember? Oh, and I think you've had a little accident. Here, I'll help you back to your room." Mr. Blair examines her face, like she's an angel or the flickering memory of previously forgotten, soft, scented and sheltering female flesh. A wife. A lover. Perhaps a young daughter, now grown, who once recklessly flung her arms around his neck, called him daddy, and professed the limitless depths of her love for him. The flicker fades. "My god," he says, to the nurse, "you look sick. You need a doctor..."

"If you need assistance with anything," the nurse cheerfully calls back to Storm, as she pilots Mr. Blair away, "there should be someone over there." She points to an unmanned desk. He does need help. His stomach is rising. He reaches for a waste basket. And he feels the strangest sensation in his head. Like he's on an elevator. And the bottom has dropped out.

Storm Baker hits the floor. He has seen the future. And be damned if it doesn't look hauntingly like the past. What was it Yogi once said: Déjà vu all over again?

You Can *Go Home*

WHEN IT CAME *to the supposed formative years of my childhood, when it came to my family — in particular my mother — Ali was insatiable and tireless in her pursuit of "context and color, nuance and knowledge."*

Are all women that inherently and charmingly curious? She wanted to know everything. Every little thing. Marathon nights spent entangled on the couch in our apartment, in the dark — or, rather, bathed in only as much light as the prevailing moon afforded — talking until we were talked out, or overtaken by sleep, or until a red band rising across the horizon trumpeted the turning of night into day and generated a fierce desire for breakfast. She soon knew the details of my childhood, growing pains included, about as well as I remembered them...

Months into our relationship she began to pester me, in a sweet and endearing way, to whisk her away on one of her road trips. Only on this excursion we would have in mind a destination: my hometown. It was her contention that regarding my birthplace I was mired in state of "absolute avoidance." Untrue. As I endeavored to explain, given the emotional trauma I'd endured within those city limits, and the morbid and ghoulish reminders that lurked around every corner, I'd simply, understandably, fallen out of love with the city. Frankly, the place just brought me down. Contrary to her assessment, it was not like I was paralyzed on any level, or at all incapable of returning....

Undeniably, I found Ali's enthusiasm for her proposed road trip to be contagious, despite the destination. She gushed about wanting to explore the house in which I grew up, the only house in which I'd ever lived, the schools I'd attended, and the places where I'd hung out.

"I want to eat at the Copilot Restaurant and talk to Jimmy (proprietor/cook) who took pity on your youthful scrawniness and gave you extra portions at no extra cost."

ANDY JUNIPER

She wanted to see where my friends lived and the street corners where the Hazard successfully busked for change to support his under-aged addictions. She wanted to see the cinder oval where I ran from teen angst under the guise of high school track and field; the local movie house — twice suspiciously razed, twice resurrected under new management; the dilapidated, ancient arena where I had my first date, ushering Candy Larson – such a sweetly named young girl, redolent of Juicy Fruit gum and Herbal Essence shampoo — up to the shadowy rafters of that dangerous old firetrap.

"I want to see that arena before it gets torn down so that the story Harland told of you planting that first kiss, so clumsily that poor Candy's lip began to bleed and swell, comes to life right in front of my eyes.

"I want to see The Review offices where my Clark Kent got his start as a newspaper scribbler. I want to see Fritzies, the trailer turned mobile fast-food restaurant. You can't tell a girl about the best French fries on the planet and not expect her to want experience that salt-and-vinegar sensation on her tongue… What are you, Storm Baker, some kind of tease?"

She wanted to see the people and places and things that helped shape me. Most of all, she wanted to meet my father. It was "high time", she said. After all, I'd met her mother. And hadn't that gone well.

She knew from our late-night ramblings that my father had returned to live in the house in which I'd grown up – two or three trial separations, a divorce, and a death removed from having resided in it with us as a family; the Baker family patriarch, who seemingly grew more endearingly and blubberingly sentimental with each passing year, said he loved the diminutive war-built bungalow he'd purchased for a song at the top of the crescent and could not bear to see it sold to strangers. After my mother's death — for our family, and in memory of my mother who he truly never stopped loving despite their glaring incompatibilities — he parted company with the woman he charmingly called Squirrelly Shirley (his lady-friend at the time who, he sheepishly confessed, was becoming a bit of a wet blanket anyway) and moved home.

"I told Janeen the whole story about your mom and dad."

"The whole story?"

"All of it. Their love. Meeting at a war-time dance at the bandshell on the beach at Grand Bend. Their wedding after he returned from the war. Their incompatibilities. His so-called wandering eye."

"And what insights did she impart?"

ANGELS IN THE ARCHITECTURE

"*That the problem wasn't that his eye was wandering so much as a lower body part. And that they'd have been fine if he'd just kept his pecker in his pants. She said that people really need to realize that they are not required to act on their every single impulse and urge...*"

Silence.

"*Your mother's one to talk about acting on impulses.*"

Silence.

"*He's a good man.*"

"*Absolutely. When his pants are on.*"

Silence.

"*I promise you'll never have that problem with me.*"

"*I believe you.*"

"*I'm a better judge of right and wrong.*"

Silence.

"*And I saw what it did to my mom...*"

The trip from Toronto normally would have taken ninety minutes. Three highways: the Gardiner-QEW combination out of Toronto, the 427 north, and then onto the 401 west — this in the days before the handy 403 extension. Alas, we got turned around at the QEW-427 juncture and somehow ended up on a road called Brown's Line.

"Brown's Line? How the heck did you manage that?" she wondered.

"You were navigating," I reminded.

"No, actually I was talking, and sightseeing, and listening to a little *Van the Man*, the always amazing *Astral Weeks. Sweet Thing, Sweet Thing.* You're at the wheel."

"Well, damn it, I'm on Brown's Line."

When we finally arrived home my father was not there. A note was taped on the back screen door: "Out running errands. Back by dinner. Key in usual. Make yourself at home."

"Running errands?"

"Pete-speak for 'at the pub.'"

"Key in usual?"

"Here, under the welcome mat."

"No burglar would ever think to look there..."

I let us in and at her request I gave her a pseudo-grand tour. A one-thousand-square-foot bungalow; how grand could it get? Down twelve steep steps to the basement, with its permanent underground musty smell. Two rooms: *a cozy TV room with an ersatz fireplace and a games room, replete with a ping-pong table and a dart board. The entire basement had been finished — partitioned and paneled and painted — by my father and Henry, his handyman brother, who'd handmade the ping-pong table.*

"Ahhh, memory lane." *I said it with forced levity. But the weight of so many memories truly made breathing difficult.*

"Don't look so sad. Embrace the memories. All things considered, you had a wonderful life here."

And I had, but I still missed her so much it physically hurt.

I could not remember the last time I'd been home. In recent years, visits with my father were infrequent and tended to occur in Toronto on my adopted home turf when he was in town on business, or to catch a baseball or hockey game. When we did congregate in our hometown it was usually at my brother's country home, two miles outside the city limits.

Back up the stairs, through the tiny kitchen that we could tell by the fresh lacquer and the lingering smell had recently been repainted, a sunny and optimistic yellow. Through the living room, down the hallway, the sunroom that was once Paris' bedroom before she flew the coop at an early age, the back bedrooms. My room. Undisturbed. Every book on the bookshelf, every framed photo, every poster, undisturbed. Even my bulletin board, busy with high school memorabilia (photos, ribbons, awards, and such), undisturbed. All undisturbed and yet, to my surprise, dusted, polished. A spotless shrine.

At some point in the tour, I'd fallen conspicuously silent. My mother's practical and aesthetic touches remained everywhere, from the window dressings to the pictures that hung on the walls to the knickknacks on every table. How that woman treasured her knickknacks.

But my room, my room was a four-walled vacuum that simply sucked me into the past. In that room it was as though I'd never left home, never attended university, never written a word for any newspaper, never met Ali, never fallen in love. I was a teenager. In my bedroom. With a woman.

"It's like a time capsule," *Ali said.* "A room where time has magically stood still. I look around and I see you at sixteen, seventeen, eighteen, this magnificent young man." *She smiled, flirtatiously, being all what she called 'girlie-girl.' Flitting about the room. Looking very desirable in a white blouse, short plaid skirt, black heels.* "This beautiful, randy young man who is forever lusting after all the girls in his classes — cheerleaders, prom queens, otherwise insufferable drama queens — and who is everlastingly encumbered by this screaming..." By this time, she was up against me, her arms around my neck, her breath against my face, her voice a husky whisper. "Erection."

She giggled something about self-abuse, an entire boyhood spent in chronic pathetic postures of self-gratification. I attempted issuing denials, but even to my ears they sounded untrue. Further, my voice box was by then coated thick by desire.

"Speaking of screaming... You've done it, Ali Reynolds... Now I must have you."

"Whoa, randy-boy: your father."

"No, honestly, I'd rather have you."

I pulled her closer. We hugged for an eternity, as I gauged her mood, her interest. She remained deathly still, her breath warm on my neck. I could not read her, but I knew with certainty that the atmosphere was gradually shifting. Sobering up; all giggles were gone. She pulled away. Then, a little too businesslike — a pinprick into the balloon of boyhood erotic fantasy — she unbuckled my pants and pulled them down, kneeling on one knee to tug them all the way off. She glanced up.

"You know, babe, there's a place we have to go. We have to."

She stood, lifted her skirt and slid cotton underwear down her legs.

"I don't think I can. I really don't."

The Hazard's voice, scrabbling inside my head, advancing one of his incalculable theories. Sex as currency. Sex is currency. This for that. That for this. I wanted her so badly. And yet. My desire ached up against my abdomen. And yet. My eyes welled as she lifted a leg and awkwardly took the ache inside her. Quick intake of breath. The intensity near unbearable. Every nerve ending alive, taut, quivering.

I wept on her shoulder. Wept as we slowly moved in rhythm, my tears divided – tears down the back of her blouse, down her arm, down to meet her breasts. Our embrace desperate, frantic. Weeping uncontrollably, like a desperate, mute baby.

Two Blocks Away

It's astonishing, just how much disregard that car had for her.

And at the time of the accident, Storm was only two blocks away.

"When I want to ratchet up the corniness quota, I always note that there I was, an innocent young man with a wonderful life and my whole promising future stretching out before me…"

"God," she says, biting her lip and fighting tears, "you could have scored big points using that as a pickup line. Otherwise strong, moral, *chaste* girls turned to putty."

"I did. I did. I got all the putty-girls. All the pity-girls a young man could desire. Girls who wanted to write poetry dipped in the ink of my grief. Girls who wanted to hold my hand and drown with me in the deep end of my sorrow. Girls determined to nurse me back to mental health. Girls intent on replacing or *being* my mother…"

Freshly graduated from high school and freelancing for the summer for the local newspaper before he was scheduled to enter university, he was leaving the home of an eccentric octogenarian he had just finished interviewing for a feature story — a light, fluffy piece on the spry eighty-two-year old whose hobbies included beekeeping, cribbage, taxidermy, whiskey distilling in his backyard shed, and clicking about town all summer long on stilts. And this active elder lived only two blocks away from the scene.

It was early afternoon. The streets were sun-stroked, steamy, the air sticky and inhospitable.

"I heard the sirens," he says, wistfully. "I was a cub reporter, walking down the street with notebook and pen in hand. Naturally I followed the sound, chased the sirens to right here where a crowd was gathering." He opens his arms to the intersection of Fuller and Fife. "I can't say I knew, but… I really think that on some level I must have suspected something. My stomach was in my throat."

Ali and Storm: rumpled, sticky, redolent of a stolen moment of fraught sex and pervasive sadness. That intersection is the last place in the world that Storm wants to be. She brought him here and now she's beside him, supportively close. She hooks an arm through his arm. She's lost the fight, tears streaking her cheeks.

"Remember the adage, 'life's hard, then you die'? If only it were that easy. Life's hard, then you witlessly step out between two parked cars and get broadsided in broad daylight. And even then, you don't die. Even then God won't release you from your contract."

No release.

The car awkwardly propelled her, twisting her body, reshaping her visage, and sinking her into a coma from which she would emerge irreparably scarred and damaged. Doctors analogized how the brain is like Jell-O in a bowl. Doctors apologized: her bowl had been tipped, her Jell-O spilled, and there was nothing they could do beyond measures to keep her comfortable. She was, and would remain, one future ailment or infection from death, relegated to an unfathomably depressing palliative ward, in a hospital bed for nearly one full godless year before she would finally receive her walking papers. Before she would close her eyes for sleep one last time and simply fail to wake up.

He visits her, devotedly, each visit a lifetime in hell. There exists no light in her eyes, certainly no love. A veil has descended. He is convinced that she does not know who he is. And in his mind, his mother — his sweet, kindly mother — died on that street; he has no clue who the imposter is in that hospital bed. Still, he dutifully wipes the sleep from the imposter's eyes, the snot from her nose, the drool from her chin. And the nurses contend that she seems markedly improved when he's around; never affording him the out he so desires, that she would never know the difference if he did not show up at all.

As planned, and pushed by Pete, he departs for university in a neighboring city about forty-five minutes away. His heart is not in it, and neither is his head. But he dutifully attends. Twice weekly he drops his studies, hitches a ride, or catches a bus or train, and he visits. The trips are often perilous in winter on black-iced roads with diminished visibility, snow squalls and white-outs. Honestly, the trips are hellish in all seasons.

ANDY JUNIPER

The very sight of the hospital turns his guts. His Pavlovian response. He knows the location of all the fourth-floor washrooms in relation to her room; by rote he stops off in one before each visit to throw up. And sometimes, if anything is left in his guts, or the visit is particularly harsh, he makes an identical pit stop on the way out.

And each night back in the university dorm, where his reputation amongst mostly oblivious classmates is that of a manic-depressive killjoy, the freshman world whorls around him. He closes his eyes and prays for quiet, and prays for sleep. The image of her twisted frame and unrecognizable face, swollen and discolored, tucks him in and kisses him goodnight, ensuring that even if sleep comes it will be fitful, troubled.

He feels sorry for the driver. It wasn't his fault. He was just running an errand... sober, alert, cautiously under the speed limit... when she appeared seemingly out of nowhere and fate bounced off his car's grille.

He feels sorry for his father. His guilt-laden vigil, the hours he spends at her bedside, head in hands, contemplating countless what-could-have-beens, should-have-beens, and more to the point for Pete, what-should-not-have-beens.

He feels sorry for his siblings. Sorry for Mackey. Definitely sorry for Paris, across the Atlantic, pregnant (with complications) at the time of the accident — angst-ridden, bedridden, unable to fly. And then, her joy of becoming a new mother so sorrowfully stifled.

He feels sorry for the Hazard. In many ways, she was his mother, too. She was the woman who did everything in her power to harbor him from harm until he was old enough to take his guitar, flip-off his father, and follow the fugitive sun south. And Harland and his no-fixed-address existence had to hear about her fate in a letter that bounced around before finally reaching him too late: fourteen months after the accident. Two months following the afterthought that was her funeral.

And, admittedly, he feels sorry for himself. Some days he cannot believe his own sacrilegious prayers: that he'd dare fall to his knees and ask God to please, show mercy, show pity. To please, just let her die.

It's astonishing, just how much disregard that car had for her.

As If The Gift Of Birth Was Not Enough

It could not have been any more painfully obvious to Storm Baker — and to anyone with whom he shared his dilemma, and whose advise he so needily sought — that the odds (and, apparently, the gods) were against them ever meeting again. He did not know her name. She did not know his. And identifying and tracking down a Jane Doe in such a sizeable and sprawling metropolis would be akin to finding one particular grain of sand on an extended stretch of beach, regardless of how distinct that grain was to him.

However, what he also knew with painful certainty was that he *had* to find her because on the day he met Ali Reynolds in High Park, in the ephemeral moment they shared, he not only found his future, but he also felt that he had reconnected with his past. Felt that he had rediscovered his voice: not the sound fashioned through the mouth in speech or song, rather, the voice that resides within a person. The voice that *is* a person, that is his or her *essence*. The voice that had been muted for years, abruptly resurfacing and resonating within the walls of his head. A crisp, clear, concise voice endowed with power, purpose, and life.

He had always thought of it as the voice his mother had bestowed upon him. As if the gift of birth was not enough...

With the passage of time, considerable portions of a person's childhood become blurred, forgotten outright, or even buried. Although the family photograph albums through which people periodically thumb, and the repeated nostalgic recounting of corresponding family history, may well provide us with the illusion of knowing our infancy and youth, of possessing memories of events that we might otherwise have zero recall.

ANDY JUNIPER

All memories are colored and oftentimes distorted by age, personality, and personal point of view: it's not uncommon for close siblings to have completely contradictory remembrances of moments they shared. Further, memories are flimsy and fluid, easily embellished or diminished, and occasionally they are entirely imagined — figments of desire or overactive imaginations or the pure product of the power of suggestion (when someone says, "Surely you remember," the mind naturally attempts to accommodate: "Oh, yes, I guess I do remember...").

On Storm Baker's dresser, a framed photograph of his mother snapped during a boat ride: his mom, a passenger in a sleek motorboat in what he came to think of as 'better times', during a family holiday at a cottage in Georgian Bay. It's a close-up, the camera lens tight, practically reaching out and caressing her face. The wind is blowing her hair back, and on her face exists a carefree expression and a peaceful, relaxed smile; she obviously knew the photograph was being snapped but was not at all intimidated or concerned. That's how he often remembers her, on that lake, in that boat, wearing that expression. However, he is fully cognizant of the reality. That he was not yet born when the photograph was taken, and he personally never vacationed at that particular cottage with his family.

Storm has another photograph. Taken around the same time, possibly on the same outing, only for this picture the photographer has backed off to capture all of Katie Baker in the picture. She is wearing black-framed Jackie O sunglasses and a dark and stunning one-piece swimsuit. He keeps the photograph in a drawer, perhaps unconsciously uncomfortable with just how gorgeous his mother looks. Sleek, sensual, perfect. Even as an adult he takes occasional comfort in holding that photograph in his hands and in telling himself that it was undoubtedly his father who took the picture; that, at least back then, they were a singular and solid family unit.

For her, for his darling Katie, his father always had a certain sparkle in his eyes. Each Christmas, under the tree, a tiny package. Inscribed. From: Santa. To: My Love, Katie. Two or three or four pairs of the skimpiest underpants imaginable. Their style and brevity at once a fantasy and a desire; and, if worn, an assurance and a promise. She would open the package, then exclaim at the contents ("Oh, my!") and hold the briefs up for all to see, as blood of embarrassment rushed Storm's cheeks.

Storm Baker fully believes that everyone has some genuine remembrances from childhood that are indelibly etched in the mind and that form the foundations of our perceptions regarding what we are, who we are, and from whence we came…

Storm Baker was born in the predawn hours of a September morning, in a small Southwestern Ontario city, in the midst of a thunderstorm. And while he never attached any significance or symbolism to the fact that he entered the world during such meteorological turbulence, as a writer he was able to appreciate the rich hokeyness inherent in his birth: his story, in essence, beginning like the 1830 Victorian novel *Paul Clifford* by Sir Edward Bulwer-Lytton — and, perhaps more culturally significant, like countless tales chronicled by the cartoon beagle Snoopy: *"It was a dark and stormy night…"*

It was a night during which only the deepest, deadest of sleepers slept soundly, or slept at all, a night in which the tenuous calm was repeatedly shattered by heart-stopping thunderclaps and bolts of lightning that penetrated and shocked the darkness as the unusual heat of persistent, lingering summer collided with an incoming front of cooler and more seasonable September weather.

A light sleeper with an anxious, weary history of insomnia, Kathleen (Katie) Baker lay atop the covers, reclined on her side with two generous pillows crammed between her legs, and another supportively stuffed up under her swollen belly. Unable to sleep, and suffering all the indignities of the homestretch of pregnancy – heartburn, bloating, muscle aches, anxiety – she listened to Mother Nature's wrath, her stomach occasionally rumbling seemingly in sync with the thunder, and she watched the minute hand on her illuminated bedside clock turning tauntingly slow circles as night took its sweet time ticking toward dawn. Inside her, a full-term baby kicked and jabbed. Beside her, Pete Baker, snoring sonorously, erratically.

At 3:15 a.m. a particularly fierce clap of thunder was immediately succeeded by the sick *thud* of flesh hitting hardwood. As quickly as possible considering her condition, she propped herself up onto an elbow and then hoisted herself out of bed. She hurried (the pregnant-penguin-on-ice gait) down the hallway and into the room of Mackey Baker who was kneeling on the floor, as if in prayer, still half-asleep, whimpering and unconsciously rubbing the rising goose egg on his head.

She helped her eldest son back into bed. For a moment she took advantage of the situation and hugged the five-year-old close to her chest and stroked his warm, flushed face. It was only in one of those semiconscious, middle-of-the-night moments that Mackey allowed her such closeness. It was as she was pulling his sheet back up over him, tucking him in tightly to lessen the odds of him crashing out of bed again, that she experienced the initial pain, a wicked, searing stab across her abdomen. She winced, bit her lip, and tasted her own blood. A second contraction immediately followed.

Having experienced two previous births, she knew the routine. She sat on the couch in the living room under a single lit lamp and began timing both the duration of the contractions and the time lapse in between. This textbook timing lasted less than ten minutes before she surrendered to the knowledge that this was going to be no model labor; this was to be labor contracted, intensified.

Back in the bedroom, between the piercing pains, she struggled to roust Pete from his slumber. At least tonight he is home, she thought. With Mackey — granted, always in a hurry, Mackey was two weeks early — he'd been in an out-of-town curling bonspiel and was inexplicably unreachable for a full day after the birth. When Paris was born three years later, he was on the road selling encyclopedias that no one was having any trouble resisting. Pete would determine that at the precise moment his wife was pushing his daughter into the world, sans his comfort or support, he was motoring through the bucolic town of Paris, Ontario.

"Pete," she practically shouted, shaking her husband, hard, rough. "It's time." More shaking, more pleading, before he finally willed one of his eyes open. "Come on, Pete, damn it, wake up, it's time!"

By the time Pete was fully coaxed from his coma and into consciousness, then convinced that he did not have time even for a quick shower, by the time Mrs. Fitch, a neighbor, was summoned to stay with Mackey and Paris, it truly was time.

Daniel (Storm) Baker, a scrawny, screaming, five-pound, two-ounce baby was born in that thunderstorm, on a gurney, as his mother — cursing both her predicament and her husband — was being wheeled by attendants into hospital while Pete was off parking his Mustang.

Storm's mother, in a collage. Impeccable appearance, indisputable beauty that remained virtually untouched by the tensions in her marriage and that union's slow dissolution, undiminished even by age, or the rigors of having carried and delivered three babies. Minty breath and intoxicating scent; without diving into Oedipal pools, Storm Baker would gladly have spent a warm, woozy eternity in her fragrant embrace. Then there was her seemingly boundless love in tandem with her absolute "mom-ness." That is, the way she transformed a house into a home and the way that home so naturally gave the impression of being not only the most inviting place in the world, but, also, the safest: "The world's lone safe sanctuary," in the words of a grateful young Harland Hazard who frequently sought refuge in that sanctuary. Finally, there was her openness which begat openness. Storm could talk to her about anything. And he did, a practice that was not without pitfalls, a boy engaging his mother as his confessor.

Not surprisingly, considering their closeness, Storm and his mother agreed on most everything of importance... In her words, two peas in a pod. And, not surprisingly, his initial clear memory of her is his earliest memory of anything. He has no idea of precisely how old he was when she delivered the monologue that would be repeated to him over time and that, in his fertile mind, would eventually take on a life of its own.

He does know for certain that the first time he heard the story, he was sick — feverish and temporarily bedridden as he was so often in those days. Nothing serious, he was simply the scrawny, prone kid who caught everything going around, sometimes more than once. Years after his immune system matured and he outgrew that sickly phase, Harland reflected that, forget Storm's frailness, perhaps he had actually willed himself to fall ill. Because illness, psychosomatic or otherwise, allowed him to miss school and remain at home, wrapped in that protective, loving cocoon. With her.

"Mercy," the Hazard once said to Storm, "you and your mother... Freud would have had a field day..."

In his love of Katie Baker and the homey cocoon she so lovingly created, Storm Baker was not alone. The Hazard liked to say, "If this was my house, and she was my mom, I'd be praying for chickenpox, or measles, or something really nasty like, I don't know, gout? You name it. Forget ever washing my hands. I'd French kiss strangers and lick the buggy handles at the grocery store. I'd welcome the germs..."

Harland Hazard. Pete Baker tabbed him 'the adopted son' and joked that he'd magnanimously invited young Harland over for lunch on the day the Hazards moved into the neighborhood and "the crazy little bugger" never left. Having spent so much time under the Baker roof, he basically became a Baker, ingratiating himself into most aspects of family life, from the everyday to the intimate. He comfortably called Katie Baker 'mom';

granted, she insisted. Truth be told, the Hazard's strained home life was known to make Storm's mother more anxious and miserable than her own marital woes.

Storm's mother, his memories, her story…

"When you were born," Katie Baker began, "I told your father that I wanted to name you Daniel. I got it out of a book of baby names. Your father, on the other hand," she laughed, "for obvious reasons, wanted to name you Storm. My senses had been dulled considerably by childbirth, but I still had the common sense to fight him on this issue…"

The initial time the story was related, she was busy reducing her son's temperature with damp, cold washcloth compresses across his feverish forehead.

"In the end," she continued, "we compromised: we named you Daniel and made Storm your middle name. Of course, Daniel quickly went by the wayside. Your father won out as he always seems to win out and it was Storm that stuck.

"Now comes the hard part," she said, tucking an errant strand of her wavy black hair behind her ear. "If you're going to walk around with such a usual name, a name no one will ever forget, then you have to become an upstanding human being, a person worthy of being remembered."

So, the voice was tethered to the story his mother recounted regarding his name. The voice was tethered to his mother who, for all intents and purposes — in spirit if not body — passed away on a prickly hot summer afternoon on the heated asphalt of a side-street back in Storm's hometown. Love lost and, along with love, Storm's voice.

The voice found its way back to him on a hillside in High Park… How, he wondered, how to find one woman in a city of some four-million souls?

He wrote about their encounter in his column. Surely, she reads newspapers, he thought. The column garnered interest and feedback, but zero returns. The city has more than one newspaper, he considered. Maybe she doesn't read any newspapers at all. Or maybe, his confidence wilting, maybe she religiously reads newspapers, just not his column. He bounced his dilemma around the newsroom, off editors and reporters alike. He was in conversation with his editor, Penny Lane, when who should crash the conversation, but Lydia Beaver, recently returned from a week-long vacation in Western Canada.

ANGELS IN THE ARCHITECTURE

"Look what the cat dragged in," she said, pointing at Storm's roughed-up face. "Listen: I was off last week for all your giddy girly-boy theatrics. But the Good Life Mind & Body Spa in Manguard Springs, Alberta, where I was rejuvenating myself – two-hundred-and-fifty-smackers a night, by the way, but I'm worth it and I'll just expense it anyway – had a copy of your embarrassing essay of personal woe. Fittingly enough, I read it as I was getting a buttermilk colonic gently administered by a spicy Swedish meatball named Sven." She glanced at Penny and winked, conspiratorially, one sister to another.

"Hi Lydia," Storm said. "Welcome to my private conversation. Feel free to barge in at any time."

"Well, I've been eavesdropping for five minutes so it's not all that private, you think? You know, when your face is all bruised and swollen like that it usually means you got hit by a bad date, not *l-l-l-ove*."

"I fell, Lydia, in the woods, that's how I got scratched up and bruised and, if you could just go away, I was in the middle of a discussion with Penny."

"Penny," she scoffs. "Like Penny's going to be of any use. If you want to know dull things like how many politicians are in Parliament, or why ocean water is salty, or how to properly peel a banana, ask Penny. But if you want to know about real stuff, real-life stuff, come to me.

"What you experienced is common in a city the size of The Big Smoke. It's called a 'sighting': you know, man meets woman, woman meets man, on the street, in the laundromat, in a bar or, heaven help them, in church. Sparks fly. But the two parties either don't talk or just talk briefly. Anyway, they neglect to exchange phone numbers because of whatever, maybe they just have poo-poo for brains, and they go their separate ways…"

"We couldn't exchange…"

"Defensive. Always tight-assed defensive…. I didn't say, necessarily, that *you* have poo-poo for brains, did I? Anyway, they go their separate ways and then down the road, a little light clicks on. Wait, that may have been Mr. or Mrs. Right."

"So?"

"So, what these people do is place a personal ad in all the papers, especially the commuter freebie rags. Have a bold, catchy teaser, something like 'Feeling Low in High Park.' Then, say, 'I'm the desperate, tight-assed defensive. Saw you in High Park, rolling down hill. Thought we connected. Like to jump your bones. All apologies, I have a ridiculously small appendage.' Sign it, "Squirrel Dink in The Park', or something. Then you get a voicemail mailbox at each paper that she can contact you at..."

Advice dispensed. She then announced in a voice that carried clear across the newsroom that she had to run and "tend to the grim whims of Aunt Flo" and teetered off on her heels. Storm watched her departure, impressed by her balance on those precariously elevated and impossibly narrow spikes. Penny Lane rested her head in her hands, like she was on the brink of a migraine, or grieving for all womankind.

About to return to his desk and the work of the day, Penny grabbed him by the wrist: "If it was me and I was truly interested in this guy, if I thought such a connection had been made, I'd go back to the park. Sooner or later, she'll return to the park. Women," she sighed, "women are romantic enough, or foolish enough, to believe in lightening striking twice in the same place."

If Only I Had Somebody (Part II)

A NURSE STANDS over him, concern and confusion imprinted on her face. Taking stock, he is still nauseous, clammy, thoughts still clouded. He wonders where he is and how he got there. He hears a voice, a broken record. Goddamn it, someone stifle that voice…

"I'm all alone, in this great big world, all alone…" Right, right, if only you had somebody… Please shut her the hell up, make her go away. The voice, the pervasive smells, twig recall. He touches the sheets, crisp, starchy. He's on a hospital bed.

Think. Think.

He recalls being summoned earlier that morning. A nurse from Toronto General, a call that rousted him from sleep.

"Storm Baker? Hi, I'm Dorey-May Bell, an eighth-floor nurse over at Toronto General. Doctor Mackenzie, Redic, asked me to call: a Janeen Reynolds has been admitted."

"Janeen? Oh, no… what happened? Is she okay?"

"Actually, police brought her in two nights ago. She was out wandering in the middle of the night in the snow, in nothing but a trench coat. They found her attempting to break into a car, for warmth, I suppose. I mean, she doesn't exactly strike me as a car thief. We've had her under observation and testing ever since. We had her listed as a Jane Doe. She refused to speak to us, other than to let us know that she's miffed. Miffed with police, with us, the world… Luckily, this morning, Dr. Mack happened to see her on his rounds and identified her for us. Somehow, he knows her, and you're her next of kin?"

He's never thought of it in such exact terms, this reality: "Ah, Dorey-May, I'm all she has…"

Throwing on some clothes, the phone rang again. Redic.

"Sorry, sorry, sorry, man. She's had a series of small strokes. I really believe we're looking at vascular dementia. I've got a Dr. Corey Lincoln, who specializes in this field, coming to examine her anytime now. His work is renowned, we can count on him. Storm, it's a pretty slippery slope she's on… Listen, I can't see you at the hospital this morning. I'm booked. But let's catch up at lunch after you've seen her, and we'll compare notes and try to formulate some sort of game plan."

Both feared going in that the game plan they'd be formulating would involve strategies for watching her slowly lose her mind.

"I think I'm going to throw up again." The nurse hands him a pan. He cradles it, takes deep breathes, squirms, sweats, and concentrates on not vomiting. The nurse, fresh on the ward and unbriefed, is perplexed: in street clothes, he's obviously not a patient. When his stomach settles enough for him to speak, he advises: "I'm here to see Janeen Reynolds, my mother-in-law."

"Janeen Reynolds. Well, soldier, that would be me." She's in bed four down from his, appearing frail and insignificant under the covers, and she's staring not at Storm or the nurse. But, rather, at the picture on the wall across from her, the close-up of the cow.

"Either that picture goes," she announces, "or I do…"

Only Janeen, at a time like this. Only Janeen, that sharp tack, paraphrasing Oscar Wilde's alleged last words. Storm does not know whether to break out in laughter, or tears.

Judas Finds Pegasus Or, Solidarity

JUDAS IS PROCRASTINATING. In Toronto General, procrastinating. Wandering aimlessly, mindlessly, the length of corridors down which he has no business, down which he never previously ventured in the eight weeks that he has been coming here every day. Eight weeks of having the life sucked out of him. A veritable tap on all life's vitals, including hope. Particularly hope.

The slippery slope. Tell him about it.

A gunshot victim is wheeled into Emergency. Judas, suddenly witness to a real-life episode of a television hospital drama, only with more grit and none of the glamour. A woman clutching an IV pole leans against an obliging wall for support, liberated beads of sweat gathering on her forehead. A man gingerly pilots his pregnant wife toward the admitting desk; she whimpers and her vicelike grip on his hand tightens with each unworldly contraction, to the point where they whimper in unison. An elderly man exits a washroom, modestly clutching the back of his Johnny, staring at the floor, and cursing aloud the recent disappointments of his bowels: "Wind and water," he mutters. "Seven godless days. Nothing but wind and water." Thanks, Judas thinks, thanks for sharing that.

Elevators ding. He smells coffee from the main-floor café. The incongruous homey aroma of baked goods. He watches a man in the lobby laughing over something amusing he's reading in *The Toronto Times*.

He thinks, I can't do it. Paralyzed. Can't get on that elevator, can't get his spineless body up to the eighth floor where she is waiting, where they have packed her essentials and readied her for what they've been euphemistically been calling – for five days now — her "little trip." Her little trip. What a euphemism. Like she's heading off for a spa weekend. With Judas behind the wheel, chauffeuring.

ANDY JUNIPER

Today is the day. Redic had pulled all the strings he could possibly pull; the marionette has run out of tricks.

"Honestly, I can't find any further reason to keep her here a day longer." They'd run all the tests imaginable, primary, secondary. She isn't *sick* per se; she isn't in need of treatment because, frankly, no true treatment exists. Caregivers will be advised to administer two coated baby aspirins daily to assist in the prevention of further strokes. But, nevertheless, she must go. They're overrun. They need her bed. In this ongoing health-care crunch, they have patients sleeping in hallways. They need the resources she is draining from the system. Cruel as it may seem, they need her out.

Today is the day Judas breaks his own heart by breaking the solemn promise he'd made to her.

Redic: "What were you thinking, making her a promise like that?"

Judas: "I thought she'd get better. And if she didn't, that I'd be able to take care of her. I didn't think she'd sail this far south this fast. Really, who did? You're a doctor, you didn't. So, I promised." That he would never put her in a home. Never, Janeen, not in a nursing home, I promise. Her hand in his hand, her eyes searching his soul, and trusting; he's all she has.

Earlier in the week, when word filtered down from administration that she had to be discharged, he feebly pitched to her the wonders of The Plaza Vista Retirement Community, a gleaming, modern facility just north of the city. Luckily, he'd been told, the Plaza had an opening. Yeah, luckily someone died. Honestly, how could you beat such good fortune? His reedy Judas voice was an unbearable screech inside his own head, all the fingernails in the world drag racing down chalkboards: and look, Janeen, a garden patio where you can sit out. Had he mentioned the swimming pool, the always fucking empty swimming pool? Like she was suddenly going to run out Speedo shopping, take up swimming, and spend her twilight days absentmindedly backstroking through over-heated, over-chlorinated water.

Don't think of him as callous, don't think of him as he thinks of himself. As Judas. He did what he could. Including the research. Don't think he wasn't completely cognizant of the rapid deterioration suffered by dementia patients in nursing homes and care facilities, of the godless mortality rates when people are moved from their homes into these "homes".

Redic, choking up, taking his forearm in his own caring hands: "You have no choice, friend. It's the only thing you can do."

ANGELS IN THE ARCHITECTURE

"Please, Redic, for the sake of our friendship, please don't use the words 'slippery slope.'"

By mid-summer, nursing-home management will be proffering an ultimatum: either she enters their "secure care" – locked up, Janeen, trapped, imprisoned, drugged into submission, a veritable life sentence — or she simply goes. Granted she still has good days, bad days. However, for the most part, she's trying to escape at every turn and she's becoming all-too belligerent and, frankly, too dangerous. To herself, and possibly others.

Belligerent? Naturally. A woman from whom everything has been taken away. Her freedom, her cigarettes, her dignity, her gin.

"My whole life," she shouts in a moment of clarity.

Dangerous? Naturally. People with dementia who remain even vaguely aware of their own condition, and demise, their loss of the ability to fully function as human beings, are the patients who suffer emotional breakdowns. Piques and fits of resentment and anger, lashing out verbally and physically. Rising up, raging against the descending darkness.

Is it possible for a human being to run from his future while at once running from his past?

He beelines down a hallway not knowing where he's going, simply going. The corridor leads to the pediatric ward, to the ward's waiting/admitting room, a recently renovated, spacious, glassed-in area. Twenty paces away, he spies it through the glass, and he cannot believe his eyes. It's like an apparition, it seems that unreal. If he had subconsciously been seeking some sort of sign, a mystical nod that he was in fact in the right place doing the right thing, surely this would qualify.

There, perched impressively, imposingly in a corner, a five-foot-tall papier-mâché. Of Pegasus. Created, he will learn, by a local women's charitable organization and a local art society in an attempt to cheer up what he believes could certainly qualify – renovation or no renovation — as one of the most depressing places on the planet.

He enters the room and cautiously advances upon the winged-wonder. The room is busy, albeit not overcrowded, and nervously quiet. Parents glance up from their magazines or from their laps, where their fingers have been anxiously dancing, to witness the newcomer. There's a rather stern-looking woman behind a desk sipping a V-8 and shuffling papers in a thick file. And on the carpeted floor there are little people awaiting their turns with the doctors who practice their trade, who try to work miracles and magic in the inner sanctum, beyond two closed doors. Some kids fuss around their parent's ankles, others play. There are shelves across one back wall, stacked with second-hand toys, games, magazines, books; again, jazzing up the whole environment to make it seem to be anything other than what is truly is.

Judas sidles up to Pegasus. Touches the horse's head. A young girl, sitting on her mother's lap, curiously watches. Judas senses her eyes on him, but is captivated by the patchwork art. The creators have painted their creation a shiny silver and given the mythological steed a peaceful pose and a sly (hopeful) grin. There's a tugging at his pant leg. The little girl. Gazing up with bold, expressive eyes.

"His name is Peggy-sis. But he's not real. He's a myth."

She's bald, not even a shadow of hair on her pale head. Precocious – Three or four-years-old, he guesses — diminutive, sunny, smiling, and bald. And bald long enough, or at a young enough age, to be impervious to (or able to ignore) the awkward sidelong glances and the outright staring.

"It's so... nice..." Glancing from girl to horse, horse to girl. How familiar she looks.

"I'm here for cancer in my blood," she says. "What are you here for?"

He doesn't know what to say.

"I just took a wrong turn and saw the horse."

Satisfied, she climbs back up on her mother's lap. There are peculiar undercurrents in the room. Vague confusing sensations. He knows with a measure of certainty that he has never been here before. And yet... He glances at the girl's mother, seeking clues to unlock the mystery of the déjà vu that is toying with his head and giving him butterflies. The mother smiles, distractedly. He smiles back and nods, acknowledging the cutie on her lap. The cutie who is grinning ear to ear, devilishly. The cutie who...

Tugs her mother's short blonde hair.

The hair comes off in the girl's hand.

Remarkably, the mother seems unruffled, neither surprised nor terribly embarrassed or upset. Obviously, they've played this game before; perhaps not in public, but they've played. She takes the wig back from her daughter, shakes her head and whispers: "Angel, no." Then running a hand over her own shorn scalp says, in a quiet explanation: "Solidarity."

"Angel's just finished her last round of chemo. We're hoping for a good word today from her pediatrician and her oncologist that all tests are fine, that she's cancer-free and then... then we get on with our lives, right sweetie..." Her voice, the pull of an undertow; there's more emotion in that voice than words could possibly contain. He gets it. She's saying that she can't lose her Angel, that she could not live a moment in this world without her baby. Oh, how he gets it.

"Solidarity," he nods. Then adds: "I've got to go, my mother-in-law's up on eight. She's waiting…"

The mother is now staring. He's uncomfortable but stares back. She's processing, mentally thumbing through the pages of her life. He bends slightly to say goodbye to Angel. He wants to say, "good luck", but doesn't want the young girl to ever think she needs to rely on anything as fickle as luck just to survive.

"Goodbye, Angel."

"You should say goodbye to Peggy-sis, too."

He faces the horse: "Goodbye, Pegasus." Back toward the mother, "goodbye…"

"You," she says, smiling, recognition suddenly alight and dancing in her eyes: "You don't remember me, do you?" She laughs, the sweetest sound these walls have heard in ages. "Maybe it's the lack of hair." Sighs, "or the surplus of years. All that water under the bridge… But you really should still remember me, Storm Baker."

She could remind that she once saved him. But that was not what she initially recalled when she recognized him. "You," again she laughs, then lowers her voice to an amused whisper, "you used to spend your days on the floor, cowering under a table, under the pretense of needing to hold onto my legs for comfort, but really just… looking up my dress."

His face is on fire, reddening by deeper degrees with each moment that passes.

"Stealing peeks…"

My word.

Christian?

Matthews?

All grown up. No quirky dress. No patent-leather saddle shoes.

Christian Matthews.

He can't believe his eyes.

"Guilty," he pleads to an audience of intrigued onlookers, his embarrassment in full glorious bloom, but at once a generous smile spreading across his face. "Guilty as charged…"

Hearts Broken On The Monkey Bars

STORM BAKER, ODDBALL, outcast, Mark Haven's perpetual punching bag. Glasses, runt-skinny, nervous habits of frequent blinking, tearing up, and tugging his corduroys up ridiculously high with his elbows. Oh, and named Storm. *Storm*, for goodness' sake. Such an easy, obvious target.

Many of the boys who mindlessly harassed Storm on a daily basis — for entertainment, for sport, for the sheer intoxicating joy of forcing a weakling to eat paste — had long since physically outgrown their school grade, having experienced premature growth spurts, or having been held back once, twice. Three times in the case of the school's biggest bully, the hirsute Haven, a particularly dim and small-minded boy-man.

Haven's claims to fame were various, but all rooted in incongruity. Not the least impressive was his need to shave by grade seven — granted, less impressive when one does the math and realizes that, if not for past failures, he'd be in grade ten — or that he was able to legally drive to his own grade-eight graduation. Further, Haven possessed unnatural mastery over his bodily functions: this was a guy who could fart at will the opening bars of Tommy Roe's *Oh Sweet Pea* (although most notes fell predictably flat); this was a guy who was somehow, magically, able to turn his own urine orange by a mysterious, magical manipulation of his penis.

So impressive was this feat that whenever he had to pee, the washroom filled with the curious and, subsequently, the awed. Haven packed 'em in. Young boys gathering solemnly around the urinal, fully aware that just by coming so close to the Neanderthal they were potentially placing themselves in harm's way. Haven, with admirable showmanship – how he milked the moment – facing the urinal, unzipping, pulling his penis out and then, contorting his face as though in the full throes of a seizure, and dramatically twisting his manhood. Then, presto. Orange piss.

Storm Baker, six-years-old, meandering home from school, head in the clouds, unconsciously disobeying his mother's strict instructions not to dally and to come straight home — and disregarding the street-proofing rules she had so diligently, fearfully drilled into his head. The first, of course, being the buddy rule. He's alone; easy pickings for hyenas.

Mindlessly, he detours: a familiar shortcut between two duplexes, the walkway into the park, the new subdivision being constructed just beyond the park. An enclave, twenty-two new homes, a few finished, the others in various states of creation. How he ends up in one of those unfinished homes, he will be at a loss to say. Fascination? Curiosity? Stealthily peering this way and that to ensure he was not being watched, then tentatively entering. Standing frozen (heart beating up his chest) for a moment and listening to determine for certain there are no workers were inside. Then showing himself around.

The smell should have triggered alarms. Cigarette smoke, thick and damning, but he descended the stairs into the basement. Right on into the smoky cloud. Right on into the lair of hyenas who had difficulty articulating their feelings upon seeing the interloper.

"Fuck. Fuck. Ah, fuck. It's little Baker the little wanker. Fuck."

Storm could not fully comprehend what he was seeing through the smoke. Haven, some kid named Thompson, a bruiser named Buckner, and an older kid he'd never seen before. But why were their pants down around their thighs? Their penises liberated, all ugly, gross and stiff.

Was Haven teaching them the secret of the orange piss? Because Storm would love to know how that magic works.

"Grab him. Grab the little fuck."

They threw him on the floor. It was then that he noticed the magazines on the dusty, cold concrete. Spread open, glossy, revealing… body parts, spread open, glossy. One under his knee, another under-elbow, another under-face.

He wanted to scream but no sound came, not even a peep. Not as they busied themselves pulling up their underwear, pants, Haven's foot on the small of his back. Not even when they yanked his pants down. Not even when they pulled his underwear up so high it bunched and burned his backside. Not even when he heard his underwear ripping, or when they tossed the torn briefs across the room, all practically pissing themselves laughing.

He felt like crying, but his eyes were strangely dry. He swallowed and swallowed, pushing down on the lump working its way up his throat. His face, glasses awkwardly askew, was pressed against a glossy woman showing no sympathy whatsoever. Young Storm, so far from knowing a seductive look, from understanding the garter and stockings or why the crotch was cut out of her underpants, or even why she was holding up her breasts. Couldn't they support themselves? Then there was that dark, curly thatch. What in heck was that? His leaking spittle was on her belly, his snot on her neck.

And Haven's voice in his ears.

"Fuck it, we've got to kill him. He'll tell everybody, little shit.'

"What about his brother?" "Fuck, big athlete Mackey. I can take that twerp. Kill him too."

Storm didn't budge. Too afraid to move. Too scared to even breathe.

Someone expressed Lord of the Flies-like bloodlust and approval for Haven's plan. The other two, their nervous silence voicing timorous dissent.

Haven was bent over and picking Storm up by the scruff of the neck when Storm heard sounds he was not aware a person could actually hear: wood being wielded, cutting through air; a small bone breaking; Mark Haven screeching. Like an excitable young girl upon finding her pet hamster dead in its cage.

Haven unceremoniously dropped Storm and crashed to the floor beside him, writhing, cursing, clutching his wounded ankle. The remaining hyenas took shocked steps backward, putting some safe distance between themselves and Haven and Haven's assailant.

Storm pulled himself up off the floor and turned to see Christian, in a flowered dress, and those adorable shoes she always wore, but appearing decidedly, unmistakenly… un-Christian. Feverish, fearless. Looking possessed and capable of anything. Still slowly, menacingly waving back and forth that imposing piece of lumber.

"Pull your pants up, Bud. Let's get out of here."

"God, she broke my fucking ankle. Twat. Oh, god, shit, shit, fuck… Do something you fairy assholes, oh fuck, get her. Call an ambulance. Oh god, shit…" But they stood openly disobeying their fallen leader, whose power over them was surely incapacitated by degrees with the initial girlish screech.

Storm and Christian fled. Out of the house, the enclave, through the park until they were certain they were safely in the embrace of a highly populated subdivision. Then they walked home, slowly, hand-in-hand. Christian talked, a non-stop ramble. Storm listened. And she told him who she was, who she really was.

An only child whose young mother had long ago abandoned the sinking ship of her imprudent marriage.

"Before I can really remember. Now it's just me and my dad."

They reached her house.

"Are you okay?" she asked, touching his cheek.

Fine, he nodded.

"I'd better get in. I'm late and my dad worries."

"My mom, too."

"See you at school tomorrow, Storm Baker." She smiled, winsomely, touched his elbow, then turned on a heel.

"Hey," Storm called to her departing back, "you're amazing… you saved me… thanks."

She turned to him; again, that smile: "I'm glad I followed you." Then a demure admission: "I follow you a lot."

For the next two months they followed each other a lot. Everywhere. Then one day at the playground in the park she broke the news: her father had been transferred. They were moving out west to Calgary in two weeks.

Six-years-old and already a bitter taste of heartbreak, of looking down from atop the monkey bars and seeing his fragile heart on the ground, shattered, looking like gravel, a thousand-plus tiny pieces.

Nights At The Round Table

IF NOT A *photographer, I think she would have been a chef. Ali could cook. I know, I know,* anyone *can cook. Anyone can prosaically follow a recipe to the letter and create a meal that is satisfying, albeit (possibly) equal parts insipid, undistinguished, uninspired, and unchallenging to the palate.*

However, to fashion food into something superior, to make a meal that is memorable as Ali could do practically effortlessly... that takes passion. It takes creativity, a sense of culinary curiosity and a willingness to experiment. It takes confidence, savoir-faire, and intuition. Knowing, or sensing, *what ingredients can be triumphantly engaged. How much of* this *and when to lay off* that.

Ali often compared cooking with jazz: a riff here, a riff there, and then out of the chaos and clutter, notes rising, melding into something beautiful and, on occasion, transcendent; likewise, out of the chaos and clutter of a chef's kitchen... She spoke of the essential elements of taste and a cook's desire for balance in food and wine pairings. She would note the factors that can alter that dynamic, such as flavor and texture, and also note that wines should invariably be the dominant taste, slightly heavier than the food.

"Close your eyes," she instructed. *"Now sip this wine. Get a sense of its essence. Oak, peach, melon, fig, whatever. Got it? Now, take a small bite of prosciutto. Now, try the wine again. Well?"*

"Unbelievable. First sip, the wine was notably unspectacular. Second sip, after the prosciutto, transformed..."

"Logic, babe, logic. When it comes to wine and food, some flavor contrasts work well, and some flavor complements succeed. Just a matter of finding perfect pairings that form their own unique, harmonious, and heavenly tastes...."

Yes, she loved to cook. She said the process was therapeutic: the slow, savored creation of a simple Asian stir-fry, an anodyne to assuage the effects of

ANGELS IN THE ARCHITECTURE

a particularly trying day. Her kitchen savvy was certainly not inherited. Poor Janeen had difficulty toasting bread — "It's always getting stuck in there, stuck in the damn toaster!" — *or even heating canned soup.*

"Merde! It's all salty and thick and lumpy."

Did you add water?

"Why would I add water? I want* soup, *not tap water."*

Says right on the label, add one can of water.

"Oh, poof, who reads labels for goodness' sake? Honestly…"

Oh, poor Ali. How did you survive a childhood with this delinquent woman?

"I learned to cook for myself at a young age. Prior to that… peanut butter and jam."

Many an early Saturday morning spent down on Front Street at the historic St. Lawrence Market. Open for business by five a.m. for the traditional Farmer's Market, an institution that began on that very site in 1803 and that has survived societal transformation, building reconstructions, and even The Great Fire of 1849.

Ali, chatting up specialty vendors, half-heartedly haggling over prices and buying all the essentials for that evening. Fresh fruit and vegetables, meat and fish, and baked goods. No, she never baked. While professing a profound love for desserts, in particular chocolate desserts, she always said that the exact science of baking was best left to the bakers.

Back home. Ali in the kitchen for the remainder of the morning and into the afternoon while I was relegated first to cleaning up the apartment and later to "just staying out of the way." I was proficient at both. As fastidious as I was on a day-to-day basis, there was never any horrific catch-up clean to be done, a simple tidy, a dust cloth run here and there and a once-over the bathroom. Then it was onto the couch. Initially sitting and thumbing through the thick editions of the city's Saturday newspapers for column ideas, and then reclining and indiscriminatingly watching whatever sport was in season.

"Watching intently," Ali liked to say, "with eyes closed…" I would fervently deny snoozing through these telecasts, as she asserted. Although admittedly I occasionally found the need to rest my eyes, if only for a moment or two.

When she had advanced meal preparations as far as was practical, assuring that when the guests arrived, she would be able to spend more time with them and less time in the kitchen, she would ease me over on the couch and curl up beside me. Catlike, careful not to interrupt my intense viewing, and nodding off in what always seemed to be seconds.

ANDY JUNIPER

Late afternoon, awakened by the stove timer she'd set, then into the shower. Ali in front of the mirror, applying deft touches of makeup (none needed, little used), styling her hair and, honestly, never looking better. Irresistible. My arms around her waist; Ali glancing at her watch. Sometimes there was time, other occasions she rain-checked me. Soon after, the buzzer, the guests at the door, greetings, and appreciative gushings on the welcoming aromas emanating from the kitchen.

Nights at the round table in the kitchen/dining room. The conversation, the food, the wine, the conviviality and contentment of being surrounded by what Ali deemed "good flesh."

One night, however, one Saturday night near what I would come to think of as "the end", the regular glow around the table was dimmed through no fault of the chef. Frankly, Ali had outdone herself, doting on the details. All elements were in place. The mood and the meal. Good flesh surrounding us: guests with whom we were truly pleased to be spending time, relaxing over drinks, getting caught up, exchanging anecdotes, gossip, discussing current events, music, books, movies, sports, theater. And all anticipating the meal that Ali had informed would be ready in a matter of minutes.

I popped into the kitchen, grabbing a wine bottle off the counter to offer refills. She was at the stove, staring ahead at the backsplash tiles and mindlessly stirring a dish on an element; gorgeous in a black skirt and black blouse, protected by a long, frilly white apron. I stepped up behind her, playfully pecked at her neck.

"Wait... Are you crying?"

I was joking. Sure, there was a tear on her cheek. But I assumed she'd been affected by smoke or cut onions, not emotion.

"I told him seven. It's 8:30 and still no sign, not even a heads-up call. I know you don't like me talking about it, Storm, but I'm telling you and I wish you'd pull your head out of the sand for long enough to listen: we're losing him..."

Exaggerating. Much ado about nothing. He'd never been on time for anything in his life. Hell, my father used to kid that he'd be late for his own funeral. Losing him? What was that supposed to mean? It wasn't like her, had never been her style, ersatz drama being her mother's forte.

We finally started dinner without him, but it was awkward. Seven people around a table that seated eight. One seat empty, one place-setting undisturbed. Ali refused to remove it, glaring and noting: "Didn't you insist he'll show up? So, we're keeping his place."

ANGELS IN THE ARCHITECTURE

All that tempered the awkwardness was the fact that everyone at the table knew him. His tardiness failed to shock or even surprise. These were his friends, too. And one, Sally Hayes, was (rather obnoxiously) calling herself his date for the evening.

"I don't know what's going on in his life, but Perry-Dale and I saw him at The Blue Parrot the other night and both of us said afterwards that he's seemed particularly, I don't know, needy *and kind of desperate of late?*"

"*Detached...*"

"*Yes,*" more than one agreed. "*Detached...*"

"*Unhinged,*" I threw in. "*But then we are talking about Harland, right? And no one here is really suggesting the leopard might change its spots...*"

"*Not funny, Storm. Yes, we realize he's always been the waif, the tortured artist, but it's degrees we're talking about. He's taking this thing — or this thing has taken him — to whole new levels.*"

"*You're right,*" I jested, "*perhaps we should contemplate an intervention.*" *To my dismay, the idea wasn't summarily dismissed.*

"*Or an exorcism...*" *I was stared down into defeated silence.*

Around 9:30, the buzzer rang. I buzzed him up. Two minutes later he was off the elevator, and I was letting him in. Black eye. Disheveled. Stinking of booze and body odor.

"*You're drunk,*" I whispered, "*and unshowered, and late...*"

"*I never get the terms right,*" he smirked. "*Drinks equal drunk, drugs equal stoned. Fuck... I'm droned. Er, stunk...*"

Ali now at my side: "*Harland, my god, what happened to your eye?*"

"*Tussle. Disagreement. But you should see the other guy,*" he laughed, shrugged: "*Unmarked!*"

By then, everyone was greeting him, the return of the prodigal son. Patting his back, hugging him, tossing pity all over that eye, scurrying to get him ice for the slight swelling, a rum for his tremulous hand, and dessert. Dessert he'd never touch, although he was quite captivated by the rum.

"*Despite my... setback... I knew I had to get over here or you'd all be gossiping about me behind my back....*"

"*No, Harland, we'd never do that,*" *everyone chimed in. But he knew. It was obvious and maybe it was just me, but I think that knowledge somehow pleased him.*

I'm no drinker, but about that time I reached into the fridge for a cold, brown bottle of relief and drank it down. And when that soldier had fallen, I reached for another. Honestly, I may have downed one or two more bottles just in the time it took Sally, sitting behind Harland and staring at him rather adoringly, puppylike, to remove his worn New York Yankees baseball cap, run her fingers through the knots in his hair and, eventually, braid a few of the longer strands. That's right, fucking braids...

It was 2:30 in the morning when our guests finally departed, shooting sympathetic gazes Ali's way. Harland had been in the bathroom since 1:30, throwing up, the door open a crack so everyone could clearly hear and wince at his every violent hurl; he claimed to be too claustrophobic to endure it fully closed.

"Must be something I ate," he repeatedly confessed. Although consensus around the table was that no one had seen him eat much of anything in months. And Sally, anxious for everyone to know that there had been a night when she had actually seen her adored unclothed, talked of his boney chest, arms, thighs, the concave contours of his stomach.

"I swear," she said, "he's down to about ninety pounds soaking wet." Then, head tilted toward the table, voice lowered, voice choked. "The other night I confronted him. I asked him if he had some sort of death wish. I flat-out asked him if he was trying to kill himself."

"And?" Five breathless voices, practically in unison. "And..." Sally looked up, all wounded-doe eyes. "He was a bit drunk, and I couldn't really tell how serious he was and all, but he said: 'When you know the ending, why keep reading the book?'"

Silence. Heads shaking.

"I think we're losing him," Ali mumbled.

And there were nods of agreement.

What drama, I thought through a beery haze. How incredibly overwrought.

I put my throbbing head to bed. In the early morning, as the sun peeked into our room, my pained bladder rousted me. I slowly, steadily, gingerly navigated to the bathroom, the ache in my head sickeningly turning my stomach upside down, and there they were. Daisy and goddamn Jay. Zelda and fucking F. Scott. In the bathroom. Ali asleep sitting up, back against the tub, and Harland asleep in the fetal position, like a big baby, his head on her lap.

The Cutest Kimono Imaginable

Seven o'clock on a weeknight. She picked up on the first ring. Like she knew he was going to call. Like she was waiting by the phone. Like it was destiny calling. Or the Hazard would submit in his recurring role as devil's advocate, like her apartment was compact enough to ensure that she was never more than a ring or two removed from answering, unless absent or otherwise occupied.

His voice, tentative. Conversely, her greeting confident, cheerful and friendly, conveying open delight in (finally) hearing from him.

"Hey, I'm the guy from the park; unnecessary, she intuitively knew from the initial hello... "Storm, actually... No, seriously, not Norm. *Storm*."

Mutual self-conscious laughter.

"Storm what? "Storm Baker."

"Storm Baker from the *Times*?"

"Yeah, that Storm."

More laughter.

"I guess the odds are against there being more than one Storm Baker out there. Honestly, I'm a huge fan. I read you faithfully save for the past six weeks when my carrier mysteriously went missing and I haven't seen a single edition since... despite persistent calls to your paper. Unlike your circulation department, which continues to bill my credit card for papers I'm not getting, you're very good at what you do."

Buoyed, he dried a sweaty palm on his jeans and began describing the hoops through which he'd leaped just to find her. Sheepishly and selectively describing. Not wanting to exude naked desperation, or to come across as a woman's worst nightmare. You know, unbalanced, obsessive. In short, a stalker...

ANDY JUNIPER

He related how he frequently walked through High Park, a confession that fell considerably shy of the reality of his fixated vigil. For two-straight weeks he was there every day, rain or shine, for as much of the day as he could possibly afford and diminishing autumn daylight would allow. He even took a few floating days off. And when he was working, he did so from home to maximize the time he could spend running across Bloor Street and into the park, trolling up and down beaten paths, along less-traveled trails, scanning the hillsides and horizons for any sign of her. And when the improbability of his mission began to pessimistically cavort in his mind, he'd conjure up Penny Lane's voice: "Women are romantic enough, or foolish enough, to believe in lightening striking twice in the same place." And then he'd pick up the pace and his search.

"I know it sounds crazy, but I felt a connection with you. Please don't hang up. Don't think I'm nuts. I'm not. I swear, I'm not nuts…" An odd, unsolicited confession that made him sound, in his own mind… certifiable. Sweetly, she insisted that she did not think he was nuts. In fact, she'd felt that connection and she had been trolling, too — an admission that propelled him into a flushed, light-headed, palpitating orbit. In the park, as much as her life would allow. Searching for the man she knew only as Norm.

"We probably just missed each other. Although, it's a big park. And (gentle self-deprecating laughter) I'm a small girl."

"No, no, you're the perfect size (oh, man, probably too personal). Can we meet?"

"For sure. And maybe this time we won't be disrupted by a theft in progress…"

They talked for nearly three hours. About everything: pertinent particulars, life histories, hopes and fears and dreams, about life in general. Also, about nothing: five minutes somehow spent picking apart pistachio pudding. By the one-hour mark he was certain it was forever love. At two hours, he felt he knew her intimately, as though he could pluck her beautiful beating heart out of a lineup of a million lesser hearts. Closing in on their third hour of conversation, he was considering the logistics of an entire life spent like this — with her on the phone, with the rest of the world effectively shut out — when he heard a door slam on the other end of the line and a male voice grumbling invasively the background. She had said that she did not know her father and that she was an only child and was therefore brother-less.

ANGELS IN THE ARCHITECTURE

"The voice? Ah, he's a friend." Quickly followed-up by, "*Not* a boyfriend... More like boy who is a friend. Friend who happens to be boy. However, you'd describe this bony dufus hovering beside me. Listen, I guess I have to go, my extremely impatient and very rude *boy* friend keeps making obscene gestures and insisting he needs to use the phone."

They started making plans to meet. He ventured that he was available the next day.

"Tomorrow's perfect. Come over anytime, I'm home for the day." Having offered up her address, she added: "We'll find something to do. Or maybe I'll just sit you down and pick your brain a bit more. Oh, but listen: if you knock and there's no answer, let yourself in and make yourself at home, I'll just be in the bathroom developing film."

He was hanging up when she practically shouted: "Wait. You never said. How did you find me? How did you get my name and number? Did you do a Woodward and Bernstein and go all Watergate on me?"

In the woods, on the fourteenth day of his vigil, with hope and daylight waning, wearily walking on the road alongside the hill she'd rolled down much to the amusement of a young boy and the amazement of Storm. Striding up the hill. Entering the woods where she'd chased the reprobate who had so brazenly stolen her bag in broad daylight, and who would eventually abandon that bag, probably upon realizing that he could run forever and never divorce himself from his determined pursuer. Once again retracing their steps along the paths through the park. And there, amongst fallen leaves, apparently treaded upon by at least one muddy shoe, but nonetheless intact and ultimately readable, a business card.

Eclectic Images
Ali Reynolds
Freelance Photographer

Of course! The black bag was a camera bag. He'd been accompanied by enough photographers on enough assignments to be fairly certain. The business card invited, indeed urged: Call 416-537-2177.

So, he did. Not immediately, mind you. He walked home from the park, rolling her name over his tongue, across his lips. Ali. Reynolds. Ali Reynolds. Immediately loving the moniker, whispering it, absent-mindedly saying it aloud, pondering it, playing with it.

ANDY JUNIPER

His father would one day inform Ali that, although the spelling differed, her namesake (Allie Reynolds) was a stellar New York Yankees' pitcher in the 1940s and '50s, a flame-thrower who tossed two no-hitters. Not one, two! Pete would marvel, shaking his head. While Janeen would never produce a definitive answer as to how she came up with the name – a character's name in a fiction piece in *The New Yorker*, she hazily recollected – it was obvious to anyone who knew her that her daughter was not named after any baseball pitcher, stellar, flame-throwing, or otherwise.

He picked up the phone and promptly hung up several times in fits of abrupt gained/lost nerve. He stood in the bathroom, staring in the mirror and admonishing himself, then administering but another pep talk. He procrastinated: shaved, showered, brushed his teeth, flossed, cleaned the sink, took deep fortifying breaths, then a leap of faith, dialing her number.

And when he finally got off the phone, stretching and manipulating the telephone-cord-kink in the muscles of his neck, he was overcome. He believed he had found what it was he'd been seeking, what had been missing from his world. And the very next day he was going to see her again. Lovestruck. Euphoric. Slightly nauseous with excitement and anticipatory anxiety. He paced about the apartment in an effort to settle his stomach before eventually deciding he had better get to bed.

Sleep proved elusive. Snippets of their three-hour conversation replayed in his head. Butterflies flitted about in his belly. He stared at the ceiling. Chewed fingernails to the quick. Struggled to remain in bed, needlessly reminding himself: you need sleep. You're anxious and punch-drunk stupid when you don't get enough sleep. Get to sleep!

He once had an irascible editor who, with the approach of crucial deadlines, would scream at all those working the deadline: "Relax!" Naturally, this bellowed command only ratcheted up the newsroom's intensity and stress levels, further fraying already frazzled nerves and, of course, ensuring that no one had a prayer of passing through the deadline's threshold in a state even vaguely resembling calm.

Similarly, insisting to yourself that you must sleep only ensures a night of infernal sleeplessness. He surrendered at four a.m., rose and brewed a pot of strong coffee. He thought he'd read a book, wait out the night, wait for as long as he could tolerate before heading out to her apartment, but the book was soon set aside in favor of delicious daydreams of adventures with a woman he'd met but once, and briefly at that.

ANGELS IN THE ARCHITECTURE

He knew it was unsociably, idiotically early. But he felt confident that he would be able to adequately explain himself and — if not, he had greater confidence in her ability to empathize with his rather sad, pathetic and, he hoped, *endearing* explanation. That he simply could not wait any longer. Any more of a delay could result in him... he did not know what, but he knew it would not be pretty. And had she not clearly stated, come over any time?

She did not live far away, a few miles at most. Definitely within walking distance. Purposely delaying his arrival, he stopped twice en route. He aspired to the grand gesture: minimally he desired to arrive with expensive chocolates and a dozen red roses in hand, but no florist would be open at this hour and the best chocolate he could track down would be an Oh Henry bar. He entered a convenience store, lingering in the magazine section and finally buying an issue of *Life*. Not quite the grand gesture, but he hoped an appropriate and appreciated offering for a photographer. For another thirty minutes he loitered in a coffee shop where he ate a honey-glazed donut and drank a rank cup of coffee that anxiously descended over the two cups he'd had at home. Still, as he faced her door — breath labored, heart beating like an Allie Reynolds' fastball, high and hard in his chest – as he timidly knocked with his knuckles, it was... seven-forty-five a.m.

Good grief.

No answer. He hesitated, then knocked again, albeit even more faintly. And when he received no response, he contemplated aborting the mission, to return later at a more respectable hour. Then he recalled that she had said she was a habitual early riser — something they had in common — and that, if he knocked and received no response, to enter and make himself at home, that she would be busy in the bathroom-darkroom, coaxing photographs to life. Reluctantly, he palmed the handle and opened the door.

And stood at once facing his future and his past.

There on an area rug across the room, cross-legged and in their underwear: Ali Reynolds, side-by-side with his childhood friend, Harland Hazard. Deep in meditation. Although Harland would later reveal that by the time Storm interrupted the session, he had actually nodded off. As ungodly as the hour was. As hungover as he was...

Harland?

Storm?

Storm?

Ali...

Ali nimbly rising, covering up with a thigh-length, floral-print kimono. Harland content to meet and greet in his boxers.

Frenetic greetings, introductions, only slightly less confusing than the explanations that follow, that spill forth until all parties eventually believe they have at least a tenuous grasp on the uncertainty that is their current reality.

"Storm... it's (quick glance at her watch): 7:47."

"Sorry, sorry. Really sorry. Really..."

"Sorry?" Hazard interjects.

"Hold on. Storm? Harland? You two know each other?"

"Hold on is right. You mean the guy you've been blathering on about is Storm Baker from my wayward, woebegone childhood? My... brother in kiddie crime? God, the world is shrinking before my eyes."

"Ali, you know Harland... how? Ah, *how?*"

There is discomfiture in the way she glances at Harland and how he stares confrontationally — or, at least, challengingly — at her, and how they simultaneously turn and focus on him, still standing in the doorway, magazine in hand. A few days later, when Ali and Harland find themselves alone, Harland will question why she acted so out of character, why she substituted a lie of omission in favor of the truth. And she will respond that in that instant – when her dream-come-true asked how she and Harland had met – a strident warning bell sounded inside her head, and from that alert onward she simply followed her instincts, her heart, and the sentiments of a Joni Mitchell refrain she was fond of quoting: "There are things to confess that enrich the world, and things that need not be said..."

And so, the story went that Ali and Harland met on a photo shoot. She had been hired by *The Underground,* a popular indie music magazine, to capture the reluctant indie god on film. Seeing him at the shoot she apparently felt sorry for the poor waif who was looking like he hadn't eaten in a week or slept for that matter. That was about a year-and-a-half ago. These days she still takes him in from time to time, feeds him, nurtures him, you know, gets him back on his feet.

"Like a stray," Harland laughs. "Feeds me milk out of a little saucer and at night I lay by her feet, content, licking my paws, and purring."

They're all giggling, giddy. Storm has entered the room, dropped the magazine on a chair, and is bear-hugging his scrawny friend. There are reunion tears. Joy running down their cheeks. And Ali has become part of the hug — because the moment, she gushes, is too beautiful to not jump in and join. Fate, she will say, has kissed them all, 'plein sur la bouche.' That is, full on the mouth. And with some tongue, too, the Hazard will add.

Storm cannot possibly process all that has just happened, all he is feeling. His friend, with whom he had lost contact now for more than two years — after previous years of mostly unsatisfying, spotty communication — is now present in the flesh. The woman of his daydreams is here in the flesh – flesh modestly covered by the cutest kimono imaginable. Storm is dizzy, overcome with love, intoxicated by their first embrace. Even if it is communal, shared with his friend.

Worlds are colliding. And who, in such a rapturous moment, could concern himself with the assorted implications and consequences of such a collision? Who?

Her arm is around him. Her scent, a fragrant meadow in which he'd like to be lost. Her face, a beauty he would like to possess. And on that face, an expression of unadulterated, almost childlike bliss.

She is truly engaged in the moment. And she will disengage only for an instant to slap at Harland Hazard's wandering hand that has stealthily, adroitly inched up her kimono, furtively crept across her underwear, and lightly landed on her beautiful backside.

Not even the rain has such small hands

WE WERE MARRIED *at dawn. A cool, crisp, clear autumn dawn. Fiery sun easing up in the east, ghostly pale moon still wide awake in the west. Ankle-deep in dew, atop 'our hill' in High Park. Dressed in sneakers, jeans, a sweatshirt, and a windbreaker, with Ali in a white cotton peasant dress and a jean jacket gallantly proffered by Harland in defense of the morning chill. My love with a lone daisy tucked into her hair.* In the Hazard's words: "All very bohemian."

We were more inclined to describe it as "very casual." Which is what we desired. From our initial discussion about weddings, we were in perfect sync: casual and intimate. However, when we actually started planning in earnest, things quickly spiraled out of control, as things tend to do. Everyone began offering unsolicited opinions and before we knew it the logistics were causing insomnia and the wedding we were confronting was failing to resemble the wedding we wanted to embrace.

"This," Ali said, clearly vexed, "is turning into a circus." So, she took charge.

"It's our wedding, we'll do it our way." And we did...

We were married at dawn. Bonded, till death do us part, by the woman who, only one-month previous, had steam-cleaned the carpets in our apartment. Ali, being Ali, kindled a conversation with the carpet cleaner and then further connected over a cup of tea — discovering that Miriam was a recently ordained minister who was cleaning carpets to afford herself time to contemplate precisely where she wanted her ordination to lead; heart and head leaning toward missionary work in Africa.

"And do you not find it ironic," the Hazard queried, "given your twisted sexual proclivities, that you are to be married by a woman who wants to dedicate her life to... the missionary position?"

ANGELS IN THE ARCHITECTURE

I had proposed six months previous in our apartment on customary bended knee. Again, very casual. I'd returned from work on a Friday night after a particularly long week and a frustratingly long day to find her in a brief white teddy with white-lace ribbon in her hair and big furry slippers on her feet. Before I had the apartment door closed, she had her arms around me, babbling about how she'd missed me and kissing me with an urgency that abducted my breath. It wasn't a secret that I was soon to pop the question; we'd shopped together for the engagement and wedding rings. My plan, however, was to whisk her off to Niagara-on-the-Lake for a weekend: wine and dine her at the quaint Riverbend Inn and then propose following a romantic dinner. I don't know if it was the sexy teddy, the cute ribbon, those goofy slippers, that kiss, or my own impatience to get us moving on with the rest of our lives, but I excused myself, fetched the ring from my nightstand, returned and ambushed her. There were tears – her tears, my tears – as I laid out the truth: that I had never been as happy as I was at that moment, or the past six months for that matter, that I loved her more than words could express, and that I wanted us to be together forever.

We were married at dawn — nearly one year to the day after she rolled into my life — with God, Miriam, Janeen Reynolds, and a shivering and hungover Harland Hazard as our witnesses.

During the simple ceremony, we faced each other, locking hands and eyes, and Ali recited e.e. cummings' I carry your heart with me. *Concluding stanza:*

Here is the deepest secret nobody knows
(here is the root of the root and the bud of the bud
and the sky of the sky of a tree called life;
which grows higher than soul can hope or mind can hide)
and this is the wonder that's keeping the stars apart
I carry your heart (I carry it in my heart)…

Then, her hands still in mine, I recited cummings' classic Somewhere I have never traveled gladly beyond. *Concluding stanza:*

(I do not know what it is about you that closes and opens;
only something in me understands the voice of your eyes
is deeper than all roses)
nobody, not even the rain, has such small hands…

Janeen openly wept. Miriam, presiding, smiled radiantly throughout, later confessing to feeling truly blessed to have been asked to participate. Harland, solemn, silent Harland, surrendered a single sentence before handing us our respective rings: "You know that I love you both. But now, in the church of your hearts, I can plainly see that the choir is on fire."

ANDY JUNIPER

Before placing the ring on my finger, Ali said: "I want to die with this man loving me. Storm Baker, you are my heart, my soul, my earthly link to the sacred..."

Before placing the ring on her finger, I said: "I want to die with this woman loving me. Ali Reynolds, you my heart, my soul, my earthly link to the sacred..."

Janeen whispered, "My baby, my girl." And Miriam glowingly pronounced us husband and wife. We kissed. Both sun and moon blessing our union. Early birds sang. Two passing joggers, a young man and a young woman, stopped to applaud. The Hazard mumbled something about "tracking down" a little of the "hair of the damn dog" that bit him. And off in the distance, someone set light to the first fire of an autumn day.

Part Four

Loves Lost & Found

The Beach Girl's (Almost) Endless Summer| Or, Roots To The Sacred

I LOVED TO *hold her close and… inhale. Slowly, furtively, inhale, indulge. Her bare skin, every electric inch of her body, her intoxicating essence, from breeze-blown hair to sandy-soled feet. I loved to breathe her in before she had opportunity to step into the shower, or soak in the cottage's deep Jacuzzi tub, before soap and shampoo, body oils and lotions had eliminated all traces of her day — smelling the lingering scents of the sultry breezes that had caressed her, the sun that had colored her skin and hair, the persistently frigid waters of Lake Huron that had provided relief from the relentless, record-setting hammerlock of a heat wave gripping all of Southern Ontario.*

She would have made a perfect beach bum. Had her hair been blonde and her eyes blue, she would have been the consummate Californian femme, neo-poster girl for the Beach Boys' endless summer. Ali, hair sun-streaked, skin lightly bronzed, beautiful lips emboldened by daring red lipstick. She loved lake breezes. She loved staring out at the water and watching the waves. She worshiped the sun and could lounge under its focused glare all day long. She seemed so naturally at home barefoot on the beach, so relaxed and content, having temporarily relinquished our urban attire and our urban existence — the frenetic pace, the activity overload, the traffic and the imagined purpose in which most everyone in the city was invariably whisked up ("Like gum wrappers in a Bay Street breeze," she once analogized) – in favor of the briefest of bikinis, short-shorts, tiny t-shirts, a particularly playful polka-dot mini-dress, and the whole laid-back, outdoor, idyllic beach/cottage, sun/surf lifestyle.

While it took me a few days to shift gears and leave the city and work behind, her metamorphosis was admirably immediate and seamless: as we left sweltering the city limits, as we motored along the shimmering asphalt of

ANGELS IN THE ARCHITECTURE

the 401 highway heading west, her sandals came off – tossed unceremoniously into the back seat – and then those bare feet, toenails painted an endearing summery coral, were ceremoniously placed up on the dashboard. She meticulously rotated the radio dial until she found a station playing classic summer rock and she cranked the volume. And then she faced me with a smug smile and shouted above the music and the wind rushing in open windows, in a fabricated gloating voice: "We is on holidays." We was, we was on holidays.

We lunched in Stratford, the quaint town where the spirit and words of the Bard live on. We picnicked on a bench by the gardens, aromatic and in boastful full bloom, along the Avon River. We shared our food with bold, shameless ducks and geese that waddled right up to us and demanded handouts. By mid-afternoon we were in the charming port town of Goderich, buying groceries at the local IGA, an undersized, overstocked store bursting with perspiring and impatient tourists and locals cursing under their breath the lineups that would vanish come autumn. We stocked up on holiday essentials ("Not a holiday," my traveling companion asserted, "without a few trashy tabloid magazines and some Twizzlers.") Twenty minutes outside of Goderich and we were on the twisting gravel road that led to the Hazard's treed haven, arguably the most aesthetic of the three properties he owned.

And that's where we parked ourselves, taking advantage of Harland's largesse for two glorious sun-drenched weeks in the striking baby-blue cottage that sat postcard-perfect behind a cluster of soaring, sky-bound trees, atop a hill that overlooked a pristine stretch of beach on the seemingly endless sandy shores of Lake Huron.

As would be repeatedly driven home during my later convalescence in Florida, I'm not a bona fide beach person. I've never worshiped the sun. Sea breezes inflame my sinuses and tend to make my head ache. I'm clumsy with spare time, intolerant of the uncertainties inherent in unstructured moments. That said, at the Hazard's hideaway, even I was able to ease into the lazy rhythm of cottage life. The weather helped. It was too hot and humid for extended thought, let alone activity; even lazy beach walks or woodland explorations were more prudently undertaken in the early morning hours, or just before sunset.

The Hazard's cottage was equipped with air conditioning — the Hazard suffered neither fools nor the vagaries of Mother Nature gladly — but Ali insisted it not be switched on.

"Just open the windows and let the lake breezes in," she'd say. "There are always cooling breezes by the lake." There were definitely breezes, slow and dimwitted, but none that could be considered cooling. Truth be told, during *that particular stretch of weather, the breezes were cumbersome, pregnant with humidity, and about the best that they could manage was to grudgingly push the stifling air about.*

On the second day of holidays – after a first night spent tossing and turning on sheets of perspiration — I suggested that a little blast of air-conditioning at dusk might facilitate sleeping. Ali said, forget the manufactured chill. She had a plan to help us get a better night's sleep. That night and every night thereafter, after the sun sank spectacularly into the lake, she would coax me into the unappealing darkness, down the fifty-odd wooden stairs to the beach where, with further coaxing – the night air suddenly seemed cool on my sweaty, burned skin; the water black and uninviting – we were out of clothes and mad-dashing into the water.

The nightly ritual, meant to cool our body temperatures so we could sleep, ironically invigorated, jolted us back to life after a long day and a naturally somniferous happy hour and barbecued dinner, leaving sleep as the last thing on our minds. Those swims were heavenly.

Harland Hazard often opined that religion is forever getting in the way of God, but by 'religion' I think he meant 'organized religion' or 'the church.' Ali once informed that the word 'religion' is Latin, meaning roots to the sacred, to reconnect with the spiritual, with the realm of the spirit — not necessarily in a church or on your knees, but, rather, via the everyday. Laughter and joy, music and dance, literature and poetry, sex and love…

One night under a glorious full moon, we swam about, treading water, breast-stroking, until our bodies adjusted to the initial shock of the water. Then she came to me. I was standing far out into the lake on a sandbar. She brought her arms around my neck, her legs around my waist. And under the moonlight, under winking stars, we kissed slowly, softly. She kissed my face, my neck, nibbled on my ears, teased me with her tongue, with whispered enticements, endearments. And then she took me inside her and we bobbed in the gentle waves, connected to each other, to the universe around us, to a moment that was beautiful and timeless, spiritual and sacred, our only bonds to earthly flesh being our eventual shared shudder, and her sharp fingernails pressing into my shoulder.

****

Over the course of the holiday, we made love often, to the point where one afternoon when I suggested we forgo the beach in favor of the bed, she raised the white flag in surrender and declared that she was "all sexed-out." Conversely, over the course of the holiday, we made war but once — one fight, one blow-up, a molehill that Ali noted I managed to turn ("as only you can turn") into a mountain.

Ali, you see, had a young admirer on the beach. One morning early into our holiday as we were spreading towels out on the sand, a lanky, tanned teen paraded by, slouch-shouldered and smirking, in an embarrassingly brief black Speedo – embarrassing for me, I should say; for his part, he seemed altogether unembarrassed, quite cocksure in regard to the embracing brevity of that swimsuit. A shameless double-take of Ali's behind in her flowered bikini as she bent to straighten her towel and he continued his trek up the beach.

Later, when I'd headed back up to the cottage to break from the sun and fix sandwiches for lunch, he returned and struck up a conversation with Ali. Apparently, his name was Marco — I say 'apparently' because frankly I didn't trust anything that spilled out of his mouth. Apparently, he was spending the summer at his grandparent's cottage a mile or so up the beach from us. Apparently, his parents were warring over an affair his mother was having with her boss – an entire family of fucking clichés! — and wanted their preciousness out of the line of fire. Apparently, he was lonely and bored (oh please, break out the violins), missing his friends and his social life back in Toronto and finding beach life with well-intentioned grandparents to be excruciatingly dull — at least that's what Ali relayed when I asked why he insisted on parking himself beside her towel every day. Marco: as unwelcome as rain clouds, as persistent as the deer flies that persecuted us, unrelentingly buzzing about our heads whenever we ventured up into the surrounding woodlands.

During their first encounter, I watched them from the cottage through Harland's powerful binoculars: Ali and her admirer, amiably chatting. From his body language it was obvious that the young poseur was endeavoring to impress and she, my Ali, was rather girlishly… Flirting?

Of course, she denied it. Just as soon as she finished expressing disbelief that I had been 'spying' on them. Then she made the mistake of articulating an honest thought: "He's a beautiful boy. That full head of black curls, his smooth mocha skin… Maybe that's what I will call him," she teased, "Mocha Marco."

If I was with her when he showed up, Mocha Marco could barely contain his disappointment. He would greet her warmly, nod unsociably in my direction and then, for the remainder of his visit, ignore me completely. If Ali was reading, he wanted to know in detail about the book, themes, plot, author. If listening to music, he asked to sample her songs and discuss what he was hearing – perfectly natural, after all, that a teenage boy would rather wile away a summer day discussing Joni Mitchell with an older woman then, say, wander up the beach in search of under-attired and over-eager girls his own age. But there he was at her side, always appearing flatteringly attentive; always seemingly absorbed by everything she had to say. If Ali were applying sun lotion, he would be up off his towel with embarrassing alacrity, offering a helping hand for those hard-to-reach spots. Leaving me virtually alone with my fecund imagination, my thoughts, and insecurities.

When he would eventually leave, sometimes to just wade out into the waves where he could show off his swimming skills — captain of the provincial-champion high-school swim team; his rationale for the postage-stamp Speedo — or perform daredevil tricks on his windsurfer, we would talk about him. I would condescendingly refer to him as "that boy."

"Why does that boy *come here every day?" And with each day we repeated this conversation, Ali became increasingly annoyed.*

"It's a free beach. Anyone can come you know. Besides, he's a nice kid. You should try to be pleasant to him. He's going through a rough patch. And you know, Storm, he has a name. He's not just 'that boy', he's Marco. Marco. Say it, Mar-co."

"Mar-cock," I responded. "Sorry, Freudian slip. Honestly when he's around I don't know where to look..." And that's what I took to calling Speedo Boy, immaturely, I'll now readily admit: Ali's Mocha Marco, Marcock, or plain old Cock for short.

It was obvious to me that the kid was smitten with my wife. In love and in lust. I'd catch him staring at her. I'd note his stealthy glances at her breasts. His pleasure at seeing her stretching. His unabashed delight when she bent to snatch a skipping stone from the sand. Once I watched him watching her doing beach yoga, and I was concerned that he was going to require medical attention for eyestrain.

"He's innocent, an innocent boy," Ali would say, rising each day to his defense.

He was but a boy, only a few years beyond the cracking voice. But what did she know about boys that age? Innocence did not even enter the picture. Hell, I'd been a boy that age. I remembered how it was. I recalled with clarity that overcharged time in life when the male world is singular, when everything – every little thing – is about sex. When rock hard young men determinedly attempt to act upon the urgent urges and testosterone perpetually pulsating along their genetic wiring. Nothing between boys and girls, and certainly

ANGELS IN THE ARCHITECTURE

nothing between a boy in lust with a woman in a bikini could be construed as innocent.

"His attention is nothing, except perhaps flattering." Adding, "He's harmless. Lighten up."

"He wants you. And," I added in a feigned amused tone, "maybe you want him." Then, (again) maturely, I started to hum Mrs. Robinson.

"Oh, hilarious," she said. "Honestly, I can't believe you are jealous. He's seventeen, tops. Besides, my adult needs are being more than satisfied by the guy who brought me to the dance." Great sex, every day. Regardless… still, on the topic of Mar-cock, like an idiot intent on sabotage, I persisted. Apparently powerless to get out of my own head; powerless to stop myself.

Two days before we were to leave, he presented her with a bouquet of wildflowers he'd ever-so thoughtfully picked. She thought it was endearing and cute. I thought otherwise. Back up at the cottage, we fought. I said all the stupid things I could conjure up and then she uncharacteristically blew. Her vitriol bounced off my back as I spinelessly retreated, grabbing the car keys off the kitchen counter and bursting out the back door. Head clouded, adrenaline charging through my body, I pointed the Dart toward town, just to put some distance between us.

It was as I entered Goderich that I first noticed the clouds, thickening and bruise-colored, multiplying and ominously congregating over the lake. I flicked on the radio and caught the first of many repeated and urgent severe-storm warnings. I got out of the car in the town's charming, circular downtown, stopping only long enough to sprint into a flower shop to purchase a dozen long-stemmed red roses. Because even then I knew that I'd been dead wrong, that I'd been an idiot, that my jealousy was unfounded and untenable and blinding, the poison river that ran through my mind.

Back on the highway, the winds were increasing. The epic heat wave was finally breaking, right before my eyes. The windshield was dotted with plump raindrops. And thunder and the lightning were starting to roll in off the lake. We were in for it — it was obvious to me and to the birds that flew low, dive-bombing the ground and squawking in protest. I drove faster. The rain picked up. I took reckless chances on the wet curves. I passed a lumbering truck when prudence, and oncoming traffic, dictated I lay back. I was at once sweating and shivering. I was afraid. Afraid for my wife. For her intense, irrational fears, her personal hell, phobias of thunder, of lightning.

By the time I reached the cottage, the rain was horizontal, driven madly by the winds and reducing visibility to next to nil. Trees were bending *unnaturally, and the sky was one long angry rumble punctuated by jagged electric jolts of lightning. Out of the car, soaked before I had the door closed, I raced for the front door, roses nearly ripped from my hands.*

"Ali," I called, as I tore into the cottage. "Ali, where are you?"
I stopped dead at the sounds of rustling, muffled moans. But no response.
I thought of Marcock. My heart leapt into my throat.
I felt frozen, but panic propelled me, methodically, room to room.
I found her in the bedroom.
On the sandy, hardwood floor.
In the fetal position.
In her still-damp swimsuit.
Quivering. Whimpering. Tormented.
And, it goes without saying, alone.

Unspeakably vulnerable, tears and snot across her face, she was curiously hugging – clutching, for dear life, like a security blanket — one of Harland Hazard's old sweatshirts he'd left behind in a closet.

In the company of misery

JANEEN SLALOMING ON the slippery slope. Janeen in flux.

And Storm uncertain of what he'll discover each day upon his arrival at The Plaza Vista Retirement Community. Uncertain of *who* he'll find. Old Janeen. New Janeen. Good Janeen. Bad Janeen. Lucid Janeen. Confused (or Incoherent) Janeen. Happy Janeen (pills working). Sad Janeen (pills covertly discarded, spat up, thrown out). Stoic Janeen. Emotional Janeen. Pleasant Janeen. Paranoid Janeen. Independent Janeen ("Oh, poof!"). Needy Janeen. Reflective Janeen. Capricious Janeen, multiple moods compounded by multiple personalities.

Who will greet him, or fail to greet him, or confront him – smilingly, sullenly, silently, smolderingly? — with appreciation (a smile, a rare hug), or acrimony (accusations, invective, abuse)? With love or with hate? One day she forgives Judas for delivering her here. One day she has no recall of Judas or the nature of his crime. One day she is simply impervious to her circumstances. And one day she hurls whatever is handy at his head, prompting rage management, the forcible application of restraints, sedatives.

At no time can he forgive himself. He has broken one promise to her and as she deteriorates, he dreads the inevitable: that he is destined to break another. He should have known better; had life taught him nothing? Like a fool he had promised the impossible.

Death with dignity.

There is an ephemeral period during which she appears to enjoy being told stories and viewing pictures. The stories, or perhaps it is simply the soothing tone and calming cadence of the storyteller's voice, temporarily allay her agitation better than the ineffective Ativan she is forever being force-fed, along with assorted other medicinal jellybeans designed to make her feel better or at least make her more pliant and manageable for the Plaza staff. As for pictures, she takes pleasure in staring at the images, although occasionally a picture triggers an unexpected response: an incongruous spasm of laughter, an outburst of anger, an emotional meltdown.

To entertain her and help them both pass the time during his marathon visits, he brings in photo albums; there are no shortages of still-frames in his baggage. They sit in her room, or in the Plaza's comfortable common room, and he thumbs through the pictures in the album and narrates accompanying stories. Oftentimes she listens in childlike silence so rapt he is never certain whether she is wholly absorbed or entirely oblivious, disconnected and off in a private sanctuary somewhere inside her own head. Sometimes over the course of viewing an album, she interjects a comment that makes perfect sense in the context of his monologue and sometimes she contributes a glaring non sequitur. Occasionally her chin gently drops to her chest, and she succumbs to a narcoleptic-like urge for sleep.

To him, some of the photo albums prove particularly unsettling, arousing memories and flinging open doors and windows he's carefully boarded up. Likewise, the accompanying stories he recounts. And, of course, some stories must be edited or rewritten as they are being recounted in consideration of the audience. She is his mother-in-law, after all. And regardless of how confused and forgetful she might be on any particular day – pointing to a picture of her daughter cradling a kitten at an open-air bookstore in Santa Cruz, California, and heartbreakingly inquiring: who is the cutie-pie with the kitty? — she still need not be privy to intimate details of her daughter's married life.

"From our honeymoon," he says, one afternoon, opening a thick white album bursting with memories. "Two weeks in California, traveling down the coast. Honestly, the trip of a lifetime…

"Our plane tickets," he says, pointing to the souvenir-stubs Ali had taped to the inside cover of the album. "Air Canada, Flight #757. Departing Toronto at 9:20 a.m., arriving in San Francisco at 11:50 a.m. I always love that, flying across the continent and, by leap-frogging time zones, getting to California in two-and-a-half hours with most of the day still ahead of you. Granted, on the return, it's payback: according to these stubs, we left Los Angeles at 8:20 a.m. and arrived in Toronto at 3:45 in the afternoon, although I recall it was considerably later on account of a small earthquake in L.A., and the runway having to be examined for fissures before we could take-off. Regardless, minimally seven-and-a-half hours for a five-hour flight and the day shot."

He says: "We spent four nights at the Four Seasons Inn on Market Street, a hotel so out-of-our-league we could barely afford the expected tips. Fortunately, our room was comp, a wedding gift from the management of the *Times*, or I'd still be paying it off. Here's a picture of the Inn with a doorman standing out front. And here are a few shots inside our room – *room*, it was more like a suite. We spent our days touring the city and our nights, ah…. what an incredible city…"

But he thinks: We spent our nights taking in the nightlife and then returning early to our room and making love. Ali Reynolds Baker, my beautiful bride, knocking my ever-loving socks off. We were on our honeymoon, after all. And she was Ali…

And then he recalls: On their first night at the Inn, an urgent knock on the door. They are fresh out of a shared bath, steamed pink and perspiring and clad only in the plush white housecoats provided by the hotel. Reluctantly, he answers and in barges an imposing woman dressed in a standard hotel uniform and carrying a compact portable stereo like it's a football. Complimentary room service, she announces in a husky voice as she plugs in the boom box. Ali and Storm face her in stunned silence as the opening licks of Rod Stewart's *Hot Legs* fill the room and she begins determinedly removing her uniform. In an instant she has her jacket off and is pawing the buttons on her blouse and a few things are apparent. For starters, she's an Amazon. Six-feet-something atop her heels. Impressive shoulders, upstanding breasts. And… the beginnings of a five-o'clock shadow scuffing her jaw.

It's Ali, yanking the boom box cord from the socket, who kills the music and convinces her to stop, stand still for a minute and explain. Insisting: there has been some mistake! Amazon maintains there is no mistake. She was hired for this room on this night with explicit instructions to strip all the way down, no matter what. Confusion abounds for an instant and then at once Ali and Storm understand. Storm ushers Amazon to the door, handsomely tipping the guy (honorable 'exit' pay), while Ali thanks Amazon for coming over – like she's politely saying goodbye to company. And when the door closes, they crack. Laughing until they ache. Three-thousand miles away and he's still goofing on them. Flipping Harland, ever the lunatic.

More pictures. Explaining the significance of the photographs, not the least of which is that Ali is in them: photographers are never *in* pictures; they resist the lens like musicians resist the light of day. However, he had insisted she be equally represented in their honeymoon photos. Further, she was not allowed to critique any of his shots, even if one was grossly overexposed or appallingly off-center, or too prosaic or grainy, or even if his thumb roamed into the frame, she was sworn to just let it be…

Ali on a trolley car. Ali in front of Saks Fifth Avenue, holding her wallet upside down and open to illustrate that she did not possess the kind of coin or plastic needed to shop there. Ali with the Golden Gate Bridge behind her. Ali at Fisherman's Wharf, depositing change into the open guitar case of a dreadlocked busker covering Marley in a medley. Ali at Pier 39. Ali at Alcatraz, behind bars in a cell, tin cup in hand and her face an exaggerated, expressive plea for freedom.

"From San Francisco," he says, "we rented a car and headed south down Highway 1, the Pacific Coast Highway that's considered to be one of the most picturesque coastal highways in the world. It's a road with a storied history but when you see it you can't help but think it isn't long for this world. It appears in peril of being buried by landslides or of being swallowed by the Pacific.

"And, as you can see by all these pictures, we made slow progress down the coast because we kept stopping and jumping out to photograph all we were being awed by. Ali was beside herself, clicking pictures as fast as the camera would allow, even shooting on the move from inside the car. But, it's obvious why she was so enamored. Look at this: the ocean, the craggy cliffs and the highway hugging the contours of the landscape. We had to stop for a couple-hour breather at one point since Ali was carsick-green from the rollercoaster road, the hairpin turns and from shooting those photos out the window…

"But, you know, we would have stopped anyway. At every town, village, and hitching post along the way," he laughs, thumbing through the pages, "you know, given Ali's curiosity with everything.

"Santa Cruz – this picture was taken along the Santa Cruz Boardwalk. Monterey – no way could we pass Monterey without detouring to see Doc and Mac and the boys on Cannery Row and pay our respects to Steinbeck. Of course, we had to visit Carmel-by-the-Sea, the renowned artists' colony, just to see if Dirty Harry was home. The scenic region of Big Sur where the Santa Lucia Mountains jut abruptly out of the Pacific;

ANGELS IN THE ARCHITECTURE

the best of Ali's coastal pictures were taken in this area. San Luis Obispo, about halfway between San Francisco and Los Angeles. Santa Barbara with all its amazing Spanish architecture. This is a sunset shot of the Mission Santa Barbara, 'The Queen of the Missions.' And then on down to Long Beach…

"Sorry, Janeen, pardon?"

From her lips, a barely audible and wistful whisper.

"A curiosity, *her* curiosity… an insatiable thirst."

"Ali? Ali's curiosity? Insatiable?"

She nods and smiles, pretty and demure. He doesn't mean to stare, but it is a startling statement laced with clarity. Further, she looks so sweet today and civilized — civility not having been assured for some time now. Sitting attentively in a chair, in a fresh pair of silk pajamas, lipstick neatly applied and even her hair washed and styled that morning at the Plaza's beauty parlor. In recent weeks she's been alarmingly indiscriminate with the basics of hygiene, particularly reluctant for no rational reason to brush her teeth or allow anyone to help her brush. However, today her teeth are sparkling and her breath minty fresh. And today, a god-given bonus, there is even honeylike sunshine spilling into the Plaza. With that welcome sunshine, his photo album on his lap, his memories, with Pretty and Attentive Janeen, he is content and almost happy to be here.

Almost. While he is always glad he has come, it is always difficult, if not impossible, to be genuinely happy to be there. To be frank: no matter how the Plaza gussies it up, *here* is a bit of a hellhole. *Here* is the land of the living dead. Men and women with vacant eyes, in various stages of whispering, whimpering the so-called long goodbye, and their loved ones spilling blood and tears on the floors. That is, when they are not diligently flogging themselves senseless with grief and guilt.

Regardless of how clean the hallways are kept, how fresh and cheerful the paint is on the walls, how adorably the rooms are decorated and how homey the patchwork bedspreads appear on the beds, regardless of how quaintly the main-level pharmacy and café and beauty parlor and common room have been made to resemble the four corners of a small town's downtown core, circa 1950, or how admirably the odious smells are masked by air-fresheners, like all things in life, the Plaza Vista is what it is. When you enter through the front doors and are greeted by security, all senses stand on guard and detect the despair and utter hopelessness of the place and you innately understand that until security signs you back out, until you hop into your waiting getaway car and squeal from the parking lot, you are in the company of misery.

Nonetheless, Storm fully appreciates all the Plaza does in its persistent attempts to disguise. Before placing Janeen, he'd visited other less-concerned, less-fastidious long-care facilities that did not even bother with the mask and the results were unbearable and gut-wrenching. In mere minutes, the other residences – cold, cruel sanatoriums; leper colonies — sank him so deep into depression he could barely climb out. But he climbed. For Janeen's sake. Because he is all she has looking out for her.

Still, in touring those facilities he relearned a life lesson, one that is reinforced each visit — even in a facility as modern and polished as the Plaza Visa. Death with dignity? Oh, for god's sake man, just open your eyes, just ask yourself: if any of the "residents" in any of these "homes" could have foreseen their fate when still of sound mind, do you think there is a single soul who would not have put a bullet into their own head?

There is no dignity.

It's death.

And, like birth, it's messy.

Dignity is a human construct. And humility is the eye of the needle through which everyone must pass…

Her agitation abruptly springs to life. Body coiled, she points a tremulous finger at the last picture in the album. Ali at LAX. Soon to bid adieu to California and board for Toronto. On her face an ambiguous expression: pleased to be homeward bound? Saddened that their honeymoon adventure is over?

"She," Janeen says, sadly, "she looks so much like her father…"

Storm is stunned.

"Ali's father, Janeen? You've never mentioned him before. Ever. Who…" he begins to question, but she cuts him off with a wave of her hand.

The tension seeps from her body. She slumps back on the couch, retreating and appearing fatigued and aged beyond her years. She points to the door.

"You must go now, Harland, I'm performing in one hour and I need to collect my thoughts and don my stage face."

His head spins in disbelief.

"Janeen, I'm Storm…."

"Jesus. Christ. Go!" she commands.

Not Forgiven, or Forgotten

HARLAND NEVER STRAYS far from Storm's thoughts, is never completely out of mind. Ambivalent thoughts that run the gamut, run the gauntlet — admiration to disapproval, beholden to affronted, love to hate, from attempting to convince himself that he really doesn't care (screw you, Harland Hazard) to being painfully aware that he is incapable of not caring. How else to explain the abrupt onset of a migraine aura and the nauseating acid burn in his stomach whenever he considers his boyhood friend's fate. Wondering: how does someone simply fall off the face of the earth? No one in their circle has heard a word since Ali's death. He knows, he's asked.

Fearing the worst: Harland has followed her. Then attempting to calm himself with the thought that this isn't the first time he's disappeared. In fact, he has a long history of falling off the face of the earth.

Where are you, Harland, you bastard? You don't forget your blood brother. You don't stop caring even if you feel the jagged blade of betrayal in your back. You don't get him out from under your skin. You certainly don't extract his blood from your blood.

He remembers with fondness the spring day when Harland blew into his life. The new kid, the American from Minnesota. Harland easing on up the Bakers' driveway, hands crammed in his pant pockets, hair long and unruly, that trademark impish grin on his face. Harland introducing himself. Even at age ten he was a precocious magnet for people of all ages with his laid-back manner and easy charm and that coolly delivered, wry, self-deprecating humor.

"My word, he's a little Johnny Carson," an amused Pete observed.

And when his new neighbor befriended him and eventually effectively adopted his family as his own, Storm's social problems disappeared.

Overnight, the kid who was once every bully's punching bag was suddenly off-limits, safe and untouchable — immunity granted via association with the charmer everyone was anxious to befriend. Even that moron Mark Haven backed off. Granted, Haven was never quite as antagonistic (or mobile) after his bone-crushing humiliation at the hands of young Christian Matthews.

Storm and Harland, attached at the hip.

Storm could effortlessly misplace entire hours adrift in memories and contemplation of the 'good old days', the times they shared, the camaraderie that transcended even the awkward and otherwise unbearable moments of adolescence.

He ruminates on the concerns that Ali had voiced near the end, concerns shared by all their friends, by all but Storm: that Harland was no longer simply being Harland. That he was inching toward an encroaching darkness. His disappearance suggests perhaps Ali was more right than wrong. Storm considers that perhaps there were cries for help that he chose not to hear or was too preoccupied to hear. Or maybe over the course of their friendship he had just heard the wolf cry one too many times. And maybe, he considers, maybe this time the Hazard truly needed help in saving himself from himself. Guilt resides in Storm's anxious guts. However, every time that guilt begins its languid ascension up the walls of his stomach and into his throat, it is hammered back down by the brute force of an image…

Storm's thoughts of Harland tend to begin and end in the same place. In High Park on the morning of the day Ali died. The image — the image that won't die, that not even time will kill, that remains too clear, too distinct, too definitive despite its age and the thick and eerie autumn mist that surrounds it.

Storm is halfway done his constitutional walk in the park when he sees them through the morning mist, in the parking lot off in the distance. And the sight stops him dead in his tracks. Legs shaky and weak, suddenly unable to support further movement and barely supporting his weight. His heart stutters, but still he watches, transfixed, unable to avert his eyes from his worst nightmare. Harland Hazard, familiar slouched shoulders, windbreaker riding high against the godless morning damp chill. And with him, Ali. Yes, it's her, he's certain. He knows her from any distance.

They are conversing, deep, intense — oddly enough, Ali with her back to Harland. There are times when replaying this scene where he wishes

ANGELS IN THE ARCHITECTURE

he possessed the Hazard's innate skepticism, that his mind was not so fertile where his wife is concerned, that he could question himself. How could you possibly discern from that distance, through that thick mist, that it was definitively her and that they were talking – let alone engaged in conversation, *deep and intense*? Fuck off. It was. They were. And how could you discern that he was weeping as he distraughtly grabbed her by the shoulder turned her toward him and leaned into her like a spooked child seeking sanctuary in the flesh of a parent? Fuck off. He knows what he knows, and he saw what he saw. And for the record: his wife, who sheltered all strays, charitably accepted him in her arms and embraced him. And she was weeping, too.

Some days he is certain she returned his kiss. Some days he thinks she did not. Eventually, she *did* push him away, and eventually she *did* run. A sprint across the parking lot to her car, climbing in and squealing off. And Harland stood there, body and hopes deflated, staring defeatedly at the parking lot pavement, trembling, until she had retreated from sight. His gaze then took in the horizon. Silently asking for forgiveness, before he got into his Celica and drove away. Slowly, slinking, skulking, like he'd never been behind the wheel of a car.

Why, Harland, why?

He may never know. There was a period when he thought for sure that he would never know. Who could possibly enlighten him with both Ali and Harland gone?

Then the onset of the telephone calls. Always in the dead of night. Slashing the silence, wrenching him from sleep. Sitting up in a cold sweat, surrounded by equally icy darkness, his worst fears erupting in his head – an accident, an emergency, a death — his heart and head racing out of control.

"Hello…"

No reply. Never a reply. Dead air for a minute or two until… click. He's fairly certain. Blood brothers know. So, he takes to calming himself by addressing the silence and filling the dead air.

"Harland, I know it's you. We need to talk. I need to know. I saw you in the park and I know you know I saw you. Harland? Before you got into your car, you stared right at me…"

No response. Nothing.

Maybe he is dreaming – the ringing had indeed roused him from a very deep sleep – but he believes he hears the Beach Boys faintly harmonizing in the background… Sloop John B.

ANDY JUNIPER

Well, I feel so broke up, I wanna go home...
Maybe he reads too much into it, but his heart interprets it as a plea.
"Harland... You can come home." All is not forgiven, or forgotten, but... "We can talk. Harland..."
Click.

****

For his part, he's been preoccupied. Thinking until it hurts. Thinking from his perch atop a rattan barstool in The Sunset Grill outside of Long Beach, California. Mostly he contemplates suicide, although he believes the act would be, to a degree, redundant: that an integral part of him has already died. He contemplates pills. Considers a rope knotted like a tie around his neck. About running a razor across the wan underside of his wrists. However, for the most part he remains preoccupied with the Pacific as a means to an end. He is preoccupied with the ocean's mournful voice and the soothing rhythm of its waves slapping the shore. Waves he'd like to run out and embrace.

In sober moments – granted, few and far between — he's been conducting research. Studying rogue waves. He knows that extreme rogue waves can capsize ships, occasionally even sink a supertanker while smaller rogues are a regular occurrence along the coast. People on shore, on dry land, on a jetty or rock, believing they are watching the waves from a safe distance, suddenly ambushed and dragged into the depths of a body of water that is both unpredictable and unforgiving. Experts advise don't ever turn your back on the ocean. Rogue waves, he read with interest, strike in any kind of weather at any time of day in any coastal area. That said, there are stretches along the rugged northern California coastline where these waves are as common as surfers to the south. He considers that maybe he should head north and try to catch one of those waves. Rogue Roulette. Let the game decide his fate.

And, yeah, there are nights after B.J. has closed the Grill and escorted him out the front door that he meanders home, pours himself a heavy-handed superfluous nightcap, strips out of his clothes, turns on the stereo, cloaks himself in the wistful genius of Brian Wilson and is overtaken by rogue waves of sadness, homesickness, hopelessness and a need not necessarily to converse, but to simply hear a brother's voice.

Biking In The Beaches

THE TELEPHONE RINGS. The timing is perfect. It's mid-afternoon, moving day. God how he loathes moving days. He knows cup-half-full personalities view moving as an adventure, the beginning of a fresh phase. Lately he finds the cup-half-full people and their unfounded optimism particularly tiresome, and he views moving as something else altogether – exhausting and depressing, another of life's doors being slammed shut with finality. Which in part explains why he welcomes the ringing diversion. Granted, about now he would welcome anything that offers reprieve from the daunting task of unpacking.

He has finally checked-out of the Harbour Castle. Settling the bill for his extended stay that very morning, graciously thanking staff at the front desk for everything, and leaving a forwarding address and telephone number. How long, he'd wondered can a man continue to reside in a hotel? By definition hotel life is for those seeking temporary accommodation while traveling on holidays or business. Hotel life is for the rich and restless and the terminally transient. In his mind he came to equate moving out of the hotel with moving on with his life. Wanting to believe that he is indeed moving on, he invested his savings — and Ali's considerable life-insurance payout — and he bought a house. Outright. Sans mortgage in a red-hot housing market.

Moving on. Despite compelling evidence to the contrary. No strategies in place to resurrect his professional life. Social life still dormant. Taking little joy in any given moment. Nary a plan beyond driving north each day to the Plaza Vista to visit Janeen.

Despite an obvious lack of all the usual enthusiasm for the home-purchasing process – apathy that drove Jane, his particularly cheerful realtor, absolutely twitchy – he nonetheless hit the jackpot. In a whirlwind twenty-four-hour period that made his head spin, Jane found the perfect house. Storm viewed it for all of fifteen minutes, loved what he saw, got entangled in a bidding war, and won. And, for sure, it's a beauty. A two-story, three-bedroom house on a mature, treed lot on a likewise mature street in the distinctive district known as the Beaches, in the city's east end, just a stone's throw from the renowned boardwalk and Lake Ontario. The charming old house has been recently renovated – finished basement, upgraded kitchen, swimming pool sunk into the backyard — and is wanting for nothing.

"Even a fireplace in the master bedroom for… romantic, intimate evenings," Jane cooed.

"I'll bet that will get a lot of use," he cooed right back.

"Just our luck," she'd said, up front, "the couple living here is splitting and in the midst of an ugly and acrimonious divorce."

Which prompted his reply: "I have nothing in my life, if not luck." Which later got him wondering when he had become so unbecomingly snide and sarcastic, so Hazard-ish, only with less humor and more of an unsavory edge?

The movers miraculously managed to unload everything by noon. What he had with him at the hotel and what he and Paris had long-ago stashed in storage. However, for some inexplicable reason, when Storm stepped out to finalize paperwork at his lawyer's office, they haphazardly dumped most of it in the kitchen. The one room to which access is essential. It's discouraging to say the least, seeing boxes stacked near to the ceiling. Boxes that will have to be unpacked, their contents cleaned and organized and put away should he need anything as basic as a glass of water from the sink, or an apple from the refrigerator. That is, once he can clear a path to the fridge to actually stock it with apples.

There's a strident ringing. He locates his newly connected telephone under a pile of crumpled packing paper.

"Hello."

"Do you ride a bike?"

"Not particularly well, but, yes, I can ride a bike. I'm not ready for the Tour de France, but… Wait, we're talking the pedal kind, not the motor kind, right?"

"Absolutely. And do you own one?"

"Oh yeah. Ninety-nine-buck special. A real hog."

He hasn't seen her since their fortuitous reunion at the hospital. They had hurriedly exchanged telephone numbers as her daughter was being summoned by the receptionist and ushered in past Pegasus to see her doctor. Ever since, she has been on his mind, a welcoming and buoying beam of thought. He's considered calling her, but something/everything always reins him in, and life keeps intervening.

"It's good to hear your voice," he says. "Really, really good…"

"You could have heard it sooner, you know. I thought you might call. Get caught up. Invite me out for dinner."

"That would have been so very forward of me," he jokes. He hadn't called, of course, because to call would have meant overcoming both his paralysis in this area and any notions he harbors that such a call could be conceived, at least in his own mind, as unfaithfulness to his past. He takes a reassuring breath and plunges in: "You know, in this day and age, a woman can call a man. That's right, you could have called me."

He expects a laugh, or retort, but hears only clumsy silence. Then a snivel, stifled but evident. Sorrow streams across the connection and his mind leaps to worst-possible conclusions.

"Christian, are you okay?" Panicked. "Is it Angel? Is she okay?"

"Angel's okay, Storm. Really. Terrific and, thank God, cancer-free. And I'm okay. Sort of. It's just, well, I could really use a friend right about now, an ear to bend, shoulder to cry on and all that. And I thought of you." There's a pause as she steadies herself. "My… my divorce is complete, final, as of about twenty minutes ago. My lawyer, Mr. Good News Himself, called. Hey, I'm a free woman. Free of that prick. Free." She is crying freely now. She endeavors to pull herself together.

"I'm sorry, you've got enough going on in your life without me balling in your ear. It's just, just that I loved that bastard, and he *is* the father of my daughter, and he just walked out on us and right on into a new life without so much as glancing back. Even though she was sick. How wrong was I about him? Think of it: what kind of a person abandons…" She lets the sentence trail off in the stark light of its own obviousness.

"And it hurt. And it still hurts, even though now I swear I wouldn't cross the street to see him, unless it was to run him over, and I wouldn't take him back no matter what…" A muffled sob. She excuses herself. He hears nose blowing, unabashed honking, before she returns to the phone.

"Sorry… He screwed around on me on so many levels. He was ten years older than me. He was amazing, attentive, loving and he used every bit of his considerable persuasive powers to bowl me over. I was a nurse, a young, harried nurse working too many hours in an understaffed hospital.

We met and within months he convinced me to quit my job, marry him, have Angel, and become a stay-at-home mom. A few weeks – *weeks* – after she was born, I knew he was having an affair, one of many. I just knew, not that he ever did much to hide them. Oh, and icing on the cake: just last month the smug bastard called to gloat. He and his new eighteen-year-old, very-pregnant secretary are moving to Australia. Pity the poor girl. Pity their baby. Pity the unsuspecting Aussies. I'll bet he won't even find time to drop by and say goodbye to his daughter. Oh, listen to me prattling on…"

He doesn't know what to say. Her hurt has his guts knotted in empathy and her anger has him wanting to track down and kneecap the worthless philandering prick she called her husband. But he honestly can't think of a thing to say. Finally, he blurts: "And biking is the answer? Biking, with me biking badly. This will pull you through, get you over the infidelity, the abandonment, the divorce, the cradle-robbing hubby…"

She laughs through her tears and the thickness in her throat.

"Biking is the key," she agrees, brightening. "It's just, Angel's at a friend's place for a playdate until eight tonight. I'm alone in this, The House That Dickhead Bought, with poison thoughts in my head and the walls closing in. For sanity's sake, I thought of companionship and exercise almost simultaneously, right after I considered consuming copious amounts of red wine which I don't think would be wise right now."

"Not wise at all. Biking with a companion would be far healthier. *Followed*, perhaps, by copious amounts of red wine…"

She informs that she got his new number from the Harbour Castle and asks about his new digs. He talks about the travails of moving day and about his home in the Beaches, and how wonderful the prospect is of postponing the unpacking in favor of a little fresh air and exercise.

"Why, in the grand scheme of our sprawling metropolis, we're practically neighbors," she gushes. "My bike is already strapped onto the bike-rack. I can be at your new house in thirty-minutes, God and gridlock willing, and we can bike on the boardwalk. Don your spandex, Storm Baker. We're going biking, blow out all my anger and grief."

"Spandex?"

"That was a joke. Spandex was a joke."

"Oh, thank god."

"Geez, now I've got a mental image in my head that will haunt me to my death…"

"You and me both…"

A Little Left Of The Dial

CONTRARY TO POPULAR *wisdom, I don't believe that everyone has skeletons in their closets. Real life is rarely that theatrical. People are rarely that dramatic. And more often than not, those who lay claim to the extreme and the exotic are eventually exposed as liars, high-school drama queens, or con artists selling snake oil.*

In this day and age, in our comparatively civilized corner of the world, life seldom comes down to the kill. Rather, closets become cluttered with the insignificant and the irrelevant, the personally memorable but otherwise mundane: in one corner of the closet, for instance, reside gravelly bits of your own heart and the faint melody of James Taylor's Fire and Rain, *borrowed from your sister's record collection and obsessively spun after your heart was shattered in the vice of an adolescent crush (eventual epiphany: so,* that's *why it's called a crush). Okay, I'll grant that if you are an exception – if you've lived life at all on the so-called edge – then maybe, just maybe, your closet contains the odd skeletal fragment, a random bone or two.*

I acknowledge, and endeavor to accept, that in every relationship there may well be secrets. Secrets that stealthily ride in on the backs of a man or a woman eager to locate the missing pieces of the jigsaw puzzles that are their lives, keen to couple and understandably reluctant to open the love match by lobbing a lurid confession over the net, disclosures the likes of those witnessed daily in shameless detail on syndicated television talk shows or soap operas where skeletons overpopulate every character's closet.

Am I being fanciful, romantic (I'm certain the Hazard would say 'naïve') in saying I believe that Ali entered my life cleanly? No skeletons, no secrets? I grew to know her so intimately — momentous moments in her life and, likewise, her everyday everythings. And I wanted to believe that Ali Reynolds was all admirable openness and gushing, brutal honesty.

Pessimists would be disinclined to concede the possibility of two people sans secrets coming together. And even then, I can just hear them submitting: what is to prohibit the future, furtive pocketing of secrets? Cynics are quick to point out that people are imperfect, that most are inherently secretive and, ultimately, not to be trusted — a Darwinian survival trait, according to you-know-who. At the very least: small deceits, insignificant indiscretions occur, and what perhaps should be dragged out into the light remains cowering in the dark. Personal secrets. Then there are the assorted secrets that couples endeavor to keep from the world, or not...

I can divulge a personal secret: two weeks before she died, I had a dream so vivid that upon waking I could only believe it was real; so vivid I carried it with me like an unassailable truth until it finally faded with her death and the onslaught of more pressing thoughts — and more unassailable truths. For the record: we were not going through a rough patch, there was no marital discord to speak of, so don't even go there in your tiresome psycho-babbling analysis of what follows.

The dream:

I return home unexpectedly early from work and hear noises emanating from our bedroom. You know what's coming. I know what's coming, the foreshadowing in my dreams is about as subtle as the costumes in a gay pride parade. I walk the doomed slow-motion walk of dreams toward the sounds. I open the bedroom door, peer in, and see my wife, facing me and wearing nothing beyond an expression of ecstasy on her face, astride a similarly clad male. They are having at it. Like rabbits. On oysters. So vivid is this dream, from the doorway I smell her pungent sex, I see the perspiration beads across her forehead, and I see the pendant Pegasus bouncing between her breasts, just as clearly as a feel my world being blown apart. She abruptly stops her wild bucking, opens her eyes and looks over at me, nonchalantly; he twists his head my way, too, smirking prick. My wife and my best friend.

The dream disconnects. Once reconnected, he is gone wherever — maybe I've killed the bastard — and she is collapsed on the bed, her nakedness wrapped like a mummy in bed sheets. I am going off on her, the cuckold exploding in fury, all barrels of my pain blazing. Her back is to me, but as I continue my rant, she slowly rolls over and interrupts, in exasperation: "I've had a long afternoon of wine and sex, you've got to leave me alone..."

ANGELS IN THE ARCHITECTURE

Like my confronting her is the problem.
For the next two weeks I sleep on a bed of nails.
After that, of course, I don't sleep much at all.

And since I'm playing True Confessions, I guess I can tell you Ali's little secret. That became our little secret...

The south wall of our apartment was continuous glass — two large windowpanes with thick sliding glass doors to the balcony between them. We had blinds — inexpensive, plastic, standard-issue verticals — but like the majority of our neighbors, we rarely closed them save, in our case, on mornings when the sun threatened to transform our apartment into a hothouse suitable only for the most temperamental orchid. Open-blind policy. Indigenous apartment-dwelling entertainment. Life in full view.

You could stay up through any night and witness humming humanity illuminated by lamplight: watch the action as midnight quickly approached and slowly departed and life drifted off to sleep. Watch people around dinner tables, at personal computers, on exercise equipment, people breaking the spines of books, people stationed in front of television sets; people watching the Blue Jays or Leafs or Argos in season, the spiritedness and animation of their actions revealing the level of their inebriation and the fortunes of their beloved boys in blue. People fighting, people loving, people winding down after a long day, people gearing up for a long night, people on the treadmill of simply existing and, occasionally, for color and flavor so associated with city life, exhibitionists putting on an exhibition....

Late one night shortly after we were married: relaxing on the couch by that very wall of windows when she enters the room. Bare feet, tight blue jeans, thin white T-shirt and, it's apparent, no bra. She stands before me, unbuttons the jeans, unzips, offering a teasing glimpse of white undies. She turns her back, slips thumbs into the waistband of the jeans and slowly, sensually peels her denim skin....

It's part of living in a metropolis, in sky-bound apartment complexes, feeling anonymous enough to trash inhibitions, to walk around in your underwear, to scratch places you wouldn't normally scratch in public, to make love or war, secure in the knowledge that the odds are stacked in your favor. Not against being observed — of course someone's going to see you — but of ever actually encountering the person who witnessed your moments of surrendered inhibitions, or dignity... And even if such a potentially embarrassing encounter *followed, the odds are highly favorable that the two parties meeting up would not recognize each other up close, let alone know each other. Under the covers of sweet anonymity.*

"Ahhh, babe, we're not alone. Blinds are open." And a quarter moon is watching.

She smiles, a flirty, truth-or-dare-and-I've picked-dare smile, reminds of the live wires witnessed one week previous, in Building Two, sixth floor up — dressed like Leatherman of The Village People and acting like feature performers in City TV's Blue Movies — then she suggests you stand. And as you stand, she bends over, and reaches back for your hand...

Ali liked to be spanked. As the world watched. I know, I know, in the cosmopolitan cityscape such a fetish barely registers on the radar of kinky. And in a world of sexual deviancy, of dog leashes hitched to clitoral rings and potentially lethal asphyxiation sex, this behavior was blushingly tame, or what Harland Hazard called "only slightly left of the dial".

Yes, I confessed to the Hazard. I had to tell someone. And his reaction, delivered surprisingly sans his usual ironic grin – suggesting that my wife on some "subconscious level" thought she was a "bad girl" who needed to be punished – made me wish I'd never opened my big mouth. And made me want to cuff Mr. Pseudo Freud. "Not crazy-wild behavior," he added, "not Zeppelin with the mud shark, by any means. Not really even out there..."

For me, it was out there. Nearly off the dial. When she initially guided my hand, smacked it against the tight underwear that was stretched across her backside, I was a flushed fluster of rustic roots and relatively conservative upbringing, wondering from where this desire had sprung and worrying about who may be watching. That she had her mother's free-bird exhibitionist blood coursing through her veins should not have surprised me; had we not made love in, among other venues, the dunes on the beach at Hilton Head, South Carolina, in the sensual shadows of dusk, and the purposely stalled elevator of the Hyatt Hotel in downtown Montreal at four a.m.? That she was uninhibited, resourceful, and creative when it came to sex was obvious to me from the first time we made love.

Still, somehow, this was different. Which is not to imply that I did not surprise myself and, well, enjoy...

For clarification, they were tender spanks, not meant to bruise, wound, or inflict pain. Nothing sadomasochistic, a sensual sting at most. She would take my hand against her backside until tears dampened her face — tears she could *never satisfactorily explain (and demanded I ignore), although she once said they were "Good cleansing tears. Not bad tears."*

Eventually a purr would rise from the back of her throat. Goosebumps would ride her soft flesh. Back would arch, muscles tighten, and our secret would dissolve for the night in a liquid shudder.

Revelations, The Beauty, The Body

"You know," she says, absentmindedly twirling grey hair around her fingers. "He visited you in the hospital."

"What? Who?"

"*You*," she says, emphatically. "In Florida. He called me before he left California. Said he was going to rescue you from some hurricane. A regular Errol Flynn. He arrived late, though. After-the-fact. Typical. But he still checked up on you in the hospital. Give him credit. It wasn't easy for him to even be in Florida, what with so many memories tied up there." She pauses. They lock eyes. "It's where they met."

There is something at once innocent and ominous in those eyes.

"They knew each other for a long time before you came along, you know. Harland and Ali, they did. Yes, they did..." She folds her hands in her lap.

It's too much. His head spins. California? Calls? She actually spoke with the Hazard? The Hazard was in Florida at the hospital? Never. Nonsense. She never talked to him. He was never there. As for Harland and Ali meeting in the Sunshine State...

It's Crazy Janeen, he thinks. Talking gibberish. And yet she is exhibiting none of the accompanying characteristic unruliness or abrasiveness he typically associates with Crazy Janeen. Conversely, she is primped, sitting demurely on a chair in the common room. She appears perfectly regal. She's on new meds. Her eyes are clear and focused, even twinkling. And up to this point she has been admittedly lucid: requesting a Ginger Ale, suggesting they be seated near a window, so she could watch the world, imparting in a maternal tone that he appeared tired and that he really should be taking better care of himself. Granted, for a moment early on in his visit she did misplace her slippers and the associated word.

ANGELS IN THE ARCHITECTURE

"I can't find them, my... you know, the *things*, the things that go on my feet..."

"Only a bit more than a year, Janeen. That's not too long. They met at a photo shoot in Toronto..."

"*No*," she interrupts, brusquely, in a tone armed with forceful certainty. In lucid moments, she is forceful concerning anything she feels confident about; in lucid moments she is cognizant of just how fed up she is with being told she's mistaken and being treated like she is either not in the room, or nuts. "They met in Florida — Lauderdale, I believe, years and years before. And he saved her. Harland saved my girl from..." She waves her hands dismissively. "He was her knight in shining armor."

Beyond disconcerted, beyond flummoxed. The walls close in. The smells of the Plaza Visa overwhelm, nauseate. He sweats. Palpitates. Considers acting upon a sudden, urgent urge to *escape*. He feels unhinged, fears he's suddenly surrendered all control. He thinks she's crazy, but he also wonders whether she may be talking truth. Crazy truth. How the hell could she have made that up? But it's his world she's discussing. The very foundation of his world. Ali met Harland at a photo shoot. That's just part of their reality. Start screwing with that and you are screwing with his world, rewriting his relationship with his wife, revising their whole history. Wait...

"He saved your girl from what?"

Clear eyes clouding. Fingers nervously rising, dancing. An anxious facial twitch.

"What?"

"Harland," he snaps, with more agitation than ever intended. "You said Harland saved your girl from.... But you didn't say, saved from what?"

"Who?"

"Harland!"

"What?"

"And then," he informs his dinner companion, "then the whole conversation collapsed into some ridiculous semblance of *Who's on First?* You know, the old 'What's on second? I Don't Know's on third.' I finally had to buzz for assistance to escort her back to her room and I cut short my visit. Retreated outside and helped myself to a panic attack. I must have been a sight to see, sweating buckets, shivering, hunched over and hyperventilating in the parking lot. It was all I could do to not lay down in the fetal position on the asphalt and suck my thumb..."

ANDY JUNIPER

They are ensconced in Ellas on Pape, one of the first Greek restaurants to open its doors in the Danforth area. She's been dining here for years; it's his first time. Pink tablecloths, ersatz Corinthian columns, multicultural conversations buzzing amid savory restaurant aromas. They are self-consciously — quick and insistent in acknowledging — *not* on a date. Who needs that kind of pressure? They are simply and innocently out together, two friends, dining on succulent rack of lamb, sipping a full-bodied Merlot, watching trays of flaming sambuca surfing by and conversing over the candles.

"So, what do you think? What do you make of it?" she asks.

Honestly, it's the last thing she wants to be discussing, the relationship between his former wife and his missing best friend. But she wants to be there for him, as he's been there for her of late. She can only hope that this topic, which so obviously unsettles, will not entirely undermine the evening. As a single mother, she does not have the luxury of many nights out. Furthermore, with the time and care she invested in preparation for this *not*-a-date — the thought she took in choosing an outfit and accessories, the attention paid to styling her hair and applying makeup – she'd prefer his thoughts be affixed to the here and now, not meandering in the past.

"I think more than ever that I need to talk to Harland wherever the hell he is. Back in California? Still alive?" He sighs. "Is it possible they knew each other, years previous, in Florida? I know he did spend a few years there before moving to California. And," he's thinking aloud, his thoughts are running in circles like a dog in hot pursuit of its own tail, "she did vacation there: winter break, I think she said, in her first year of university, but..." He glances across the table at his companion, his *not*-a-date bathed in candlelight, empathy etched on her face.

"But what?"

"But, you know what I really think? I think that I'm a fricking idiot for even talking about this with you sitting across from me looking so very, very... incredible. I may be out of line, but Christian, you were a damn cute kid and now you are a very beautiful woman."

"You're right," she says, with a flirty smile and a timely comedic pause, "you do need to talk to Harland."

"And you are beautiful..."

"She *is* beautiful, empirically speaking, no doubt about it. And you are miles out of your league just being here with her." They glance up from their conversation to see a svelte, smiling man standing beside Christian, looking across the table at Storm. "I can see why you've dropped out of the game. You've obviously got better things to do with your time then chase after quotes from people with precious little to say."

Storm stands in welcome greeting, shakes the man's hand, and offers up introductions.

"Christian, this is Allen Abel. Al, Christian."

"I won't keep you from your meal, or each other," he grins and self-consciously adjusts his glasses. "I just wanted to drop by and say hello and tell you that those of us still toiling in the business miss your sunny smile. Not your purple prose, mind you, just that sunny smile. Seriously, you need to get back into the saddle, my man. You're too good to be on the sidelines. That's my two cents. Nice meeting you, Christian. Enjoy your meal," he says, winking at Storm and departing.

"Abel?"

"Used to be with *The Globe*, now out on his own. Good guy. Incredible writer. And he could coax a quote out of a rock, I swear."

"Maybe he's right. Maybe you need to get back in the game. Maybe *you* should write a book."

"And maybe that big dufus derailed my train of thought."

"Which was…"

"How incredible you look. Oh, and the notion that when this meal and this bottle of wine are finished, maybe we should go to my place for dessert."

"Storm Baker, you're actually flirting."

"There is hope for me yet, right?"

"By profession, I'm a nurse. I tell everyone there's still hope."

"Even the terminal patients?"

"*Especially* the terminals…"

He's sitting on the edge of the bed in the master bedroom of his new house, in the soft illumination of the gas fireplace that's purring on low, in an otherwise darkened room. She stands before him. After an indecisive, diffident moment between them, she self-consciously unbuttons and removes her blouse, briefly blinding him with the whiteness of her bra and by the topography and beauty of her tender flesh. She whispers that she wants him, that despite herself, she cannot not have him. She unzips, steps out of her skirt. Again, blinded. By the whiteness of her underwear, by her courage, and more of that soft, inviting flesh. She comes closer, then straddles him on the bed: her eyes closed, smoky mascara, bold lipstick, face rapturous, she takes his head in her hands and begins to squeeze. To the point where… where she is hurting him. The previous sensual expression on her face replaced by something akin to torment. She abruptly releases him and sighs.

"This is not going to be easy. It's so hard for me out here on this limb. I want you; I need you. But there is still… still so much anger, rage, fury…" Hands clenched. She exhales through pursed lips… "Men…"

Just when he is resigned to her imminent retreat, she reaches back, unhooks her bra and deposits it on the floor. She takes his hands and guides them to her breasts. Her skin is welcoming, nipples at attention. She leans forward and kisses him, tenderly, soulfully, over and over. She kisses his hair, his eyes, his cheeks, lips, earlobes, neck. His temperature rises with each kiss. There is no questioning their connection or denying his desire. His heart is aflutter, butterflies are flittering in his stomach. Hands shaky. Perspiring, light-headed, silently considering the possibility that he's consumed too much wine. She stands, steps out of her panties, playfully covers herself with her hands, and advises that the time is now or never. That he really, really had better get naked.

"Before I get cold feet… or other body parts…"

He should stand. He should get naked. His head pulsates. He fears the pressure in his skull and chest might actually kill him, that this beauty, this body might be an unwitting accessory to murder. For an instant he closes his eyes. The room spins; his head swims. How he desires her. Wants to possess her, devour her, to feel her on top of him, beneath him. Wants to be inside her, touching her essence, her soul. Wants to make love with her more urgently than he has wanted anything, *anyone* since…

"Ali…"

She has gathered her clothes and is not even attempting to disguise her sobs from behind a locked bathroom door before he fully emerges from his trance and fully realizes what he has done.

In the aftermath, they sit civilly at the kitchen table. She has ceased crying although her eyes remain bloodshot, her mascara's a runny mess, cheeks streaked. He stares at the floor, searching for a crack in the ceramic tile, anything he can disappear into.

"It was a bad idea, anyway," she says. "I'm obviously still incensed with your entire gender. You're obviously still obsessed with Ali, and we were obviously idiots to think otherwise." She shakes her head, sadly. "I think we need to say goodbye. At least for now. I need to deal with me, with my issues. I need to become a whole again for my sake and for Angel. And you need to deal with… your loss. No one will ever be able to compete, Storm, she's too high up on that pedestal. You can keep her up there with the angels, but for the sake of those of us here on Earth, you'll have to come to grips that this is not a competition. No one should ever be expected to compete with her.

"Actually, Storm," she continues after a moment of further reflection, "what you really need is to deal with yourself. There's something depressing about a man who has the perfect love with a woman he adores who is nonetheless forever undermining and sabotaging that love with insecurities and pettiness and jealousy. That's what I think you did with her. And I think you need to figure out why."

Insecurities. Pettiness. Jealously.

This, he thinks, could be Ali talking. And yet, he was never able to stop himself. Powerless to rein himself in. He loved her as much as anyone can love another human being. And, yes, he knew she loved him, too. With all her big, beautiful heart. And yet, even in attempting to fully embrace her hello he remained forever fearful of hearing her goodbye.

"From all you've told me, Ali was special. She was something else. Just from what you've said, I wish I knew her. She didn't fool around on you, dumb man. I know it and deep down I think you know it. Maybe there was something going on between her and Harland, but it wasn't romance, it was not an affair. In your twisted mind, in your darker hours, you might think it was. For whatever reason, you've conjured up and used things like this to prevent yourself from fully appreciating and enjoying what you two had. For whatever reason, consciously or otherwise, you held back and never fully lived in the here and now. Maybe afraid of getting hurt, of losing her, or of putting yourself out there – of being, you know, fully human and vulnerable.

"Yes, you need to find Harland. You need to find the truth. But, most of all, you really need to find Storm Baker… If you ever want to be with anyone again, if you ever want to experience anything even resembling happiness, you're going to have to let her go, move on, throw yourself into life and begin to really, truly, put yourself out there…" She picked her purse up off the table. Adjusted her skirt. Lightly kissed his forehead. And whispered: "Goodbye, Storm…"

Around In Circles

He's squatting in a dusty and cramped storage cubicle in the basement of the CrossRoads, examining a sizable painting he discovered in a corner wrapped and protected from the environment, dust and mites and mice, by only a ratty old blanket cinched by string. He's spellbound. The painting is luminous, even under the unflattering flat light. Complex. Intricate. Circles interlocking on the canvas. Untamed colors on a canary yellow background. It's art with breath and muscle all of its own. Art that draws you in, envelopes you. Art that toys with you or claims you as its own. He averts his eyes. Turns the painting over and finds the inscription:

From the desert
From the brush
Of your Chairman of the Board
I call it: 'Jazz and Janeen'
Love, Frank

He whistles softly.

It's one of many treasures he's uncovered. One of many he's forced to pack. Janeen's lease is up. There is no way in hell she will ever be back here. In recent weeks, her descent has hastened.

Redic is upstairs assiduously boxing up her belongings – efficiently creating three piles: one for charity, one for keeps, and one for garbage; the garbage pile keeps multiplying. It was the superintendent, dropping in to see how they were progressing, who reminded that each tenant has access to a basement storage area for bicycles, excess furniture and the like, and that they'd better check out Janeen's space.

ANGELS IN THE ARCHITECTURE

No, Storm did not expect to find priceless Frank in this cubbyhole, not exactly cosseted from theft by a thrift store padlock he was easily able to pick with a hairpin. Nor did he expect to find Ali's father. However, he is here, in a box labeled in bold, black letters: "Private."

A creased and faded black-and-white photograph. And once he studies the picture, it is obvious. The facial features, particularly the cheekbones and chin, the winsome smile. And if it had not been obvious that he begat her, the accompanying paperwork conveys the whole story. Written in legalese, but nonetheless discernable and dated one week after Ali was born: his paternity sworn never to be revealed, the details of his proposed monthly child-support payments, and three signatures — his, that of a witness, and Janeen's, a flourish of impatient and impetuous ink.

At home, sitting up in bed. 3 a.m. Mind racing. He's been thinking about Janeen and all she has divulged in recent visits. Crazy Janeen? Lucid Janeen? He is reluctantly connecting dots, engaging in giant leaps of logic.

The old man, his neighbor back in Turtle Cay. Whatever the hell was that amiable oldtimer's name? Brady? Remembering his whisky voice: "You get knocked on the back of the head, clunk, you fall flat on your face, unconscious, right? Then you drown. The water gets you, fills your lungs, steals your breath. End of story... No, sir. I found you right-side up. Right-side up." Could he possibly have been there, providing divine intervention, flipping his friend... right-side up?

The young nurse, Carlotta Swift, saying a friend of his had dropped by to visit while he was sleeping. Said the friend asked a lot of questions, said he'd come back, but didn't. But didn't. Typical. So very, very typical.

Then... Pegasus. The pendant, its whereabouts a mystery since her death, suddenly reappearing – casually tossed by Carlotta onto his bed in the hospital along with his other valuables. The connection of this particular dot is accompanied by its very own visual: someone charming their way into the area of the hospital where valuables are stored and no, not stealing, but, rather, adding an item to the cache. My god, he thinks, Harland. The Hazard had Pegasus. How else to explain its reappearance without introducing and leaning heavily on the mystical? It's his imagination conjuring up the how and the why of him having that pendant that triggers panic.

Out of bed, pacing, in the full throes and on the verge of throwing up just to calm himself when the phone rings. Rather than ignore it, he practically attacks the receiver.

"You'd better not hang up this time, you son-of-a-bitch. You're making me lose my fucking mind with these calls. We're goddamn blood brothers and you've screwed me over for far too long. I need answers, you bastard, and you'd better provide, or I swear I'm going to reach through this goddamn receiver and strangle you…"

"Hey man, stop, wait. Mistaken identity, man. Is this the number for Storm Baker? Are you Storm?"

Unfamiliar voice. Not Harland. Panic, anger decelerate. In a mortified whisper he declares: "This is Storm speaking."

"Ah, Storm, my name is B.J. If you can take your meds for a minute, I need to talk to you about your friend…"

Harland quit Long Beach. Three nights previous he informed the bartender that they would not be seeing each other again. He shook his hand, mumbled goodbye, and departed as abruptly as he had arrived. On a breeze. With only minor theatrics.

"And here's the odd thing," B.J. said. "Actually, there's a couple odd things, but here's the first. He said he was going north, up the coast to surf. I've had about a thousand hours of conversation with him, and I'm a surfer. I can tell you with certainty: he is not one of us. I don't think he's even a swimmer for that matter, despite the amount of time he spends staring at the ocean.

"Second odd thing. He left me a note, a letter in a sealed envelope. He said he was certain that one day you'd come looking for him and when you did, I should give this to you. Man, I've been thinking about him non-stop since. I'm worried sick. He talked about you a lot. I knew you were a journalist in Toronto, so I decided to find you. It took me this long to track you down. Give me your address and I'll courier the letter to you."

"Forget the courier, B.J. I need you to read me Harland's note. I need you to read it to me right now."

"Harland? Didn't know that was his name. He's been Rocky to me. Rocky all this time…"

"He's rocky, for sure," Storm mumbles. "And that's why I need you to read the letter to me now."

Crinkling at the other end as B.J. opens the envelope. Storm is about to hear from Harland. He thinks he'd better sit down.

"It's hard to read."

ANGELS IN THE ARCHITECTURE

"Chickenscratch?"

"Yeah. And it's, ah… it's epic. Across the backside of three menus and both sides of two napkins and there's a spill…"

"Rum?"

"And Coke…"

"Gently bathed in ice," they say in unison.

Storm feels that gently bathed ice navigating through his veins.

She Loved You, Ya, Ya, Ya

Storm. Storm. Storm.
Where to begin, how to explain?
She loved you, ya, ya, ya.

SHE LOVED ME, too. Just "not in that way." Never in that way. Not once. She couldn't. She wouldn't. Her, me, could never be. No Zelda to my F. Scott. A little Daisy to my Jay, I guess, considering how things ended; although, by the book, it should have been me shot, dead, drowned in the proverbial pool. But never, really, truly in that way. That's what she said in the parking lot in High Park. Yeah, I saw you. I'd betrayed my best friend, and he was a witness to my betrayal. How Thomas Hardy. How fucking unlikely. How fucking unlucky is that?

I don't expect you to understand, but I need you to *know*. I'd been traveling down this dark road that was taking me places nobody should ever have to go. Nameless places that can't be described with words, not by me anyway. I reached the point where I figured I had only one shot left, one way out, one hope for survival. Ali. She always knew how I felt about her. I think that was painfully obvious. But did she know how deep those rivers ran? I'd been saying for weeks, saying we needed to talk. I think she knew what I wanted to say, psychic soul. Reluctantly, she finally agreed. It was your day to jog around the park, not walk through it! Guess you busted out of character and changed-up your schedule. Anyway, we met in the parking lot, and I poured out my heart, one last time. She listened. We hugged. I kissed her and, I believe, she kissed me back, empathetic soul. My pain tearing her apart. Then she told me it could never be. Not in that way.

ANGELS IN THE ARCHITECTURE

Said she loved you, ya, ya, ya. And she said she'd never thought of me in that way, never felt that kind of attraction to me, the obnoxious chemistry that you guys shared, the chemistry that had your lips forever locked and all that jazz. Personally, I think it was more because of what we'd been through together. What I'd seen. Hard for a woman to love a man who has seen her down like that…

Picture. Her and two friends at a table up front in the Flamingo Club in the bowels of the Hilton on the beach in Fort Lauderdale. They were down from U of T, winter reading week, or some such, and I was the monkey in the suit playing for bananas. Strumming my guitar and singing other people's songs and pretending to give a crap about any of it. Her friends were giggling and grooving and batting back martinis because it was the promotion night where femmes drink for half-price.

If you promise not to tell a soul, I'll admit that I was doing a Neil Diamond medley as requested by management and spelled out in my contract. But there was one in the audience who seemed impervious to my haunting Neil, and my charms for that matter. Our Ali. I took it as a challenge. After I closed the set with a killer Solitary Man, I stepped down off the stage and right into their dreams, asking the ladies if I could join them.

I could tell you how beautiful she was, Storm – she had her hair up, and these cute wisps had fallen — and I could go on about how when I talked to her it was like everyone else on the fucking planet thankfully disappeared. But I know how that kind of thing messes with your head. If I wanted to really mess with your head, I'd tell you exactly what she was wearing, down to the dangly star earrings, and God how heavenly she smelled. Sorry. I shouldn't be pushing your buttons. Not now, not ever, brother. It's tempting though, knowing the huge worlds of fiction your head produces out of tiny kernels of truth.

I'll just say that she and I, we got along. Started with the old reliable "Canadian connection" and went from there. Her friends, realizing they'd been effectively boxed out of the conversation, decided to jump ship, go next door to another bar or wherever. I had a final set to play, a tribute to folk legends, or some such. She stayed to watch. At some point in the set, in the middle of Gordon Lightfoot, she broke my heart for the first time. Talking to some muscle-bound hulk in a tank top who'd sidled up to her. I can't tell you how the folkie-shit suffered when she got up and left the club. I watched Hulk finish his drink and her drink in two greedy swallows and follow her. I was tossing daggers at his back with my eyes.

When the set ended, I hauled my guitar and my depression outside for a bit of air behind the club before heading back up to my room for another long, lonely night. I was wandering aimlessly in the parking lot, one of those that just extends forever into the night, and I thought I heard a cry, this... squeak of distress. I walked toward the sound.

He had her down. Pinned in the darkness, on the asphalt, with most of her clothes torn off or ripped open and his fucking sweat sock stuffed in her mouth, and he had his prick out and... the asshole was pissing on her. And do you want the kicker? She later told me that the only reason he was pissing on her was because he was unable to do what he really wanted to do, which was crap on her.

It's a fucked-up world, Storm. Mankind is a club you'd have to be crazy to even want to join. With more fucked-up people than I can handle or even imagine. And what men do to women. What crazy goddamn bastard men do to women... I mean, we're supposed to be in this together, you know. Fuck, how my heart bleeds for women...

I bashed his brains, Storm. I knocked that prick and his prick right into next week with my Guild Dreadnought. My solid wood six-string sweetheart. Typically, not much give in that baby, but I gave him enough of a swing that my baby busted. Then I grabbed Ali, gathered up her clothes and we were on the run. I looked back twice and if the asshole moved at all, even twitched, I never saw it. I don't know, maybe I killed him. I never heard, but a guy can hope.

We lived together for five days and nights. Shacked up in my hotel room. With me as Florence Nightingale and her as my patient. She cried, I comforted. She blamed and loathed herself and I struggled to inject sense into her. She said she felt dirty. I poured her baths. Steamy foamy bubble baths. Harland Hazard trademark baths, for god's sake. So steamy the water turned her skin scarlet.

And while she soaked in the tub, we surrounded ourselves with beauty. She got me listening to, and actually appreciating, the essence and splendor of Brian Wilson and the Beach Boys. I read to her from the only book I had with me. But then, you know what book... And how she loved it. In a way, it was her saving grace, the beauty and poetry of F. Scott's words in stark contrast to the ugliness of this world.

ANGELS IN THE ARCHITECTURE

You can relax, my brother, nothing happened. I know you're chomping at the bit, your head turning in mad circles like Linda Blair, wondering if anything sexual was going on. True, I saw her naked ever day, but it's not cause for jealousy. It was the least sexual thing I've ever experienced, a nude woman overdressed in her own sorrow.

Rereading what I just wrote I see a few mistakes. Correction #1. We *were* intimate: once she invited me into the tub. She needed me to hold her steady while she cried until no more tears would come. Correction #2. *Something* did happen. I fell in love. And she knew it, even though I never said a word. And she said right then and there that it could never be like I wanted it to be. She said something, all Ali-corny like, you'll always be my hero, Harland, but not my honey… I think, by that point, she'd already had the dream about you in the park.

Two days before her holiday was to end, we were scheduled to split. She was going to back to join her friends and I was supposed to fly up to Nashville to meet some record guys and demo some material for them. I think you know what happened, though. She dreamed that my plane would go down and she convinced me to remain grounded. When that plane crashed, I became a full-fledged believer. A card-carrying member.

I stayed with her. At the end of her holiday, she returned to Toronto, and I forgot about Nashville and moved on to California to coat my sadness in sunshine. We didn't communicate all that often after that – you know how I am with… communication. But we stayed connected. There were nights when she'd call and read me a passage she'd re-discovered in *Gatsby*. There were nights when I'd call her and be rejuvenated just by the sound of her voice. Time found me back living in Toronto after I'd tired of California, or California had tired of me. Some magazine requested a story and photo shoot, and I insisted she be the photographer.

I know you, Storm, I know what you're wondering: why did she lie about us in the first place? You tell me. Could she have just stated the simple truth? Harland saved me from some guy who was trying to literally crap on me? I honestly don't know how you would have reacted, you, being you. There were other reasons, too. I know, because I pressed her on this, asking her repeatedly: Why the lie? Why not clear up the lie? It was so unlike her. So un-Ali. And how did she respond? She offered up three things…

One, basic instinct told her that you would never be able to handle that truth — even in the infatuated infancy of your relationship, she was reluctant to place such a roadblock, especially since she knew you would have to carry on your shoulders the burden of her premonitions. Secondly, some crazy thing about a Joni Mitchell quote along the lines of "there are things to confess that enrich the world, and things that need not be said." And, finally, you know that little secret that you told me, that thing you were doing between meeting her in the park and later tracking her down? Well, I let it slip. I told her that you were so smitten and desperate and determined to make an impression on her if you ever found her that you practiced smiling in the mirror for hours.

"Well," she said to me, "that's just so goofy." Of course, I fully agreed. Then she added, "and charming and sweet and…" I told her she'd already nailed it with goofy.

I'm sorry, my friend. I did not want to take her from you. I just knew I needed her for me.

I followed her out of the park. But you know that. Despite her head start, I caught up to her on Keele Street, heading south. I knew she had an assignment down the highway in Oakville, so I tailed her along the QEW. We were speeding, stupidly. She knew I was behind her. I knew, she knew. She was crying. I was crying. Things were just so royally fucked up. She was doing goddamn dumb things behind the wheel to…to try and lose me. I was doing stupider things to stay close.

Storm, Storm, Storm.

It's astonishing, just how much disregard that transport had for her. The truck nailed her on a blind cutback she had no chance of executing and it rolled her car and bounced it off the guardrail. The sound is still stuck in my ears. The transport driver helped me pull her out of the wreckage through a shattered window. The car was smoking, black choking smoke. We were afraid it would blow. When the driver ran back to his truck to radio for help, I held her. Cold. No pulse.

I once read in one of those flakey books she loved that in the moments after death a soul hovers over its body. In my dreams she is watching over me as I kiss her flesh goodbye and take Pegasus from around her neck. Then, as more and more people gathered, as sirens began wailing in the distance and chaos ensued, I vamoosed. Fled the scene.

Took it — Pegasus — to give to you. But once I sped from the accident, I knew I couldn't part with it. It was my last connection to the woman I loved. The woman I had killed. I know forgiveness is too much to ask. So, I only ask that on your deathbed, you don't still hate my guts.

ANGELS IN THE ARCHITECTURE

Wouldn't you give anything just to see her?

Wouldn't you give anything just to say you're sorry for all the shit we put her through?

They say love is the seventh wave. It's the wave I plan on catching.

Take care of yourself, Storm Baker. Without you, I'd have never even made it this far. Who knows how far I'll make it from here. But then, who cares?

God, as Janeen once said to me, protects drunks and sparrows. This sparrow can only hope. This drunk can drink. Brother, if you're ever wondering just how much I love you… I stayed sober for two-straight days – in a bar, for god's sake — just so I could write this…

h.h.

Until The Trail Went Cold

IT'S TRUE, I suppose. You can run, but you cannot hide. I still run every other day. Many days I find myself running as though in a trance. So in-the-moment that I am unaware of everything around me save for my own breathing and the pendant that bounces off my chest in rhythm with my strides. However, when I eventually stop, when I emerge from that trance — regardless of how fast I've been running and how much ground has been covered — I am often overcome by the illogical sensation that I have actually been standing still. Anchored. And spinning my wheels. It's still me and her and everything I lost. On my deathbed, even if I live to be one-hundred years, I will still be missing her. Her absence is everywhere.

She believed in reincarnation. While I cannot say I believe, I do find myself gazing into the innocent eyes of infants I encounter. Expecting what? That one day, one of these beautiful saucer-eyed babies will let me in on his or her secret with a sly wink, or a conspiratorial nod? The rational side of me shakes its cynical head while my flighty side reminds the rational that it did not believe in the prophetic nature of Ali's dreams, and we know how they turned out.

So, I hold out hope. Yes, hope is still alive.

Ali had a refrain that she would recite to herself each morning: *The best times of your life have not been lived.* Imagine: regardless of how good life was, even better times were still ahead. She lived with that kind of optimism, with that kind of hope. This despite her dire premonitions. She knew that hope is all anyone has.

Hope piloted me to California. That I would find him, the needle in the haystack, one lone soul in an expansive state, and that he would be alive.

ANGELS IN THE ARCHITECTURE

I met B.J. I sat in Harland's place in the Sunset Grill and the bartender explained how the Hazard had always insisted the seat next to him be kept empty – waiting, I suppose, for her to walk through the doors and back into his life, waiting for her to rescue him — as he once rescued her — from this living hell.

B.J. and I rehashed conversations the two had, seeking clues as to what he might have been thinking and where he might have gone. Before I set off on my own to track Harland's trail up the coast, B.J. told me that each day the Hazard entered the Sunset Grill, the bartender would ask him how life was treating him. On good days, the Hazard would reply: "The universe is flirting with me." On bad days, "The universe is fucking with me." For the last few months, B.J. noted, the universe had been doing nothing but screwing him over.

Alas, there were no surprises. In no time at all, the trail turned stone cold. Like he had disappeared into thin air, like he'd waded out into the vast Pacific. As one state trooper said: "Listen, mister, if a guy doesn't want to be found in California, trust me, he won't be found. Not even if you're some super-sleuth."

I only had one week. That's all that I could allow myself away from Janeen. After all my broken promises to her, I sure as hell was not going to have her die alone. Just before I flew west, she had muttered, apropos of nothing: "The world is not long for me." Seven days were all I could spare. North up the coast, nose to the ground sniffing for his scent and not allowing myself even a moment to wallow, not even an instant to think of how I was retracing the route of our honeymoon, only in the opposite direction. Still, cities, towns, landmarks leaped out at me. Triggers were everywhere and at times I swear she was with me, offering advice, pointing down dusty sideroads he'd be inclined to take. Ali, riding shotgun.

As promised, I called B.J. from the San Francisco Airport. Nothing, I said, forlorn and defeated, not a trace. I've left my name and number up and down the coast. And, of course, if I hear anything I'll call. He said he'd keep up the search at his end. I hung up feeling slightly comforted, that the Hazard had spent his nights with a soul as caring and compassionate as B.J.

God how we need family, friends, protectors.

Two Broken Flowers

"Hello."

"Sorry to be calling so late. I just need to know. Are you still angry, in hate with all men?"

"Yeah, absolutely, although somewhat tempered. Are you still obsessed with... your obsession?"

"Yeah, absolutely."

"Guess we remain two broken flowers... I'm in therapy."

"One broken flower, one broken weed... I'm not."

"Storm, what is it? Your voice. What's the matter?"

"Janeen." The pressure in his head and the weight on his heart are unbearable. Eyes stinging. Choking on words that are under intense pressure to spill out. "She's dead. Janeen died."

"Oh Storm. Oh, Storm, I'm so sorry... Where are you?"

"The hospital. Waiting for a coroner. Papers to sign..."

"Don't budge. I'm on my way..."

"Christian... I put myself out there. I did. Really, truly, for Janeen. So far out there and, goddamn it, it hurts, it hurts..."

It hurts. How it hurts. He's gutted.

Three days previous he'd arrived for a visit at the Plaza Vista and discovered her propped up, strapped into a chair and unresponsive to his voice and to his touch, gently shaking her arm, finding her skin clammy. His heart leaped into his throat. He shouted for help.

For the past two weeks he'd noticed she was becoming increasingly less alert. Less and less alive. He took his observations to the administration, and he blamed their drugs. He accused Plaza doctors and staff of overloading her in response to her burgeoning anger, belligerence, fits of violence. Upping dosages. Effectively drugging her into submission, into a stupor. Plaza administration repeatedly denied any such allegations and took umbrage at the very suggestion. Plaza administration said – again the damnable phrase – that Janeen was simply on an inevitable slippery slope, and this was merely the next phase in her wicked degeneration.

Comatose, she was rushed to hospital. Three days in that coma with Storm steadfastly at her side, an intense bedside vigil. Willing her to awaken. And then, deep into the third night, as he sat watching her, she opened her eyes. Eyes that seemed remarkably clear. Focused.

And with those clear, focused eyes she gazed not at Storm, but rather out the hospital window at the night sky, then spoke with a parched voice.

"The stars," she said with a weak half-smile, "the stars seem so happy to see me."

"Janeen…" He leaned forward and clutched her hand as her breath grew noticeably faint, barely there. "Janeen… I love you. Janeen…"

She looked so tiny on that bed, a wisp of the woman she once was. Her eyes remained fixed on the window. A single tear made its way down her sunken cheek. For an ephemeral instant, he believed her grip tightened ever-so slightly on his hand. And then she released.

"I have to go now," she said. "There's something beautiful out there…"

Epilogue

Angels In The Architecture

I WATCH AS she flits about the house, a butterfly in a breeze. What a beautiful child. A miracle. Thin, lithe, perhaps a few inches undersized for her age. She has big, bold, expressive eyes, an infectious smile, and a full head of sandy-blonde hair. She is always ebullient and forever engaging. Today she turns ten and, as if those double digits are not enough to hyper her into a frenzy, she is also keenly aware that Christmas is only weeks away. Even more than most children her age, our birthday girl absolutely loves *Christmas.*

Surrounded by opened storage boxes, she's unpacking our festive decorations to display around the house. In a few hours, five of her "best-est" friends in the whole world will arrive for a sleepover. Adorably, they will hug and kiss cheeks, their own little greeting ritual, and they will help her celebrate the anniversary of her entrance into the world. They will play games and watch movies, fussily pick at pizza, and messily demolish cake. Gabbing, gossiping, giggling, they will make more noise than is customary in this home that houses three — five if you count the hounds — deep into the night. Until I finally (unsuccessfully, laughably) attempt to silence them with idle threats of there being no more sleepovers. Ever!

Currently she's a bundle of barely pent-up energy and anticipation. She can't sit still, not even for a minute. Not even if she wanted to.

We live in the Beaches, in a pleasant neighborhood, in an old house that has been modernized for comfort and convenience. Outside there is a doghouse — although I don't think either of our dopey dogs has ever seen the inside of this structure — gardens and an in-ground pool, closed for the season and

ANGELS IN THE ARCHITECTURE

beginning to ice-over, and bordered by stately cedars. Last weekend, on a cold, grey day, she had me up on a ladder, teetering in a hostile wind, stringing those cedars with hundreds of Christmas lights. A trouper, she stood out there with me in the elements, shivering in a white winter coat that she hates – she says it makes her look "puffy, like a marshmallow" – encouraging me, untangling rows of lights, and otherwise assisting wherever possible. And when we finished, she made us cups of hot chocolate. That's what kind of girl she is, self-sufficient, generous, and compassionate. Her heart is huge.

She has an aversion to silence. As she decorates, she talks. For all she knows, I'm out of hearing range. For all she knows, she's talking to herself. Doesn't matter to her, she just likes to talk. A gabby girl, this one. Truth be told, I am listening because what comes out of her mouth is as precious as she is precious.

By noon, she's dressed for the party. On Halloween she went out costumed as a fashion disaster. Honestly, I have trouble discerning the difference between what she wore that night trick-or-treating and what she's wearing now: chopsticks in her hair, dangly earrings and an outfit as outrageous and mismatched as anything ever worn by Janeen Reynolds, another true trouper. But then, I'm a man. What do I know about fashion? Really, what the hell do I know about anything?

I know with certainty that I have regrets. About things that happened in past lives, things I honestly could have changed — and about things in my new life, regrets over events that were wholly out of my control. Regarding the latter: there are days when I regret that I wasn't part of her life at birth, wasn't there to see her being coerced into the world, wasn't there to hold her hand and help her in any way possible throughout her treatments. Days I just simply regret missing those first years. However, these regrets do not make me feel any less blessed. And now, whenever I'm with her, I have this sense of urgency, like we're making up for lost time.

My mother used to say to me, "Storm, if you're going to walk around with such an unusual name, a name no one will ever forget, then you have to become an upstanding human being, a person worthy of being remembered." For years I thought this meant that to be worthy of being remembered, I needed to forge a career that would net me a measure of fortune and fame. Now, I finally get it. Each day I strive to be an upstanding human being, a decent father for this girl, a decent husband for her mother. And each day this precious girl tells me – with a gesture, a hug, a kiss on the cheek – that in her mind, in her heart, I am worthy of being remembered. Just as I remember, near every minute of near every day, those so very worthy of my remembrances…

Janeen, of course. And my other angel, Ali…

ANDY JUNIPER

Her eyes are alight. The dogs are barking. The garage door is opening. Chaos erupting. Her mom is home. Back from her Saturday morning guitar lesson in the city's west end — she's intent on becoming proficient at the instrument and she has an excellent instructor, at least when he's not being a wanker and hitting on her. After the lesson, an errand run. Party supplies, party food, including the birthday girl's favorite, a chocolate ice-cream birthday cake. Ice-cream in December? She insisted, and she has prodigious powers of persuasion.

She greets her mom in the mudroom, dances around her with excitement, then solemnly places a hand (as if in greeting) atop her mom's slightly swollen belly. They hug. My girls. My little girl, our precious pixie, who turns ten today. And her expectant mom who is, without exaggeration, my savior. One of the angels in my architecture.

"Harland says hello," my savior says, as she places a few shopping bags on the kitchen counter and slips out of her coat. "He was in a particularly reflective mood today and only hit on me once. This is his anniversary, you know..."

Don't I know. Five years ago, to the day, I opened the front door looking for the morning newspaper, and found him curled up, dead drunk, and nearly frozen to death on the porch. I rushed him to the hospital. And from there he went directly into rehab. Five years ago. Five years of being stone-cold sober.

In his words: "Five years of being the death of the party..."

While I won't argue against the refrain that I have heard so many times in my life that I now know it by rote, we are indeed "borne back ceaselessly into the past." However, here in the Beaches, we keep our eyes cast on the horizon and we endeavor to hold in our hearts Ali's endlessly sunny belief that the best times of our lives have not yet been lived.

— 30 —

Acknowledgments

Thanks to The Fam. Nuclear, extended, in-laws, and outlaws — the winsome, the wonderful, the wackadoodle (you know who you are). All amazing, all inspiring.

To Maureen Juniper, who has supported me on so many levels over so many years. To Matt Juniper, for repeated reads, endless edits, and sage editorial advice. To Scott Juniper, for being a sounding board for the prose (and the cons) and the process. And to Haley Juniper, for all the encouragement, for burning brain cells on publicity and marketing strategies, and for bringing andyjuniper.com to life (along with web designers Gillian Miller and Borna Najafi).

Thanks to my siblings, Denny and Guy — lifelong supporters — and their spouses, Fred and Jacinthe. Also, thanks to the dedicated readers of my early drafts: Matt Juniper, Patrick Kelly, Christopher Kelly, Catriona Kelly, Andrea Paetkau, Tim Holmes, Judy Sinclair, and Nigel Miller. Special thanks to Scott Morrison, Doug Lincoln, and Corey Ellis — cool, creative souls who just naturally guide and inspire. Oh, and one guy who has known me practically forever. Roger Hall has been with me through every draft of everything I've ever written – the good, the bad, the ugly; happy to tell me what works, unafraid to tell me when I've missed the mark. I trust this man to tell me how many yards it is to the pin and what treachery awaits beyond the dogleg; likewise, to read, review, and proffer advice on any given word, sentence, paragraph, and chapter in my life. And to always ask the question that energizes writers and propels fiction: "Hey, what if?"

Finally, huge thanks to Howard Aster, who gambled on me back in 1994 when he published my first novel and continues to roll the dice. And to his staff at Mosaic Press who diligently worked to bring *Angels* to life.

About the Author

Andy Juniper has written three novels: *Sweet Grass*, *The Sunforth Chronicles*, and *Angels in the Architecture*. Over the course of his career, he worked for *The Globe & Mail*, contributed a weekly sports humor column to *Sportsnet.ca* and *The Huffington Post*, and penned some 1,500 family life/humor columns for Metroland newspapers that have been compiled into two editions: *When You Get Done Bleeding, Can You Get Me A Snack?* and *Strangled Eggs*. Andy is currently working on a fourth novel, *The Party Line And Everything After*, based in the world of professional hockey, and *Wild Life* — a memoir *of* and manual *for* country living — a lighthearted look at his family's 20-plus years living in the hamlet of Moffat, Ontario. He can be contacted at andyjuniper.com.